O. Henry: Obscenely and Outrageously Obliterated

O. Henry: Obscenely and Outrageously Obliterated

By

Jay Dubya

www.bookstandpublishing.com

Published by
Bookstand Publishing
Pasadena, CA 91101
3070_7

Copyright © 2023 by Jay Dubya
All rights reserved. No part of this publication may be reproduced or transmitted in any form or by any means, electronic or mechanical, including photocopy, recording, or any information storage and retrieval system, without permission in writing from the copyright owner.

ISBN 978-1-58909-677-6

Other Books by Jay Dubya

Adult Fiction

Black Leather and Blue Denim, A '50s Novel
The Great Teen Fruit War, A 1960' Novel
Frat' Brats, A '60s Novel
Ron Coyote, Man of La Mangia
Pieces of Eight
Pieces of Eight, Part II
Pieces of Eight, Part III
Pieces of Eight, Part IV
The Wholly Book of Genesis
The Wholly Book of Exodus
The Wholly Book of Doo-Doo-Rot-on-Me
Thirteen Sick Tasteless Classics
Thirteen Sick Tasteless Classics, Part II
Thirteen Sick Tasteless Classics, Part III
Thirteen Sick Tasteless Classics, Part IV
Thirteen Sick Tasteless Classics, Part V
So Ya' Wanna' Be A Teacher
RAM: Random Articles and Manuscripts
Mauled Maimed Mangled Mutilated Mythology
Fractured Frazzled Folk Fables and Fairy Farces
FFFF&FF, Part II
Nine New Novellas
Nine New Novellas, Part II
Nine New Novellas, Part III
Nine New Novellas, Part IV
One Baker's Dozen
Two Baker's Dozen
Shakespeare: Slammed, Smeared, Savaged & Slaughtered
Shakespeare: S, S, S and S, Part II
Suite 16
Time Travel Tales
Snake Eyes and Boxcars
Snake Eyes and Boxcars, Part II
UFO: Utterly Fantastic Occurrences
The Psychic Dimension
The Psychic Dimension, Part II
Modern Mythology

First Person Stories
PLOTS
PLOTS. Part II
Twain: Tattered Trounced Tortured and Traumatized
Poe: Pelted Pounded Pummeled and Pulverized
London: Lashed Lacerated Lampooned and Lambasted
Hawthorne: Hazed Hooked Hammered and Hijacked
Hawthorne Hacked, Shakespeare Sacked & Thurber Thwacked
THEMES
The FBI Inspector
Prime-Time Crime Time
The Arcane Arcade
Thirteen Tantalizing Tales
Homer's Odd Sea Odyssey
HOMER'S ILL ILIAD
The Timeless Time Machine
War of the Worlds
The Invisible Man

Young Adult Fantasy Novels

Pot of Gold
Enchanta
Space Bugs, Earth Invasion
The Eighteen Story Gingerbread House

Contents

Description

O. Henry: Obscenely and Outrageously Obliterated is a collection of eighteen classic William Sydney Porter "surprise ending" short stories that have been rewritten and satirized into adult parody form featuring adult content and language. When author Jay Dubya was a New Jersey public school English teacher, he often enjoyed teaching and reading O. Henry's "influential literature" to his sometimes-enlightened middle and high school students.

Even though O. Henry (1862-1910) had died at a very young age, the author still managed to remarkably write over five-hundred short stories and anecdotal sketches. W.S. Porter's fiction often occurs in familiar environments and settings that the writer had known well during his short tenure upon this Earth. O. Henry was very familiar with New York City. And so, his famous stories "The Gift of the Magi", "The Last Leaf", "The Furnished Room", "After Twenty Years", "The Higher Pragmatism", "The Cop and the Anthem", "The Green Door", "The Caliph, Cupid and the Clock", and "Mammon and the Archer" all take place in Manhattan at or around the turn of the twentieth century, during the emergence of the exciting Golden Age of science and technology.

Porter was born in the South in Greensboro, North Carolina, and so the prolific author was quite familiar with the culture of the post-Civil War Dixie states, and some of his popular stories are set there: "The Whirligig of Life" (Tennessee), "One Dollar's Worth," "A Call Loan," "The Pimienta Pancakes" (in Texas), and "The Emancipation of Billy" also take places in the American South.

Most interestingly, many of O. Henry's terrific short stories were authored while he was in jail. In 1892, Porter moved to Texas and soon became a teller at an Austin bank, where the institution's officials accused him of illegally manipulating funds into his own account. Porter fled to Central America, but upon returning to the States after his wife became very ill, the on-the-lam author was captured and then convicted. Thus, one of O. Henry's most famous stories "A Retrieved Reformation" involves safecracker Jimmy Valentine getting out of prison, and also, the writer's humorous stories "Shoes" and "Shoes and Ships" take place in Coralio, an imaginary seacoast village in Central America.

It is widely believed that the unique writing name "O. Henry" had been conceived in honor of a certain security guard named Orrin Henry, who had been employed at the federal penitentiary where the literary genius William Sydney Porter had been serving his sentence.

"Shoes"

Just look what the hell the legendary Lotus Plant had done to the noble Odysseus and his men in Homer's famous *Odyssey!* The larger-than-life hero's crew had eaten from the fabled shrub, and immediately, the ancient mariners fell into a dismal, melancholy, mental state, subsequently refusing to leave the artificial security of the Land of the Lotus Eaters, and consequently not returning to their sarcastic wives and juvenile delinquent, disobedient children back on the island of Ithaca.

In Coralio, Central America a certain mediocre American who was content idling-away his un-ambitious life was wastefully suffering from a similar dilemma as was Odysseus's dysfunctional, mentally-disillusioned, lost and unmotivated warriors.

John de Graffenreid Atwood had symbolically eaten of the tantalizing Lotus Plant, root, stem and delectable flower. The Central American tropics had easily gained possession of his preoccupied distracted and whimsical mind. But nonetheless, valiant Johnny energetically pursued his principal emotional obstacle, which was to try and forget all about his most-attractive girlfriend back in Alabama, a gorgeous example of femininity (possessing a terrific pair of titillating knockers) going by the rather-poetic-sounding name Rosine. Paradise and the Tropic of Cancer had collaborated to be realistically cruel to one John Eugene de Graffenreid Atwood.

Atwood and his loyal associate Billy Keogh would nightly occupy the veranda of the little consulate house, and drunkenly roar-out the catchy lyrics to popular turn-of-the-century songs, until the area natives puffing-away on microscopic marijuana joints, would shrug their shoulders, scratch their testicles, and mutter indiscernible profanities about the "fucked-up Yankee assholes".

One fine morning, Johnny's favorite delivery boy Pedro Burrito entered the consulate; awkwardly tripped over a very noticeable ottoman, and then clumsily dumped the daily mail onto a flat coffee table. Johnny slowly leaned from his comfortable hammock, and casually scrutinized the assorted letters and junk solicitations. Meanwhile, the all-too-carefree Keogh was trying to decapitate a lazy centipede with his exceptionally versatile Swiss Army knife, after vainly failing to amputate the critter's many squiggly legs. As Johnny casually perused the newly-arrived stamped stationery, his brain was totally absorbed in that perplexing state of Lotus-eating, where the entire world seemed bitter to his sensitive taste buds. Atwood was indeed in a very negative mood.

"Same old nonsensical bullshit!" Johnny nastily complained. "More nutcase naive Americans writing me for pertinent information about this God-forsaken, minuscule, insignificant country. The foolish shit-heads desire knowing all about raising indigenous fruit, but even more stupidly, the fools inquire about how to make a colossal fortune without lifting a goddamned fingernail to earn it. Half of the dopey freaks and brain-dead buffoons don't even exhibit normal courtesy in sending an adequate number of stamps to guarantee a prompt reply from their Coralio Consul."

"Maybe the ludicrous assholes are too busy playing with their girlfriends' love tunnels, while *their* unfaithful wives are being hammered by their frivolous husbands' best friends," Keogh laughed in self-amusement. "Cheating husbands always have pussy-pounding buddies and acquaintances. That's an axiom of early twentieth century existence! It's just emblematic of the times!"

"The moronic Imbeciles think that an essential Consul like me has nothing better to do with his valuable time than to write boring letters describing the myriad benefits of residing in this horrible hellhole! Gently slit open those precious envelopes for me, Old Man, and we'll see exactly what absurdities this new batch of un-illustrious Idiots are inquiring about."

Keogh conscientiously maneuvered his chair up to the table with a rosy smile adorning his happy-go-lucky countenance, and next began to recklessly slit open the envelopes with a broken, rusty scissors. Four of the lackluster missives were from citizens living in various sections of the United States, all of whom apparently regarded the young Consul at Coralio as an encyclopedic fountain of irrelevant knowledge. The curious letter of inquiry authors asked lengthy interrogatives about the climate, the indigenous fruits and vegetables, the laws, the business opportunities, the drug distribution networks, the destitute indigent residents, and the solicitors of information also sought intricate knowledge concerning rumored "notorious whorehouses" abundantly situated all throughout impoverished Coralio.

"Write back to the mentally-challenged Assholes, please Billy," the minor U.S. government official instructed and declared. "Feed them several immaterial statistics that'll refer the voracious Ignoramuses to the latest consular report that's conveniently available for the mere sum of one-hundred-and-fifty American dollars. Tell the inquisitive tycoon wannabes' that the State Department will be absolutely thrilled to the level of intense orgasm to share additional pertinent misinformation, after they've digested and comprehended my initial materials. And Billy; you have my royal permission to sign my full name, and provide my official seal at the bottom. And don't let your annoying pen scratch, Billy. Even when you scratch your fat ass, the nuisance noise keeps me awake for hours-on-end."

"Don't snore and inhale every freakin' flying and crawling insect that's buzzing, creeping, and flitting around Coralio," Keogh amiable replied and snickered. "I wholly promise to do your tedious work for you, if you consent to buying me some scandalous porno' pictures of Matthew Brady Civil War sexy bitches, ha, ha, ha! Truthfully Johnny," Billy elaborated. "You need a corps of subordinates to assist me in completing your numerous, arduous responsibilities! Hey Pal, wake-up a cotton-pickin' minute! This is too fucked-up to believe! Here's an inspirational letter from your old home town, Dalesburg, Alabama."

"Is that so?" Johnny reflexively uttered and mumbled, demonstrating a mild element of bland interest. "What's it about? Some demented freak of nature wanting to open an illegal munitions factory out here in the middle of the primitive jungle?"

"It's from your town Postmaster, who's apparently writing for one of Dalesburg's more respectable criminal citizens," Keogh facetiously related with a smile. "The memo says that a certain impractical jerk-off has a wild notion of coming-down here to Coralio and opening a much-needed shoe store. The Postmaster wants to know if you believe such a popular-type of U.S. business would be profitable. Says that the Gent he's representing has heard that there's been a keen economic boon along this remote disease-infested coast, and that the anonymous genius wants to get in on the ground floor while the poker's still hot! What do you think of that happy horseshit? Makes you wish you had dysentery, doesn't it?"

In spite of the high heat and his predictable mercurial temperament, Johnny's hammock swayed with laughter, until gravity-being-defied had the Consul tumbling head-first upon the filthy, wood-planked floor. Keogh was boisterously laughing, too, in response to Atwood's unexpected plummet. And the pet monkey on the side top bookcase shelf chattered-away as if the animal were enjoying a period of sexual heat; its gibberish intonations being projected in a total vocal dissonance that seemingly paralleled the humorous human reception of the zany Dalesburg letter.

"Great city sewer shit!" Johnny guffawed and shouted from his new-found position on the floor. "A mega shoe store to be located right here in metropolitan downtown Coralio; population two-thousand-five-hundred-and-three, including you and me! What'll they ask about next I wonder, a freakin' igloo or iceberg factory? Tell me Billy; of all of our stellar inhabitants fartin' around here in Coralio, how many lucky people have actually ever even worn a pair of bona fide shoes or sandals?"

Being somewhat theatrical, Keogh (feigning seriousness) pondered the great intellectual question as if he was a contemporary Descartes. "Let's do a quick evaluation, My Man. There's you and me, and the regional priest, and the macabre undertaker and…"

"Don't you dare stereotype me, you brazen nauseating Pervert," Johnny objected, holding-up a foot flaunting an authentic well-worn Indian moccasin. "I haven't worn an ordinary shoe down here since the last leap year elapsed. My painful bunions and spurs won't allow such a dumb-ass ridiculous practice!"

"But you own several standard pairs though," Keogh politely corrected. "And then there's that no-good bastard Blanchard; that gay faggot Geddie, who thinks he's a lesbian; that old womanizer Lutz, and don't exclude good old Doc Gregg; and let's not forget that hideous Italian gigolo, who's an agent for the renowned Mensa-Mensa Banana Company, and also let me mention that sinister rogue Delgado; no, that dumb-dick proudly wears women's open-toe high heels. And oh yes," Billy chuckled and added. "There's obese Madame Ortiz, who runs the town brothel at night that functions as Toddler Town Kiddy-Land during the daytime: She had sported a pair of polka-dot slippers at the community '*ho*-down' last week. And, oh yes," Keogh pontificated. "There's also Miss Pasa, Madame Ortiz's voluptuous daughter, that studied male prostitution along with group homosexuality while a dedicated sophomore at Beaver Navel Academy back in the States."

"You're giving me a damned splitting headache that's really quite-beyond the solution of me downing a full bottle of powerful aspirins," Johnny laughed. "Stop your incessant litany right this second! Have you no fuckin' cultural scruples? Learn to be more civilized. Act like petroleum, and be less crude and more refined!"

Keogh deliberately ignored Johnny's blatant criticisms. "And let's not forget Mrs. Geddie, who wears a size five on her left foot, and a size nine on her right, and that about takes care of the most prosperous local ladies! Let's see," Billy continued his comedic analysis. "Don't some of the barracks' troops wear protective footgear? No, unfortunately, not so! The who-gives-a-shit soldiers ingeniously prefer walking on grass and weeds, when they aren't actively smoking grass or weeds in their bunks! I'll be perfectly square and honest with you, Johnny; whoever your deranged Postmaster had to scribe that crazy letter for, must be suffering from brain cell deficiency!"

"True to form and par for the course," Johnny readily agreed, while imagining a beautiful green golf course fairway in his fanciful head. "Not over twenty of the town's burgeoning population wears necessary leather on their walking apparatus. Oh yes, Billy," Atwood frivolously concluded, "Coralio *is* the ideal hamlet to support an enterprising shoe store. That is to say, one queer retail emporium that doesn't want to part with its exotic merchandise. Wonder if my silly Uncle Obadiah Patterson is trying to pull my chain by sending me *that* abominable joke-type letter? The old geezer has a notorious reputation for always intentionally playing pranks and tricks on unsuspecting Dalesburg victims. I just got a mild brainstorm, Billy. Let's write him back a fictional narrative that I'll authoritatively dictate. We'll competently jolly good old Uncle Obadiah back with a few juicy words of our own."

Keogh industriously dipped his fountain pen into a nearby desk inkbottle, and applied the articulated language to paper at Johnny's illustrious command.

Mr. Obadiah Patterson
Postmaster
Dalesburg, Alabama, USA

Dear Sir:

In response to your meritorious letter of July 2nd, I have the distinct honor to inform you that according to my professional opinion, there is no place on the entire globe that presents to the naked eye stronger evidence of the need for an aristocratic-type shoe store than does the colorful town of Coralio.

There are almost three-thousand worthy residents walking the streets of our thriving pueblo, and not a single (or married) shoe store to service the growing number of much-in-need wealthy customers. The direness of this extraordinary situation literally speaks for itself!

This splendid coast is rapidly becoming a vital destination for enterprising businessmen, but evidently, the shoe industry is one that has been carelessly neglected. In fact, a considerable number of our gentry are actually without substantial walking arrangements as I diligently compose these bona fide words.

Besides the drastic need above cited, Coralio residents are also clamoring for a college of higher mathematics, an operational coal-yard, a dynamic cannon and cannonball plant, a mahogany-wood toothpick manufacturing and distribution facility, a hemorrhoid shrinking and breast reduction clinic, and finally, a legitimate and sensational Punch and Judy puppet show. Needless to say, I have the honor to be, sir,

Your obedient civil servant,

John de Graffenreid Atwood
U.S. Consul at Coralio

P.S. Hello Uncle Obadiah! How's the old Southern burg doing at the beginning of this exciting new century? What would the inefficient government be doing without dedicated public servants like you and me keeping Washington afloat? Look-out for a green-headed iguana and a retarded parrot with a yellow banana nose coming your way soon; all originating from your favorite and most-distinguished only nephew,

Johnny

"I specifically included *that* creative postscript," the jocular Consul incisively indicated, "so that impish Uncle Obadiah won't take umbrage with the sophisticated and official tenor of my inane letter! Now Billy," Johnny stipulated. "Have the grammar, spelling, vocabulary, and punctuation of that fine piece of correspondence fine-tuned, and then get Pedro's skinny ass over to the post office for its immediate delivery. According to my fiscal calendar, the *Ariadne* takes the mail out tomorrow morning, if the local lazy stevedores come out of their drunken stupors and haphazardly load the ship's hull with fresh-picked fruit."

The social nocturnal activities in Coralio were without a doubt monotonous and dull. The people's recreations were few, and indeed, totally unimaginative. Most of the dreadlock-haired men staggered around barefoot, randomly cursing to each other in Spanish, and simultaneously smoking illicit, homemade, drug-laden cigars and cigarettes. In some distant shacks and shanties, the strumming of mournful-sounding guitars saturated the already sad and distasteful environment. Enormous tree frogs that were too fat to croak, fought for species' dominance up in the high foliage, but by nine p.m., the town's dirt and gravel main street, its secondary trails, and its ancillary paths were virtually deserted.

But most matters remained rather tranquil inside the centrally located consulate. Billy Keogh would habitually arrive nightly, and open a bottle of sweet bourbon for personal consumption; for the village's only cool evening spot was the small seaward veranda of Johnny's special hideaway asylum.

After fully downing the delicious, intoxicating liquor, each night around midnight, nostalgia would gradually develop in the self-exiled Consul's lonely heart. Then Johnny would invariably repeat the all-too-familiar background to the empathetic and disciplined Keogh, who would patiently listen to his colleague's woeful, disenchanting, redundant monologue.

"But Billy, don't think for one iota that I've actually forgotten *that* fickle bitch," Atwood would summarize his mirthless speech. "And I want you to know that I've entirely forgotten *that* sexy broad. The memory of her seldom enters my lousy mind. Now Billy, you must fathom that I've forgotten all about Rosine. If that stunning and dazzling doll would enter through that door right now," Johnny stated in almost a trance, "my pulse wouldn't jump a notch, and I certainly wouldn't manage to achieve half a hard-on. That troublesome female infatuation of mine has been virtually fully extinguished. Call me selfish if you wish, but I've decided to keep all of my testosterone, and all of my sperm juice all to myself!"

"Don't I know it, too," Keogh would automatically and sympathetically respond. "Of course, you've forgotten all about that lovely vixen. I gotta' commend you for that! That's the appropriate thing to do. It wasn't quite kosher for that amorous Babe to entertain the likes of that ruthless Dalesburg villain, Dink Pawson!"

"Pink Dawson, you mean!" Johnny volleyed-back with obvious contempt in his tone of voice. "That obnoxious, rich son-of-a-bitch owned five-hundred-acres of fertile farmland, though, and in Rosine's old man's microscopic skull, *that* particular bullshit was all that really mattered. Maybe I'll have a chance to enact some well-deserved retribution upon that dastardly shit-head Dawson someday. Once upon a time, the Dawsons weren't anybody in Alabama. Every hick and hillbilly throughout the entire state has heard of the patriotic Atwoods. Say Billy Boy; did I ever tell ya' in confidential conversation that my blessed mother was a de Graffenreid?"

"Is that so?" Billy would predictably answer. "I thought that there was only one Blessed Mother! But that's special news to me!" even though Keogh had listened to Johnny's pouting litany at least three hundred times. "Say, Johnny. If your mom was your blessed mother as you just aptly divulged, does *that* significant relationship make you Jesus Christ reincarnated?"

Johnny overlooked Billy's sacrilegious verbalization "It's a provable fact that can be easily documented and confirmed about the haughty and respectable de Graffenreids of Hancock County. But I never think of or mention that voluptuous Bitch any more, do I Billy?" Johnny melodramatically slurred before violently imbibing the remaining ounce of bourbon in the bottle.

"Not for a New York minute," Billy sarcastically announced to the disconsolate Consul. "You've got a bad fuckin' case of amnesia as far as her extraordinary feminine charms are concerned! Why don't ya' just go over to Doc Gregg's cottage and have your useless dick fully amputated? I really think that a basic sex-change operation would do you a world of good. You need a nice pink vagina, and a swollen, aroused clitoris; that's what the hell you really need! Then you could both piss and shit sitting-down."

At that point in their often-repeated and inebriated verbal exchange, Johnny would gradually fall into a welcomed slumber, and Keogh would gingerly rise, stumble over the ancient wicker furniture, and then instinctively cough his way back to the confines of his own shabby domicile.

In a long day or two, the impulsively organized letter to Obadiah Patterson constituted major, literary non-history to the two Coralio/American misfits, but on the twenty-sixth of July, the forbidden fruit of Johnny's hilarious written reply suddenly appeared upon the proverbial Tree of Ignorance.

The *Andador,* an archaic and obsolete fruit steamer that dropped anchor in Coralio Harbor rather regularly, showed-up in port right on schedule. The local sandy beach was instantly crammed with an array of gawking spectators, while the overzealous quarantine doctor, and the conscientious customhouse appointees assiduously rowed-out to comprehensively enact their highly-specialized and important duties. In this particular instance, the arrival of the very familiar steamship was a major event.

An hour later, Billy Keogh ambled into the consulate looking totally refreshed, and especially cool in his white linen attire. The likeable fellow was grinning like an infamous Cheshire cat.

"Guess what has occurred, Dear Master of the Universe?" Keogh boldly addressed Johnny, who was still occupying his hammock, with his idle body arranged in the classic fetal position.

"It's too goddamned unbearably hot to guess anything!" Johnny vehemently protested. "Stop playing childish and adolescent mind games, Billy! Get to the goddamned essential point!"

"Your weirdo shoe store man has arrived, coming all the way from Alabama," Billy giggled and informed, completely relishing the wonderful moment. "And the flamboyant jerk-off has a fantastic supply of goods large enough to provide for the entire hemisphere as far south as Tierra del Fuego. The dock-men are busily transporting the bald-headed numbskull's cartons over to the customhouse as we speak," Keogh further explained. "Six amazing barges full that they've already brought ashore, and they've paddled-back to retrieve the rest of the non-sellable retail products. Oh my; glory absolutely does reign supreme throughout the usually uncertain tropics, Mr. Consul! Ha, ha, ha!" the euphoric aide gleefully conveyed. "I can't wait until the old stubborn Asshole has an earnest conference with *you,* my exquisite Superior! It'll be worth nine fabulous years laboring on Devil's Island, just to eavesdrop on that one sensational discussion between the two of you! Ha, ha, ha! What a fantastic blast! Ha, ha, ha!"

Billy Keogh was entirely enthralled; his giddy mind dizzily swimming in his own self-generated levity. The felicitous fellow soon chose a clean area of the matting to lay upon the floor, still laughing indulgently. The thin walls shook as William Addison Keogh coughed and choked convulsively. Johnny turned over in his hammock, naturally shocked at hearing the incredible morning news.

"Don't tell me that any red-blooded American dementia-oriented senior citizen was foolish enough to take my nutty letter seriously!" Johnny exclaimed. "The insane guy must be the ultimate asshole of stupid moronic assholes!"

"A ten-thousand-dollar stock of dress shoes and loafers!" the all-too-ecstatic Keogh exhaled. "I took a long gander at the fanatical codger while the dumb-ass was standing like a statue on the crowded beach. You should've been there when the old curmudgeon looked around and squinted his eyes through his thick-lens specs, and then avariciously peered at the barefooted natives' feet. I wish I had a reliable newspaper reporter's camera in my possession to effectively capture the strange phenomenon on film."

"Are you maliciously prevaricating again, or are you telling me the God-honest truth?" Johnny Atwood demanded. "What the hell ever happened to fairy tale endings? Why does Cinderella have to now get screwed before she gets married? Why does she have to get balled before the ball? Why does innocent and pristine Snow White have to contract venereal disease by osmosis before having intercourse with any of the sex-starved, long-dicked Seven Dwarfs? And I hereby insist that you stop your bothersome chortling, Billy!" the agitated Consul admonished his aberrant silly underling. "I hate to see a grown adult asshole like yourself successfully making a laughing hyena out of himself!"

"And the narrow-minded old-timer's dark-skinned daughter has good looks, too, and her physical charms appear to be in ultra-fine cherry condition! The Old Gent's last name is Hemstetter," Keogh enthusiastically elucidated. "He's a_____! Hey Johnny, what the hell's wrong with you now? Your pallid face looks like you've evolved into an albino! Are you turning into a spooky Halloween hog-goblin right before my eyes, or what?"

Johnny's moccasin footwear struck the floor with an abrupt thud. "Get off the damned matting, you toad-faced Nincompoop! You've just accurately described my precious Rosine, and her dumb-assed father! What a complete knucklehead Uncle Obadiah is! Now get-off the shit-eatin' floor and help me, Billy! What the hell are *we* gonna' do? Has all the maniacal world gone even more maniacal? What the heck ever happened to rationality? Tell me, Loyal Friend. Has all dependable reason abandoned the Earth while I was napping?"

Billy rose and dutifully saluted Johnny in a mock military fashion. "Let's run away like bona-fide cowards to South Africa, and go on permanent safari!" Keogh promptly suggested. "Or better yet; let's become avowed transvestites and enter a Catholic convent. I think you'd make a terrific bossy Mother Superior!"

"Cut the immature bullshit, Billy! This drastic, ugly situation must be resolved!" Johnny emphatically reprimanded his chief advisor. "Why the hell couldn't you be Sir Isaac Newton or Nostradamus, or somebody else good at problem solving?"

"Honestly, Johnny. I never once considered the possibility that the new arrivals would be your old flame and her gullible pop. I'll tell you what I'll do!" Keogh humbly promised, now submissively on his knees like an ancient Greek suppliant. "I'll get the girl and her dad some decent living quarters, while you go-down to the pier and face the weird music that you've so inadvertently orchestrated. Yeah," Billy resolved. "I'll scurry over to Mr. Goodwin's Jungle Lodge and arrange for *his* wife to wholeheartedly take them in as valued guests.

I surely hope that this confounded dilemma doesn't escalate into a bizarre debacle!"

"Bless your remarkable soul, Billy!" Consul Johnny gratefully acknowledged. "I knew all along that you wouldn't desert me on my death bed! Maybe we can stave-off impending disaster before this fucked-up world stops spinning and revolving all around the fucked-up Solar System!"

Keogh deftly hoisted his battered white umbrella, and then ambitiously trekked-over to Goodwin's Jungle Lodge. Johnny hastily put on his coat and hat. Next, the besieged Consul methodically marched-down to the crowded beach, all-the-while contemplating that he had neglected to brush his teeth, shave his whiskers, and comb his hair.

Amidst the dark shadows of the decrepit-looking customhouse, Johnny Atwood eventually located Mr. Hemstetter, accompanied by the alluring Rosine, both of whom were surrounded by a gaggle of gaping and gossiping locals. The customs' officers were engrossed in their individual responsibilities, precisely tabulating the newly itemized imports, while the *Andador's* lethargic crew was unloading more merchandise.

Rosine was very animated-but-composed as the gorgeous doll cautiously surveyed the eccentric-but-impetuous ship captain, who was picking his nose and then flicking the disgusting boogers one-by-one onto the rain-drenched ground. A blush quickly appeared upon her rosy cheeks when the Alabama beauty queen noticed her old Dalesburg admirer approaching. Mr. Hemstetter eagerly extended his hand in a very friendly manner. Immediately, Atwood perceptively fathomed that his former prospective father-in-law was indeed a fatuous and asinine get-rich-quick, fickle prick, who was forever dissatisfied with *his* current economic circumstance.

"I'm delighted to see you, John; may I call you John?" Mr. Henry Hemstetter began his garrulous salutation. "Let me thank you for your instant reply to our postmaster's general introductory letter. That feeble-minded coot Obadiah Patterson volunteered writing to you on my behalf. I had been studying this part of Central America, and selectively searching for something in the way of a business opportunity where the profits would be, how should I say, would be more-than-adequate. I had observed in the newspapers that this isolated region had been getting the attention of big Wall Street investment firms. I'm extremely grateful for receiving your honest advice to establish a shoe store right here in downtown Coralio," Hemstetter expounded. "I had sold every tangible asset that I owned and parlayed the money into the finest assortment of men's and women's shoes available. You have a picture postcard-like town here, Mr. Atwood. I hope and trust that my shoe revenues will be as substantial as your encouraging letter had led me to believe."

Johnny's gut-wrenching anguish was miraculously abbreviated with the swift arrival of Keogh, who intelligently dispensed the pertinent news that Mr. Hemstetter and Rosine would be initially staying at the very accommodating Goodwin's Jungle Lodge. Billy suavely recommended that the aide should escort the young lady and her bound-to-fail father over to the aforementioned inn, so that the new arrivals could thoroughly inspect their respective rooms.

After the three others departed the area, Johnny decided to saunter over to the customhouse to determine that the shoes' shipment had satisfactorily passed the traditional entrance examination, and that the merchandise had been safely stored inside the government warehouse (that incidentally featured a leaky tin roof). In the meantime, Billy "the Kid" Keogh anxiously scrambled about Coralio's main street, attempting to find the Goodwins in order to tell them not to divulge to the Hemstetters (waiting at the lodge) the ostensible truth about the rain forest town not being the ideal scenario to open a bound-to-fail shoe store.

'Johnny needs a chance to redeem himself,' Keogh imagined with a grim, sober expression ruling his facial features. 'I'd hate to see my good friend castrated by his old girl's livid father, who at one time might've been an accomplished butcher.'

That night, the apprehensive and desperate Consul and the consoling Keogh held a frantic consultation on the consulate's breezy veranda. "Send them back to Dalesburg," confided Keogh. "If you want to avoid assassination, or an on-a-mission father-daughter firing squad, immediately deport them both back to Sweet Home Alabama!"

"I would," Johnny confessed with undeniable remorse. "But I've been lying to you Billy all along. And I don't mean that I was lying in my goddamned hammock either."

"All right about the veracity of those stark words," Keogh almost-apologetically agreed. "Everybody's entitled to make an ass out of himself by growing exaggerated donkey ears at least once in his miserable life!"

"What an absolute catastrophe I've ignorantly perpetuated Billy! I've deliberately told you at least a hundred times," Johnny vividly recollected and elaborated, "that I had forgotten all about lovely Rosine and her robust bust," Atwood declared.

"About three-hundred and seventy-five to be more exact," verified the staunch pillar of patience. "Yes, my delicate ears do not deceive me! My hearing has listened to approximately a full year's worth of your radical and preposterous bullshit!"

"I lied every time," Johnny regretfully disclosed. "I hadn't forgotten *that* knockout chick for one tiny second. I was a stubborn jackass for running away from reality once, and I was too proud of a charlatan to ever return to Dalesburg like a defeated and disconsolate grown man. Just this afternoon, I found the time to discuss the deplorable past with Rosine. And I actually enjoyed a few treasured moments over at Goodwins. Do you remember that wealthy farmer dude back in Alabama that was always trying to harass me, and win over my girl's affections?"

"Dink Pawson?" Keogh said, systematically attempting to aggravate his boss and further break Johnny's already supersensitive testicles. "Wasn't his name Dink Pawson?" the naughty comrade forcefully reiterated.

"His gruesome name was Pink Dawson; not Dink Pawson!" Johnny angrily shouted. "Well, anyway. I've just learned that the muscle-bound punk wasn't even a hill of pork and beans to my beloved Rosine. And my girl didn't believe a syllable of the contrived things Dawson had told her about me."

"Like you being a transgender male with only half a penis, and only a third of a gonad?" foolishly jested Keogh. "If I were you, which I'm glad I'm not, I'd be mighty fuckin' pissed-off too about that shit! With a limited-sized penis, and only one tiny testicle, I'd say that you'd be a veritable Johnny-come-lately! Ha, ha, ha!"

"But my fate is sewed-up now, Billy!" Johnny sulked. "That absurd letter we had dispatched ruined and killed all hopes of any suitable reconciliation. I suspect that Rosine will positively despise me when she discovers that her vulnerable father had been made the victim of a destructive crank prank that no half-decent eighth-grader would be guilty of formulating. Shoes! Why Mr. Hemstetter couldn't sell twenty-seven pairs of shoes here in Coralio if he kept his doomed shoe store open for twenty-seven centuries."

"Send them back to Alabama, and if you're lucky, you'll only be hospitalized for a month with your legs in traction. But on the plus side, you'll still be breathing!" Keogh objectively evaluated. "Send them both back to Dalesburg, and start living a new inspired life devoid of debilitating grief!"

"If I tell them the truth and send them back to the USA," Johnny reluctantly speculated and stoically opined, "what'll Rosine think of my foolish nature then?"

"Who the fuck cares!" Keogh uncharacteristically yelled in demonstrable frustration. "You'll still have *me* as your supportive bedroom companion!"

"I love that luscious doll more than ever, Billy, despite the fact that I've never had occasion to even once rub her hairy pussy, or get my middle finger wet inside her warm love tunnel," Johnny intimated and shared. "But now I've lost her devotion forever, because I tried being a dim-witted simpleton bozo when the thermometer's temperature had reached 102 degrees. Billy, please check my vital signs when you have time!"

"I'll show you some savory porno' pictures of naked, aborigine women with magnificent split beavers. And if you get an erection, the odds are that you'll live to see tomorrow," Billy assured.

"But what can we do? That is, given the inferior lowlife human material we have to work with here in Coralio?" Johnny questioned. "To tell you the truth, I'd rather be a condemned asshole shoveling tons of hot shit into furnaces down there in Hades' domain."

"Keep cheerful and try jerking-off at least three times daily to settle-down your frayed nerves," Keogh optimistically remarked. "And let the Hemstetters open their glorious shoe store. We can stir up a temporary rush in footwear demand. I'll start off the frenzy by purchasing six pairs of cheerleader saddle shoes, as soon as the front door swings wide-open to conduct commerce. And I've debated and mulled over the evolving crisis with several trustworthy citizens. Our friends will buy shoes as if they were overly anxious centipedes getting ready for fall and winter weather. Mr. Goodwin has agreed to acquire three cases. The Geddies want eleven pair between them. Clancy and Doc Gregg each desire procuring three pair of alligator-hide slippers; and that flirtatious Frenchman Blanchard wants a dozen pair to impress future lady visitors that accidentally land in Coralio. The Hemstetters could even improve their anticipated prosperity by selling cotton socks, elastic suspenders, and peds."

"That's only a dozen prospective customers for a tremendous inventory of imported shoes," objected Johnny. "That harebrained solution just won't work! There's a gigantic problem here that I must assess, attack, and solve!"

"Maybe if you take a healthy shit, your confused mind will be clearer!" Billy constructively offered. "I contend that your erratic one-shit mind has been challenged by a two-shit conundrum!"

"Go home Billy, and please leave me the hell alone," retorted Johnny. "I gotta' get my stalled cerebrum going in the proper direction. I'll sit quietly here inside the consulate, and be painfully constipated until I finally find the most viable answer to my perplexing riddle. If there's a solution," Atwood conjectured and stated, "I'll use my perseverance and my guile to doggedly locate it. If I fail in my endeavor, then *that* defeat will constitute another terrible shipwreck attributable to the enigmatic tropics."

Keogh obediently left the front porch of the consulate, feeling extremely depressed and rather impotent, although the aide never before had ever experienced any symptoms of erectile dysfunction. Johnny soon stretched his limp body inside a steamer chair, and began randomly hypothesizing and pondering. When dawn finally broke on the eastern horizon, the still-puzzled Consul remained slouched-down in his chair. Then, the despondent fellow slowly rose from his seat, sneezed into a dirty handkerchief, and persistently whistled as Atwood took a quick bath.

At precisely nine o'clock in the morning, the formerly-bewildered Consul paced down to the dingy, miniature cable office and groggily stood above a blank piece of paper. Then, Atwood began scribbling-down an inspiration that his fertile mind conceived. The U.S. Consul officially signed the brief statement, and then handed the message to the affable employee, which was transmitted at a cost of thirty-three American dollars. 'There's nothing like having an old nagging problem (like Pink Dawson) solve a new one,' Johnny theorized.

To Pinkney Dawson
Dalesburg, Alabama

Draft for a hundred-dollars to be forwarded to you via the next mail shipped out of Coralio. Please have delivered to me immediately five-hundred-pounds of stiff, dry cockleburs. The prickly objects have a new innovative use here in the local arts and sciences. Current wholesale market price is twenty cents a pound. Further orders are likely. Please rush delivery.

John de Graffenreid Atwood
U.S. Consul at Coralio

"Shoes and Ships"

A week after Rosine and Mr. Hemstetter had made their surprise appearance in Coralio, a modest storefront had been secured on the Calle Grande (Great Street), and the enormous stock of shoes was then carefully transferred from the sweltering dockside warehouse and into the new retail business's premises. Curious onlookers passed by the oddball establishment, wondering if all traveling Americans suffered from the same insanity that Mr. Hemstetter, Johnny Atwood, and Billy Keogh amply demonstrated.

But Johnny was quite fortunate to have loyal friends that were sympathetic to his romantic plight. Keogh aggressively bought a new pair of shoes every hour the first day the footgear emporium opened its doors; eagerly purchasing a pair of elevator alligator loafers, crocodile tennis shoes, floral decorated rubber boots, and dainty tan dancing pumps, all before high-noon. The other English-speaking Coralio residents nobly and liberally mimicked Keogh's admirable example, thus reinforcing the grand illusion that a capitalistic American shoe store could easily thrive and prosper in the sweltering Central American jungle port town.

Mr. Hemstetter was thrilled beyond belief at his shoe inventory's initial success, but the elderly codger expressed to Rosine his alarm that the inhabitants of the mosquito-infested village seemed to be "boycotting his all-essential merchandise".

"They're basically shy and timid, Father," Rosine supportively declared. "The local citizens have to first adjust to us being here, and then they'll actively patronize your Grand Opening, once they get used to us being enterprising Caucasians."

"I hope you're right," Mr. Hemstetter tentatively replied, showing his grave concern. "What more could we expect at first contact with uneducated, and introverted natives? Perhaps I should obtain a bilingual dictionary, and start learning how to speak fluent Spanish. I could make-up some multicultural jokes by saying such goofy remarks as, 'Mira Aqui', while amusingly holding the store's *key* in the palm of my hand. Ha, ha, ha!"

One sultry Tuesday afternoon, congenial Billy Keogh stepped-into the Consul's consulate office to consult with and console the rather beleaguered consul. "Got any non-liquid solutions up your sleeve?" Keogh asked Johnny. "If you can grab a magician's hat, and make a bevy of new shoe customers come-out of it, instead of an anemic-looking white rabbit, I suggest that you perform that slick trick immediately to salvage your bound-to-disintegrate relationship with your Alabama sweetheart. I'm glad that I'm now celibate, and don't have to worry about such dangerous, amorous-type bullshit."

"If I was an accomplished magician, I'd gladly travel back in time and turn into my driveway in familiar Dalesburg, Alabama; hitch my horse to its stable post, and then merrily drag and park my buggy into the rear red barn," grieved and wished the disconsolate Consul. "And furthermore, noble Sir William. I wouldn't want to pull an antagonistic, belligerent hare from a black high-hat, or else risk being pulverized with a flurry of low-blow rabbit punches that might effectively incapacitate me for life!"

"Well, all the boys have already expended their spare dough negotiating for shoes, so regrettably, Good Buddy," Keogh sadly noted, "it's now exclusively up to you to save your worn-out *sole,* without making a complete heel out of yourself. I mean, after Clancy preposterously bought seven pairs of ballerina slippers for his homosexual boyfriend, it's sad to say that there's been only one pair of shoes sold since then!"

"What about the rest of our sympathetic friends?" Johnny asked.

"Blanchard had obtained a pair of gaudy-fur-lined slippers, when the notorious womanizer thought he had seen Miss Hemstetter enter the front door, but then when the voyeur found-out that Rosine wasn't anywhere near the termite-infested building, the Peeping Tom became disgruntled; and sprinted at full-speed to the lagoon, and violently tossed the newly-acquired footgear into the stagnant, deep swamp area! But Johnny Boy, isn't a fruit steamer from Mobile scheduled to arrive in port tomorrow? Perhaps we can stealthily kidnap Rosine and her senile old man, and have the pair stowed-away as cargo, if we can handsomely and generously bribe the ship's captain and crew."

"Billy, I certainly would appreciate any constructive help you could provide; that is to say, after you get over the excessive immaturity you've been suffering from ever since early childhood!" Johnny skillfully chided. "If you can't act your age, Sir William, then I recommend that you act your shoe size, no pun intended!"

"Well, my good, Scholarly Pal. Since my mind is as barren as a New Hampshire deciduous tree in the height of winter, exactly what do you intend to do about your unenviable predicament?" Keogh impudently and indignantly inquired. "Commit sudden suicide?"

"Since we can't create any more demand for Mr. Hemstetter's irrelevant foot products, I shrewdly plan to create a necessity for the demand," Atwood obtusely answered. "That's what the hell I plan to vigorously do. I'll scheme a way to generate a necessity for the now-limited demand."

"I gotta' admit. A man's love of hairy vagina can make any normal guy's dick get erect," the aide humorously reminded the Consul. "I remember I once had a big crush on a gorgeous brunette when I was a young stud, living out in Phoenix, Arizona," Keogh facetiously intimated to his government boss.

"How did you handle it?" Johnny wanted to know, both accidentally and incidentally biting the dangling bait.

"Well," Keogh elucidated with an impish chuckle. "I got my bowels in an uproar when the doll shaved her luscious pussy, so I cleverly removed my toupee from my head; slit the sucker down the middle with a sharp carving knife; glued the furry object to where her bush should've been, and then screwed the hell out of the squealing bitch just for spite and Old Glory!"

Two weeks had now elapsed since the thoroughly-neurotic Consul had sent his strangely worded cablegram to the rich muscular Dalesburg farmer, Pink Dawson. The first Wednesday morning in August, a huge, mysterious, cumbersome burlap bale was routinely delivered to Johnny's front porch, which by the way was tattered, unkempt, and desperately in need of new insect-resistant screens. The minor government official surreptitiously dragged the strapped-but-heavy cube into his main storage closet, to be secretly stowed-away for future utilization. But eventually surrendering to temptation, late that night, Johnny ripped-open a corner of the smelly bale to privately inspect the quality of its contents.

'These prickly burs will help me get some fine satisfaction from that prickly prick Pinkney Dawson,' Johnny introspectively surmised as the Consul keenly examined the wonderful antidote to his present difficulty. 'How cunning can I possibly be? These son-of-a-bitches are as sharp as needles, and will easily penetrate any barefoot; no matter how friggin' thick the victim's goddamned skin is! If you want to get under someone's skin, this foolproof bur method is definitely the perfect remedy, ha, ha, ha!'

When all of the drunken, sleep apnea town natives were snoring away in deep slumber, Johnny roamed the Grande Calle with impunity, and generously distributed his cockleburs all along the narrow dirt streets, and also inside the even more-narrow dirt and grass walkways. The crafty prankster even dispensed the skin-piercing items inside the skinny alleyways that channeled between the houses, where the *cerveza*-drinking men often emptied their filled-to-capacity kidneys before re-entering the village saloon to imbibe some more brew, thus pissing-away every last peso left inside their shallow pants' pockets.

The following morning, the ordinarily apathetic market vendors predictably assembled near the seaport docks to sell their food and wares at the southern end of the Calle Grande. Soon, Spanish shouts of "What the fuck's this shit?" and exclamations of "My fuckin' toes are bleeding!" saturated the entire scene of confusion.

At first, the random loud squeals were quite ambiguous in nature, but soon the shrill intonations became much more specific and defined. "Shit! I haven't screamed like this since I had my first genuine orgasm!" one swarthy-skinned overweight woman yelled. "I must be fuckin' masochistic, or something like that! I actually think I'm enjoying the damned severe pain! It reminds me of the time I lost my virginity by repeatedly shoving an overgrown cucumber up my crotch when I was a mere eight-years-old."

Another even fatter-but-shorter lady hollered-out in Spanish, "Mother fuck! I haven't had excruciating pain like this since I was pronounced the first octo-mom in Coralio! And believe me, and I swear to God on a pile of Catholic and Protestant Bibles when I say, I haven't gotten laid once since the gruesome eight baby delivery! Hey somebody; get me a Koran!"

Soon, the aggregate of hurting and cursing natives either plopped-down onto the dirt and gravel main-street, or sat upon the grassy turf sidewalks, intensely scrutinizing the new-found source of their mutual discomfort. Jabbering lamentations could be heard coming from all possible directions, and soon the aggrieved adult males in attendance commenced hopping and dancing around in circles, as if they were intoxicated frogs, toads, and chirping crickets; all of them responsively uttering flurries of expletives to vehemently express their general unhappiness and overall duress.

"We've been bitten by invisible, poisonous, evil spiders of an unknown variety!" the vociferous village mayor proclaimed. "Holy cow shit! My fuckin' swollen ankles and toes don't now feel very swell at all!"

Soon, howling and crying bratty children, fresh victims *of* and participants *in* the recently-developed pandemonium, all in unison ceased their former wild romping. And then, a brief moment later, the obnoxious little tykes clamorously began proclaiming very audible Spanish chants of: "Shit!" "Fuck!" "Cock-sucking hurt!", and finally, dissonant unrehearsed classic choruses of "Who needs this shit?" and "Mother fuck!"

Dona Maria Castillas Buenventura de las Casas, the corpulent and sassy village chief prostitute, emitted a loud howl as the corpulent harlot gingerly bent over, and then savagely plucked a large bur from her right foot's little toe; her hairy, naked asshole being exposed for everyone's examination. But unfortunately, the men of the sex-crazy community were too preoccupied removing piercing thorns from their own tender feet to ever take notice of the woman's very familiar (but still now-ignored) ultra-wide split pink taco. Then, the distressed "pay-for-play" whore got-down on her hands and knees, and rapidly crawled into the local panaderia, and after removing six painful burs from her aching feet, the notorious bitch discovered two large loafs of bread. She quickly sliced the dual objects open with a sharp cleaver, and then imaginatively used the recently baked, very hot oven products, as improvised shoes.

"That'll be twelve pesos," Senor Sanchez, the local baker demanded. "Twelve pesos, or else take them off and get the fuck out of here! Quit loafin' around, Bitch! You oughta' know a good bargain when you see one!"

"Fuck you, Viejo Verde!" Dona Maria Castillas Buenventura de las Casas loquaciously retorted. "You still owe me fifty damned pesos from the last time you naughtily stuck your sticky tongue high inside my raunchy, smelly, love tunnel, trying to locate my goddamned G-spot. So, Jacketta; don't expect any dough from me, you goddamned demented sex pervert!"

Senora Dora Madonna Naomi Clarissa Valdez, the popular village whore who screwed for pleasure and not for money, simply because the woman was a devout nymphomaniac with an insatiable sexual appetite, began crying aloud as if the sought-after harlot had a family of lethal scorpions spontaneously bite (and take a massive chunk of flesh out of) her hyperactive clitoris. The extremely-ugly bitch swiftly meandered on her fingers and knees through a wicked obstacle course of stumbling, hopping, limping, and noisy frantic men, women, and children; all of whom were energetically emitting ear-shattering vituperations.

The first-person observant enough to realize what the hell had happened was Esteban Delgado, the esteemed aged barber, who had experienced a similar unpleasant event while he was taking a healthy crap ten-years-earlier inside a vacant farm field down in Argentina. "These are not the bites of venomous insects!" old Esteban cried out, remembering the Gauchos' complaints on the pampas. "And they're not the earth droppings of constipated pigeons or eagles, either! These nasty swellings are the remnants of ordinary cockleburs, and the only fuckin' remedy as far as my limited intelligence knows is zapatos for our toes! Zapatos, I say!" the barber shouted about the chaotic din. "We should've all been born with shoes on our fuckin' club feet!"

Everyone that had been suffering from their individual harrowing agony instantaneously rushed in the direction of Mr. Hemstetter's shoe store, with the entire herd of Coralio residents stampeding one another while attempting to collectively barge into the building. That noteworthy day, the jubilant shoe merchant sold over three-hundred pairs of footgear with the "necessity for the demand" having been ingeniously caused by the remote seacoast town's inimitable U.S. Consul. That evening, the happy government official paid a visit to the disheveled Grande Calle shoe business, which had cardboard boxes, cartons, and wrapping paper strewn all over the floor. The owner of the establishment was ecstatic.

"What a fantastic sales rush we had today!" Mr. Hemstetter informed Johnny, nearly hyperventilating as the greedy entrepreneur fanned himself incessantly. "Yesterday, I had only three customers all day long, but today, over a hundred times as many patrons scrambled through the front portal. I worked my fat ass off this afternoon, so if you find my rectum lying somewhere inside the stockroom," the old geezer grinned and joked, "give the sucker a much-needed enema, before attaching the indispensable organ back onto my ultra-wide posterior. What do ya' think, John?"

"If you recall, I had told you the natives would eventually spend their whole salaries on beautiful leather shoes, instead of on the usual booze and sex venues, once the citizens had acclimated themselves to the attractive idea of finally adjusting to modern civilization," Atwood proudly bragged. "And you, Mr. Hemstetter, coincidentally were in the right place at just the right time to efficiently zap the local population with *zap*atos, ha, ha, ha! What a wonderful travesty!"

"I gotta' order at least three dozen new cases from my New York supplier, simply to keep my dwindling stock at a respectable level," the naïve old codger insisted. "This new prosperous business of mine has really turned into a virtual 'shoe-in,' ha, ha, ha! I can't wait to open my next store in the little town down the coast."

"Don't be too impetuous or optimistic while anxiously exploring your unbridled euphoria!" the wary Consul counseled. "Wait a few days to see if your orders and sales slack off! Better safe than sorry; that's what I prescribe!"

Within the next week, Johnny again abundantly disseminated his cocklebururs at midnight, all throughout the primitive village. And the following morning, bright and early, Mr. Hemstetter's store business was spontaneously rejuvenated to the extent where three-quarters of his goods had been successfully bartered for pesos. Johnny immediately cabled the muscular bully, Pink Dawson, for another ample five-hundred-pound bale of cockleburs at the international-wholesale going rate.

Mr. Hemstetter ambitiously made-up a lengthy order for shoe stock replenishment, and Johnny-on-the-spot wisely volunteered to dependably deliver the itemized form to be dispatched from Coralio in the next morning's mail. But before the wily Consul reached the vicinity of the tiny post office, Atwood deliberately destroyed the white envelope containing the urgent shoe request, fully honoring the dictates of his very guilty conscience.

At eight o'clock that evening, and beneath a majestic full moon, Johnny slowly escorted naïve Rosine under the neighborhood mango tree to register a sincere apology for his blatant letter-writing indiscretion involving the girl's very susceptible father. His humble apology was not-too-well-received.

"You're a wicked, deceitful no-good, son-of-a-bitch bastard!" Rosine nastily balked and accused. "You oughta' have your horny pecker re-circumcised and re-shaped, for being such an utterly detestable practicing asshole! You pathetically say it all was a terrible joke!" the infuriated girl squawked. "I say you oughta' die a slow agonizing death from five different kinds of insidious venereal diseases, all eating away at your genitals!"

"I'm very sorry I fumbled the ball and lost the game," Johnny replied and sobbed in a low tone of voice. "Is there no mercy, no forgiveness in your heart?"

"When you had solemnly and sanctimoniously entered the shoe store as my father's first customer, I thought at that moment in time that you could be trusted," Rosine recollected and verbalized. "But when you held up a pair of black suede loafers, and pompously said 'I think I could take a shine to these handsome shoes,' I knew right then and there that you were the same obnoxious asshole I had known and resented back in Dalesburg! You make Pinkney Harold Dawson look like Mr. Good Guy!"

But as luck would have it, love gradually prevailed, after a half an hour of difficult-but-then-affectionate dialogue ensued. When the argument segment of their discourse finally terminated, the two lovebirds were now fondly discussing the implementation of either blue or pink wallpaper for the guest bedroom inside the old colonial Atwood family mansion. Marriage plans and wedding bells suddenly became an unavoidable inevitability, and in the tranquil end, Cupid's arrow had dramatically triumphed over human contempt. Heavenly bliss had been fully achieved.

* * * * * * * * * * * * *

On Thursday morning, Johnny trekked-over to the still-thriving village shoe store to conduct a confidential conversation with Mr. Hemstetter. After listening to Atwood's shocking confession about the Consul's deviously contrived letter, and after learning about the true prospects of sustaining a viable shoe store in downtown Coralio, Rosine's irate daddy said to his tormentor while squinting through his thick lens' spectacles, "Your overall demeanor is one of a prankster-type-asshole; a troublesome scamp unworthy of ever courting my dear sweet daughter, and then presumptuously escorting her to the altar. It's positively amazing that I haven't gone fuckin' bankrupt while obediently following the false advice of a quixotic, young, arrogant jerk-off such as yourself! Now that the local shoe market has been completely saturated," Rosine's livid father quipped, "how do you suppose I should liquidate the remainder of my inventory?"

"I'll think of some workable solution, and if the solution is poisonous enough, I'll absolutely drink the toxic substance down!" Johnny bluntly replied and exaggerated. "Stop making me fuckin' suicidal! If I suddenly die, it'll break your daughter's tender heart!"

The next Monday, the second cocklebur invoice arrived from Dalesburg via express boat shipment. Johnny wasted no time in loading the five-hundred-pound burlap bale (along with the cargo of remaining unsold shoes) into a rented schooner, and then the youthful dreamer proceeded to sail ten-miles down the exotic-looking coast to Alcazar Village, where the unsuspecting, isolated natives all walked-around the sandy village barefooted.

That evening, in the same clandestine, diabolical manner as Atwood had exhibited in Coralio, the unscrupulous Consul spread the new supply of cockleburs all along the hamlet's main dirt thoroughfare. The brave fellow victoriously returned to Coralio the next afternoon with a bag full of pesos, and not so much as a shoestring was left over to boot. Then, the joyful Consul promptly resigned his official government appointment that Johnny had indicated in detail in the form of a brief letter, thus deciding to abandon his infatuation with Lotus-eating, for the sake of re-uniting with the standard spinach and cress commonly associated with distant Dalesburg, Alabama.

Later that same day, Billy Keogh reluctantly accepted the lofty position of Acting Consul at Coralio, *pro tem*, and the now-vindicated Johnny Atwood, accompanied by the comely Rosine and her fairly satisfied father, cruised back to the good old USA aboard the rusty tub *Andador*. The Spanish Main had instantly lost one of its most intriguing and exceptional residents, the departing Ex-Consul.

'I can't stand responsibility!' Keogh reasoned inside the inadequate consulate. 'I wholly hate this pretentious title of Consul, and the all-too-formal prestige and status bullshit that goes along with it. I understand from newspaper accounts that there's an upcoming revolution brewing down in Peru, so I just might desert my myriad duties as Consul and accompany that loudmouth Clancy to Lima for some high adventure.'

Then, Keogh ruminated some more. 'Clancy and I could become part-time mercenary soldiers of fortune, engaging in wild sex for pleasure orgies, rather than participating in dangerous fighting-for-honor bullshit!' Keogh pragmatically reckoned. 'And I'm now convinced that the only way to keep me stationary here in Coralio is for a fucked-up but effective graft scheme involving *mucho* under-the-table cash, along with plenty of free promiscuous quality pussy-munching, too!'

Then Billy reflected some more on his present circumstance. 'Perhaps I could become a local riverboat gambler. No, that's a silly illusion! There aren't any damned riverboats down-here in *this* lousy shit-laden hell pit! Holy crap! I sometimes wish I didn't possess such an inventive imagination! I mean,' Keogh rationalized. 'Who the fuck wants to maintain a typical job earning an average piss-poor income! Why the hell couldn't I have been born fourteen centuries ago, and actively kicked every villain's ass as one of King Arthur's intrepid Round Table Knights? On second thought,' Keogh mentally paused and realized, 'fuck the elusive *Holy Grail!* If I had lived during the Dark Middle Ages, I would be fuckin' dead and buried in some obscure European cemetery now!'

Three days after Johnny's unheralded departure from Coralio, and also after Keogh's unexpected simultaneous appointment as Acting Consul, two small schooners docked in port, and unloaded some unusual cargo deposited in front of the antiquated, rickety-walled customhouse. And then, a tall strong-looking muscular man climbed onto the short pier, and his steel blue eyes gazed about, perceptively evaluating the alien jungle environment.

The confident stranger asked around, and was escorted by Pedro to the village consulate office/residence. Keogh's random reverie was interrupted by a loud knuckle-knock upon the front door. The preoccupied man immediately ceased drawing caricatures of deformed naked women with distorted tits, and the newly-appointed Consul *pro tem* alertly swung his feet out of the hemp hammock, and deftly plopped them onto the filthy and unpolished wood-planked floor. Billy then sauntered over to the door.

"Is this where that varmint skunk Johnny Atwood hangs out?" the sunburned visitor wanted to know. "I'd kick his ass black and blue, and yank his midget dick off, if I wasn't here to explore a good business proposition that'll give me sufficient cash to supplement and enhance my burgeonin' stock market portfolio!"

"Gone!" Keogh answered with a degree of trepidation originating from his vocal cords. "Atwood's not here anymore!" the Acting Consul apprehensively added, while straightening-out the tight knot on his elaborate Uncle Sam necktie.

"That's just like that no-good craven bastard," the powerful-looking young brute concluded and remarked. "That cowardly punk is always gallivantin' around in circles, and not getting any goddamned constructive thing done. Will the craven instigator be back soon? The yellow-bellied cock-sucker needs a long and painful beating for all the accumulated grief he's caused me in the past!"

"Er, I doubt it!" Keogh nervously answered after some serious deliberation. "Johnny Atwood's not too dependable when it comes to things that involve accountability!"

"I suppose the asshole weakling is behind some village shanty workin' his diminutive erection up to producin' a tiny ejaculation," the tall, tough visitor assessed and opined. "That worthless psychotic freak is a born-loser from the word 'go'. He'd piss into the jaws of success every fuckin' time opportunity presented itself!"

"I concur with your accurate depiction of the creep," agreed feckless Keogh. "It's right on the money!"

"Well then; where's the goddamned factory?" the angry visitor mentioned, indirectly threatening the new Consul, as the harasser clenching his enormous fists in an intimidating manner. "I'm askin' ya' as fuckin' politely as I can. Where's the goddamned factory?"

"What factory?" Keogh wondered and asked. "The only factory around here that I'm aware of exists in the word satis*factory*," the new Consul weakly jested.

"Wise guy, huh? Why, I mean the goddamned factory where the owners use all of the freakin' cockleburs that I've been sending here," the incensed behemoth clarified. "Those two ships out there anchored in the harbor were loaded to the gills with numerous bales of cockleburs. Now, I'm willing to sell them to either Johnny Atwood or to *you* for a bargain price; let's say fifteen-cents a pound. Back in Alabama I had hired a hundred lazy derelict kids playing hooky from school to gather-up the millions of burs and deposit them into the five-hundred-pound burlap bales. Ya' just gotta' fuckin' appreciate my incomparable business acumen!"

Keogh was totally incredulous, as a look of extreme consternation dominated his beet-red countenance. "Are you by any chance the infamous Dink Pawson?" Billy neurotically stammered and misspoke to the visiting brute. "If so, your fabulously excellent reputation has preceded you!"

"My damned name happens to be Pink Dawson, and not Dink Pawson!" the muscle-bound Goliath aptly corrected. "What the fuck do I look like? A freshman punk from *Harvard* flaunting a tiny round dink on my skull?"

"The Spanish Main is graced with your royal radiant presence," Keogh complimented and lied. "It seems that Johnny's out of town on business, and won't be back for several weeks. As for me," the new Acting Consul informed. "I'm heading straight down to Peru with an old friend to conduct an archeological dig into recently excavated Inca Indian settlements. How would *you,* Mr. Dawson, like to have the privilege and honor of being the designated temporary U.S. Consul until the government eventually finds and assigns a qualified replacement?"

"A Call Loan"

In the late 1880s, most of the uncivilized Wild, Wild American West had been tamed; the most rebellious Indian tribes had been impressively subdued, and the now-triumphant cattlemen declared victory over their adversaries, the lowly farmer/homesteaders. Beef ranching had emerged as the vanquisher, and was thriving as the dominant economic force west of the Mississippi. The spectacular "cattle rush" brought to the prairie-land territories a veritable stampede of eager entrepreneurial speculators, with each ambitious newcomer (to the former frontier) being blind-eye infatuated with his own get-rich-quick, self-employment scheme. Many money-seeking beef-herders rapidly became exceptionally wealthy, driving their branded stock to distant railroad stations to load the awaiting cattle cars with future meat, which was swiftly transported to stockyards in Kansas City, and to slaughterhouses in Chicago.

Some adventurous men new to the cattle business spent their profits too freely. Then others used their earnings to wine and dine gold-digging women. Still others either treated themselves to diamond-studded gold watches with expensive fob chains, or the "new money" generously bought rounds of "drinks on the house" for all the grateful cowboys and card-counting gamblers fortunate enough to be standing at the local saloon's whiskey bar on Friday or Saturday nights.

Such a manly gent coming-out of the desert chaparral was one Long Bill Longley, who stood six-foot-ten-inches in stature, and who was rumored to have the longest and widest pussy stuffer in the entire Midwest region. The only bad feature of Long Bill Longley's sexual apparatus (as the legend goes) was that the notorious cowpoke was impotent, and had difficulty achieving (let alone sustaining) a healthy erection.

Back in 1889, Long Bill Longley was conservatively estimated to be worth over a half-a-million-dollars, not counting his most recent fantastic financial triumphs involving clever prime real estate acquisitions, and their subsequent profitable sales. The affable cattleman was sole proprietor of the Bar Circle Ranch; was a champion lariat twirler and lasso hurler at various rodeos, and was easily recognized in public places as a famous cowpuncher. Longley was also reputed to have knocked out (with his bare fists) at least four-dozen steers and eighteen bulls during one particular fit of rage down in El Paso.

A good portion of Long Bill's fabulous fortune had been accumulated with him purchasing stolen livestock from enterprising-but-deceitful mavericks, and from trusted cowpoke desperadoes before *the malo-hombres* could be caught and hung either by the law marshals or be lynched by vigilante-posses. But as the 1880s neared conclusion, Longley became more legitimate in his manifold endeavors, capitalizing in the ongoing trading-and-selling cattle boon, and consequently, again greatly enhancing his proliferating personal gains. Thus, Long Bill had successfully made the difficult transition from being an ordinary working-stiff cowboy, chowing-down around the old chuckwagon, to becoming a prosperous cowman owning every chuckwagon within a ten-mile radius of his renowned and treasured Bar Circle Ranch.

Showing-off his affluence, Long Bill shrewdly built a fantastic eighteen-bedroom whorehouse in the frontier town of Chaperosa, Texas, where the conscientious cattleman was doomed to gradually evolve into a reputable leading citizen. 'I'm gonna' hang-up my quirt and spurs and diversify into other forms of prosperous businesses,' Long Bill reckoned. 'No more whippin' the daylights out of wild mustangs, and breaking-in ornery, temperamental broncos for me. I plan on organizing the First American Bank of Chaperosa, because I'm a decent chap from the high chaparral country, with chapped lips, and presently chaperoning a popular bordello for other sex-starved chaparral chaps. Since I own the goddamned newly-constructed First American Bank,' Langley hypothesized, 'I think I'll appoint myself President-at-Large.'

One hot July morning, in 1889 (a Wednesday, according to documented and corroborated newspaper accounts), a short, fat, baldheaded government representative, wearing a dark-blue three-piece suit and bulky spectacles on his snout, featuring inch-thick lenses, identified himself with his official card and accompanying badge at the First American Bank's high-barred teller counter. Immediately, the self-important fiduciary examiner was conducted into the private office of the eminent Long Bill Longley, who skeptically received his unexpected caller.

"Mr. Longley; my name is Mr. Ignatius Edgar Todd, and I'm here in Chaperosa to produce a major report on your operation's accounting records. Naturally, the government oversees all banking procedures conducted throughout the United States of America and its attendant territories. And indubitably, Sir. It's my distinct responsibility to ascertain whether or not your institution's methods and standards of good banking are consistent with established federal guidelines," the self-important visitor declared. "Now I want you to be aware that I happen to take great pride in my very tedious work, Mr. Longley, and I assure you that my final analysis is always thorough, comprehensive, and ostensibly quite efficient."

"What the fuck did you say?" Long Bill wanted to know. "I'd freakin' understand you plenty better Mr. Todd if you were speakin' Chinese, or maybe even regular slang English. Now tell me without wrapping your thoughts in a blanket of Latin bullshit," the self-appointed bank executive demanded, "exactly what the hell has your so-called report decided?"

"Generally speaking, your bank for the most part is not in any grave jeopardy as far as your deposits, your credits, and your debits are concerned," Mr. Ignatius Edgar Todd knowledgeably informed. "However, there remains one rather-suspect caveat that I must bring to your attention. You have in your portfolio of accounts a certain Call Loan of $10,000.00, made-out to a man named Thomas Merlin, who is some sort of a traveling maverick magician no doubt. Anyway," the fastidious inspector continued his polite criticism. "Not only is the huge amount that you've lent your customer in excess of the maximum allowed, but also, I'm obligated to communicate to you that the Call Loan had been dispensed without adequate security or endorsement. In other words, my dear Mr. Longley, you haven't been guaranteed sufficient collateral to legally extend the loan to this elusive anonymous fellow, Thomas Merlin. I presume that this certain individual in question is living somewhere on the planet, and is not a dead person planted out on Boot Hill, or a macabre ghost nightly haunting your bawdy Texas house of ill-repute across the street."

"So, what the hell could the consequences of issuing this irregular Call Loan be?" Long Bill vehemently challenged. "Ya' gotta' realize that I'm a good friend of Mr. Thomas Merlin, who incidentally is an aspiring cattleman, and not a commonplace fucked-up travelin' magician or roaming minstrel havin' his menstrual periods as you've so haphazardly accused. Now to get back to my main idea, Mr. Todd. The only damned security I need to obtain from my fine acquaintance Tommy Merlin is his goddamned word. That's the way I'm used to conductin' business out-here in no man's land, Mr. Todd. A man's handshake is his bond; especially a firm one given by a proven friend, and in my mind, that's all that I need to go to bed at night, with a goddamned clear conscience."

"Well now, Mr. Longley," the now-exasperated, itinerant federal bureaucrat declared. "Since you're pretty new to the very intricate machinations of the banking industry, I'll cut you a break. It's plainly evident that you've inadvertently violated one stipulation of the transactions' statutes, and I'm held liable by the public trust to promptly deliver a detailed report to Washington. And then thereafter, the Department of Justice will authoritatively act on the essence of this particular matter. Now listen carefully, Sir. Here's what I plan to do to help alleviate this rather embarrassing situation. I plan on heading out to…."

"Look here, Mr. Todd," the now-vitriolic William Longley abruptly interrupted the short fat man, who was then sweating rather profusely from emotional stress, and from the sweltering hundred-degree heat. "Tommy Merlin had heard of 2,000 head of two-year-old-stock ready-for-market, down near Rocky Ford on the Rio Grande. The herd was for sale for eight-dollars a head, so that's an investment on Tom's part of sixteen-thousand-dollars to initiate the deal. The cattle were apparently smuggled across the border, by Larendo Garcia's taco and enchilada gang, I believe. Eight bucks a head is a steal, because the pilfered animals are worth at least fifteen dollars each on the open market up in Kansas City. And so, Mr. Todd, just follow the math': thirty thousand minus sixteen thousand will yield a bonanza of fourteen-thousand bananas for Tom Merlin," Long Bill explained. "Now I know both Tom and Larendo like I know my own handsome face in the mirror, and both fellas' wouldn't be involved in any wicked plot to cheat one another, even though they're mutually engaged in the possible transportation of animal contraband. Both of those God-fearing men are decent and outstanding and…."

"Look and listen carefully, Mr. Longley," the perspiring and fatigued bank investigator indignantly sneered. "The only aspect of law violation that concerns me at this difficult and vexing moment involves a specific questionable dealing in the banking industry at a certain Chaperosa, Texas location, namely yours. What the heck goes on in the procurement of the aforementioned money that goes into your bank deposits is not part of my bailiwick. And thus. is out of the scope of my domain. Do you now fathom my drift?"

"Not even if you were a heap of twelve-foot-high snow during a fuckin' super-intense Colorado blizzard," Long Bill indulgently laughed and then sneezed, fully relishing the gravity of his direct insult. "But good old Tom had six-thousand-bucks of hard-earned seed money in his pocket. So, me being his good amigo, naturally I let him have the additional ten-thousand advance in good faith. The whole thing's no big fuckin' deal, Mr. Todd! Tom's younger brother

Ed took the two-thousand cattle up to Kansas City three weeks ago, and should be back with the seven bucks per head profit any day now. When Ed safely returns from his journey north, Tom will pay-off his outstanding bank note, and then everything in *our* cozy gentlemen's exchange will be peaches and cream, and also honeysuckle and roses."

"Hear me out on this sensitive issue, Mr. Longley, because your barbaric diatribes I find both inexcusable and intolerable. Now then, Sir. I'm going to proudly step-out of this federally licensed building of yours, march down to the telegraph office, and send an urgent wire to the Comptroller," Mr. Todd threatened. "But I'm trying my best to be civil and cooperative with you! You must assist me in avoiding a devastating catastrophe that will most certainly be descending like a fiery meteor on your all-too-vulnerable First American Bank. Now then, for the final time," Mr. Todd emphatically stated. "I'll give you one last chance. Listen to the loophole that I propose, or else be prepared to do some serious sitting, and then growing fantastic hemorrhoids, inside a lonely cell at the nearest federal penitentiary."

"What in tar-nation do ya' have in mind?" the now-worried Long Bill Longley insisted on learning. "You're pretty lucky that no one out West has brutally beaten the living shit out of you. We Western men folk aren't totally domesticated and law-abiding yet, Mr. Todd; no siree. But I'll probably heed your unwanted advice, if I think your plan has any merit in it! What's your big idea?"

"Despite the fact that I abhor your insolent demeanor, Mr. Longley, I'm takin' the afternoon train, out to nearby Hillsdale, to perform another routine bank inspection," Mr. Todd revealed. "On my way back, I'll get-off the train here at the Chaperosa Depot, around noon tomorrow. You'll have until then to straighten-out this outstanding Call Loan on your books, or else you'll be facing government prosecution. If you can succeed in doing that simple arithmetic," the agitated-obese gentleman stated, "then I'll not report Mr. Merlin, you, or the illicit Call Loan incident to my demanding superiors in my summary review. Fair enough?"

"Fair enough, Mr. Todd," Long Bill acceded with a broad smile appearing upon his handsome countenance. "But you, Mr. Todd, and the goddamned railroad have one fuckin' diabolical thing in common. Ya' both have narrow one-track minds!"

* * * * * * * * * * * * * *

After the immensely aggravated Mr. Ignatius Edgar Todd left the First American Bank's front door, the President, having his feathers ruffled, leaned back in his red leather chair; put his feet and shoes up on his fancy desk; placed his hands with interlocking fingers behind his head, and zealously contemplated the huge dilemma that had developed involving his close friend Thomas Merlin and the "by the book" federal banking official that had just departed the premises. 'I'll pay my loyal buddy a visit, and disclose *our* little troubling circumstance with him. Tom's usually a level-headed guy, and if we put our thick skulls together, then my round dense head might just become level, too!'

"Tom," Long Bill said inside Merlin's modest residence on the outskirts of Chaperosa. "Have you heard any encouragin' news from your brother Ed yet? He's got the potential to be a real pistollaro, in spite of his many fucked-up peccadilloes, yes, he does! Young Ed's been gone for three whole weeks now, and has not returned from Kansas City. I hope Eddy wasn't robbed by Indians coming-down from Cleveland, or that he hasn't met a pretty gal and eloped to either Atlantic City or Coney Island!"

"Can't elope, or should I say 'wouldn't elope', because Eddy don't know too much about growing melons and the like," Tom quipped and chuckled as the novice cattle bargainer continued plaiting his quirt. "I'm sure Eddy is eddying around somewhere on his pinto! I guess my little brother must've hired a small posse to protect him and his cash that he received selling the two thousand longhorns. That is, unless some devious heinous whiskerando gave him a bum steer, ha, ha, ha!"

"This is no time to be joking around," Bill sternly cautioned his jocular (none athletic) buddy. "A certain bank examiner named Mr. Ignatius Edgar Todd was snoopin' around my establishment this morning, and the coy bastard discovered our little ten-thousand-dollar loan negotiation. Now, you and I both know that everything is copasetic, and will work-out all right. But this short, fat, baldheaded government asshole claims that what we did is against banking regulations," Longley explained. "These confounded letter-of-the-law guys really suck the big one! Now Tom, whatever happened to the goddamned spirit-of-the-law?"

"I suppose that either the Good Lord or Satan must've spirited it away! But Bill, can't we just stave this dumb fuck Todd fella' off for three more days?" Merlin asked, adopting a more serious attitude and expression. "That strategy ought to help solve the problem, I'm practically sure!"

"I'll try to be level-headed with you, Tom, even though some old-time local British jerk-offs say I look like one of Oliver Cromwell's Round Heads," Bill awkwardly jested. "Those three absurd English jaspers that recently arrived in town, hobo vagabond triplets, I believe. Those three varmints also claim that they had lost two-hundred-pounds each while playing blackjack inside a London casino, but surely; I think that Nigel, Angus, and Elton are entirely overweight at three-hundred-pounds each, and are all totally full of liquid and solid crap as it is. But getting back on topic," Longley proceeded in a more solemn tone of voice. "I'm a trifle short on cash myself; otherwise, I'd easily put-up the damned dough just to get this shit-talkin' troublemaker Todd off *our* damned backs."

"What could be done?" Merlin worriedly asked.

"Now Tom, I've got up to noon tomorrow to raise the ten thousand cash, but if I fail, it looks like certain curtains for me! I understand that Uncle Sam has pretty damned big feet, and I don't want that sneaky son-of-a-bitchin' jerk jumping on my stomach with his giant clodhoppers while I'm horizontal sleepin' in the sack. I don't know if you're aware of it, Tom," Bill added. "But despite my great success and fine reputation, I still sleep in a common bunk bed; upper tier in fact!"

"I'll try and raise the friggin' money, even though it's harder than raisin' corn, which I tried and miserably failed at doin' when I was a dumb-ass vegetarian homesteader," Tom Merlin confessed while still focused on braiding his short horse-whip. "Say Bill, ya' got a couple buckets of milk! I might just use my trusty quirt here to make a few gallons of whipped cream, ha, ha, ha!"

"All right, Tom," Bill somberly replied, shaking his head in mild disgust. "I suggest that you do what that famous British playwright fella' William Shakespeare recommended. Get your' fuckin' act together, and don't make a goddamned scene."

Fifteen-minutes later, the now very determined Tom Merlin tossed his small whip onto the kitchen table, and sauntered a mile into Chaperosa. The distraught cowpoke entered the only other financial institution in the remote desert town, which was a private enterprise operated by Cooper & Craig. There, Merlin spoke with Mr. Daedalus Cooper, a former barrel, cask, and hogshead manufacturer. "Mr. Cooper. I've got to have ten-thousand-dollars by tomorrow noon, or else I might be financially ruined. My modest dwelling and land are worth about six-grand, and that's about all of the collateral I can muster right now," the anxious visitor disclosed. "But I've got a big cattle deal in progress that's sure to bring me twice the ten-thousand loan I'm requestin', as soon as my brother Ed returns from Kansas City with his saddlebags loaded with loot."

Daedalus Fennimore Cooper, who was not a typical fly-by-night businessman/banker, suffered from consumption, and suddenly began coughing his lungs out. First green mucus filled his handkerchief, and then some red blood spewed from his mouth. "Ya' got me coughin' my goddamned way right into my mother-fuckin' coffin!" the bank partner complained between sporadic gasps. "I need a new fuckin' set of lungs! Wish the hell I was a fish, or a loan shark, having gills to breathe out of! I've always felt like a goddamned fish out of water, cough, cough, cough!"

"Please, Sir. Don't deny me the ten-thousand-dollars!" Merlin melodramatically pleaded. "My Call Loan with Long Bill Longley over at First American has been exercised, because Bill lacks sufficient funds to cover my recent debt; or should I say, *our* recent debt. Bill needs the money desperately, and I've gotta' make good for it, or else we'll both suffer the consequences. Ya' gotta' help me, Mr. Cooper, or else, I won't try savin' your ass should ya' stop breathin' and stop coughin'! I was once a lifeguard ya' know, up in Rockaway Beach, just outside New York City. And I know all about the ins and outs of performin' artificial respiration and the like!"

"No doubt about your avid sincerity, but I've got a stubborn jealous partner that I gotta' convince, and also deal with," Cooper confidentially divulged and intimated without getting too intimate. Thereafter, the sick banker nearly convulsed and regurgitated his trachea and bronchial tubes right out of his irritated throat. "My business partner, old Icarus Craig, is a no-good bastard, who despises *our* only banking rival in town, Bill Longley, with a passion. Craig will never go along with your deal in two centuries! Cough, cough, cough'! Shit Tom!" Daedalus Cooper exclaimed. "I wish I'd just die right here on the floor, and get it all over with!"

"Can't you do something drastic to help me out?" Merlin shrieked and then also began coughing. "Why should you care one hard turd dropping about what the hell that two-bit cock-sucker Craig thinks in regard to my Call Loan problem? I understand the shit-face is out of town, buying a marijuana factory down in Tijuana."

"Because Tom, Icarus Craig and I just put up fifteen-thousand smackers to finance those fearsome Myers Brothers over in Rockdell," Daedalus Cooper explained while attempting to recuperate from his lengthy gagging and blood spitting attack. "As I was sayin' earlier, Icarus and me don't run any cheap fly-by-night operation here!" Daedalus maintained before again loudly coughing and wheezing. "And Mr. Merlin, Sir. I gotta' tell ya' something else that's mighty pertinent. Those enterprising Myers' boys that started-out as destitute paupers are buildin' a colossal-sized sex recreation and amusement park over there in Rockdell, and after floating the iron-clad deal, this reputable bank at present has no money left to lend anybody. Maybe in retrospect, Tom, I should've invested in a horse-drawn ambulance and a mule-pulled hearse, or put my bucks in a goddamned frontier hospital instead, cough, cough, cough."

Tom Merlin despondently returned to his humble home where the cowboy-turned-entrepreneur spent three long difficult hours deeply meditating about his unsavory Call Loan predicament, all done while finishing-up the rawhide braiding on his prized quirt. Later that afternoon, Merlin paid a visit to the First American Bank of Chaperosa where the disenchanted fellow again met with Long Bill Longley, and promised to satisfactorily deliver the ten-thousand Call Loan by noon the following day.

* * * * * * * * * * * * *

At eight o'clock that evening, Thomas Merlin stepped-out of his small frame bungalow on the outskirts of Chaperosa, the outskirts being a fairly long distance to trek from Petticoat Junction. The disguised bandit-impostor toted two silver six-shooters, and wore a black silk bandanna, with his new-imposing getup also sporting matching black shirt, pants, hat, boots, and jet-black dyed chaparrals. The desperate fellow owing the bank Call Note swiftly ambled-down the lonely sandy side trail that ran parallel to the hamlet's main dirt and gravel street.

Soon, Merlin followed the familiar straight railroad tracks, until the trekker eventually arrived at the very isolated train depot's water tank tower. 'In approximately ten minutes, the locomotive will be arrivin' at the platform, and thank God, my cousin Jake is the choo-choo's conductor, who had wired me sayin' that this connivin' eastern jasper Ignatius Edgar Todd had changed his plans, and is gonna' be a dumb-shit passenger in one of the arriving Pullman cars. I gotta' act fast. This is my only risky chance.'

As soon as the steam locomotive rounded the distant bend, and came into Tom's view, Merlin confidently rose from his cover behind several shrubs and cactuses. Immediately, two very strong and formidable hands latched on to the gunman's shoulders. Quickly, the robber-pretender was roughly hurled onto a rather prickly stationary tumbleweed. A heavy knee was forcefully pressing against Tom's back, and soon, two iron-like paws were grasping and immobilizing the surprised hostage's wrists.

"What the heck's goin' on?" Merlin yelled and squirmed. "Who the hell are ya'?"

"Ya' ain't movin' an inch, until the train's engine takes on all its water, and after all the passengers get-off and vacate the area," came a very familiar voice. "I gotta' save ya' from destroyin' yourself, you bungling insane Asshole!"

"Bill, what the hell are ya' doin' here interruptin' my clandestine activity?" Merlin uttered in astonishment. "I thought you was my friend! If I didn't know better, I'd accuse ya' flat-out of intrudin' into my personal affair!"

"I *am* your friend, you harebrained Imbecile!" Long Bill Longley confirmed. "And just like that train over there, I had accurately theorized that you had some 'loco-motive' up your sleeve, and so I came down here to stop you from doin' something terribly crazy. Now, what the hell are ya' up to?"

"Well Bill," Tom panted and then deeply exhaled from his subordinate position upon the dry sandy ground. "I found-out from my cousin, who's the conductor on this train, that Mr. Todd was secretly arrivin' back in town on *this* particular excursion. I had planned to board the train; find the dumb-ass hardheaded bank prick; kidnap the bureaucratic fuck-head, and then lock-him up in the caboose and keep the interferer captive for three days, until Ed arrives from Kansas City with the highly-anticipated cattle dough. That way Bill, this intruding Todd dick-head wouldn't..."

"Wouldn't be able to telegraph the authorities in Washington and report *my* bank as being in violation of federal statutes," Bill Longley eloquently finished Tom Merlin's incomplete statement. "You was always schemin', when you weren't dreamin', as far back as I can remember, Tom!"

"I was ready to pistol whip the wimpy jerk-off, and then three days later, toss the mean-hearted, power-huntin' asshole out of the caboose, and then make him eat his own shit while sittin' his fat bare ass on a chopped-down saguaro cactus! But now, Mr. Bank President. You've totally destroyed the genius of my foolproof plan! We only got a meager sixteen hours to find ten-thousand non-counterfeit U.S. legal tender buckaroos!"

"You faithless, stupid-assed, Bastard!" Bill laughed, releasing his firm grasp as the locomotive chugged out of the deserted desert depot right on schedule. "You were makin' so much fucked-up nonsensical static that I couldn't get a word in edgewise. Young Eddy just arrived in town with the vital cattle funds, just in the nick of time, before I have to confront Mr. Todd tomorrow at noon. I thought I'd tell ya' the good tidings before ya' suffered a massive heart seizure, and then have to be in an infirmary bed lyin' right smack next to that tuberculosis-coughin', loathsome, son-of-bitch Daedalus Cooper. Old conniving Icarus and Daedalus never quite learned how to adroitly straighten-up and fly right!"

"Ed's a real capable youngster," Tom drawled as the greenhorn cattle-trader gingerly stood-up and clumsily began dusting himself off. "I gotta' give Eddy credit, because I can't give him cash!"

"How does it feel makin' your first big cattle deal?" Bill innocently asked. "I predict that some-day you're gonna' open your own bank and whorehouse, and give me some serious competition!"

"If ya' wanna' know my gut instinct, I do think I'm actually gonna' stick to bein' a simple-ass, commonplace, cowboy, happy ridin' the dusty range. If ya' want my opinion, Bill, I don't think I can take much more of this perfidious, pressurized cattle-dealin' business that *you* seem to relish. I think I'll just leave that type of psycho' jeopardy up to brave, illiterate varmints like you, Bill!"

"Okay Tom, if you say so!" William Longley answered with a definite degree of swagger. "But if you're ever interested in bein' my foreman and partner, just let me know when you finally regain your sanity. My next logical goal is to drive those two unscrupulous fuck-heads Daedalus Cooper and Icarus Craig out of business, and then out of Chaperosa altogether."

"One Dollar's Worth"

The judge presiding over the United States Court of Brownsville, Texas, geographically situated just across the fabled Rio Grande from Mexico, discovered the following anonymous threat letter in his morning mail:

> When you had mercilessly dispatched me off to federal prison four years ago for committing a minor theft crime, you had angrily and viciously referred to me as a "dangerous rattlesnake". Maybe I am one, who the fuck knows? But you can hear me rattling my tail right now, and let me add with confidence that my fangs are poisonous and lethal, at least to you!
>
> One year after I got thrown into the goddamned slammer, my poverty-stricken daughter had died of some mysterious, unidentified, sexual disease, and she was buried in total disgrace in a lousy pauper's grave. Now, I know Judge from reliable sources that you too have a beautiful daughter that you love and cherish, and I feel it's my solemn duty (now that I'm out of jail and on the loose) to make you aware of exactly the same kind of pain that I had suffered under the duress of your harsh sentence.
>
> I'm a free and roving rattlesnake now, Judge. I don't say too much anymore, but you're reading my toxic-sounding rattle right this very minute! Look-out when I decide to lash-out and strike! And in case you're wondering, I've hired an unemployed American high school English teacher to write this graphic warning letter to you on my behalf, just for me to make sure that it's perfectly legible and very grammatically (although not politically) correct.
>
> Yours in revenge,
> Rattlesnake

Judge Aristotle DeWitt placed the nasty letter on the left side of his desk, with his dour facial expression showing little sign of alarm. A half-hour later Justice DeWitt brought the missive to the attention of Douglas Littlefield, whose charming sweetheart Nancy DeWitt had been explicitly referenced in the literal threat from the anonymous and affronted 'Rattlesnake'.

"Doug, you and Nancy are to be married in the fall, so you might want to be aware of this typical kind of direct threat," Aristotle related to his protege. "I get plenty of these nasty notes from nefarious individuals each year, so I've become quite accustomed to receiving them. But this particular one struck me as being very malicious in intent, mostly because it was my daughter that had been alluded to and not just myself."

"I guess such unpleasant things come with the territory," Douglas Littlefield diplomatically answered. "I won't tell Nancy about it, if you won't. But I'll assiduously perform some preliminary research for my own satisfaction, just to narrow-down the field as to whom the possible mendacious culprit might be."

An hour later, Douglas Littlefield entered the county clerk's office to curiously conduct his document files' investigation. After scrutinizing forty unique cases, and laboriously comparing the gleaned data with the specific information provided by Rattlesnake's iniquitous letter, the newly-appointed county prosecutor concluded that the mailed item had been sent by "Mexico Sammy", a half-breed Caucasian/Hispanic border desperado, who had been imprisoned for committing manslaughter four years before, and who had just gotten out of jail "on good behavior". But within a week, the threatening letter had been mentally relegated to "back-burner status" in Douglas Littlefield's busy and all-too-cluttered mind.

Another Monday morning came around on the docket calendar, and the Brownsville Court was again "officially in session". Most of the mundane cases to be tried involved amateur smuggling, counterfeiting, smalltime swindling, post-office fraud, and thwarted robberies, along with other sundry and minor federal border violations.

The third case heard by Judge DeWitt and being prosecuted by Douglas Littlefield was aimed at convicting a young belligerent Mexican of low morals; the cited personage going by the birth name of Jose Morales. Ralph Kirkwood, the deputy serving as bailiff, escorted the accused petty theft suspect into the crowded court chamber. A reputable druggist was prepared to assume his seat upon the witness stand, and cooperatively testify on behalf of the Brownsville District Attorney's Office.

"This man paid for prescription medicine using counterfeit silver dollars," Fabian Duncan alleged, pointing an accusative finger at Jose Morales. "But upon closer scrutiny, I readily determined at the store's front counter that the strange-looking coins were actually rather poor counterfeits, which were composed mostly of a softer metal than silver; possibly zinc or lead, or a combination of both."

"Not much more is needed to prove that Jose Morales was responsible for passing-off illegal tender, does it Judge DeWitt?" Douglas Littlefield competently expressed to his future father-in-law. "Now in my palm is the hard evidence in the form of three rather soft-feeling fake dollar coins, that certainly weren't legally minted in Carson City or anywhere else in the United States of America for that matter. And I do strongly believe that, Jose here, is a well-utilized pawn for a ruthless Mexican counterfeiting gang that's terrorizing towns and villages all along the other side of the Rio Grande."

"I understand you have a pretty girlfriend, and that you plan to get married," Judge Aristotle DeWitt indirectly admonished Jose. "This court will be adjourned for two hours, because I have an emergency dentist appointment, and my bottom left jaw is really hurting like crazy from an infected tooth. We'll continue with the sentencing when I return after lunch. Too bad I won't be able to enjoy eating any food until suppertime. And I really was hungry for a few tacos, a little brown rice, and a scoop of baked beans, too. Sorry for the inconvenience, Mr. Duncan. I'll tell you what Fabian. I'm going to adjourn court until tomorrow morning, nine a.m. sharp, so that you can get caught-up on your busy pharmacy agenda. Court's adjourned until tomorrow morning!" Judge DeWitt announced and decided as he pounded his gavel on his abbreviated forty-five-degree angled lectern. "See you all manana!"

Ralph Kirkwood accompanied Jose Morales back to his grimy jail cell, where the suspect would await his temporarily suspended justice. Then, District Attorney Douglas Littlefield and the overworked bailiff began discussing the various remaining cases listed on the court docket, when voluptuous Nancy DeWitt unexpectedly entered the district prosecutor's small office.

"Oh Doug; sorry to interrupt your impromptu conference with Ralph, but I just heard out on River Street that court won't be resuming until tomorrow," Nancy reviewed and alertly stated. "Now I just have to remind you Doug, that you had promised to take me out in the countryside to go plover shooting, whenever the opportunity presented itself. Well, Dear, in terms of time management, that glorious opportunity happens to be right now!"

"Knowing how organized you generally are," Doug said to Nancy while giving Ralph Kirkwood a quick wink, "you've probably gotten the entire bird-shooting excursion arranged already. I'm willing to bet a pork rib dinner at the Canteen Café on it!"

"Oh Doug, you're smarter than the average pedigree hunting dog, that's for sure," complimented the judge's pretty blonde-haired daughter. "The men at the livery stable have hitched-up old Fly and frisky Betsy to the company's finest leather-seated buckboard, which incidentally and ironically, the shiny rig will only cost you a mere one buck to rent. Just don't pay Mr. Sheen with any counterfeit American silver dollar, or with any fraudulent Mexican pesos. After all, you have a good Brownsville reputation to maintain!"

The slightly blushing Douglas Littlefield keenly assessed the overall situation with a rational mind, which coincidentally was mostly based on biological emotional attraction. The happy pair was to be married in the fall, and the carnal attraction between the two lovebirds, along with the glamorous element of romance were both at their respective independent heights.

The decision-making process about bird shooting was suddenly interrupted with the sound of a gentle rapping upon the district attorney's office door. A beautiful, dark-eyed Mexican lady entered the room, wearing a black shawl that had been tightly wrapped around her swarthy-skinned neck. The disturbed young woman began speaking in Spanish, and dependable Bailiff Ralph Kirkwood, who had passed Spanish III in high school with a less-than-mediocre D average, interpreted the female's words for both the district attorney and his rather concerned fiancée.

"Doug, her name is Maria Sanchez," Kirkwood deciphered and related. "And she's apparently mixed-up with our ignominious ward Jose Morales, who Maria claims is totally innocent of the frivolous charges filed against him. Miss. Sanchez also claims that she's the manufacturer of the counterfeit dollar coins, and that she's responsible for compelling Jose to attempt to pass them off at Fabian Duncan's pharmacy. As you know, Doug," Ralph Kirkwood added, rendering his own personal opinion, "this is the way it is with these amorous Mexican girls. They'll lie, steal, smuggle, exaggerate, or even kill just to protect their passionate lovers. Never trust the words of any Mexican woman that's been hit by one of Cupid's errant arrows. That's an axiom that reflects the honest-to-goodness truth."

"Ralph, that's an unwarranted generalization you're making based on false stereotyping," Doug Littlefield verbally reacted before human rights' advocate Nancy DeWitt could ever open her mouth in defense of womanhood. "Stop excoriating this poor innocent girl, at least until Jose Morales is found to be villainous as publicly charged.

As you know, Ralph," Littlefield editorialized. "In America, under the aegis of the Constitution and its First Ten Amendments, suspects and so-called 'people of interest' are regarded as innocent until found and proven guilty."

"Doug, you're so gallant!" Nancy DeWitt abundantly praised her special beau. "In fact, without sounding too medieval, I'll go as far as calling you chivalrous! I know in my heart that you sincerely and genuinely believe in liberty and justice for all!"

Then, sobbing Maria Sanchez continued her maudlin Spanish recitation. Kirkwood again volunteered to serve as the multicultural translator, pretending to be extensively fluent in the dual Romance Languages on display.

"Maria here says she's perfectly willing to take her boyfriend's place in jail, if you'll let him out," the self-assured bailiff explained. "Senorita Sanchez insists that she had been extremely sick, and was down in bed with a terrible fever, and the family doctor said that she was a candidate eligible for death. The young woman didn't have the proper medicine to recover from her severe malady, so that's why she got Jose to use the three counterfeit silver dollars to exchange for the necessary medications, which she now maintains saved her life. I gotta' admit Doug," Ralph Kirkwood again deviated from being the interpreter. "Her talk is loaded with mushy love references, and this here Mexican doll really has the hots for her incarcerated Jose!"

"Tell her that unfortunately, I can't do anything to release her boyfriend, and please relate that her wish could only be granted by the Honorable Judge Aristotle DeWitt," Littlefield instructed Kirkwood. "The case will be tried tomorrow morning. And then, and only then, will the outcome be determined. The worst-case scenario is that Jose will get three days in the calaboose, but it's not in my power to prevent that from happening."

Maria Sanchez listened carefully to the bailiff's stilted Spanish words, and then the aggrieved suppliant did a little curtsy before the three flattered Americans, and next exited the tiny room saying some bizarre phraseology in Spanish slang. Ralph Kirkwood again did the loose translation.

"Maria said in leaving that if the life of the girl that *you* love, Mr. Prosecutor, is ever in danger, then please remember the honorable name Jose Morales. Then, you'll finally be able to identify with *his* crisis and his suffering from being separated from Maria, while rotting away in a jail cell."

"Ralph, don't you have some urgent police business to address down the corridor in Marshal Platt's office?" Doug Littlefield reminded the very gregarious public servant.

"Sure do, Mr. Littlefield! Have a good afternoon flirting with your wonderful woman out in the wild shrub country, pretending to be shooting-down those totally doomed plovers. Wish I could come along for the ride, but this tedious police-law-enforcement labor stuff is the big disadvantage of being a salaried Brownsville public employee." Then the good-natured deputy tipped his hat in deference to the judge's attractive daughter, and casually strolled-out of the prosecutor's office.

"Are you absolutely sure, Doug, that you can't do anything to mend Maria Sanchez's shattered heart?" Nancy futilely begged. "I'm afraid that the upset girl's going to turn suicidal if you don't act in a timely fashion! Doesn't the law know the feeling of pity? I thought that the law was supposed to be based on mercy!"

"Don't allow your surging sentiments to interfere with what constitutes logical good judgment!" Doug cautioned his idealistic sweetheart. "That's precisely what the law is founded upon; rational sane discretion! But I hereby pledge to you that my prosecution of Jose Morales will not be vindictive. And furthermore, I guarantee that your judicious dad is going to calmly convict the unsavory Mexican based on the valid statements of observant witnesses, especially those of Mr. Fabian Duncan. And Nancy, I've got one of the counterfeit dollars in my pocket that I had kept to show you. This round piece of poorly designed lead will be my 'Exhibit A'."

"You've always been an exhibitionist," jested and giggled Nancy. "Now, Douglas Littlefield. I'm absolutely and wholeheartedly convinced of *that* relatively truthful allegation."

* * * * * * * * * * * * *

"What's out beyond this vast wilderness on the other side of the northern horizon," Nancy DeWitt academically asked Douglas Littlefield on the scenic buckboard ride out to plover-shooting country. "I've never been too good at studying geography, or reading maps. History and gym class were always my strongest school subjects at Brownsville High."

"Oh, over the northern horizon are just a vast tundra and some huge melting polar glaciers," Littlefield cutely replied and fibbed. "At least, there'll be voracious growling grizzly bears, and plenty of herbivorous caribou, but very few if any lethal rattlesnakes."

"I wonder what's going to eventually happen to Maria Sanchez?" the fiancée conjectured and inquired. "In my heart, I still feel sorry for her plight."

"That cute little coquette is an absolute tease that could make your mind detour from reality," Douglas honestly opined. "I hate to admit it, but in my brief courtroom tenure, I've seen hundreds of sentimental Mexican ladies that behaved just like her. Now Nancy," Littlefield continued his observations. "Why don't you take that beautiful Senorita under your quixotic wing, and teach her some basic American values and culture? I'm convinced that *that* sort of positive guiding-light education would work wonders for the emotionally devastated girl."

The recently polished buckboard was deftly steered along a bumpy, grassy road, and then it passed along a piece of rolling prairie land until a heavy timber-line had been reached in the vicinity of Piedra Creek, the favorite area sanctuary for mating plover. The bird shooting expedition that afternoon went smoothly, and soon the travails of the Brownsville courtroom and its daily parade of violating personalities became lost in the excitement of the challenging sport.

The intermittent shooting was crudely interrupted when a black haired-man, riding an awesome-galloping black steed, was hurriedly approaching the dense woods from the south.

"I've seen that fellow somewhere before, but I just can't place him right this second in an exact setting," Littlefield noted and said to Nancy DeWitt. "Maybe he's just a delirious rancher with agitated intestines, needing to find the nearest outhouse."

Douglas Littlefield abruptly stopped the buckboard and the two momentarily shell-shocked occupants clambered-out, and quickly hopped-down to ground level. Immediately, the pair began bagging plover with Nancy's reliable twelve-gauge, and her expert steady aim soon remarkably downed three squawking birds in ten minutes.

A half hour later, the shotgun-toting lovebirds started their eight-mile odyssey back to the material comforts of "Alamo-land civilization". The two horses gentle, synchronized trot was soon overshadowed with the same mysterious, in-a-rush, sinister-looking horseman appearing directly ahead; his magnificent black stallion moving at breathtaking speed.

"That's the same man we saw a half an hour ago," Nancy astutely pointed-out. "And the way he's riding, I don't think he's searching for any available lavatory facilities."

"That ugly son-of-a-bitch has drawn his Winchester and is aiming it right at us," Littlefield apprehensively and hysterically yelled. "I now recognize that dirtball mother-fucker! That hombre is Mexico Sammy, and he's seeking revenge while bearing-down on our asses."

"Douglas Littlefield; I've never heard you use such uncouth language before. I demand an immediate apology for your breach of good manners! I hope you don't intend on using such vile vulgarity after we're married!"

"Look here, Nancy. This crisis is no time for cultural formality," the alarmed boyfriend lectured. "That diabolical cock-sucker is the same lousy bastard that had written an obnoxiously obscene epistle to your father, where the selfsame culprit who's presently pursuing our asses, Mexico Sammy, had threatened to physically hurt you and then evilly watch you intensely suffer and helplessly writhe-around on the floor in excruciating pain."

"Why that no-good son-of-a-bitch, bastard!" Nancy DeWitt loudly shrieked. "I'll blow his fuckin' balls off with my twelve-gauge if I can get a few decent shots off! That detestable Mexican fuck-head is messin' with the wrong damned Protestant chickadee! I'll personally pull every single pubic hair off his balls, one by one!"

When Mexico Sammy came within the shooting range of *his* pointed rifle, the crook let loose with a barrage of bullets. The dastardly varmint was indeed knowledgeable about the limitations of certain firearms, and was aware that the bird-shooting weapons carried by Nancy DeWitt and Douglas Littlefield were not capable of hitting him, or his horse, from the current distance separating them and him. Ducking down beside the buckboard with Nancy at his side, Littlefield reached into his pasteboard box and quickly loaded two cartridges into his overmatched shotgun.

"Keep behind the horses when that despicable jerk-off starts firing away again," the take-charge district attorney commanded. "If that wise-ass prick comes into range, I'll try blasting his asshole right out of his rectum!"

"I'll fuckin' do far worse than that!" Nancy promised. "That ruthless fuck-head will be ass-less, ball-less, and dick-less after I fuckin' get done with him!"

"Nancy, I've never heard you talk like that before," Littlefield remarked in a stunned tone of voice. "But I think I kind of like your new speaking style."

"An emergency situation tends to bring out a person's true character," the former DeWitt family female saint stated. "Now let's kick some Mexican butt, before I lose my goddamned tits and you lose your goddamned manhood! Let's fuckin' terminate this extended vendetta right now!"

The incensed pursuer kept entering and exiting the yonder woods at unpredictable intervals, thus forcing Littlefield and his lady companion to shift their positions back and forth on either side of the buckboard. Several of the besieged district attorney's birdshot pellets whizzed-by the charging black horse, which then promptly pranced into the safety and cover of the adjacent timber woods.

Minutes of silence were followed with the lunatic desperado firing a close shot that ricocheted-off of the buckboard's right front wheel, and then glanced across Nancy's cheek. Blood trickled-down, weaving a narrow path, winding around the fiancée's open mouth. "Don't fret! I'm not injured badly, Doug. It's only a splinter from the wheel. But I can't wait to shoot and strangle that heinous mother-fucker! That cowardly ruffian will have no sperm left in his worm when I finally get my sweet revenge!"

Another well-aimed shot from the determined attacker hit old fearless Fly in the neck, and immediately, the likeable horse crashed to the desert ground in a cloud of dust. Betsy then broke away from her traces, and galloped swiftly away into the far-right hand section of the timber woods. During the ongoing pandemonium, a bullet caromed-off of Nancy DeWitt's thick shooting jacket.

"Get on the ground next to Fly!" Douglas screamed at his panic-stricken love-mate. "Our only chance of survival is to trick the fanatical son-of-a-bitch! Don't lose your cool, Nancy! Fly's dead and won't fart in your goddamned face! Now get-down on the friggin' ground I said!"

But then certain implausible, arcane words that had been expressed by Maria Sanchez (when she had rushed out of the district attorney's small office) suddenly made very clear sense to Doug Littlefield. 'If the life of the girl you love is ever in danger, just remember the name Jose Morales!'

"Stop lying face down! Roll over on your stomach and open fire on the heinous psychopath," Littlefield instructed his chosen girl. "Wait a minute! I just got an inspiration on just how I can mortally wound that no good dangerous prick!"

While the intimidated girl aimed and fired away at the demented Mexican aggressor, Littlefield removed his handy pocketknife and deftly exposed the object's sharp blade. Meanwhile, the crazed desperado pulled his heavy black Stetson down over his eyes to protect his peepers from a lucky scattered birdshot volley. Again, the maniac seated upon his black steed fired at his motionless victims, wondering if the Brownsville sweethearts, just like the incapacitated horse, were on their way to visit St. Peter. The ruthless assailant tugged and re-directed his impressive stallion's reins, and the obedient animal slowly advanced toward the stationary buckboard.

When the obsessed killer and his snorting stallion were a mere fifty feet away, Littlefield very deliberately rose to one knee, aimed his trusty shotgun at the astonished villain, and then fired his round. The shotgun blazed, and Mexico Sammy sighed, as his left hand rose from the saddle's pommel, and three seconds later, the viperous rattlesnake fell from his steed; his heavy body plummeting-down to the dry, arid, desert sand.

* * * * * * * * * * * * *

At nine o'clock sharp the following morning, distinguished Judge Aristotle DeWitt, with a very noticeable swollen bottom right jaw, promptly convened his Brownsville court. "The State of Texas versus Jose Morales," Bailiff Ralph Kirkwood called-out in a very clear voice. The district attorney, with his left arm in a sling, gracefully stood and respectfully addressed the court.

"If it may please Your Honor, I wish to enter a *nolle pros* in dispensing of this rather ordinary case," the encumbered county prosecutor surprisingly requested. "Even though the defendant Jose Morales might be guilty as sin, the government possesses insufficient evidence to pursue and secure a just and equitable conviction. Consequently, I can no longer locate two of the counterfeit fake silver dollars, and the third false coin is no longer available to be presented as direct evidence. I therefore, ask Your Honor, that this particular case be stricken-off the court's record."

"Permission granted!" the venerable Judge Aristotle DeWitt determined. "God, my mandible is really aching! What's next on the docket, Bailiff Kirkwood?"

* * * * * * * * * * * *

At the noon recess, Ralph Kirkwood ambled into the district attorney's less-than-adequate-sized office, and the beleaguered bailiff asked for a brief consultation. The versatile sheriff's department deputy desired learning more about what had happened to the three counterfeit silver dollars, especially the third one, which from Kirkwood's alert observation, the bailiff remembered had been in Littlefield's pants' pocket just the day before.

"Well Doug, what the hell happened to the three bogus silver dollars that Jose Morales tried passing-off at Fabian Duncan's pharmacy?" Kirkwood wanted to know. "Why in God's holy name are they missing-in-action?"

"The first two coins are tucked-away inside the far-right corner of my desk drawer," Littlefield admitted with a broad grin showing on his recently-scarred face.

"Well then, what about the third one?" the somewhat-shocked bailiff asked. "Where the heck is it?"

"Exhibit A was effectively used to be carved into lead pellets," the irascible prosecutor answered, tongue-in-cheek. "I employed my pocketknife, and crudely cut the soft metal coin into six usable slugs. I then very scrupulously put several of the pieces into my shotgun, rose to my right knee, and blasted the goddamned life out of that worthless rattlesnake son-of-a-bitch, Mexico Sammy."

"Then you've actually committed first-degree manslaughter!" the bailiff exclaimed.

"Yes, but it was done in self-defense," the district prosecutor argued and insisted. "And nobody's ever going to discover the plaintiff's body that's buried out in the desert, eight-miles away over near Piedra Creek. I'm hereby swearing you to secrecy on the whole touchy subject, Ralph. If you ever wreck my future, I'll surely come after you, too!"

"Amen!" Kirkwood answered before clearing his throat. "Amen!" the bailiff nervously verified and repeated.

“The Pimienta Pancakes”

I had always liked good-natured old-fart Judd Odom, mostly because the partially-insane chuckwagon cook once honestly admitted to me that the varmint was full of shit, and that I shouldn’t pay too much attention to any of the incredible bullshit he ever uttered in my direction. And I also valued Judd’s singular company because the inimitable, dirty ranch rascal was the only person I’ve ever known that had adequately mastered how to successfully whistle the entire unique melody of “Old Susanna” out of his hyperactive asshole. Of course, the irascible fool had to first swallow-down several pounds of hot baked beans.

Anyway, while some rogue cowpokes and I were assiduously rounding-up a herd of the Triangle O’s cattle, just north of the Rio Grande, a projecting branch of a dead mesquite caught my stirrup. And the impact wrenched my right ankle really bad, so bad that at the time I wished that the son-of-a-bitchin’ aching appendage would drop right off my leg. I was laid-up in the camp bunkhouse for a whole week, trying to learn and master (by means of trial and error) how to whistle popular tunes out of my untalented asshole, but all of my dedicated fucked-up efforts were to no avail.

On the eighth day of my compulsory recuperation, I hobbled-out to the chow wagon and got my hands warm near the morning fire. Old Judd, an avid conversationalist and nationally acclaimed professional bullshit artist, was in need of a captive audience to listen to his asinine verbal crap. So naturally, I was very accommodating in that particular regard. My belly was pretty damned famished, and on the verge of starvation, so I inquisitively asked the senile old fuck, “Hey Judd, can ya’ make me up a chimney of some scrumptious pancakes?”

Judd laid-down his shiny six-shooter, which the zany storyteller was intending to use to pound-down a tough antelope steak. The cook’s head turned toward me, showing a menacing sneer on his heavily bearded face, which confidentially made the unkempt geezer look like an adolescent of only eight decades old, instead of being his real ninety-three years of age. Odom’s sourpuss reflected an aura of being extremely pissed-off as a result of my very ordinary request about simply asking for some savory pancakes for breakfast. And right then and there, I got the distinct impression that “the cantankerous one” resented me even being present, believing that my sinister purpose for attendance was to basically aggravate his ass.

"Say you there, Scoundrel," Judd began speaking in his standard pessimistic disposition. "Are ya' tryin' to hook the gaff into me like I was some pathetic sea bass ya' just hauled onto your raft? Have some of the bunkhouse boys been tellin' you about me and my fucked-up adventurous pancake experiences? How'd you know I had a big connection with pancakes somewhere in my past?"

"No, Judd. I'm just hungry, and I had a cravin' for a heapin' stack of some delicious griddlecakes, that's all!" I respectfully insisted. "I don't care if they're generously crowned with some Vermont or New Hampshire maple syrup, or smothered with some delectable New Orleans' slow molasses in January. I even don't give a shit if you substitute some sarsaparilla for those other damned tasty fruit topping ingredients that's historically been your moronic pleasure!" I firmly emphasized. "I'd even swap my coveted saddle and dependable pony for a stack of buttered brown flapjacks right now," I boldly exaggerated. "Tell me Judd, you got a story about pancakes that I don't know about?"

"Well, it's a true *short* story, rather than a fictitious *tall* tale," Judd nastily answered and snarled like a hostile wolf. "I'm about to disclose to you what really happened between a pink-eyed asshole named Jackson Bird and me, involvin' a ravin' beauty contest queen named Miss Willella Learight. Now, don't interrupt my serious monologue," Odom gruffly warned. "Otherwise, Young Fella'. I might lose my temper and viciously break your other goddamned ankle in two with my five-pound frying pan!"

"Okay, Judd. I'm game for listening to your outlandish hyperbole, which would make really good church pulpit material," I commented and then grimaced, anticipating mental pain and emotional anguish that my head and ears were about to suffer. "Just tell me your little narrative that ain't recorded in any history book, newspaper records, personal journals, or secret woman's diary. And please make sure I don't yawn myself to death either out of general boredom!"

"When you was just a young whippersnapper no higher than a grasshopper, skunk, or a horny horned toad, I was occupied and employed punchin' longhorns for the venerable Mr. Bill Toomey over on the Bar Zero Ranch in San Miguel," Judd explained as the prevaricator provided me with logical-but-important background setting. "One sunny day, a Thursday I reckon, my mind became all worked-up about consumin' some luscious pancakes, just like you and your stomach are actin' mesmerized and homed-in right now! Anyway," Odom involuntarily farted loudly four times and then continued his monotonous rhetoric. "I hopped-on my mongrel bronco and headed east out to Uncle Emsley Telfair's store, which was inconveniently situated at a remote place known as Pancake Crossing, or Pancake Junction, or Pimienta, or some other asshole geographic nomenclature like that!"

"Good exposition has been established for your lengthy, real-life story!" I facetiously complimented. "Now, let's get to the interestin' part, so that you can start preparin' my fabulous pancakes! My gut's growlin' so loudly that I think I'm turnin' into a goddamned grizzly bear! Cut the flagrant bullshit and hurry-up with your damned nutcase story!"

"Enough of your' annoyin' pony-shit jabberin', and your fickle cock-suckin' gibberish," Judd sharply disciplined and reprimanded my apparent insolence and disrespect. "Now then; about three in the afternoon, I threw my bridle over a mesquite limb, and walked twenty-or-so yards. And I'm not speakin' back*yards,* but a distance of sixty-feet mind you. And then," Odom returned to telling his tale, "I nonchalantly sauntered into Uncle Emsley's disorganized general store, that truthfully looked pretty-much like a condemned shanty that needed to be demolished. Immediately, I got out my rusty pocketknife, and meticulously opened-up cans of apricots, pineapples and cherries, which of course I planned on usin' on my pancakes as fruit toppings. I was feelin' a little like Adam must've felt before he spotted the fabled apple tree in the Garden of Eden, when I looked-out the window, and my eyeballs perceived a chickadee; a beautiful hunk of blonde-haired femininity. The doll was just standing there in her tight jeans and calico shirt, tryin' to induce a hard-on inside any man's pants that might be alertly checkin' her nice tits, tight ass, and solid crotch!"

"'Did your Uncle Emsley know who the hot-looking doll was?" I asked, crossing my thighs to conceal the recently formed bulge between my legs. "I mean, what was that hot-lookin' bitch doin' out there in the middle of nowhere?"

"Sure, the ancient fossil did know her identity!" Judd Odom promptly confirmed. "Uncle Judd revealed that the cute babe was none other than his niece, Miss Willella Learight, who had come down from Palestine on a family visit, even though she was no Israelite. Then, my cornball relative, through marriage on my mother's side, volunteered to introduce the sexy prom queen to me!"

"Well, how did you manage to strike-up a conversation?" I asked, thinking more about my prospective pancakes than about one irrelevant Miss Willella Learight.

"After ten minutes flew by like a falcon in attack mode, Willella and I got acquainted a little bit. Then, I said to her, 'I hear you're from Palestine. Do you know some important guys like King David, Joshua the trumpet fella', or that abominable savage villain Goliath of Gath? How about that psychologically-disturbed nutcase homosexual freak, Ezekiel?' I commented, attemptin' to impress her with my Bible acumen."

"I'm from Palestine, Texas, you dumb-ass, silly fool!" the sultry-lookin' prim and proper Miss Learight corrected and criticized my noteworthy sense of humor. "The town's northwest of Dallas, and not too far from the Louisiana border. I come down here to Pimienta Crossing once a year to visit Uncle Emsley at his general store, because the hot climate in these parts is more conducive to maintaining my health than the summer weather back up in Palestine. I've got a mild case of asthma, you see," Willella explained, seeking to exploit my non-existent compassion. "And the wonderful dry air down here near the Mexican boundary is also on the average forty degrees warmer than the moderate temperature back home!"

"Yes, the girl from Northeast Texas sounds like a real winner," I remarked, wondering when Judd would start mixing-up his special-formula batter. "What were you thinkin' about at the time besides poppin' a huge load of sperm juice into Willella's hairy slit?"

"I was hopin' and prayin' that sweet little Miss Learight wouldn't run out of breath while experiencin' a long female *organism* because of her asthma condition, and that's precisely what I was meditatin' about at the time besides me bein' an enormous sperm whale in heat," the great philosopher/cook intimated and then smiled. "But standing there inside Uncle Emsley's dilapidated general store, I didn't have the courage to convey to the gorgeous, unmarried damsel my true impulses, if ya' know what the fuck I mean!" Judd yelled, fully losing his mercurial self-control. "I was thinkin' about screwin' her and her bronchitis like a bucking bronco right through a dozen or so mattresses! The store just wasn't the proper setting or atmosphere to ask the sophisticated Miss Willella if she wanted to get laid and have her wet, pink, pussy personally pumped-dry by me, while screwin' away like two minks in heat inside that termite-infested trading post's back storage room. Does that graphic reality make any fuckin' sense to you?"

"It's quite a fairly-decent story that you are tellin' me so far; that's for damned sure," I diplomatically evaluated. "But what the hell does this Miss Willella Learight bitch from Palestine, Texas have to do with pancakes? That's what the hell I wanna' learn!"

“You have no goddamned patience whatsoever!” Judd exclaimed and vociferated. “I’m getting to *that* indispensable part of my goddamned recollection. if you’ll just shut the fuck up and give me a chance to elaborate! Anyway, on the third trip over to Uncle Emsley’s grotesque-lookin’ emporium, I told Willella that before I became a rough and tumble cowpoke, I had been a sophomore at Harvard University, and was President of a fraternity called Signa Phi Nothin’. And the gullible belle believed my superior bullshit. And furthermore, the pristine Miss Learight was so enamored with my phenomenal wit, and so infatuated with my suave personality, that she gave me a big kiss on my cheek. But that’s just about when that yellow-bellied coyote Jackson Bird popped onto the scene, and maliciously interfered with my dynamic courtship.”

“What happened between you and this untrustworthy Jackson Bird character?” I questioned the loquacious pancake cook, with my creative pleasure-oriented mind then imagining me vicariously screwing the living daylights out of the incomparable nightingale Willella Learight. “How did Miss Pump-right, er, I mean Miss Learight get to cozyin’ up with this lowlife fella’ Jackson Bird?”

Judd took a very deep breath. “Well, Uncle Emsley reported to me that Willella had been goin’ horseback ridin’ with that uncouth varmint Jackson Bird, who was a primitive derelict, and a no-good sheep man, which as you know, is a cattleman’s worst enemy, besides the always-rebelling homesteader farmers that terrorize the plains. And now, getting’ back to that Jackson Bird dwarf,” Judd Odom ranted. “That cowardly thievin’ sheep dealer was raisin’ four thousand head of the finest Merinos south of the Arctic Circle,” the infuriated cook shouted.

Judd was really wired-up. “Well, I quickly excused myself and left my crazy uncle’s company, and reconnoitered the area environment. And while engagin’ in the process, performed some savvy reconnaissance, surreptitiously spyin’ on Uncle Emsley’s general store from a rocky ledge a half-mile away. An hour later, the craven son-of-a-bitch sheep rancher finally rode back to the about-to-implode trading/grocery store emporium with beautiful Willella. And then, ten minutes later, the fucked-up sheepshearer rode-off alone in the direction of his Mixed Mule Ranch. Well now,” Judd said to me and then imbibed six big gulps of rye whiskey from a brown bottle. “Despite my bad ankle with six broken bones, I deftly leaped onto my bronco from a nearby boulder, and took off like a bat out of Hades in hot pursuit after *that* dreadful deadbeat asshole. Two miles away from Uncle Emsley's eyesore store, I finally caught-up with the midget loser."

"Well, what happened next?" I asked the potential asylum case, who was now well-beyond livid. "Hurry-up with tellin' me your tale, or I'll possibly die from starvation."

Judd Odom quickly resumed his totally-boring recollection. "Good afternoon, Asshole!" I intrepidly addressed the love encroacher with a degree of bravado vibratin' out of my masculine vocal cords. "I'm mighty happy to meet you, Mr. Jackson Bird. And I strongly suggest that you wipe that sheepish smile off your hideous-lookin' face before I ram and disintegrate your glass jaw with my famous lightnin' quick right cross!"

"You must've been pretty damned intimidatin'!" I praised.

"Well now, after I took the time to formally introduce myself to my fucked-up new-found adversary," Judd Odom proceeded with his exhilarating romance/war novel plot. "I decided to greatly frighten my goofy-lookin' rival some more by givin' him a persuasive gun shootin' demonstration. My keen eye spotted an unbelievably fast roadrunner movin' quick as a cheetah down a hill with a huge tarantula in its mouth. So, I pulled-out my trusty silver gun from my holster, and blasted the speedy predator between the eyes with one amazin' shot. And then, with my other superhuman eye-vision," Judd bellowed and dramatically paused to see if I was still awake. "I viewed a jack rabbit runnin' quicker than a greyhound and passin' my sittin' position atop my bronco. The critter was really hard to follow, zippin' through the shrubs and brush rather irregular-like in a zig-zag pattern across the prairie. And then bingo; I easily killed that evasive hare, too, with my second round fired."

"Mr. Bird must've been pretty damned impressed with your uncanny marksmanship," I congratulated the still-farting storyteller. "He was probably scared that your third round would be comprised of goddamned *bird*shot, ha, ha, ha!"

"Damn tootin'!" the gossipy, volatile camp cook stated before scratching his smelly ass and then his sweaty balls. "Bird commended me on my shootin' accuracy, all right. But then, I warned the intrusive shit-head that he had a bad habit that I was payin' close attention to, and that misbehavior-type deportment was his late afternoon tendency to greedily accompany Miss Learight out horseback ridin' in the country."

"Did the weak-hearted sheepherder promise to lay off from seein' your heartthrob?" I incisively asked Judd, all the while pretending in my mini-mind that I was a world-famous prosecutor skillfully interrogating a key witness to a major crime. "What the hell does your freakin' story have to do with pancakes?"

"That lousy scoundrel son-of-a-whore told me that I had jumped to the wrong conclusion, and that his platonic purpose in dating Willella was purely gastronomical," the chuck wagon guru informed.

"Astronomical!" I yelled, laughed and corrected, deliberately busting Judd's already-vulnerable testicles. "You should've counted your lucky stars that Jackson Bird was surrenderin' to your awesome prowess, and in the meantime, promisin' not to compete with you for the young lady's hand. But tell me Judd," I urged. "What did Jackson Bird actually mean when the critter had mentioned that his intentions exclusively dealt with food digestion, and that his seeing Miss Willella was not love or sex motivated? Was Bird some kind of fag, or what?"

Judd thoroughly explained to me that (according to Jackson Bird) Willella made the "best damned pancakes in the entire world"; and that both Jackson and Odom were each hankering to obtain her secret recipe; and that the ingredients had been carefully handed-down in her family since the time of Christopher Columbus; and that the exact secret information (besides being memorized by Miss Learight) had been locked in a Palestine, Texas bank's safety deposit box for the past seventy-five years.

"And let me tell ya', Son; *that* petite arrogant jerk-off had the unmitigated audacity to say to my teeth that all Bird really and truly wanted from Willella was her well-kept secret recipe, and that he, meanin' Jackson Bird, had no nefarious designs of getting laid with Willella or getting his 'bird' blown and sucked by her succulent lips, and I tended to believe the simple-assed fuck-head because my two guns were pointin' directly at the petrified Idiot's goddamned egotistical head," the camp cook convincingly conveyed.

In his haste to escape the mighty Judd Odom's wrath, Jackson Bird had cunningly asked Judd to help him pilfer the pancake recipe from lovely Miss Learight. Jackson then said to Odom, "Maybe Willella will tell ya' Judd the magic pancake formula, rather than tellin' me, because the gorgeous hussy had already let me know that she trusts *you* more than she does the United States government, Judd," the wily Bird said to Odom.

"Well, what occurred next?" I inquired and then yawned.

"And so, I stupidly replied to that stealthy, dangerous, yellow-belly sidewinder," Judd pontificated and explained to his still-hungry chuck wagon listener. "I gladly agreed to try and help Bird secure the confidential pancake recipe to be shared by the both of us."

"Did your foolproof strategy work?" I asked, exhibiting for the first time a more-than-mild interest in Judd's outrageous narrative. "Did you two guys form a sacred alliance?"

"Well, around ten o'clock that same night, I said to Willella that there was nothing on the surface of the State of Texas that I craved more at that very second than a stack of mouth-waterin' pancakes," Judd confidentially divulged. "Well then, Miss Learight all-of-a-sudden becomes real-jumpy-like, as if she was one of those unpredictable Australian kangaroos, or maybe a wallaby, ya' see boxin' all comers at the circus. She then dashes over to the old dusty piano and starts playin' 'Old Susanna', which I automatically started fartin' the melody to. Then the unscrupulous bitch tried tricking me big time."

"How did Willella ever attempt accomplishing that trickery?" I asked, my fatigued brain becoming overwhelmed with abnormal, devastating curiosity.

"What street in St. Louis did you live on?" Willella impetuously asked me in order to get my mind off of passing large quantities of intestinal gas that I had been deployin' as the principal part of my improvised musical accompaniment."

"Did you answer her truthfully about St. Louis?" I asked.

"I lived at the corner of Pancake Boulevard and Syrup Lane," I cleverly replied to the enchanting doll. "That's the precise address where I learned how to fart around as an idle, worthless, lazy teenager. Now tell me, Willella," I insisted very emphatically, my articulation enunciating each fuckin' syllable of every fuckin' word. "Can you play the goddamned harpsichord as well as ya' can play the goddamned piano?"

"Well, Judd. Did Willella know that the two instruments shared basically the same keys and notes, and that the tonality of the sounds happen to be the only real difference between a piano, a harpsichord, and an organ?" I asked Odom at the front of the chuck wagon.

"Well, Son, I told her *that* exact same academic bullshit as *you* just described, but when I asked her if she wanted to play *my* organ while I ate some pancakes, well now, the neurotic maiden got-up in a huff from her piano stool, which in reality smelled like human toilet stool, after all the damned fartin' I had been doin'!"

"Did she run to be rescued from your lunacy by your Uncle Emsley?" I intelligently, verbally probed.

"She sure did!" Judd sadly related. "And that crazy psycho' relative of mine ran into the room with a large pail of cold water, and the bastard poured the entire contents onto my head. Then, I asked

Uncle Emsley if he knew the secret pancake recipe, which I had been desperately seeking real-hard, as if the normal words 'pancake recipe' were the Holy Grail itself," Judd explained to me. "And then the belligerent asshole got his erratic bowels in an uproar, and smashed me over my skull with a wooden ladle fifteen times at half second intervals, until I eventually sprinted-out of that nightmare general store, wonderin' exactly what the fuck was wrong with the mentally retarded son-of-a-bitch, and with my damaged brain also tryin' to figure-out what the hell was wrong with Uncle Emsley's equally fucked-up distant niece, Miss Willella Learight."

* * * * * * * * * * * * *

I was getting pretty damn weary and tired of listening to paranoid Judd's preposterous love story involving a mystical, alchemistic pancake formula, so I temporarily excused myself from his eminent presence to take a long, much-needed piss on the other side of the often-abused and smelly-wet chuckwagon. When I reluctantly returned to *his* illustrious company, old Odom wasted no precious time resuming his totally fucked-up, dopey rendition.

"Well, Son, as I was accurately recallin' and sayin'," Judd Odom uttered in my direction, as if I had never left his side of the chuck-wagon to drain my kidneys. "About a week later, when my spirits was feelin' much better, I met-up on the Pimienta Trail with Jackson Bird. And we exchanged civil pleasantries and some frivolous small-talk dialogue, because we were now bosom-buddy friends, with both of us sharin' the common goal of committin' a little grand larceny and stealin' Miss Willella's heavily-guarded pancake recipe. Man," the disgruntled cook said to me, "I was more goddamned *gull*ible than that lost squawking seabird flyin' up there!"

"Please tell me square-up, Judd. Were ya' ever able to purloin the sought-after chemical equation for Miss Learight's pancake mix?" I cheerfully inquired before discreetly covering my mouth with my hand between giggles and chuckles. "As the umpires say in the baseball league world, 'batter up!' Ha, ha, ha!" I laughed.

Judd exhibited a hellish frown upon his grisly-furry face. Odom stated to me that Jackson Bird had said that *he* wasn't having too much success with his exploratory espionage activities with Miss Learight, but that the suitor (namely Jackson (Jay) Bird) believed that he was almost there at the brink of accomplishment about the type of maple syrup and butter that Willella systematically used in her meticulous preparations.

"Let me get this illogical bullshit straight," I insolently and out-of-patience asked Judd. "You met Jackson Bird riding out to Pimienta on his way to see Willella Wheelwright, er, I mean Learight. Then, you're bein' put on the back burner of the stove while Jackson Bird is plannin' on stuffin' his erect bird inside Miss Learight's tight warm oven. It sounds like your sheep rancher competitor Jackson Bird is home on the range all right! That is to say, Judd, home on the range ridin' Miss Learight right into the bed's rusty springs located directly below the filthy mattress with bedbugs flyin' all over the goddamned room!"

"Stop your irritatin' quippin', or else I just might start hallucinatin' as is my wont; draw my six-shooter out of that holster hangin' over there on the wagon, and then imagine that you're a treacherous Comanchero, or maybe even *that* furtive despicable no-good son-of-a-bitch Jackson Bird bein' suddenly bird-less!" Judd threatened. "Now then, where was I before ya' so rudely wrecked and derailed my train of thought?"

"You were sayin' that your nemesis Jackson Bird was tellin' you that getting the pancake recipe out of Miss Willella was harder than draggin' a prairie dog out of its deep burrow with a broken peanut shell," I returned with an impish smirk featured on my irascible face, trying my utmost not to giggle too hard.

"Yeah, okay Son," Judd told me. "I had then very kindly told Jackson, 'You keep tryin' to get the recipe and I'll continue to pump Willella; that is to say, I'll continue to pump her about the pancake formula,' I backpedaled and clarified to Mr. Bird."

And that's exactly what Judd had said to me while finally beginning to mix his own unique flapjack batter. But then Odom was inspired to tell me some more nonsensical horse crap.

"After *that* negotiatin' parley, that wily jasper Jackson Bird and me cordially parted company, and our horses began kickin' up dust in different directions," the mentally-unstable cook somberly stated. "Everything seemed fine and dandy at that *junction*, er, I meant to say at Pimienta *Juncture*."

"Well, did you ever acquire the pertinent pancake secret?" I asked Odom. "To tell you the truth, my brain's startin' to lose focus after my ears have listened to all this distasteful hideous baloney. How the hell does this really terrible story ever end?"

"You'll find out soon enough!" Judd answered and bristled. "I'm getting to the climax of the goddamned episode, so don't start jerkin' off. Now then," the vociferous cook muttered in a more contemplative and conciliatory tone of voice. "I rode out a few days later to talk to good old Uncle Emsley about some personal concerns, in that I had heard that Grandpa Dexter had finally died at age hundred and eighteen."

"I guess your Grandpa Dexter wasn't ambidextrous enough to live longer than he did. But getting back on the relevant subject, Judd," I wondered and respectfully asked. "Did ya' find out anything essential about the mystery of the magic pancake mix?" I anxiously interrogated. "This asshole story of yours is a lot longer than your Grandpa Dexter's longevity, and certainly much longer than my semi-erect dick, that's what the fuck I think."

"Uncle Emsley informed me that *that* insidious worm Jackson Bird and Willella had clandestinely journeyed off to Palestine four days prior, and had gotten married, and were gonna' then honeymoon in Niagara Falls, Lake Tahoe, and finally, in Jackson Hole, Wyoming! Man, I was really pissed-off when my brain learned and absorbed that lousy catastrophic information!"

"Well Judd, it's mighty better to be pissed-off than to be pissed-on!" I sympathetically commented. "But this Jackson Bird fella' was a real pisser, I gotta' admit! You can say a real piss-tol, ha, ha, ha! So, Judd, despite the fact that you have this mental fixation about the tricky midget sheep rancher, tell me kindly and briefly, what was all that crazy bullshit about involvin' Miss Willella's fantastic, confidential pancake recipe?"

"It was all a big fuckin' diversion from the get-go," Judd testified with an excessively grim expression seemingly welded upon his heavily gray-bearded visage. "After the unexpected elopement had been announced, Uncle Emsley Telfair confided to me that whenever I said the word 'Pancakes', well that slippery varmint Jackson Bird had deviously told Willella and Uncle Emsley that once upon a time, some ill-tempered cowboy didn't like the flapjacks I had prepared for him, so the dumb-fuck hit me over the head with my own fryin' pan when I wasn't lookin', and gave me a permanent concussion. And as a direct result of that unwarranted violence," Judd reviewed for my empirical knowledge and gratification, "every damned time I would hear or mention the word 'pancakes', I would begin to go crazy and destroy my immediate environment, and savagely convert into a hostile Visigoth barbarian, and indiscriminately annihilate every goddamned, terrified victim that I could obliterate!"

"That's what Jackson Bird told your Uncle Emsley, and his pretty niece?" I asked, almost pissing myself, even though I had just emptied my bladder a few minutes before. "Now Mr. Chef, you were humbugged rather grandly, that's what the hell I now think! That crafty *midget* Jackson Bird had one *giant* brain, and was no birdbrain by any stretch of the imagination. And Jackson sure made a complete *imbecile* out of you," I concluded to the extremely perplexed Judd Odom in a convoluted oxy*moron*.

"Yeah, I was fuckin' hoodwinked by that confounded pancake allegory!" Judd acknowledged in a fraudulent, melancholy voice. "Uncle Emsley told me that Willella never made a goddamned pancake in her entire mediocre, spoiled, life. And in fact, the retarded bitch never ever learned how to properly boil water, either!"

"Tell me Judd, without expressin' any historic histrionics, how long ago did those hysterical events happen?" I asked the chuck-wagon supervisor, while once again my mind and tongue immaturely toyed around with the English lexicon.

"Three years, four months, six days, and seven hours ago," the defeated love warrior literally recounted. "Yes Sir; Jackson Bird and Willella are now livin' over at Mired Mule Ranch raisin' those prized Merenos."

"I guess you were a little too *ram*bunctious about pancake science during your failed courtship!" I foolishly joked before ducking-down and nearly being decapitated by a flying hot frying pan filled with sizzling pancake batter.

“The Emancipation of Billy”

One of the last prominent surviving Southern politicians from the archaic and historic antebellum period lived in the town of Elmville, in the County of Ashford, in a Dixie state that wishes to remain anonymous. Old Governor Pemberton resided with his obedient attorney/son in a Civil War era, square, wooden mansion, featuring dual parallel perimeter porches enveloping its mammoth girth. The ancient structure had numerous rotting window frames, and finally, the landmark edifice was suffering from white paint peeling-off most of the old mansion’s exterior.

In the year 1909, following the impact of the Industrial Revolution throughout the American South, the bitter enmity-residue associated with “the War of Northern Aggression”, all-but-had generally been forgotten in and around Elmville. But the somnolent community’s proud elders still refused to abandon many of the time-honored plantation-based customs, traditions, and courtesies emblematic of the cavalier and gentler days of President Jefferson Davis.

Retired Governor Abner Horatio Pemberton basked in the radiant honor and prestige that *his* loyal Confederate-status past glory had amassed. Even though the revered gentleman’s bank accounts had dwindled-down considerably since the turbulent decades following the Civil War, virtually every honor, and every award, and every plaque that the grateful state legislature could bestow upon the venerable and eminent prominent Elmville citizen had already been ceremonially conferred. The polite residents of the lazy community valued reverence for the idyllic past, and the population also cherished homage for the genteel culture that has been very specifically embodied in the resplendent phraseology “Southern hospitality”. Good manners and cultured breeding have always been uniquely characteristic of the American South in general, and of Elmville in particular.

Governor Pemberton’s monstrous decaying domicile/mansion still maintained a position of esteemed nobility on the town’s main street. The decaying structure was situated a mere quarter of a mile from the central U.S. Post Office, the Elmville High School, the volunteer fire department, and the town’s city hall and adjacent police station. Every morning, the white-goateed Governor would gingerly exit his screened-in front porch with his golden-tipped cane in hand, while wearing his signature three-piece white linen suit, looking much like an internationally known (and commercially famous) important fried chicken impresario.

The ninety-six-year-old "Governor" Pemberton, sporting his immaculate silk "blanco plug" (hat) and matching impeccable white gloves, would predictably proceed on the jagged brick pavement toward the "town square". And his snow-white hair was often the talk of both gossipy housewives, and of recently released scuttle-butting hardcore Methodist convicts, violent Presbyterian villains, and insane Southern Baptist terrorists.

Everyone that the gregarious Governor encountered on his morning stroll either saluted or greeted his excellent presence. And when the town's academic institutions were not in session, grammar school children would follow along after the distinguished gray-haired "Pied Piper" in what constituted a respectful daily procession. Some admiring acquaintances demonstrated commendably good manners by vigorously shaking hands with the venerated Abner Horatio Pemberton, and the married women and single whores, along with the young virgin belles, and assorted predator prostitutes, would formally or mockingly curtsy in recognition of a cherished anachronism from the distant past.

Every business-day morning, the hawk-eye belonging to General Dudley Deacon Diffenbaugh would perceptively notice the Governor's measured approach down the sidewalk, and the very mannerly former Civil War hero would hasten from his elegant marble-walled office inside the First National Bank and anxiously exit the building, specifically to warmly greet, chat with, and enthusiastically flatter his close friend (and relic) from a bygone era.

"Take my arm won't you, Governor," General Diffenbaugh ritualistically implored each and every Monday-through-Friday morning. "I need to guide you through the thick maze of huckster stations, farmer's wagons, kiosks, pushcarts and new-fangled automobiles cluttering the middle of Lee Avenue. It's too bad that old Robert E. wasn't alive to own one of these weirdo horseless carriage contraptions, or else out Confederate hero might put you inside the engine, because his automobile might need a *governor* to go the proper speed limit, ha, ha, ha! The undependable noisy automobile invention will never replace the bicycle, no it won't! Now please tell me in ten thousand words or less; how's your rheumatism acting, Governor?"

"I'm getting ready and rehearsin' for my one-night stint as the main attraction *stiff* playin' over at the Stonewall Jackson Funeral Parlor," Governor Pemberton loudly laughed. "That's the only place where this goddamned rheumatism will be coming in handy; preparin' me to be that stiff son-of-a-bitch lyin' horizontal in my coffin's fancy white silk interior. I've already paid Mr. Jackson for the confounded display and burial box ten years ago. Isn't the ironic truth something, Dudley?" the Governor rhetorically stated. "I popped-out of a hole when I was born ninety-six years ago, and I'm gonna' be planted in a hole at the Elmville Cemetery the day after my viewing expires. Why the hell do they call a viewing a wake anyway? No corpse ever wakes-up after bein' pumped to the gills with goddamned embalmin' fluid! Am I losin' my formerly incredible intellect, or what General?"

"It's just a convenient figure of speech, I suppose, Governor," General Dudlry Deacon Diffenbaugh chuckled and answered. "But I gotta' confess that you still haven't lost your distinctive sense of humor after all these difficult years of dealing with Reconstruction, and after enduring those countless Southern scalawags and legions of abominable Northern Carpetbaggers."

"Well now, General. I can remain standin' after most any devastatin' calamity includin' death. That is, after experiencin' disappointment and frustration at Gettysburg, Atlanta, Richmond and Vicksburg," the old fossil Abner Horatio Pemberton quipped. "And I strongly wish, Dudley, that my extreme rheumatism would miraculously convert into arthritis, go directly to my limp dick, and magically make that useless tool throb and stand at attention again. That's what I miss most about my youth, General; the wonderful sexual energy that I used to possess. I especially savored and relished getting laid in every cathouse from the New Orleans delta all the way up to the banks of the Potomac. And after making penetration and porking-away for at least an hour," the Governor bragged, "I then enjoyed wildly squirting sperm juice all over a horny bitch's bedroom ceiling and four walls. God, how I loved to again shoot-off my huge red cannon!" Pemberton ejaculated.

"Well Abner, we're gonna' have a delicious five-course breakfast across the street at the Palace Hotel, where you and me used to screw kinky bitches in separate beds in the same room back during that annoyin' distraction known as the Civil War," General Dudley Deacon Diffenbaugh recalled and mentioned, the same mealtime words he had expressed every Monday-through-Friday. "And if my weak memory serves me correctly, once when there was only one bed in the hookers' room, I believe it was on Meeting Street in Charleston, we creatively screwed the two gorgeous bitches simultaneously right there on the same single-bed mattress. And then for sloppy seconds, we switched bitches! Do ya' happen to recall that marvelous event, Abner?"

"I sure do, Dudley," the former Governor recollected and acknowledged. "But nowadays, the best thing that ever happens to my feeble body is irritable bowel syndrome, and that's on a fuckin' good day, too. But I'll tell ya'; there is a certain advantage to not bein' able to get laid anymore!"

"And exactly what the hell could that dumb-ass advantage be?" the retired General wondered and asked.

"I no longer have to worry about contractin' syphilis, the crabs, or bothersome gonorrhea, because I've lost my ability to screw pussy," the reminiscing Governor related. "And if you was smart, General, you'd also stop fuckin' around too if ya' know what the hell I mean. Women nowadays are carryin' new kinds of transmittable diseases that old farts like you and me have never heard of. I don't wanna' die on account of me not bein' able to piss or shit!"

"You're entirely right in your sage evaluation, Governor," General Diffenbaugh fully agreed. "But in genuine retrospect, I'll never forget the marvelous time back in April of 1863 that I was watchin' you while we were on a double date down in Tupelo, Mississippi. Incidentally, *that* was the temperature inside *that* Mississippi room too, *two below!* Anyway Abner," Dudley suavely elaborated. "I distinctly remember that you were pumpin' a big-titted whore so hard that your big hard head went right between the parallel brass headboard bars, and your bleeding skull wound-up right inside the goddamned plaster wall behind the bed!"

"You got a fantastic memory, General!" the former aged Governor praised and giggled. "But in *this* reprehensible mediocre year of 1909, the only way that I can ever get plastered is to drink a full gallon and a half of sweet Kentucky bourbon, ha, ha, ha!"

* * * * * * * * * * * * *

After consuming their extravagant and abundant Palace Hotel breakfasts, and after fully clogging-up their narrow arteries and intestines, retired Governor Abner Horatio Pemberton and retired Civil War General Dudley Deacon Diffenbaugh stepped-out of the cheerfully decorated lobby, descended the marble steps to curb level, and then began taking their daily relaxing morning walk along Lee Avenue. Soon, the carefree pair ambled near the wrought-iron entrance to a very familiar Elmville pharmacy.

"Let's briefly step inside this family establishment, Governor," the talkative General suggested. "I want to buy a pint bottle of that anti-fatigue snakebite medicine that Mr. Appleby R. Fenstermacher meticulously concocts in his back room. I do believe the commercial name of that stellar secret formula is Four Leaf Clover, 1909, Patented Private Stock. Of course, next January 1st, its appropriate designation will naturally be 1910, Patented Private Stock. And it only took me seven years of dedicated concentration and studious analysis to figure *that* esoteric bullshit out!"

"The liquid shit works wonders in cleanin' out the entire digestive system," the aged and well-educated Governor commented. "Be prepared, General, to spend at least twelve and a half hours on the old porcelain hopper. If ya' want an aggravated swollen asshole, then that's the right crap to drink-down. Appleby's deceased father, God rest *his* pestle and mortar, was my Masonic Hall brother Bartholomew Aloysius Fenstermacher. If ya' recall, the famed Elmville mixologist had ingeniously invented the therapeutic Four-Leaf-Clover elixir way back in 1883. And the local town folks accurately speculated at the time that an accidental overdose of that all-powerful unearthly shit had evilly dislodged, and then subsequently floated, old Bartholomew's two defective kidneys right out of the senile experimenter's asshole; thus, causing instant and excruciating death to occur in a matter of seconds."

"Yes, it's a good thing his loyal son was around and next in line to carry-on the family tradition of mixin' various chemicals into sophisticated compounds," the General deducted and contributed to the rather strange conversation. "The two generations of demented Fenstermacher druggists have in the past half-century utilized their extraordinary talents to make three-quarters of Elmville's diagnosed hypochondriac population, all totally dependent and bona fide druggos."

After purchasing their separate alimentary canal flush syrup bottles at the notorious apothecary shop, the chatty pair met-up with Judge Barnabas Ashley Calhoun; with County Coroner Jeremiah Cooper Wilkes, and with Cecil Benedict Lippincott, editor-in-chief and only reporter of the Elmville Banner Times Gazette. The three important "pillars of the community" were carrying a portable gurney in case either Governor Pemberton or General Diffenbaugh were to collapse somewhere along Lee Avenue, and then the always-vigilant rescue squad trio were always prepared-in-advance to rush the emergency victim over to Doc Mathers' infirmary on Pine Alley.

One little law office was always passed (by the frequent morning pedestrians) at the corner of Lee and Davis, and that Elmville business was the law practice of William Trent Pemberton, the intelligent-but-subordinate only child of Honorary Governor Abner Horatio Pemberton. The forty-seven-year-old introverted attorney-at-law never had the gumption to set-out on his own. Instead "Billy" chose to take the easy road, and thus inherited the law practice from his temperamental father, the former State Chief Executive, who also had appointed cowardly William as his main servant and domestic slave. And the demanding elder Pemberton constantly reminded his submissive son of *that* particular role daily.

'I'll always simply be remembered as the son of Governor Abner Pemberton, and I'll never be able to establish an important identity of my own, as long as I stay put here in Hickville, er, I mean Elmville,' Billy thought upon waving to his father's entourage as the procession of elders solemnly strolled by. 'I'll always be living in Pop's enormous shadow; and therefore, always be overshadowed. Shades of mutiny, I do declare!' William conjectured. 'If only I had the hairy balls to run away from home like any normal ten-year-old, ambitious, adventurous punk would decide to do! But alas,' the rueful son lamented. 'I must be loyal and subservient to my assigned duty; my fucked-up assigned duty being a vassal to my domineering and tyrannical Old Man!'

Despite his poor self-image, William Trent Pemberton happened to be a crackerjack town barrister, who had mastered the integral principles of federal, state, county, and local law. Upon invitation, "Billy Boy" had twice journeyed to Washington DC, and had successfully argued several cases before the United States Supreme Court. So, the shy lawyer knew that he could indeed develop a fine reputation outside the Elmville corporate limits, if he so elected to apply himself. And thus, successfully leave his father's influence and dictatorial needs behind. And William's diminutive income from his modest law practice was almost-exclusively used to support his father's deteriorating mansion, and its accompanying high property taxes, and also was spent to maintain his glorified dad's stellar reputation in the tightly-knit community.

'I'm always introduced at public events in and around Ashford County as Billy Boy Trent Pemberton; the only son of the distinguished former Governor Abner Horatio Pemberton, the pride and joy of Metropolitan Elmville. I think I'd rather swallow a bag full of chicken-shit than to attend the next county function, which according to my comprehensive diary record, is presently slated for the end of September.'

Then William Pemberton reflected some more on his present predicament. 'The only world that I've ever desired to conquer has been Elmville, but my bigger-than-life father always denied me even *that* small pleasure. That's really the reason why I've never left this one-horse town to explore bigger and better things. But as long as my dominant Old Man rules the roost,' William the Un-Conqueror regretted, 'I might as well be a small turd slowly sinking to the bottom of a giant cesspool! Why the fuck don't I have the courage to rebel against unwarranted and unjustified exploitation, just like the South had done at Fort Sumter!'

The following Wednesday, Billy was casually examining his morning mail, when a certain exceptional-looking letter from the U.S. State Department informed the struggling attorney that the President in Washington wished to appoint him as the new Chief Justice of a remote island territory in the Philippines. "Only candidates of the highest character and mental competency have been nominated, and your famous name was unanimously chosen as the designated appointee," the unexpected official government missive congratulated William. "Your confirmation is certain to have the full endorsement of both the Senate and the House of Representatives. The entire Congress has absolute faith and trust in your sincere dedication and devotion to your noble law profession and to your country."

William Trent Pemberton could not effectively subdue the genuine exultation that had instantly invaded his all-too-chaste heart. This was his often prayed-for opportunity to finally achieve liberty from his father's very tight apron strings. At last triumphant national recognition and true spirit-building-independence would be at his beck and call. The local yokels would feel proud and obligated to extend to Billy Pemberton the well-deserved honor and prestige that had formerly been primarily offered to his patriarch, the former Imperial Governor.

Inside the white wooden Lee Avenue mansion's dark and dreary library, William conducted a civil dialogue with Thomas Jefferson Clay, a likeable black servant functioning in the capacities of the estate's gardener, butler, maid, valet, and horse and buggy chauffeur. The faithful servant, for two difficult decades, had been Billy's chief consultant, sympathizer, and staunch confidante. The unique pair had always been compatible and amiable, sharing both family surprises and personal secrets, as if they were sworn-to-oath university fraternity brothers.

"Them Yankees made you a big-time judge, huh," the astounded black valet gasped. "It's about time those dumb-ass Northerners did somethin' constructive to make-up for what the hell they did to the South; ransackin', burnin', and destroyin' plantation after plantation. That's the justice of reparations for ya'. Now William, don't forget to send me a letter in one of them Manila envelopes once ya' get settled-down over there in the Philippines."

"I'd have to live there, and will probably get homesick for Elmville," Billy remorsefully replied. "Absence often makes the heart grow fonder."

"That's not what the hell my fourth-grade teacher Mrs. McGonigle would say to me after I played hooky for a damned full week," the black servant recalled and stated. "She'd always say to the class that my absence made her feel one-hundred-percent better. Even at ten-years-old, I thought that *that* hideous naggin' sea hag was a total bitch on wheels!"

"If you had your druthers, what would you wish for?" William asked Thomas Jefferson Clay.

"I'd ask to run away from Elmville and go cavortin' with you to the Philippines."

"Then poor Pop would be left all alone to die in this mansion here on Lee Avenue," the Governor's son concluded. "In two months, he'd be pushin' up daisies along with the other dead sinners out in the Protestant Cemetery."

The following evening, Billy Pemberton's soul garnered the wherewithal to bravely confront and inform the obstinate Governor of the good news that *he* had officially received from Washington. Old Abner sat idly in his favorite rocking chair, puffing-away on his pipe until the hoary fellow finally fell asleep two hours later without ever articulating a single damned word. The old egotistical coot, thereafter, remained completely silent for a full week until Abner finally orated several solemn paragraphs at the supper table.

"My chronic rheumatism's been growin' worse these past seven days, Billy Boy," the old wily curmudgeon began his lecture, showing no relevant deference to his son's recent fabulous federal appointment. "I'm now in my upper nineties, Billy, and to tell you the truth, I can't remember the names of any damned Supreme Court Justices that served in Washington during my eight-year-tenure as Governor; or maybe it was four years, I can't fuckin' remember which. But getting more to the essential point," the Governor very cogently emphasized. "If you elect to go to the Philippines in quest of some illusionary destiny, you too will in time be forgotten by your powerful political peers. In other words, Son, leave me now and your ass will be grass in and around Elmville, and all over the whole goddamned United States of America! You won't become famous! You'll be judged as being infamous!"

"You're trying to send me on a guilt trip all the way across the Pacific," William squawked and protested. "You think I'm your little puppet, your private marionette, at your greedy command every time you pull a goddamned string. That's all you've fuckin' done all your damned life, Pop! Pull strings for others in Elmville, and then pull my strings to get me to do your selfish bidding! Well, Dad, you need to know that I'm sick and tired of being your accommodating chattel! I've been your loyal son all my life, and quite frankly, I've never known or felt the real meaning of freedom and individual sovereignty until right this minute."

"Your name is always linked with mine here in Elmville. And all of the high-ranking citizens think commendably of you, just as well as they do of me," Abner coyly generalized. "And if you decide to wickedly abandon me at ninety-some years of age, during this most-dire crisis time of my life," the former state Chief Executive yelled, "then you could consider yourself a family disgrace, and for the rest of your pathetic years, you'll wear the emblem of shame on your no-good-bastard conscience. And if you ultimately desert me while seekin' exposure to tropical yellow fever, dysentery, smallpox, cholera, colitis, jungle diseases, and the like," the Old Man screamed like an obsessed banshee, "then you can go fuck yourself out there in the middle of nowhere, committin' family treason, and you should plan on never returnin' to Elmville ever again!"

Before William could present a persuasive argument in his own defense, the Governor's pipe dropped from his lap, and plopped onto the floor, and next a very noticeable crocodile-tear trickled-down his left cheek. And within a heartbeat, the old fart's mouth began incessantly snoring and wheezing.

'Oh my God!' the diffident William Trent Pemberton thought while desperately panting during his first real acute panic attack. 'I almost killed *him* with my defiant language! I gotta' watch my tongue! I mustn't be so damned arrogant!'

Then, the guilt-laden son pleaded out loud to his sleeping patriarch. "Don't worry, Father!" the sorrowed lawyer whispered as the guilt-laden son nervously touched the old shrewd codger's shoulder. "Elmville's good enough for me. I promise you, Pop. I'll never leave you stranded to fend for yourself in this rinky-dink town. You'll never be alone in this glorious historic mansion on Lee Avenue, as long as you and me are still breathing!"

* * * * * * * * * * * * *

According to repetitious and monotonous habit, on Thursday morning, General Dudley Deacon Diffenbaugh exited his plush office at the First National Bank and rendezvoused on Lee Avenue with his longtime pal and peer, former Governor Abner Horatio Pemberton. The first topic of discussion was "Billy Boy" getting a "letter of recognition" from the U.S. State Department. The General pretended to be astonished upon learning that there were now possibly two famous members in the Pemberton family.

"Sounds like a plum job for your remarkable Billy Boy to pursue," the General matter-of-factly appraised. "That incredible news should send the local real estate market sky high. I mean to say, Honorable Governor," Diffenbaugh deferentially expounded. "It's certainly nothing for *you* to be lugubrious about. Everyone here in Elmville has been absolutely blind about your Billy Boy's potential all these years. Great Gatlings! Shoot the rusty cannon in the town square! We must have some sort of grandiose reception at the high school auditorium or maybe even an impromptu pep assembly at the gymnasium. Maybe I can get the mayor to sponsor some large travelin' carnival to come to town."

"What did you have in mind?" the decrepit, ancient Governor Pemberton asked.

"I know Jim Anderson pretty damned well. We used to sing in the same barbershop quartet together over on Davis Street. Jim sang bass and I was a tenor," the general continued his petty eloquence. "But the group split-up when that fuck-head Anderson told me that my voice was so terrible that I should be singin' *'ten or'* fifteen miles away from him! What a cornball jerk-off that detestable idiot is! But Governor; I'm pretty damned sure that the town council will fully cooperate and ratify such a noteworthy proposal to edify and revere Billy Boy with a barbecue pork rib feast and correspondin' festival, if it's properly presented and advocated by you and me."

"General Diffenbaugh; I'm extremely-saddened to report that my Billy Boy has declined the government appointment. I'm sayin' that my devoted lawyer son wants to live the rest of his life assistin' the needy public here in Elmville with their legal concerns," the venerable former Governor prevaricated and disclosed to his colleague, feigning glumness. "And besides *that*-rather, very important decision, my true-blue loyal son refuses to leave me high and dry at the culmination of my old age. What a blessing that boy has been to me! What a tremendous blessing!"

"You're full of stallion manure, you fucked-up horse's ass!" the former General candidly accused. "I can vividly imagine just what had happened inside your crumbling mansion. You had more-than-likely complained to Billy Boy about your chronic rheumatism; sent the shamed fella' into an unprecedented guilt trip, and then promised that you'd exclude him from your worthless will and microscopic estate. You bankrupt, stupid-assed Bastard! I strongly recommend that you develop arthritis in both your hands, so that you can finally learn to get a grip!"

"I hope that your fuckin' flaccid dick explodes right off your goddamned torso the next time you take an hour-long piss," the livid Governor nastily retorted. "Sometimes, General Diffenbaugh, you forget you're in the South, and as a definite result, you neglect to demonstrate the appropriate genteel manners; your ego preferrin' instead to act like a retarded gorilla, not knowing what the hell to do with *his* ever-pulsating, imaginary hard-on! If ya' don't stop verbalizing your oppressive vindictive vituperations, I'm gonna' formally ask the Supreme Board of Directors over at the country club to cancel your privileged membership, even though you and I haven't played a friggin' game of golf since the goddamned clubhouse was built and dedicated back in Ought One."

Three months elapsed, and the fall season had arrived in all-too-complacent Elmville. And all was quickly forgotten about "Billy Boy's" federal government appointment, and his subsequent refusal to accept the prestigious United States Government commission.

The Retired Governor and the Retired General mutually re-established their post-Civil War truce, and peace, and tranquility once again existed every morning on Lee Avenue. But the emergence of a major surprise soon affected all serenity on that crisp autumnal morning. It was announced and promulgated via the gossip mill that there was to be an eventful visit from a touring Presidential delegation, and that the unexpected spectacle was scheduled to occur outside, and the political extravaganza was to be conducted upon the Palace Hotel's grand marble balcony.

The whistle-stop train bearing the patriotic stars and stripes' banners (that were fluttering in the wind) majestically pulled into the Elmville Railroad Station. In the meantime, the hotel balcony had been swiftly festooned with red, white, and blue bunting. Excitement instantly and dramatically pervaded the entire downtown business district. The high school's boring classes were dismissed, and soon cute cheerleaders with their waving pom-poms assembled on Lee Avenue. Then, the uniformed band played a lively medley of John Philip Sousa military march songs. The town's most illustrious citizens had been positioned on the great rotunda to officially receive the government entourage, and to hear the visitors' various monotonous speeches. Indeed, the gathering was a matter of epic and paramount significance to Elmville's civic-minded citizens.

Everybody applauded loudly in heartfelt appreciation as the U.S. President clasped hands with the noble Governor Pemberton, and next with the effervescent General Dudley Deacon Diffenbaugh. William Trent Pemberton stood at attention in the background, obediently holding his "white plug" in his right hand to exhibit his authentic respect for the President. Then, much to Governor Pemberton's dumbfounded shock, General Dudley Deacon Diffenbaugh was introduced, stood-up, and loquaciously made the following important announcement:

> "Mr. President; it gives me great privilege and satisfaction to introduce Mr. William Trent Pemberton, your recently appointed Chief Justice of the Philippine Islands. I'm confident that William will serve his country with distinction in the glorious year 1909, and will make everyone here in Elmville proud of their new most famous and outstanding citizen. People of Elmville, may I present to you, your new favorite son, the Honorable William Trent Pemberton."

“Mammon and the Archer”

Fossil-faced multimillionaire Anthony Rockwall, a retired stock market investor, and the principal shareholder of the thriving Eureka Soap Company, peered-down from his Fifth Avenue mansion’s library window, and grinned like a full-bellied shark. His pretentious neighbor to his right, the sanctimonious Dutch aristocrat G. Van Schuyflesh Suffolk-Jones, from Norfolk, Virginia, was exiting *his* extravagant brownstone. And then the pompous geezer snootily wrinkled his clogged-up nostrils at wealthy Anthony Rockwall’s Italian Renaissance Cupid-with-Arrow statue, which had been cemented to its white marble pedestal, which was conspicuously situated in the center of the sidewalk. Showing scorn and indignation at noticing “the hideous eyesore”, Suffolk-Jones from Norfolk anxiously hurried to his motorcar to quickly evade the “lacking culture proletarian monstrosity”.

‘God, how I love breaking that old skinflint’s shriveled-up balls!’ Anthony Rockwall chuckled at his neighbor’s apparent utter frustration. ‘Next summer I’ll have my resplendent palace patriotically painted red, white, and blue, just to further pulverize that old weasel’s tiny testicles. That brazen act is bound to turn the parsimonious Dutch snot-nose into a true, risk-taking American entrepreneur, who is wholeheartedly believing in this wonderful Land of Opportunity. ‘Oh, say can you see, by the dawn’s early light, ha, ha, ha’.’

And then, the always-scheming self-made capitalist Anthony Rockwall, who never much cared for bells, whistles, sex or masturbation, summoned his recalcitrant son by shouting, “Dick-head! Come in here immediately!” in the same bass voice that had once intimidated his poverty-stricken family’s mules back at the old Kansas prairie homestead.

“Tell me honestly, my fucked-up, disillusioned, apathetic Son,” the cantankerous and domineering martinet greeted Richard Rockwall, after the often-defiant offspring had slowly-trudged his way into the mahogany paneled room. “Exactly how much cash did you pay for the company’s superior soap product that you most frequently used when you were away, attending, I believe, that inferior Russian-style university up in Northern Siberia?”

Richard, who had proudly graduated from the University of Maine only six months before, was somewhat-stymied and taken by surprise upon hearing the unexpected ‘ridiculous question’. The lad momentarily attempted figuring-out his father's modus operandi in asking such a bizarre interrogative. Richard Michael Rockwell was amply aware that his flamboyant sire was more-full of feces than the average country cesspool happened to be.

"Around six-dollars for a dozen bars!" the son replied. "Yeah, Pop. Around six-dollars each time that I had shipped the item up to New England from *our* Bronx factory. I remember the exact expense, because it was the same price as the cost of a cheap blow-job provided by my favorite house of ill-repute over on Surf Avenue in Coney Island!"

"And now, please enlighten me further. How much, Mr. Cleanliness, do you pay for your average daily haberdashery; let's say, what you're wearing right now?" the insistent soap mogul demanded knowing.

"I suppose about a hundred-dollars translated into 1908 money," Richard conjectured and then answered. "Why the hell are you asking me all these idiotic, dumb-ass questions? You already have a freakin' monopoly on the whole damned soap industry, and all the goddamned money you'll ever need in this life, and also will ever need in the eternal afterworld! All you're ever concerned-about is accumulating mammon! You could also support saints Peter and Paul for the next ten thousand years, if the Lord commanded that His treasury was low, and you were morally obligated to do so!"

"You're always robbing Peter to pay Paul, but someday Peter's going to be out of both money and soap!" the father rankled and vociferously retorted.

"I have my own value system, and you have yours," Richard vehemently argued. "Let's just amiably agree that we're entirely incompatible."

"Look here, Little Dick. You're supposed to be an educated gentleman," the tallow-peddling tycoon diplomatically and suavely commented. "Now I've heard where your young blood Harvard and Yale buddies extravagantly spend an average of twenty-four-dollars a case for labeled perfumed soap, when you intelligently exercise discretion and frugality, by spending only six-dollars to purchase a case of *our* fantastic Eureka brand!" the father preached and lectured. "Our competition's poorly-manufactured soap smells as raunchy as *your* favorite prostitute's lice-infested cunt does over there on Surf Avenue in Brooklyn. I've learned through reliable sources that *that* lusty Coney Island bitch of yours shoves fat boardwalk hotdogs, and full-length extra-thick Polish sausages up her sordid crotch when you're not inside *that* fleabag bordello porking her like a mongrel dog in heat!"

"Look, Pop," Richard Rockwall indignantly and reflexively bellowed and sneered. "You're so full of crap that you need to grow a second large intestine, and then go to your proctologist and have a second asshole cut out of your fat ass! That's my conclusive assessment of you! What's with all of these pretty irrelevant questions you're asking? Are you studying to be a two-bit private detective or something?"

"Well, Son," old wily Anthony Rockwall continued his diatribe. "As I was saying, you're truly a gentleman-in-progress; one in-the-making, so to speak. You're just going through a juvenile, adolescent period of rebellion against adult authority. Now then," the self-made man and main Eureka Soap Company stockholder continued his pertinent exposition. "Certain Wall Street experts claim that it takes three whole generations for an ambitious fellow to finally accumulate a respectable fortune. And the two old-fart snobbish Dutch shit-heads living on either side of *us,* they're both abundantly jealous of *me* and my fantastic success, because I represent new free enterprise money, and those two arrogant bastards still think that the city's name is New Amsterdam and not New York. I'm amazed that the two Old World pricks no longer are walking about Manhattan in antiquated knickerbockers!"

"So, what, Dad!" young and idealistic Richard Rockwall instinctively challenged. "Mr. G. Van Schuyflesh Suffolk-Jones from Norfolk, and Mr. Vincent Van Brocklin Norfolk-Smith from Ghent, might both be envious of your wealth. But they've never hired any hit-men to have you assassinated, as I'm often tempted to do. You just don't get what the hell life's all about, Pop! There're some intangible and abstract things that money can't buy," Richard maintained. "A woman's love is a prime example of precisely what the hell I mean! You can't purchase a sincere lady's devotion!"

"You've always had a penchant for advocating immaturity!" the financial soap baron chastised. "If it weren't for my patience and guidance, you'd be a twenty-three-year-old, totally hormone driven, over-the-hill juvenile delinquent by now!"

"Pop, why are you so hostilely sarcastic and condescending?" Richard asked. "You need some refresher courses in psychology, human ethics, and sociology!"

"You don't realize it, Son. But you're inadvertently quoting your middle-class income, share-the-wealth, asinine college professors," Sir Anthony pointed-out. "Don't you understand the real world? Your mediocre-salaried, socialist university instructors wanted to permanently brainwash you, so that you'll never be able to earn and exceed their lackluster annual wages. By running Eureka Soap after I surrender my fifty million shares to you, upon my *natural death* as has been stipulated in my will," Rockwall reminded his radical son, "you'll then be able to buy and sell the entire University of Maine, along with its anti-business, and anti-American, Marxist faculty!"

"You're so damned critical that you've become hypocritical!" the son impressively argued in defense of his own suspect value system. "You have nothing on Socrates, Plato, and Aristotle, that's for damned sure! If you can't prove to me your preposterous contention that money can buy anything, then pragmatically, prove it to me by providing some observable, concrete example!"

"Okay, you stubborn and impetuous Young Fool!" the patriarch of the wholly-despised soap family agreed. "If I can't demonstrate absolute truth to you in the abstract, I'll competently illustrate and verify it to your poisoned mind in terms of genuine and bona fide real-life experience. Now, My Boy," the rags-to-riches monetary philosopher articulated and then briefly paused. "Let's sit-down and share a pot of coffee, and then you can civilly tell me all about your fucked-up quixotic idealism! All right, stubborn Mr. Caterpillar. Are you ready to have a wonderful metamorphosis into a colorful Mr. Butterfly? I predict, Richard, that I'll eventually convert your unappreciative, lazy ass from you being a primitive Java man, into you becoming a prominent Wall Street executive, ha, ha, ha!"

* * * * * * * * * * * * *

"Now Richard," old Anthony Rockwall dictatorially prefaced his next remark. "I'll bet my pocket cash on valuing money every damned, single time. In my destitute younger days, I'd study the encyclopedias from A to Z, persistently looking for something that money can't buy. And don't tell me that my youthful experience being poor is just baloney. Your Marxist philosophy is pure and simple mediocre, socialistic poppycock. I suggest that you immediately extract *that* all-too-ludicrous Communist abstraction from your underdeveloped cerebrum! As I just said," the soap baron opined. "The abstraction known as love is a lot of butcher-shop baloney! In fact, what you call *love* is really more like sausage than baloney! Your salami pumping some horny bitch right through the goddamned mattress, that's what the hell *love* really is! Love is a man's overwhelming desire to have and enjoy pleasurable, deep, biological penis penetration, and nothing more!"

"Well Pop, your marvelous New Money won't buy my admission into an exclusive circle of high society Old Money respectability," Michael insisted. "The established Fifth Avenue Dutch aristocrats will always look-down on us Rockwalls, even if we could buy lower Manhattan along with Queens, Harlem, Brooklyn, Staten Island, and with the Bronx ghettos, too!"

Old Anthony pondered Richard's contention for a moment. "Look Rich, the worst thing in the world you could ever do is to procrastinate! Hesitation usually leads to bitter disappointment! Never let indecision interfere with you achieving your personal goals!" the elder professed. "Have sperm in your worm; that's what the hell I always say!"

"Get to the point, Pop. I'm about to fall asleep."

"Now Richard, you tell me flat-out. Who the frig' is this so-called exclusive Manhattan family that you're citing? And then I'll tell you exactly which cattle-boat that their indigent, immigrant ancestors had boarded in various European embarking ports. And yes, the lucky future, capitalistic Americans eventually docked at the U.S. government's Ellis Island facility. Even the goddamned snooty Astors were disasters before descending the rickety gangplank, and arriving in New York! The indigent assholes didn't even have a copper pan to shit-in, or a tin pot to piss-in, when the ambitious immigrants stumbled-off the rusty, barnacle-laden ocean steamer at Ellis Island!"

"You're a closed-minded, old, obsolete Ignoramus!" young Richard Rockwall defiantly exclaimed. "You oughta' be stampeded and trampled by those wild running bulls over in Pamplona, Spain!"

"My dear Rich, and I respectfully use that name even though you're as fuckin' poor on your own labors as a Mexico City barrio," Anthony Rockwall poignantly and sarcastically qualified. "There's something rather strange dominating your vulnerable, adolescent mind. And I've been observing this weird change in your behavior for around a month now! Is your liver acting up again? Do you need an eight-hour enema? What about your double hernia? Perhaps you should take my yacht down to the Bahamas for a couple of weeks, and have that gender transformation operation you were thinking about when you were an asshole freshman at the University of Maine," the retired and insensitive soap czar quipped. "Now I urge that you level with me Richard. What's the stupid self-infatuated bitch's name that has your mixed-up mind captivated in an advanced stage of hypnosis?"

Young Richard Rockwall was stunned that his narrow-minded father had accurately diagnosed the exact nature of *his* secret problem. How could his doltish old man know anything about the complex sentiments of the human heart?

"Look Son," Anthony imperatively stated to fill a void in the conversation. "Why don't you simply ask the wealthy Old Family Manhattan slut living next door to marry you? This aristocratic sophistication façade stuff that you're subscribing to and believing-in is a lot of stinking bullshit; you understand me, Son! In the final analysis, money talks and the rest walks, and you've got plenty to say with my super big bucks defending and backing your simpleton ass! If you were living three centuries ago, you could've beaten Ben Franklin in authoring Poor Richard's Almanac!"

"The right opportunity hasn't yet arisen for me to propose marriage," Richard weakly admitted. "Alice Van Lantry's definitely high-society, and doesn't want her reputable name mentioned in the newspaper gossip columns. She's certainly Park Avenue material, and quite afraid of being either directly or indirectly associated with the uncultured and uneducated, non-Dutch Rockwalls of uptown Fifth Avenue! Wouldn't you agree, Pop!"

"Nonsense and horse manure!" the now-livid father violently screamed. "Take that snobbish pompous broad for a romantic walk in Central Park, or for an invigorating straw carriage ride through Greenwich Village. Or accompany the rich Dutch bitch home from church on Sunday morning; or take her on a tour of our company's newly-renovated sanitary napkin facility over in Queens! I'll advise you of an elementary fact, Son; flip any screaming naked woman onto a bed, open her legs, and you'll soon discover that the cunts all fuckin' look basically the same, rich or poor!"

"But Dad, the young lady's not a streetwalking tramp! Alice Van Lantry's part of the upper-crust New York social scene, with every minute of every hour of her busy day carefully arranged and organized into a tight time schedule," Richard dejectedly complained. "She's always on the run, and always in the company of others of her fine silk ilk. And I can't find the time to be alone with her to drop the big nuptial suggestion! What an unprecedented fuckin' bummer!"

"This mammon-seeking girl of yours might possess a high society name, but I guarantee you Richard," Anthony Rockwall adamantly argued, "I could buy her old man ten times over, if I had to do it. This greedy gold-digger woman of yours will lick your asshole every night, just for the daily allowance she'll be allowed to spend at the uptown jewelry shops and expensive gift stores. And if we put her on the payroll without working," the father extrapolated, "you'll get a decent blowjob every evening, so you'll no longer have to travel out to Surf Avenue to get your sex pipes cleaned-out. Just remember Rich: the upper crust of society is held together by a bunch of crumbs with a lot of dough!"

"Well Pop, my divine Dutch heartthrob is scheduled to sail to Europe at noon in two days, and she'll then be staying in Holland for a full year," Richard reluctantly disclosed with an element of melancholy evident in his tone of voice. "She's presently staying with her holier-than-thou aunt in Larchmont. But unfortunately, I'm not allowed to go there because of her family's austere societal constraints against Manhattan New Money lowlife. But I've cleverly arranged to meet her with a cab at Grand Central Station tomorrow evening before we have to arrive at the theatre at eight to see a Broadway play.

"I assure you, Richard. Your Old Money Dutch lady acquaintance is more interested in your future fortune than you are! She would even go to the theater with you, Dutch treat, just to try and collar you to propose marriage."

"I'm sorry Pop," Richard sadly expressed. "But this is one grotesque mess that your fantastic New World fortune can't begin to penetrate. I mean to say; rich people would live longer than other less fortunate humans, if we could buy time and tack it onto our miserable lives. But alas, neither my or your longevity can be extended by simply writing a check! And regrettably, I'll never be able to have sufficient occasion to propose a marital engagement with Miss Alice Van Lantry before she sails to the Old World. No way Jose in Santa Fe!"

"That's a very sad story you've just conveyed to me, Poor Richard without any almanac," old and crafty Anthony Rockwall sympathetically commiserated. "I strongly caution you, Son. Being mesmerized by a beautiful woman is analogous to being temporarily insane! But on the other hand, I want you to know that I'm glad your liver wasn't acting-up again, and that it's only common heartache that you're presently suffering from! But I must vigorously oppose your blatantly false convictions about money and love."

"Pop. You're from a different generation concerning the modern-day topics of love and money!"

"You just erroneously declared that money can't buy time!" Anthony Rockwall insisted. "Maybe not exactly in *that* particular context, my Poor Richard! But beyond the shadow of a skinny doubt, money *can* indeed buy you enough time to finally get good fortune on your side! Just you wait and see!" the wily soap tycoon confidently predicted. "I know human nature better than you do! Just you fuckin' wait and see! Now Son, run along to your weekly Pornography Club meeting, while I take care of some important family business. Maybe your perverted Princeton and Dartmouth post-graduate pals will appoint you Sergeant-at-Legs at the exclusive scumbag club! Ha, ha, ha!"

* * * * * * * * * * * * * *

That evening, Anthony Rockwall's ancient and wrinkled-skinned Aunt Ellen paid the rich fellow a visit at his palatial Fifth Avenue mansion. The sentimental, skinny wench interrupted her haughty nephew's perusal of the afternoon newspaper, and the maudlin woman began discussing love woes and the affairs of the heart.

"The ornery brat told me all about his fascination with some high-falutin' Dutch dame," Anthony disgustingly acknowledged. "That naïve grand-nephew of yours began knocking the significance of money, and how it couldn't alleviate his romantic escapade. What a moronic dunce with a capital D!"

"Don't be so enamored with money while neglecting the more essential things in life!" Aunt Ellen admonished her only first-generation nephew. "Really, dunce Anthony. Wealth is absolutely meaningless where the involvement of affection is concerned! If Poor Richard had only introduced his love dilemma to us earlier, the Dutch girl would never have the chance to reject or refuse our beloved Little Dick. But now Anthony," Ellen Vandersnoot wept. "I fear it's all too late. I'm afraid that all of your geld will not bring happiness to *our* poor Richie's shattered heart."

"Don't be absurd!" Anthony prattled in his normal manner, with his nose still pointed at the center of the opened newspaper. "Your grand-nephew is better off without the pain of separation, divorce, and alimony ten-years or so down the line. I'd rather see him join an Eskimo tribe up there in Alaska, than ever getting married to a Manhattan Dutch debutante. A man should honor his mind's logic; not his penis's erection; that's the excellent behavior policy that I've always advocated."

At precisely six o'clock the following night, Aunt Ellen handed Richard a quaint golden ring at their appointed rendezvous in front of a popular Sixth Avenue restaurant. "Now Richard, wear this family heirloom ring later tonight on your pinky, so that you don't accidentally lose it," Ellen instructed her very favored only great-nephew. "Your mother gave it to me the day before she committed suicide. Her last wish was for me to transfer it to you when you finally found your prospective marital mate. Thank God I never lost the tawdry son-of-a-bitchin' thing down a sink drain, or knocked it off a window ledge from my twelfth-floor apartment by mistake."

"Gee thanks, Aunt Ellen," young Richard gratefully replied. "With the stingy allowance that Pop gives me, I couldn't even afford cheap costume jewelry to woo Alice. I'll see if I can propose marriage to my special lady on the carriage ride to the Broadway theatre tomorrow night. Oh, this appropriate gift is so terrifically peachy. Ring-a-ding-ding! Ha, ha, ha!"

"That's perfectly fine, Richie," Aunt Ellen amiably agreed. "Unlike your bellicose father, I had married into social status for *love,* and from my sensational fifty-year experience, I believe that you should do so, also. You have my blessing regardless of what your abhorrent, petulant father thinks or believes!"

* * * * * * * * * * * * * *

The evening of romantic reckoning had finally arrived. Richard Rockwall promptly met the alluring Alice Van Lantry at the designated cab station, precisely where the prospective soap heir had to gently separate the convivial young lady from her chatty and jealous socialite girlfriends.

"Oh Richard, you're always in such a dramatic rush, acting like the whole world's going to abruptly end the next minute!" Alice politely scolded her chief admirer. "But then again, we mustn't keep Mamma and Aunt Harriet waiting. They've volunteered their valuable time to graciously chaperone us at Wallack's Theatre."

"To Wallack's Theatre as slowly as you can drive this miserable contraption," commanded Richard to the overweight carriage driver. "I'll give you a fifty-cent tip if you take your damned time!"

"Piss it out your ear!" the insulted driver yelled-back. "That kind of lousy tip represents a down payment on absolutely nothing! Fuckin' rancid chocolate candy bars cost more than that in even the most dilapidated five and dimes!"

The bulky carriage whirled-up Forty-second Street to Broadway, and then in the vicinity of Thirty-fourth Street. Richard courageously thrust-open the cab's trap, and intrepidly ordered the burly driver to pull his horses' reins and stop.

“What the hell’s the problem?” the corpulent driver balked. “Did you piss your pants or something? Is your lady companion sick?”

“I’ve dropped a valuable ring out the door’s window, and I must retrieve it,” the embarrassed, florid-faced youth apologized. “It was a special heirloom from my deceased mother. And I’d hate to lose the damned thing. I saw exactly where it landed, so I won’t detain you for more than several minutes.”

“Okay, but this all smells mighty fishy to me!” the already aggravated driver replied. “I hope your woman friend had taken a bath and washed her crotch before entering my impeccably clean and immaculate cab! As I’ve just said, it all smells mighty fishy to me!”

At that crucial moment of truth, a cross-town cab had stopped immediately in front of the aforementioned carriage, and then an express wagon with an antagonistic driver halted alongside Richard’s cab in order to avoid a collision. Next, a large furniture van further ceased moving, as the centrally located intersection’s traffic flow became even more clogged. Soon, over fifty vehicles were blocking the excessively-congested intersection, the irate drivers all clamorously barking vulgar expletives and derogatory nomenclature at one another. Street commerce would certainly be tied-up for at least fifteen-minutes, until the city police would finally arrive on the scene and methodically unravel the immense metropolitan tangle.

“Richard, why don’t you do something drastic? Honestly, I’m not at all accustomed to being exposed to such uncouth and obscene vitriol!” Alice decisively demanded. “Mother and Aunt Harriet will have dual French hemorrhages worrying about me, er, I mean worrying about *us,* even though they’re both of pure Dutch origin!”

The junior Rockwall felt confused, and was momentarily petrified. Then, Richard stood-up and stuck his head through the cab’s overhead trap door. The soap heir’s eyes perceived an aggregate of stationary trucks, taxis, wagons, vans, and horse drawn streetcars occupying the space between the convergence of Broadway, Sixth Avenue and Thirty-fourth Street. A classic early 1900s traffic jam had instantaneously materialized, but this urban vehicle mess exceeded any previous one that had ever developed in the city.

Richard sat-down in his seat with a bewildered expression evident on his now-pallid countenance. “I’m sorry to report to you Alice that we’re stuck right in the middle of a massive traffic knot of extraordinary proportions. It’ll take at least a half-hour for the police to eventually restore order. It was all my damned fault. If I hadn’t dropped the ring…”

"Let me see that ring," Alice requested. "Since we're delayed on making it to the theatre, I must have something to look at in the meantime. Who wants to see *Romeo and Juliet* anyway? What a silly and stupid love story!"

"Yes, Alice! Romeo's tight leotards popped more than a few threads as his pubic bulge swelled when his great love for Juliet had the insane knucklehead literally climbing the walls over at Miss Capulet's Verona residence!"

* * * * * * * * * * * * *

At eleven o'clock that evening, a very excited Ellen Vandersnoot rapped on the insomniac Anthony Rockwall's front door. The soap mogul was casually dressed in his red smoking jacket, that at the moment, wasn't smoking anything. The tallow and detergent baron had been surprised to see his wrinkled aunt standing there in the mansion's vestibule, with an abnormal broad smile that exhibited the dame's original pearly white teeth.

"Come in, Aunt Ellen. I was just intensely reading a fiction book about Blackbeard's notorious Caribbean pirate adventures. Did you know that the nautical thief was selling corn at a *buck an ear*, ha, ha, ha! What brings you here at this late hour? Has your crazy landlord finally evicted you from your apartment? He's been vowing to do so for at least three decades now."

Aunt Ellen was in a happy and euphoric mood, and up-close, looked like a gray-haired angel recently dispatched from heaven by St. Peter. The ecstatic woman had trouble controlling the powerful emotions presently escaping from her heart and throat. "Guess what, my illustrious nephew?" the thrilled woman rhetorically asked. "They're officially engaged! Alice Van Lantry has promised to marry our dear Richard after all! On their wild ride to the theatre, there was a tremendous unexpected traffic tie-up, and it was a full hour before the cab the two were occupying could slither out of the all-too-cluttered intersection. What an incredible blessing in disguise that sudden disappointment turned out to be!"

"What?" Anthony yelled. "Now, my son will have to pay years of alimony after a divorce is announced twelve months from now! He's ignorantly thinking with his throbbing erection, and not with his head, that's for goddamned sure!"

"Oh, foolish Man. Don't you ever dare brag to me about the exclusive power of money again!" Ellen Vandersnoot merrily chided. "Your deceased wife's heirloom gold ring had done the trick, and the gem worked absolute wonders during the colossal traffic jam. Our cherished Richard has satisfactorily achieved happiness and bliss, once and for all! This propitious news of their engagement is certainly occasion for us to celebrate. You must admit, Anthony. Money is often dwarfed by the awesome power of love!"

"I'm glad that the young punk can now abandon his need for lust gratification by traveling every noon out to Coney Island for the mere biologic purpose of expelling ounces of sticky reproductive fluids from his aching testicles!" loudly laughed the miserly soap entrepreneur. "Someday, my short-sighted son will realize that there's plenty more to life than routinely shooting excess sperm from his overactive reproductive glands. I hereby predict, Ellen, that the acne-faced novice will evolve into a pauper after that snotty debutante bitch eventually gets her grubby talons inside his all-too-thin wallet!"

"When will you ever learn to forget about the acquisition of mammon, and learn to nobly pursue the acquisition of true love?" Ellen bluntly reprimanded. "There's something drastically missing in your life, Anthony. And I theorize that it's *not* the vice known as the relentless quest for money! I strongly advise that you pay more attention to your splendid Fifth Avenue marble statue of that archer Cupid standing with his bow and arrow poised for shooting."

The next morning, a common pock-faced peddler with red hands, and a blue and white polka-dot tie, paid an important visit to Anthony Rockwall's Fifth Avenue mansion, where the formally-dressed butler readily escorted the expected caller into the mahogany-walled library.

"Greetings, Kelly!" the all-too-clever soap magnet enthusiastically exclaimed. "I see I owe you five-thousand-bucks for the successful performance of your indispensable services. I figure that a hundred bananas apiece should satisfy the expenses for your transportation pals' major contribution to skillfully cause that historic, contrived traffic jam between Broadway and Sixth Avenue, which my naïve son Richard foolishly interpreted as being quite accidental."

"Unfortunately, Mr. Rockwall," Kelly answered before nervously clearing his vocal cords. "I had to fork-out three-hundred additional dollars over and above my initial cost estimate. I managed to get the express wagons and cabs for five-dollars each. But the trucks and horse team drivers raised their fees to ten-dollars apiece, in order for me to convince the stubborn sons-of-bitches to participate in the fucked-up caper. And then, the hard-to-persuade streetcar motormen wanted twenty-bucks each. And the nasty-tempered loaded wagon drivers demanded similar monetary compensation. But in the end, Sir, the overall scheme worked pretty smoothly. However, I gotta' confess the honest-to-goodness truth," the shrewd street event organizer related. "If your clumsy numbskull of a son hadn't unintentionally dropped that gold ring out of the cab window," Kelly emphatically indicated, "then the entire ruse could've never taken place, because young Rockwall's cab had actually approached the designated main intersection a full ten minutes earlier than had been anticipated and planned."

"Well, Kelly, thanks again for your amazing and deft expertise!" Anthony Rockwall commended. "Here's an additional two thousand cash to cover all your miscellaneous expenses!" the soap king laughed, as the mogul very deliberately counted twenty crisp, recently-printed hundred-dollar-bills into the palm of the street peddler's right hand. "This cash sum bonus is meant to complement the accompanying five-thousand-dollar check! You don't happen to despise money and all that money can buy, do you Kelly?"

"I like money better than I do sex, and certainly, I like it a lot better than love," Kelly answered with an eyewink, his language being sweet music to old Anthony Rockwall's ears. "I positively loathe the very stupid man who ever invented poverty! That villainous and confused fuck-head had to definitely be a defective asshole of the most major magnitude!"

"You didn't notice anywhere between Broadway and Sixth Avenue a certain naked fat boy with a quiver on his back, shooting random arrows across Thirty-fourth Street, did you Kelly?"

"Why no, Mr. Rockwall!" the mystified street huckster replied. "Maybe the cops had alertly arrested the perverted nude son-of-a-bitch, before the unfortunate massive traffic incident occurred."

"Always remember this social axiom, Kelly," the great practical and erudite soap philosopher esoterically remarked without standing on a soapbox. "The power of money will easily transcend and trump the weakness of love, every single time!"

"The Caliph, Cupid and the Clock"

The poorly-clad mendicant sat idly upon the New York City' park bench, and the lonely dreg was waiting for someone interesting to come by and interrogate. Late fall was rapidly setting-in, and the windblown November autumn leaves were floating and swirling down from the Greenwich Village park's deciduous trees. A full moon was rising above the rooftops and chimneys of expensive brick dwellings that were situated across the street.

The raggedy-dressed vagrant was especially cold and quite alone in his miserable plight. The bum's ears could vaguely discern the voices of children playing on a side street, the sound of which momentarily alleviated the fellow's singular solitude. And then there was the dull face of an illuminated clock that was ensconced inside an abandoned building's tower; its shadowy appearance morosely dominating the tops of two half-barren oak trees.

The old, gray-whiskered fellow's weatherworn holey shoes were wholly tarnished and indeed in need of repair. The vagrant's stovepipe hat was a faded blue, and the headpiece scarcely provided the poor derelict with any adequate protection from nature's unsympathetic elements. The indigent fellow definitely appeared in need of public assistance; of benevolent altruism, and of charitable philanthropy. The down-on-his-luck gent's general condition could be described in one applicable adjective: "Pathetic". Impatiently, the destitute old codger waited for some stranger in the neighborhood to show-up so that the loner could hold a general conversation, and share his special companionship and keen insights. Such was the beggar's main pleasure and pastime.

Fifteen minutes elapsed, and then a dapper-looking young fellow stepped into the well-landscaped area, and soon sat down, occupying a position upon an adjacent wooden park bench. The newcomer nervously smoked a cigar in anxious haste, and the fellow periodically glanced at the distant clock tower to confirm the time of night. The young man's quiet intent seemingly wanting to make the time-instrument's ancient hands revolve in a quicker manner. Meanwhile, the observant vagabond attempted to break the prevailing cold silence, and politely commence some casual human communication.

"I beg your pardon, Young Man," the unkempt-looking degenerate began his formal salutation. "But by your stressed demeanor, you appear to be suffering from some form of anxiety, which probably concerns either the subject of love or money, or perhaps both of those entities. According to human protocol and standard etiquette, allow me to introduce myself. My name is Prince Michael, Caliph of the Electorate Valleluna Caliphate, and I'm very happy to make your acquaintance. As you may have surmised," the audacious mendicant continued. "I'm the heir to the principality's throne; sort of what you sophisticated Westerners might call a Dauphin; not the tropical fish mind you, but the next in line to be king. It is my sincere habit to render worthy opinions and advice to anyone who arrives in my presence; a perceptive individual who might naturally value heeding my illustrious wisdom."

"I think you're rather full of shit; an authentic jackass at best!" the young fellow evaluated and verbally conveyed. "Looking at your tattered costume, you certainly are the 'Chic of Arabee', ha, ha, ha! Or, maybe you're the world-famous Sheik of Caliph-fornia! Ha, ha, ha; yes-siree! This is all-too-rich for my brain to comprehend and mentally digest, all at the same time. But I gotta' admit that I do find you to be an amusing diversion that temporarily distracts me from my myriad adversities. Glad to meet you, Prince, and good luck in pursuing and acquiring your anticipated family inheritance."

"Despite your weird sense of humor, I find you to be a decent young man underneath that external façade of coldness you feel compelled to exude," Prince Michael very courteously declared. "My marital and financial advice happens to be quite famous all over this metropolis, and I'll gladly lecture my vital rhetoric and my incomparable knowledge to you, if you so desire to listen to my extraordinarily-sagacious exhortations."

"Well, Prince Michael. I don't know if I'm just yet ready to share my problems with a perfect, or in your case, with an imperfect stranger," the somewhat-neurotic young stud stated in a more respectful and cordial tone of voice. "It's all sort of a private and personal matter involving both time and unusual circumstance, but thanks all the same for your genuine concern, and for your promise of effective crisis solving. To tell you the truth," the tuxedo-dressed good sport declared, "I'm basically and fundamentally fucked-up, and I ordinarily appreciate the efforts and intentions of other fucked-up people such as yourself, who profess a certain empathy for my melancholy state of mind."

"That clock in the ramshackle tower up there has obviously captured your' attention," perceptive Prince Michael articulated. "And it seems to be controlling your thoughts and actions from afar. Its face and hands have you completely mesmerized. I mean, Sir," the impoverished Caliph elaborated. “Time is ephemeral, and its mastery of you simply represents your abject slavery to its imperial commands. Don’t allow a mass of rusty brass and steel dictate your fate. Learn to gain command of your own destiny! Now please enlighten me, Young Man. Why the hell aren’t you carrying a wristwatch so that you wouldn’t have to rely on that ugly, decrepit tower clock up over there above the oak trees to tell you the time?”

“I know I’ll sound like a stupid, asshole, Kind Sir, but in my rush to trek over to this vicinity, I had forgotten to put my wristwatch on,” the handsome, clean-shaven gentleman confessed. “So, here I am, a dependent victim of time, with my eyes keenly studying *that* gargantuan, lustrous, circular yellow object as if my entire future hinged on the outcome of a lousy half-hour interval.”

“Now, Young Fellow, I happen to possess the propensity to recognize bullshit when I either hear or see it,” Prince Michael calmly maintained. “But please be brave enough to place credence in my ability to allay your overwhelming burdens along with your unbearable emotional troubles. I do possess *that* remarkable wherewithal to attack another person’s difficulty with a certain ferocity, ya’ know!” Prince Michael proudly boasted. “Now, I must admit that I’m a particularly good judge of character, and my gut instinct tells me that I like your personality, and am intrigued by your integrity, you handsome Young Fellow, you. So, are ya’ goin’ to fuckin’ tell me the essence of your dilemma, or must I torture you by setting you on fire, or fartin’ in your face to make you reveal the full source of your damned perplexity?”

The young man glanced in the direction of the huge clock, frowned, and then sobbed. Next, the gentleman’s wandering pale blue eyes fixed their focus upon a well-constructed four-story brick mansion located across the empty street. The home’s window shades were drawn, and the room lights dimly shone through them. Yet something inside that superb residence was mysteriously affecting the young man’s vulnerable conscience and psyche.

“Ten minutes to nine, and not even a silhouette to be seen through the drawn shades and sheer curtains,” the young fellow lamented to the self-proclaimed Caliph. “But I want you to know that I’m not a Peeping Tom, despite the fact that my name is Edward. Your hypothesis is correct about my personal quandary involving either the Queen of Hearts or the Queen of Diamonds, or perhaps a combination of both royalty ranks in the separate card suits,” Edward sadly admitted. “I’ll give vivacious Priscilla ten more minutes, and then I’ll slowly vacate the premises in defeat. And Dear Prince, I promise to join your courageous dumb-assed crusade against the futility and uselessness of clocks and time. Astronomy has discovered that the Earth is billions of years old, so what's the sense of me placing weight on anyone's eighty-or-so years roaming around, and going absolutely nowhere on this damned fucked-up planet's surface? Life has no special credibility, or particular rhyme or reason whatsoever!"

"Return your rectum to your park bench seat and don't despair," Prince Michael advised his listless, now-standing listener. "Women tend to be natural foes of clocks and time. For example," the fraudulent Caliph uttered. "It took my always-constipated ex-wife three-hours to take a shit, eliminate three hard pellets from her obese flabby ass, and finally vigorously wipe her crotch. Yes indeed," Prince Michael philosophized. "My research into the matter clearly confirms that clocks and time certainly limit *our* earthly pleasures, and egregiously accentuate our follies; intensify our failures, and magnify our human frailty. Now, please conveniently relate your gloomy story to me, so that I can properly counsel you with my abundant wisdom. Otherwise, your fucked-up state of mind will undoubtedly grow exponentially, and consequently, make you become even more fucked-up than either you or I currently are!"

"Your Royal Highness," the young fellow responsively laughed with reckless abandon. "I shall spill my heart to you, as if I were a devout altar boy. Over in yonder brick house lives my precious girlfriend of six months. Well, at six o'clock this evening," Edward attested, "I had stood in the foyer of that magnificent home across the street and had to deal with her emotional accusation that I was being unfaithful, and actively screwing several ugly whores over on Twenty-second Street," Ed sorrowfully related to Sir Michael. "Being in a state of complete shock, I guiltily acknowledged to Priscilla that I had been a truly naughty cad, and I next pledged that I would never again violate *our* sacred dual fidelity. During the culmination of our heated oral exchange, my gorgeous woman told me in no uncertain terms that I should have my flaccid dick stretched, and then go and fuck myself."

"Have you ever screwed this girl, Priscilla?" the knowledgeable Caliph incisively asked as if he were a distinguished city prosecutor confidently interrogating a suspect on the witness stand.

"No, but I've gotten my finger wet several times while exploring her love tunnel, and she had competently jerked me off on two memorable occasions," the young man recollected and informed. "But out of wholesome respect for my girl's chaste reputation and good standing in society, I swear to the Almighty that I've never once pumped her hairy pussy!"

"How did your intense argument with this Priscilla end?" Prince Michael asked. "Did she violently attack your personals with a kitchen cleaver as most extremely jealous, on-a-rampage broads would do under similar circumcisions, er, I meant to say under similar circumstances?"

"Priscilla indicated in the doorway that she will either fully forgive my immoral cheating on her, or she would never look upon my handsome face again," the distraught young man revealed in a sad and dismal low voice. "At eight-thirty tonight," Ed proceeded with his tale of woe, "my totally peeved girl firmly announced, 'I expect you to be outside in the park watching my lit bedroom's middle upper window on the fourth-floor. If a white silk scarf is hung out the window, then you will fathom and assume that your cheating has been forgiven. If you see no scarf dangling, then you can conclude that our fragile relationship has destructively smashed into the proverbial siren's rocks!' Now Caliph Michael, they're the exact angry words that my treasured Priscilla had vehemently used."

"So, that's why you've been so seriously studying that brick mansion across the street," the Dauphin-in-Waiting deducted and communicated. "Let me repeat to you, Young Fellow, that women, including this pristine Priscilla of yours, are the natural enemies of clocks and time. Keep the faith Eddie, my boy. Your essential ass, your swollen testicles, and your limp pecker are still attached to your torso, so you won't bleed to death in the meantime. The doll's silk scarf signal may yet appear in the fourth-story window. Miracles do happen, ya' know!"

"On the contrary, Prince Michael. Priscilla is always on time, and she's the one exception to your obstinate women and time generalization," the jilted lover candidly divulged. "In fact, it was *that* wonderful habit that had originally attracted her to me. I should've realized at eight thirty-one tonight that my goose was cooked after I had taken a lengthy fifteen-minute gander at her bedroom window. I'll meet-up with my loyal pal, Jack Miller, at a midtown bar later on at nine. Jack's hopping on a train and heading out West to Nevada to start a new life, and I'll be occupying the seat right next to him," disconsolate Edward glumly predicted. "If my dude ranch fantasy experiment goes bust, then as an alternate pursuit, I'll probably wind-up singing and playing a banjo at a near-bankrupt brothel/saloon in either the Klondike or the Yukon. I bid you a pleasant 'good night', eminent Prince Michael, and furthermore, I wish to sincerely thank you for your patience, and for your precious *time*."

Disconsolate Edward then again sadly stared at the huge clock's yellow face situated up inside the ancient tower. "Of course, Prince, your keen assessment is right on target in one respect. Women, as a whole, are a general nuisance; always late for dinner dates, and then predictably abandoning their goddamned meal to be powdering their noses and rubbing their horny twats in the restaurant's Ladies Room. Oh well, I'm familiar with woe, all too much. It's three minutes to nine and all is not well in my love life."

"Look here, Edward! If you ever decide to marry this prim and proper Priscilla girl," Prince Michael offered and consoled, "you can meet me in this park every night, weather permitting, and we could thoroughly rehash the friggin' matter. This bench is sort of my regular hangout, if ya' know what the hell I mean. If everything is copasetic between you and this Priscilla beauty, then I'll mercifully and instantly write you a bona fide check for one-million-dollars to safely launch your marriage in the right direction. That is, after I can reclaim my foreign kingdom."

"Thanks a million, Your Benign Highness. But I believe I won't need to purchase that exquisite mansion on the Hudson in the near future after all. To be perfectly 'frank', although my name is Edward, I'd stand a better chance of marrying *that* legendary Massachusetts' babe Priscilla Mullens, who as you know from American history, has been a deceased Pilgrimette for several centuries now."

At nine o'clock, the tower clock mechanism began its standard loud bonging. At that ominous juncture, Edward gradually arose from his hard wooden bench, took a deep sigh, and then exhaled most of the carbon dioxide from his vernal lungs. But then at the end of the depressed fellow's relinquished hope came a sudden exclamation of triumph and jubilation. From the middle fourth-floor opened window appeared a wonderful white silk scarf waving in the night wind.

"Well, Edward," Prince Michael authoritatively explained. "It's precisely twenty-nine-and-a-half-minutes past your false witching hour. That dysfunctional yellow-faced clock mechanism up there hasn't worked correctly in seven years, and now it's always uselessly thirty blasted minutes late."

"I almost blew the entire reconciliation with lovely Priscilla, because I had stupidly left my expensive wristwatch on the vanity counter in my apartment's bathroom," Edward nervously and joyfully disclosed. "Oh, what a relief this wonderful silk scarf signal is! It's even a better relief than taking a very healthy shit after a huge dinner! It's even a better relief than getting laid!"

"Yes, sir, Edward my boy! That clock's always been a half-hour fast ever since my daughter Priscilla was twelve-years-old, and *that* nostalgic event was seven damned years ago."

"Don't tell me that *you* live-in and own that imperial brick home across the street!" Edward gasped in amazement. "And truthfully now; you can't be this exotic and internationally renowned Prince Michael Caliph of Arabia person, can you?"

"I assure you, I'm not a Middle Eastern Caliph, but I *am* Justin Milburn the III, affluent industrialist and jovial Wall Street tycoon. I've just returned from a fruitful moose-hunting trip up in the Maine wilderness with some old Boston University fraternity drinking brothers. That's why I have all of this stubble on my face. And as far as my poor taste in clothes is concerned," the Wall Street prince further elaborated, "I quickly changed into this humble apparel after I had arrived in my downtown brownstone from New England. Incidentally, you might consider this quirky deportment of mine as being erratically fucked-up, but I oddly like to dress this way because it reminds me of how I used to look before I became a multimillionaire," the extremely wealthy Justin Milburn the III explained. "If someone came by the park, sat-down, and afforded me some human compassion, I would as a standard habit generously reward that gracious individual with my unconditional philanthropy; or maybe even give that person a job as a new lease on life. And so, as you can plainly determine, dear Edward, I used to sit in this park and dream of owning…."

"A spectacular mansion similar to the brick one across the street," Edward marveled and finished Sir Justin's declarative sentence. "Mr. Milburn, did you know that I would be arriving here in this park for the purpose of waiting for Priscilla to give me her fantastic signal of romantic compromise?"

"No, Edward, I didn't know that particular fact until you had disclosed it to me. *That* remarkable piece of mutual destiny was purely coincidental," the formerly incognito investment king cheerfully expressed. "But from the very start of our park bench relationship, your disposition and your attitude struck me as you being a fine young fellow. And in fact, your general demeanor immediately reminded me of how I had desperately struggled and sacrificed, in a financial sense, when I was around your age. I immediately identified with you and your plight."

“Then you might just turn-out to be my father-in-law!” Edward realized and shrieked. “How ironic and how terrific! There’s nothing deleterious about that! Nothing whatsoever!”

Justin Milburn the III was now quite jovial and supportive. “Yes, indeed Edward. And now let’s go inside my humble palace, so that I can write you and my daughter a solid check for one-million-dollars to get your love boat heading safely out of port,” the Wall Street tycoon cordially suggested.

“That would be just grand!” Edward acknowledged. “This phenomenal coincidence is much better than winning a major lottery! How lucky could a young jerk like me get? I feel like I’m sitting on top of the world!”

“But I must warn you! Beware Edward!” the prominent stocks and bonds’ investor/vaga*bond* cautioned. “Priscilla has some rather peculiar traits that tend to mimic those despicable behaviors exhibited by her reprehensible mother, who incidentally, also happens to be my estranged nasty-tempered wife, Ethel! I just hope for *your* sake that my lovely daughter doesn’t transform into the same kind of despicable bossy bitch that my sharp-tongued spouse regrettably was, and is!”

"The Green Door"

The vicinity around the intersection of Broadway and 42nd Street, which is also known to the world as Times Square, represents an area of intrigue and adventure, whether the walker is a fascinated visitor to the bustling metropolis, or a hard-core native casually strolling along the filthy-but-busy New York sidewalks.

Vaudeville review matinees; a chorus of honking horns; sleazy straight, gay and lesbian bars; legitimate stage plays, and a variety of circus and carnival-like sideshows all vigorously compete for the abundant foot traffic traversing the congested area.

A plethora of beautiful enticing women, many wearing lustrous diamonds and sable furs, march right alongside scantily-clad business-seeking hookers and on-the-prowl kinky prostitutes, both of the latter female segments perfectly willing to sell their curvaceous bodies for a "cheap trick". Fresh cash is readily obtained for the streetwalkers' vital services from straight men, from homosexual men, or from devil-may-care transvestite lesbians in need of cozy feminine companionship.

Yes, indeed, all sorts of imaginative scams and flimflams tempt the senses of the busy thoroughfare's daily trekkers; the dissatisfied pedestrian masses' both expecting, and relishing, having their attention lured, which in reality represents the mobile lady vultures' first step into accessing innocent victims' wallets or pocketbooks.

All along the notorious avenue, loud-voiced hawkers incessantly bally available customers and gullible sightseers into small side street businesses. And to make the chaotic environment even more confusing, direct face-to-face solicitations along the horrendously crowded major artery are quite commonplace. The police endeavor to control the bizarre flow of legal and illegal commerce, but many people who saunter along the famous street's pavements in quest of Holy Grails, Golden Fleeces, lady loves, hot disease-free sex, and free dildos are frequently disappointed at their lack of success.

Many itinerant trekkers manage to psychologically adjust to their failed "adventure mission", and ultimately return home to their nagging wives, and to their bratty and totally-spoiled kids, the disappointed seekers mentally accepting the delay of their next exciting downtown exploit.

Oftentimes, a subsequent excursion to Broadway follows another violent domestic argument (involving a wife or a husband), compelling him or her to leave the house in desperation, and methodically search for some empathetic personage of the opposite gender to share and to allay his or her heart-wrenching marital dissatisfaction.

In the center of Manhattan, the twin spirits of Adventure and Romance often compete to attract the good, the bad, and the ugly elements of human nature. A gallery of curious-minded predatory faces often peer-down out of upstairs windows, randomly scrutinizing the endless pedestrian traffic, with the gapers' perceptive pupils looking below for vulnerable, weak, innocent prey to either con or distract. Cabdrivers vociferously yell their redundant solicitations to ferret-out prospective clients amidst the stream of impersonal humanity that clutter the sidewalks of the Great White Way between Thirty-fourth and Forty-third streets.

As far as the eye can see, sophisticated ladies and scumbag harlots drop their dainty handkerchiefs, wherever and whenever the tacit solicitor sizes-up an assumed eligible gentleman or targeted "mark". Everyone inside Broadway's surreal-perpetual motion illusion seems to be aggressively evading one basic truism: that is to say, no one sauntering along majestic-but-gaudy Times Square wishes to be (on some future day) lying on his or her deathbed, singularly regretting that he or she had neglected or missed that elusive once-in-a-lifetime opportunity to pursue and experience an extraordinarily-enjoyable human activity. No one lying horizontal and about to receive his or her last rites ever wants to remember a pallid and mediocre marriage; or a bundle of wrinkled cash idly sitting in a bank safety deposit box, or recollect a piss-poor sex partner with sleep apnea as his or her eight-decade marriage's ultimate thrill and greatest accomplishment.

* * * * * * * * * * * * *

Rudolph Steinberg was a skilled piano tuner and salesman by trade, in addition to being an after-work wanderer, prowling along the downtown glitz and glitter of magical Broadway. The fickle-but-feckless fellow was always searching for some romantic adventure outside the perimeter of his miserable marriage, and the unhappy man was also in quest of certain adult excitement far away from his obnoxious teenage son and daughter. And besides those specific aspects to Rudolph's lackluster existence, the unfulfilled, roaming salesman was also an avid sex addict and porn' fanatic.

'I really need to get laid today,' Rudolph kept thinking as the depressed fellow quickened his stride along the popular noisy street venue. 'My wife and kids are visiting her folks out on Long Island, so this is the perfect opportunity for me to show some audacity and get my noodle wet. My damned frigid wife doesn't like having wild sex, and I think the witchy bitch actually hates her own cunt! But right now, I need not worry about time being a deciding factor, because I have all-night-long to literally screw around,' Steinberg concluded with a smile. 'I just got paid cash under the table by my tyrannical boss, so I have additional bucks to spend on personal luxury, if necessary. I'll have my pick of the crop in terms of happy hookers. As usual, I'll use my guile and my charm. I just have to be shrewd enough to select a Broadway broad that doesn't have a bad case of transmittable V.D.'

Rudolph Steinberg hurried along, weaving in and out of the two-direction streams of people hastening about, and all adding to the area's general hustle and bustle. A certain contingent of the New York humanity-in-motion consisted of captivated and enthralled foreign visitors to the legendary theatrical district. The second more familiar aggregate, which included the in-need-of-sex piano expert Rudolph Steinberg, represented the daily native Broadway participants, either parading home from their places of employment, or eagerly seeking a dynamic bar lounge, or the comfort of a friendly brothel waiting room.

'I've tried most of the standard whorehouses,' Rudolph decided. 'I know what I'll do. I'll look for a good-looking doll to pork; yes, a pretty honey standing in one of the many doorways. I'll know the right one the instant I see her. If the babe's asking fee is reasonable, I'll be able to do something constructive with my nagging hard-on. Getting my aching rocks off all by myself' is so friggin' juvenile, so goddamned adolescent!' the disgruntled piano tuner imagined, shaking his head as he paced ahead faster.

Further down Broadway, Rudolph continued his thought processes. 'I'm tired of being a stupid jerk-off every time my bitch of a wife is out of town visiting on Long Island! I've read in my favorite book *Junie's* Love *Test* exactly how to pick-up the right broad on Broadway. Say; that's gotta' be precisely how this fucked-up thoroughfare got its name! To my knowledge, piano tuning is definitely not the oldest profession in human history, ha, ha, ha! Even the goddamned prehistoric Neanderthals had whores and hookers! And I've got money to burn!' Rudolph confidently chuckled as the on-a-mission pedestrian swiftly passed by a prominent New York City fire department station.

That evening, during his later-than-usual urban safari, Rudolph's attention was distracted by a set of clattering false teeth hopping around inside a glass case, which a man with a cane and red and white striped-jacket was loudly describing as a "Living dental specimen from Somalia". Glancing upward while surveying his general environment, the enterprising piano tuner observed the electric letters of a colorful dentist's shingle, automatically indicating that the chattering and clattering uppers and lowers were creatively and appropriately advertising the tooth extractor's legitimate place of business.

Standing alongside the amusing jumping teeth phenomenon was a tall-but-muscular Afro-American, who was colorfully dressed in an embroidered red fox-hunting coat; imposing yellow trousers with black stripes down the sides, and the enormous fellow was also sporting a tilted red fez atop his shaved head. The formidable-looking black giant was assiduously distributing business cards to the passing public, and anyone the disseminator chose to tacitly solicit felt intimidated, being too afraid to decline reception of the small rectangular pieces of information.

"Are you a real Zulu?" Rudolph awkwardly asked the suddenly and slightly chagrined black Goliath. "Are you a real Zulu?" Steinberg admiringly reiterated.

"Did you call me a real Lu-Lu?" the gargantuan card disseminator asked with a disdainful frown evident on his visage. "Say it again, and I'll beat the living shit out of you!"

"No Sir; you are mistaken, er, I mean it was *my* mistake," Rudolph stammered and vaguely apologized. "I didn't say Lu-Lu! I had no intention of insulting your honorable character with any idiotic, derogatory remark. I was simply making an historical allusion, my Kind Sir. I had foolishly mentioned the word 'Zulu', which is a distinguished South African tribe consisting of many noble and courageous warriors. Many of those barbarians, er, I meant to say 'brave tribesmen', are rather humungous in size, and quite similar to the famous Watusi lion hunting natives."

"Sounds like a lot of fucked-up bullshit to me!" the black Hercules answered. "But your wild theory is right on-the-money about that African shit! My mother used to tell me that our family originated from Ethiopia. Here, Sir! Here's a card that you ought not to discard, ha, ha, ha! Have you ever been to Africa, my good man? If by chance you have traveled there, you were probably incontinent on the continent, ha, ha, ha!"

Rudolph Steinberg was so thrilled and relieved at not being pulverized by the enormous black ogre that the pedestrian didn't peruse the print on the card until he had nervously traversed half a block down the avenue. One side was blank, but on the opposite side was printed "The Green Door", without any address or other pertinent information provided.

And then, being rather vigilant and curious, the self-conscious piano tuner and salesman alertly observed a man toss to the pavement a similar card that the massive Ethiopian had deftly handed-out. Rudolph carefully stooped-down and examined the rejected card, which to his surprise did not read "The Green Door", but instead had printed on its surface the name and address of the aforementioned dentist, along with the traditional boilerplate caption: "Bridge Work, Crowns and Painless Oral Operations".

'This is some sort of oddball enigma!' Rudolph conjectured. 'The other guy received from the gigantic black fellow a dental card with specific information given on it, while I had been handed a card that only reads 'The Green Door'. Hey, I get it now!' Steinberg ecstatically hypothesized. 'I'll bet that The Green Door is a new house of prostitution that's just opened its door for business! Glory be to the Highest! It's all amazingly materializing right before my eyes! This could be the exotic sex adventure I've been waiting for! I could feel intense throbbing in my lower abdomen already!'

Being intrigued by the minor 'Calling Card' puzzle, Rudolph inconspicuously crossed Broadway, walked a block on the opposite side, re-crossed the noisy avenue, and again approached the immense but handsomely dressed Ethiopian. Without making eye contact, the piano tuner accepted a second introductory business card, which much to Rudolph's consternation, exclusively had inscribed on it the mysterious phrase that lacked vital context, definition, and description: "The Green Door".

Then, a peevish male pedestrian disgustedly tossed a business card to the pavement that had recently been obtained from the awesome-looking black fellow. Steinberg bent-down and automatically read the printed language, which clearly described the dentist's practice and the exact location of his professional parlor.

'How could this be?' Rudolph wondered as his hyperactive penis shriveled inside his trousers. 'I'm pretty damned befuddled by this more-than-small riddle. I'm not exactly fully certain that 'The Green Door' is a newly established cathouse! But damn it. I'm gonna' find-out soon! I've got millions and millions of sperm that I need to shoot out of my sex pistol, or should I say blast-out of my abdominal cannon! Yes, *that* second thought sounds much better!'

Rudolph neurotically made another U-turn across Broadway, paced a block south, then re-crossed the street and again approached the hulking Negro standing next to the square glass case containing the clattering false teeth. This time the black behemoth failed to hand the befuddled piano tuner a business card, but instead randomly and courteously did so to other less interested but cooperative passersby. Gazing back at the towering Ethiopian, Steinberg received the distinct impression that the menacing-looking black gent had been deliberately ignoring him.

'I now get the apparent connection!' Rudolph perceptively realized while looking-up to the blinking electric dentist's shingle that was tacked above an entryway leading to a steep flight of steps. 'The Green Door paradise I'm dreaming about must be somewhere inside the same building as the anonymous dentist's office. No address appears on the brothel's Green Door card, because it's obviously an illicitly operating house of ill-repute. What a moronic asshole I was for not being able to decipher the essential basics to this ridiculously simple, uncomplicated mystery!'

Changing his attention from his visual recognition of the rather ordinary 'on-the-blink' electric dentist shingle, Rudolph's eyes then looked to his left, and his pupils promptly perceived the presence of a thin attractive brunette elevated in high heels, and wearing a short and provocative black dress. The alluring female was casually puffing on a cigarette and impatiently standing with her ankles crossed in the doorway.

'The building's five stories high,' Steinberg astutely counted and comprehended. 'I'll closely follow that tough-looking hooker all the way up to the fifth-floor, if I have to! I hope I can still get and maintain an erection after having to expend so much energy climbing-up to the top floor! Hope there's still enough oxygen to breath up that high! Apparently, the lady's ardently waiting to receive her next horny customer, who incidentally and wonderfully, just happens to be me!'

A moment later, after making serious eye contact with Rudolph Steinberg, the voluptuous woman slowly turned and ascended the wooden steps. The aspiring client, in need of much-anticipated sexual relief, ambled up the wooden stairs behind her.

The building's second-floor, consisting of millinery retail shops and mink-coat furriers, and the rooms had been closed-off to the public after business hours by sturdy, latticed metal gates. The structure's third-floor featured a wide assortment of still-open barbershops, hairdressers, musicians' offices, and doctors' practices, and then the more-seedy fourth-floor rooms hosted quack fortunetellers, tealeaf interpreters, palm reading rip-off artists, and several non-certified, demented, wacky amateur gynecologists and illegal abortionists.

'Oh, yes,' Rudolph alertly surmised and determined. 'The higher I go in this un-inspiring and archaic edifice, the more-cheesy the caliber of the offices become. No doubt the fifth and final floor will offer me a most excellent green door brothel, and then my brief introduction will be followed by a marvelous lewd interlude with that radiant auburn-haired hussy I had seen standing in the doorway, that's situated right next to the all-too-reputable ground-floor haberdashery emporium that my fucked-up piano company boss Mr. Snodgrass frequents quite regularly. At least, that's what the hell he tells me! But I'll bet Snodgrass uses that excuse as a deception to climb these same steps up to the sensational fifth-floor!'

Two pale overhead jets (located on opposite sides of the dingy narrow vista) eerily lit the deserted fifth-floor hallway. Directly to the interloper's right was the object that the impetuous visitor had been seeking. 'Ah, there it is; the infamous green portal! My curiosity's killing me! I just gotta' discover what's behind the Green Door! I'll nonchalantly rap three times, and within an hour, I'll accomplish tonight's destiny!' Rudolph fantasized. 'I'm sure there won't be any rowdy gamblers playing poker; any rogues surreptitiously plotting crimes, or any bloodthirsty mobsters hanging out inside. This remote haven has got to be a glorious house of sin and pleasure, and nothing more!'

A faint rustle was heard originating inside, and then the brown-haired chickadee opened the Green Door's latch. The doll wrapped her arms around her guest, closed the door, and immediately dragged Rudolph over to a ratty-looking, faded, cloth couch. The non-hesitant young woman began relentlessly kissing her new-found man on his neck and face, and next began rubbing his thighs, and then adroitly gently stroking his soon erect sex instrument. 'This is an absolute dream come true!' Rudolph considered during the height of his ecstatic reverie. 'This horny nymph must be a devoted daughter of Aphrodite! And last but not least, this lusty beauty hasn't even mentioned her fee for performing such tremendous erotic service! Holy shit! I'm about to cream my pants!'

Just prior to Rudolph reaching his first climax, the apartment's portal entrance flung open, and a colossal-sized figure rushed inside, and savagely slammed the door shut behind him. The new arrival unceremoniously lifted Rudolph up off the tawdry sofa, flung the disoriented chap against the gray plastered wall, and immediately snatched the victim's wallet from his back pants pocket.

"What the hell's going on here?" the surprised dupe yelled. "I'm an honest guy engaged in an honest transaction! I always pay my debts, and I'm gonna' pay for this current piece of ass! Say, who the hell are you?"

"I'm Rocco," the big-fisted brute insolently identified himself. "This is my sweetheart, Sally. Not only am I the doll's jealous boyfriend, but I'm also her protective pimp, so ya' better mind your fuckin' mouth, otherwise I'll bust your jaw into at least ten different fragments! Got the picture, Asshole!"

"Look, Rocco. I'm willing to pay for Sally's special talents if ya' just hand me back my goddamned wallet," the roughed-up piano tuner futilely pleaded. "Whatever happened to the history of fair commerce being practiced here on Broadway?"

"Look, Chump," Sally interrupted the melodramatic discourse between Rocco and Rudolph. "I'm having my monthly period, so I can't have sex with anybody right now. It's against my personal ethics! And Rocco and I are starving for a bite to eat, and we gotta' get some dough right-away in order to survive; that is, until my hungry pussy gets back to normal and becomes active again. And besides that, our fuckin' rent is overdue!"

"So, you devious Weasel; you perverted Deviate. This ain't no run-of-the-mill hooker's trick being done and paid for on your part; it's a goddamned robbery in progress!" Rocco effectively clarified. "Now, Punk. I'm gonna' pilfer all of the greenbacks out of your fancy wallet, because Sally and me are sailin' in dire straits and need some instant cash flow to complete the friggin' voyage. And if ya' dare run to the cops and squeal," the intimidating bully vehemently threatened, "then my big brother Bruno will find your lily-white ass and quickly turn it into pig's fodder! Ya' fuckin' understand your dangerous predicament?"

"This mark probably has an ugly Puritanical wife and a couple of raunchy ingrate kids," Sally accurately guessed and communicated to Rocco. "That's why this never-satisfied jerk-off needs a legitimate job to support that horrible mess the jerk has at home! But other than that, this mark is harmless. Go easy on the dumb shit-head, Rocco, once you've grabbed all his dough!"

Rocco rapidly removed the sum of two-hundred-and-ten-dollars from the unfortunate victim's wallet; handed the empty leather object back to its rightful owner; hoisted Rudolph up off the grimy rose-floral carpet, and then viciously punched the idyllic fool twice in the stomach for good measure. Sally skillfully opened the apartment door, and then Rocco fiercely hurled Rudolph Steinberg into the dank and dirty corridor; the airborne fellow eventually colliding with the solid brick hallway wall.

Staggering around the dark and narrow fifth floor corridor, Rudolph noticed that each and every apartment possessed an identical green entry door, similar to the one leading to Rocco and Sally's 'temporary residence'. Steinberg considered that his mandible must have been fractured, as the punches recipient slowly descended the rickety five flights of stairs. At last, the dazed and injured thrill-seeker stumbled-out onto the cement sidewalk. Above the glittering lights of Broadway, a dusky wan sky had majestically domed the area, making its spectacular, eye-appealing appearance during the city adventurer's half-hour painful absence.

'That's the last time I'm ever going anywhere near *that* nondescript, shabby, fifth-floor apartment,' the recently violated attack victim concluded. 'And up until today, I had always falsely thought that a jawbreaker was a goddamned hard round piece of candy! Say,' the piano tuner observed. 'There's that monstrous African freak-of-nature; still out there on the pavement devilishly dispensing those evil business cards!'

Instinctively, the extremely perplexed assault-and-robbery dupe valiantly confronted the fantastic Ethiopian card distributor. Holding the two distinct business cards in front of *him,* Rudolph shouted like an asylum patient, "What the hell's this shit all about? How come there's no damned information on *this* card in my right hand? Where the hell is this sinister non-existent Green Door, anyway?" the crazed molested dupe screamed in rapid succession.

"Pardon me, Sir," the imposing African suavely replied. "But The Green Door is the name of the new play that's having its debut over at the Hippodrome Theatre tomorrow night. Look over your shoulder to your right, and you'll see the handyman putting-up the new title on the marquee. I think the printer down the street was in such a hurry that the guy forgot to put the most vital information on the newly-mass-produced business cards," the dignified, well-dressed African explained. "The show's agent is a friend of mine, and the promoter asked me if I'd be kind enough to distribute his announcement cards, along with the dentist's promotions that I had been already handing-out."

“What a crock of smelly shit!” hollered back the thoroughly-upset and battered piano salesman. “I should hire you to kick the crap out of a big wise-ass palooka named Rocco.”

“Nobody around here messes with Rocco; that fighter is a former Los Angeles heavyweight boxing champion! Say Man, you’re bleeding pretty profusely from your gums and mouth,” the colossal-sized Afro-American noticed and disclosed. “If your jaw’s not broken, then certainly your front teeth have been rearranged by either a smashing left hook, or a crushing right cross. If I were you, Mister, I would immediately go up to the dentist’s office on the second-floor; and by coincidence, his office also has a green door; just like every other friggin’ room in that there goddamned, soon-to-be-condemned building that you just exited!”

"The Whirligig of Life"

Distinguished Tennessee Justice of the Peace Elijah Windhole lazily sat outside his office door puffing-away on his corncob pipe, and dreaming about all of the big-breasted naked women that the judge had gotten drunk and screwed during his wild and crazy youth. The county official turned his head and peered at the hazy Cumberland Mountains off in the distance, and the center two purple-hued peaks reminded the short, fat, wig-headed justice of his unforgettable teen sweetheart, Daisy Marie Jackson's enticing bosom. 'Too bad Daisy Marie drowned in bed when the creek overflowed during that last hurricane!' the magistrate sadly recalled. Just then the shrieking of a speckled hen crossing the dirt lane sabotaged and disturbed old Elijah's deep mental concentration.

Down the adjacent hill leading into the sleepy village came the creaky axles of a pre-Industrial Revolution donkey-cart, carrying Ephraim Bilbro and his beautiful well-built blonde-haired wife, Petula Mae. A dense cloud a dust swirled and eddied around the primitive mode of transportation as the obsolete hillbilly vehicle neared its stopping destination. After the in-need-of-repair cart halted its forward progress, the vehicle's two apparently truculent occupants hurriedly clambered-down the opposite sides.

'What's this unexpected bullshit all about?' Justice Windhole cogitated in strenuous objection at having his peaceful sexual fantasy reverie interrupted. 'I might as well look presentable to these two imbeciles solicitin' my legal jurisprudence,' the Justice of the Peace realized as Elijah awkwardly stood-up, put on his fluffy bed-slippers, and then tucked his cumbersome gray calico shirt end back inside his pants' zipper. 'I can never live far enough away from the fucked-up demands and nuances of mountain-life civilization. Why must every Tom, Dick, and Suzie's country bumpkin problem suddenly become my fuckin' problem?'

"We both wants a permanent divorce," Petula Mae adamantly and angrily announced. "Ephraim and I have both decided to call it quits after six terrible months of marital wranglin'. Our relationship has hit the skids, and there's no magic formula that can solve our present lack of harmony. I'm sorry I ever let Ephraim fondle my personals before we was hitched," Petula Mae lamented. "And I lost my childhood innocence to this hormone-driven, horny man, yes, I did. All Ephraim ever wants to do is get laid all day long while neglectin' the farm, the bills, and the animals. The chickens no longer lay any eggs; and the cows have stopped producin' milk; and the pigs have all died from starvation, malnutrition, and somethin' called skinny hog disease. And all that this lazy jasper Ephraim wants to do about all those serious problems is to pump my pussy some more," the exploited and exasperated wife grieved. "What a shit-fartin' bummer it is being married to this total loser; to this ridiculously retarded inbred Appalachian ape!"

"Well, now," the chauvinistic Justice Elijah Windhole passively replied after wrinkling and wiggling his wide-nostril, piggish nose. "I'm not so sure that being lazy constitutes sufficient litigious grounds for divorce, or even *grounds* for flat-tastin' coffee, for that matter. It's my legal opinion," the clever fellow judiciously pontificated, "that most ordinary women like to have men desirin' their bodies all day long. Answer me, Woman: are you some kind of frigid lesbian bitch, Petula Mae?"

"No, Your Honor. I am *not* frigid! And I ain't no damned promiscuous female Eskimo, either! I'm just an ordinary woman who desires to be treated like an ordinary wife."

"Petula Mae," Judge Windhole diplomatically and suavely retorted. "I used to think that you were a terrific sexy wildcat the way my juvenile delinquent nephews, Chad and Jeremy, who incidentally were also your former boyfriends before Ephraim entered your lackluster life, used to describe your amorous ways and methods in the tall haystack behind their daddy's dilapidated red barn. I mean Pretty Lady," the country judge expounded, "Ephraim here has no need to have any owls patrolling his stable loft with that magnificent set of hooters you're sportin' on your bosom; no siree! What I really mean to say, Petula Mae, is that you need to present specific complaints as evidence to establish marital incompatibility, which is law nomenclature that's better known to the public as 'irreconcilable differences,' which is the required legal basis for a divorce to be officially granted," the magistrate informed the aggrieved wife.

"I don't follow you, Justice Windhole," Petula Mae confessed. "I only graduated from second-grade."

"Now, Petula Mae. I've learned all of this technical academic terminology shit by reading the daily newspaper gossip columns and by listening to idle male chatter down at the Cattree Hollow Barbershop and Body Piercing Salon. Some legal terminology I also get from studyin' the pages of sophisticated and licentious porno' magazines. And I'm not bein' facetious or mistaken either, when I say these redundant esoteric things."

"Thanks for the backhanded compliment, Judge Windhole," Petula Mae respectfully answered. "But Ephraim's been recently hangin' around irresponsible scalawags and moonshiners, and learnin' how to manufacture illegal alcohol on his own. My husband's even feedin' his liquid concoctions to his hound dogs, making them bark all night long, and pissing yellow and green liquid waste all day long from their aching kidneys. It's a wonder those ornery dogs still have bladders and testicles! And besides those aggravating grievances, I've already cited Judge Windhole," Petula Mae indignantly continued her memorized rant, "Ephraim here disguises himself as an eligible, on-the-prowl, virgin bachelor every Sadie Hawkins Day."

"It sounds like your husband has overactive testicles, and that you can't keep him satisfied, Petula Mae," Justice Windhole interrupted.

"Well, Your Honor. Ephraim always manages to get at least three young, kinky, slutty teenagers to have their love tunnels pumped for his gratification all day long. The only advantage to my husband's participation in the Sadie Hawkins Day festivities is that I get to rest my sore, over-penetrated, pink vagina for twenty-four hours!" the spouse grieved. "But that measly one-day interval is really not enough time for me to fully recuperate and fully heal my sexual precious personal equipment."

"And what's your principal beef with Petula Mae?" the Judge inquisitively asked lethargic Ephraim Bilbro. "Your peeved wife's acrimonious protests about your numerous familial derelictions make me feel that I'm more of a Justice of the Piece of Ass than I am a bona fide and duly-elected Justice of the Peace. Let's now hear your distorted version of things."

"Well, Your Honor. Petula Mae keeps throwin' metal kitchen skillets and sharp butcher knives in the direction of my delicate forehead for no apparent reason, and the wildcat bitch continually denies me of my legal sexual pleasures after midnight chimes on our dysfunctional table clock, which chimes twelve times every goddamned hour," Ephraim recollected and testified. "I feel mighty abused, and I fear that someday in the near future, I'll lose my sexual potency. That development would surely crush my ego, now won't it Judge?"

"Judge, why don't you swear Ephraim in with his right hand on the Bible?" Petula Mae vehemently demanded. "Then, you'd surely have a big oaf under oath!"

"I'll be the county's arbitrator and chief administrator here, if you don't mind," Judge Elijah Windhole reprimanded and yelled, momentarily abandoning his regular cool disposition. "Now what else is botherin' you Ephraim concerning your wife, besides her chronic colitis that's been rumored all over the village? Let's hear the remainder of your complaints against your woman."

"Well, Judge. Petula Mae just about burns my victuals at every meal, and only just yesterday, I scalded my tongue, and as a result, I couldn't munch on any juicy pussy last night," Ephraim sulked and protested. "And every time Petula Mae spies and catches me screwin' some local whore out near the pigpen, the ornery witch rudely interrupts my pleasure by banging me over the head with her heavy iron fryin' pan. I got more goddamned knots on my head than I have on the shoelaces of my huntin' boots," the husband regretted and shared. "And just last night my ungrateful wife had the unmitigated audacity to lock me in the lonely outhouse, when I was takin' a royal dump on the wooden throne. I insist, Judge, that there's only so much unbearable marital bullshit a mountain fella' can endure! Whatever happened to the idea of the man bein' the king of his castle? Don't ya' agree?"

"Well then," Judge Windhole decisively said and momentarily paused. "You've both adequately established having legitimate grounds for divorce, even though the Tennessee Hillbilly Laws and Statutes leave the entire matter up to the local magistrate's omnipotent discretion. Now, according to the equity arrangements alluded to in the United States Constitution," the flamboyant hick Solon elucidated, "if a Justice of the Peace has the authority to marry a couple, he or she also has the power to legally separate their asses once and for all. I got volumes of proof of such duties, bein' conferred upon me by at least five-thousand rulings and decisions, all provided by the U.S. Supreme Court in a place somewhere above Virginia called Washington DC., which of course is approximately near the other side of the known world. Incidentally Ephraim," the County Justice lectured and appended. "The court cost for my rendering and dispensing my all-essential services in this commonplace matter is a mere ten-dollars. That standard fee's quite reasonable for the year 1904, I must say. But if you give me any quarrelsome annoying feedback, I'll supplement the nominal charge to twenty non-counterfeit, non-Confederate bucks."

Ephraim Bilbro nervously removed a thick brown chaw of tobacco from his front flannel shirt pocket, and instinctively popped the huge wad into the center of his cavernous, toothless mouth. Then, from his baggy pants' pocket, the chagrined husband's right hand retrieved a crinkled-up ten-dollar bill, which the distraught spouse reluctantly handed to the martinet magistrate. "That's all the damned money I got to my name. Petula Mae has spent all the rest on fancy petticoats, dildos, tight-fittin' brassieres, more dildos, girdles, corsets, suppositories, and an assortment of chastity belts."

Justice Elijah Windhole, who apparently had an aversion for any indolent person standing before him and simply farting around, quickly stuffed the ten-dollar bill into his vest pocket. Next, old Elijah authored the appropriate language that legitimized the divorce on official-looking state government foolscap, and after writing the words, read the "language of personal freedom" that had been applied in cursive upon the county document.

> Know all men in the State of Tennessee without any witness or witnesses present that the marriage vows and responsibilities that have, heretofore, existed between Ephraim and Petula Mae Bilbro are hereby legally dissolved. No longer will Ephraim and Petula Mae love, honor, and obey each other, for better or for worse, in riches or in poverty, until death, do they part, which the pair never intended to do in the first place. All of these valid and pertinent understandings have been decided in my presence, on this Fifth Day of August', 1904 in the County of Piedmont, State of Tennessee, USA.
>
> The Honorable Elijah Ezekiel Windhole, IV
> Justice of the Peace

Judge Windhole was in complete control of his courtroom's environment. The county official was comfortably sitting in his black leather swivel chair, all poised to turn the finished sealed document over to Ephraim Bilbro to apply his birth certificate name in writing, when mercurial Petula Mae had a sudden brainstorm, and audaciously interrupted the signature process before it could either commence or terminate.

"Judge Elijah, Sir," the all-too-volatile woman anxiously prefaced. "The main reason I've filed for this here necessary divorce is because I do believe that the sweet moonshine, which by the way smells like stinkin' cat piss on a boxwood hedge, is actually some sort of chemical aphrodisiac that beclouds Ephraim's vulnerable brain. The concoction makes him radically change into some sort of addicted male nymphomaniac, possessin' an excessively lustful sexual appetite that's makin' my love tunnel into Luray Caverns."

"Are you telling me, Young Lady, that you want to reconsider your initiation of this here divorce proceeding?" the wily mountain judge perfunctorily asked. "That kind of odd request would represent an inordinate deviation from normal courtroom protocol, yes, it would. Petula Mae, I detect an element of doubt and hesitancy in your nervous tone of voice."

"Well, Your Honor. This divorce matter t'aint settled no-how until I decide to sign the official paper you're holdin', and I presently have my reservations about doin' so, even though I don't own any goddamned Indian land anywhere," Petula Mae impressively stated. "Now according to the Declaration of Constitution signed in Philadelphia, I think I got my historical references right, I gotta' have my rights and privileges, that's what I maintain. Yes Judge, I gotta' have my ali-money, er, I guess ya' pronounce the cotton-pickin' word in polite society 'alimony'. I need some greenbacks to give to my kin, Jed, up on Hogback Mountain, for my first week's keep, until I find another area mountain man that'll earn a good living and get some decent greenbacks for me to spend."

"Alimony is usually a relevant factor if biological offspring, or even foster children, are involved, which they ain't in your particular situation," the letter-of-the-law Justice of the Peace determined and instructed. "However, under the existing circumstances, in that you Petula Mae have no recognizable workplace skills like runnin' a livery stable, bein' a blacksmith, or a carpenter, or workin' as an apprentice strumpet in the Best Little Whorehouse in Tennessee over there in Piney Meadows, I reckon that Ephraim here has gotta' give you some additional compensation to tide ya' over until ya' can locate another stupid man, and practice doin' your parasitic thing. It seems to me that *that* course of action would be the most meritorious route for us to pursue."

"Holy pond scum!" Ephraim boisterously balked. "Petula Mae never once hinted of receivin' any damned alimony. All she ever talked about was slicin' my hyperactive testicles off with one of them French guillotine devices, invented over there somewhere in Europe. And Your Honor; I definitely think that payin' a reasonable alimony would be the lesser of the two evils. I need my balls like you need your wallet, and your wig deodorant."

"You're absolutely right, Ephraim," Judge Windhole automatically agreed. "Cruel and unusual punishment is strictly prohibited by the Constitution, even though castration by guillotine is not specifically stipulated as a prime example of that sort of malicious torture." The Justice of the Peace's pupils then studied Petula Mae's grimy bare feet, and his mind assessed that the path going-up legendary Hogback Mountain was both steep and rocky. That germane evaluation weighed heavily upon the magistrate's ultimate judicial decision. "Petula Mae, how much does a decent pair of woman's flat shoes cost down at Griffin's General Store?"

"About the same as these here divorce proceedings; about ten-dollars, I reckon," the pretty blonde replied. "Yes, ten-dollars should do the trick, and I'm not talkin' about committin' prostitution over in Piney Meadows, either."

"Ephraim Bilbro, this infallible court hereby orders you to pay the plaintiff ten additional dollars of compensation to fully consummate and validate the execution of your mutually agreed-upon divorce," Justice Windhole declared. "Now, I command you to give your former woman the sum of ten-dollars for a pair of heavy-duty walkin' shoes, or else I'll have to terminate these here divorce papers, while scrupulously keeping my standard bargain-priced ten-dollar court fee."

"Judge, I don't have another ten-dollars," the crestfallen tenant farmer somberly and soberly confessed. "Perhaps I shoulda' thought about all the possible consequences, before I drove Petula Mae down-here to the village in the family donkey-cart."

"You dumb shit local yokel; ya' always gotta' think of the possible ramifications and of the impending repercussions of your domestic actions before ya' ever attempt doin' something drastic like filing for a divorce," Justice Windhole boisterously criticized. "Well then, Ephraim. I'll give you until noontime tomorrow to raise the prescribed cash amount; otherwise, you'll be held in contempt of this here court and forced to do a week's hard labor in my tall grass yard; in my snake-infested flower beds, and laborin' tillin' the soil in my very weedy garden," the Judge threatened the defendant.

"But Judge. I don't even do those basic things on my own mortgaged land," Ephraim protested.

"And personally, you silly-assed Clodhopper. I don't care if ya' get the referred-to money by hook or by crook. Just get the goddamned extra cash here on my clerk's desk, which is also *my* desk by tomorrow, so that I can efficiently dispose of this boring asshole marital case. Now Ephraim; *that* sage decree of mine about the added ten-dollar payment must be adhered to or obeyed, or else I'll hand-over the model castratin' guillotine tucked-away and gathering dust in my back cloakroom to pretty little Petula Mae."

Five minutes later, the disappointed couple climbed-aboard the junk heap of a donkey-cart, and then Ephraim characteristically applied the whip to the generally uncooperative Moses, his bony-ribbed, partially blind, stubborn mule. The reticent pair was soon heading out to Cousin Obadiah's (who was an inbred six-toed cousin by incest to both the estranged husband and the dissatisfied wife) ramshackle shack up on Cloudy Moon Mountain, to pout and spend the night in separate rooms.

Four hours had elapsed since the peculiar divorce initiation interview, and the craven Justice Windhole, always afraid of nightfall and roaming nocturnal ghosts, hastened to the outskirts of the sleepy country hamlet, where the wary judge lived alone in a log cabin surrounded by birch and poplar trees, situated right next to a malodorous, stagnant swamp.

Just as the fearful magistrate stepped through the familiar laurel side thicket (at the latter part of dusk), a dark masked figure intercepted the law-abiding fellow's forward progress. The imposing thug grunted, and then threateningly pointed a sawed-off shotgun in the alarmed judge's pallid face.

"Hand over at least ten-bucks, or else I'll be inclined to blow your dandruff-laden scalp right off your wig-covered noggin," the roadside villain imperatively directed. "I'm getting mighty fidgety, and my trigger finger's twitchin' something fierce. And Mr., besides *that* rather important, lousy horseshit, I got a peculiar nervous condition that the doctor calls Parkinson's disease."

'I only have ten-dollars on me, but it really belongs to the county treasury," the by-the-book judge stammered and stuttered in his tan fluffy slippers.

"Roll the son-of-a-bitch up, and stuff the legal tender in the end of this here gun barrel," the culprit demanded. "Do it quick before the muzzle accidentally discharges, because of my advanced nervous condition! To tell ya' the fair-to-Midland truth, I ain't shot nobody since late yesterday mornin'."

"Yes, sir, yes sir!" Judge Windhole quite neurotically answered. "I wanna' live to see the sun rise in the sky tomorrow at dawn. I beg you; please don't pull the trigger!"

* * * * * * * * * * * * *

At noon the following morning, Moses (the overly-exploited and abused mule) pulled the about-to-disintegrate donkey-cart into the tiny village settlement, and abruptly stopped in front of Justice Windhole's law office. The Judge eagerly accepted the ten-dollars from Ephraim Bilbro, and upon inspection, noticed that the bill had been curled-up as if it had been placed inside the muzzle of a sawed-off shotgun. 'Ah, I see that this here legal tender's serial number is exactly the same as the Alexander Hamilton I had received from that petty small-minded thief, Ephraim Jethro Judd Bilbro yesterday,' the robbery victim thought as the victim transferred the sum to Petula Mae's grateful hand. Both the plaintiff and the defendant were then given duplicate copies of the divorce document.

"I reckon you'll be moseying back to the cabin with old Moses," the former wife said to Ephraim. "I left some stale bread in the tin container settin' on the counter. And you'll find two strips of bacon in the ice box. And Ephraim, don't forget to wind the clock before you hit the hay, even though the confounded thing hasn't had the correct time for over five months now."

"You ain't a-goin' over to that pervert Jed's place?" the destitute hillbilly farmer worriedly asked. "Your retarded brother's been in a nasty frame of mind as of late, ever since his hemorrhoids and his diarrhea have been actin' up. Old reliable Doc Parsons says your kin's hemorrhoids are really pilin' up inside Jed's rectum. And that Jed had wrecked-'um by doin' too much rubbin' after taking his usual mornin',' afternoon and evening hourly craps."

"I plan to visit Jed just before dark, and I hope the lunatic's deaf mute wife Jessie is home, so that I don't have to worry about that crazy bastard wantin' to rape me," Petula Mae said, revealing her innermost fear. "And so, Ephraim, I reckon it's time for me to say 'goodbye'. That is, unless you're so bent-out-of-shape that ya' wanta' speed-away in your primitive donkey-cart without even extendin' to me the courtesy of a civilized separation. How about puckerin' up one last time?"

Petula Mae rolled-up the already abused ten-dollar bill and placed it next to her alluring bosom, when the country beauty's magnificent firm right breast delightfully popped-out of her weatherworn bra, making Justice Windhole wish that he once again was a horny, willing and able whippersnapping young stud.

Ephraim also observed the textbook-smart Justice showing carnal avarice, as old Windhole stood there admiring Petula Mae's most splendid exposed tit, and instantaneously, the former husband became a tad jealous and possessive of his former spouse's pulchritude himself. "It'll be kind of lonesome lying-in bed all by myself tonight," Ephraim apologetically admitted as the distraught former husband turned and stared-out the judge's office window at the majestic Cumberland Mountains. "But when a wife gets mad and files for divorce, there ain't much that a guilty-feelin' fella' can do or say about it."

"Nobody wanted nobody to stay in that fire-hazard shack that's been condemned by the sheriff seven times in just the last year," the former wife obtusely replied. "I guess it's now the right time for me to do the striptease Dance of the Seven Petticoats for Jed, so that my kin can get all hot and bothered before his occasional girlfriend, Lucy Ann, comes in from tillin' the corn field."

"Only *you* know how to wind the damned table clock, even though the chimes strike twelve every goddamned hour," the husband stated in a sad, low voice. "Ever since the freakin' winder fell off, only you Petula Mae knows how to get that stubborn metal sucker goin' proper again!"

"Want me to come along and show ya' how to do it," the former wife volunteered. "That fucked-up clock has a mind of its own, and needs constant tender loving care."

"Sure thing," Ephraim agreed as the downtrodden fellow reflexively reached-out his right hand to escort the inimitable Petula Mae back to the familiar, squeaky-wheeled donkey-cart. "Them dozen ferocious mongrel bloodhounds of mine will be glad to see ya' again. They'll be so goddamned thrilled they'll be barkin' until their fuckin' fangs fall-out. If we set out now, we should make it to the homestead by sundown. That is, if the old shanty is still standin', or hasn't burned-down to the ground in the meantime."

Then suddenly the Honorable Justice of the Peace Elijah Windhole made a surprise proclamation:

> "In the name of the revered State of Tennessee, County of Piedmont, I hereby forbid both of you two incorrigible nitwits to be indiscriminately defying the established laws and statues that I have especially interpreted for your mutual benefit, and which I wholeheartedly intend to uphold and enforce. Now, in conclusion, it gives my heart great sentiment and joy to witness the dark clouds of discord drifting-away, and allowing the sunshine of pure love to finally filter through again," the garrulous old coot metaphorically and loudly uttered. "But it is the solemn duty of this court to objectively preserve the trust and dignity of the State. As the court's primary representative and interpreter, I must, therefore, remind you two fickle and irresponsible, inane assholes that you two cabbage-heads have been legally divorced, and are no longer

entitled to participate in the sacred privileges and pleasures commonly associated with the matrimonial estate."

"What the fuck does all that complex wordy bullshit speech mean?" Ephraim incredulously asked. "Sometimes I believe that the more educated a man gets, the less he knows how to communicate right. That's what the fuck I think!"

"It means that the two of you are no longer married, so ya' both have to go your different ways, with no more sex, either oral or normal," the judge tersely explained. "Sleepin' together is no longer sanctioned by the all-wise State of Tennessee, or by the erudite County of Piedmont."

"What a crock of stinkin' cow piss!" Petula Mae criticized and frowned. "And you, Judge Windhole, oughta' gulp-down the whole friggin' pail of cow piss, lick your lousy lips, and then politely ask for a goddamned refill!"

The local Justice judicially re-evaluated his most recent decision, and then discreetly spoke his mind. "The court had been erroneous by making a premature judgment, and therefore, by the powers invested, er, I mean to say *vested* in me, I do declare your divorce to be null and void; and therefore, your sacred marriage to be duly reinstated and consequently, the two of you blundering lovebirds may resume your marital functions, with the full blessing of this sagacious judge and his fair-minded court."

Petula Mae reached inside her bosom for the rolled-up ten-dollar bill, and this time her left breast popped-out of her loose-fitting weatherworn bra, again catching the attention of the area's most competent tit and nipple expert, Judge Windhole. The magistrate accepted the itinerant ten-dollars with a smile, as Elijah enjoyed experiencing his first full erection in over a decade.

Five minutes later, un-emancipated Ephraim Bilbro was merrily escorting his knockout blonde wife to the primitive donkey-cart, and soon old Moses was leading the reunited couple back to the Promised Land, up on the fabled "Mountain of Love".

Ancient Justice of the Peace Elijah Windhole once again sat-down and occupied the frayed wicker chair in front of his law office; unlaced and took-off his scuffed-up black shoes; put his tan fluffy slippers on his callused and bunioned feet; lit his trusty corncob pipe, and again watched the squealing, speckled hen swagger-down the settlement's main (and only) dirt lane.

“The Furnished Room”

In the early 1900s, the red brick house section (next to the scurrilous Red-Light district) on Manhattan’s lower West Side swarmed with myriad itinerants and transients. Ragtime was the popular music of that bawdy and risque era, with women of all nationalities often chanting and singing the familiar song lyrics, especially during their monthly periods. Many cheap apartment houses characterized the crowded neighborhoods, some of the tenements featuring upper-level single rooms designed to lure aspiring and ambitious job-seeking occupants.

A diverse population of stage entertainers, Vaudeville singers, comedians, clowns, actors, and commonplace assholes, along with multiple homosexual and lesbian musicians and artists (left over from the Gay Nineties) struggled for financial survival in countless apartment house residences from Soho (South of Houston Street) to Greenwich Village. At the turn of the twentieth-century, the general New York economic climate that existed for hungry-to-succeed thespians, lesbians, and lesbian/thespians was indeed, on the rather cruel and hostile side.

Each of the standard boarding houses held dozens of strange secrets, and the various owners had countless tales and stories to tell about former weirdo oddball renters. One particular ironic episode has a zestful, young, idealistic man prowling-about the overcrowded Soho district, searching for a temporary place to dwell. The on-a-mission fellow rang the doorbell at the twelfth residence that his apartment quest had approached, dusted-off his light brown fedora, and impatiently waited for the lax landlady to answer his bell ring. The callow fellow learned from the housekeeper that there was only one remaining single room “to let” on the apartment house’s third and uppermost floor, and that the young inquirer could indeed become the suitable lodger to fill the vacancy.

“If ya’ care to inspect the furnished room, I’ll show it to ya’,” Mrs. Edith Purnell told Francis Perkins. “The place has been vacant for a full week now, should ya’ wish to look at it. The dump’s just an ordinary-looking domicile; nothing at all special about it. Single boarding-house rooms are a lot like women’s pussy; ya’ see one, you’ve basically seen ‘em all!”

“It probably beats the park bench I’ve been sleeping-on the past three nights since arriving in town by train,” Francis all-too-honestly replied. “I’m conserving all my money. until I find a dependable job as a department store manager; just like the one that I had maintained for three months at the Ridley Five and Ten store back in Des Moines, Iowa. I've decided to take a chance at the big city, where most of the high potential opportunities seem to exist nowadays. New York's the right place to be, so I hear."

"Well, the first week's down payment is ten-bucks. And the bathroom, co-ed of course, is down the hall from the furnished room. And since you seem like a decent and mannerly young fella', Mr. Perkins," Mrs. Purnell added and smiled with four prominent teeth missing from the front of her mouth, "I won't ask ya' for any fancy references. I'll even cook ya' breakfast each morning, and at nights, massage your back for ya' too, at no extra maintenance cost! Even ugly, old bitches like myself get a little horny and aroused once in a while, ya' know!"

"If I may briefly examine the room, I would certainly appreciate it," Francis humbly requested. "As long as it has a window with a view of some greenery, a functioning bureau, and a comfortable bed and mattress, I'm sure that the chamber will be adequate to meet my simple needs. But I can't stand places with stale air that smells like a funeral parlor. I suppose I have a phobia for guest rooms containing stagnant and tainted oxygen."

"The third-floor furnished room you're gonna' see has all of that crap you mentioned and much more, and by the way, Young Fella', ya' can keep and eat all of the decayin' mice and insects ya' can find in the dresser drawers and in the wall corners," Mrs. Purnell jested and cackled. "Your temporary quarters can be your contemporary headquarters, ha, ha, ha!"

After climbing several steep flights of squeaky wooden steps, the pair finally came to the all-important furnished room. To keep cordial conversation flowing, Mrs. Edith Purnell described to Francis Perkins the names and professions of several former occupants. "Some very elegant and famous stage people have lived up here, yes they have," the garrulous landlady exaggerated. "Sparrows and Mooney, a famous Vaudeville act stayed up here for three months without ever venturin' outside, and Duncan and Schultz, a notorious magic act duo, well, those tenants stayed up here too, but then disappeared into oblivion after two weeks without payin' the goddamned rent. My guests never stay, too long, because they're mostly theatre folks always on the go, and soon off to a new destination," the landlady elaborated. "Some of them were quite interestin', but I found most of 'em to be unreliable, and basically full of shit!"

"The room is all right. It meets my modest purposes, although confidentially, it looks like it should be either bombed or dynamited. It's definitely a disgusting pigsty that's somewhere between rancid and putrid on the stench scale. But against my better judgment, I'll lease this pathetic disaster for a week," Mr. Francis Perkins declared with a small forced grin showing upon his countenance. "Here's ten-dollars to cover the initial week's payment. I'd like the option to stay a second week, if that's okay with you? I'm quite depressed. In fact, I think I'm suicidal, and I've noticed that this gloomy room's atmosphere directly corresponds to my despondent attitude!"

"For all I care, you can stay until the goddamned day I die, and attend my funeral, and you're welcomed to pay for the whole damned rip-off thing, too," Mrs. Purnell morosely laughed. "And the neighborhood undertaker has already agreed to put me on his morbid layaway plan, ha, ha, ha! Life in this city is so damned miserable! And ya' wanna' know something? I just can't wait to have my decrepit veins injected with formaldehyde, ha, ha, ha! But tell me Young Man, why are you so depressed? Maybe you might consider takin' some opium to raise your spirits?"

"Several months ago, my girlfriend, or should I say my ex-fiancee, Elaine Vashner wanted me to join her and leave Des Moines, and venture here to Manhattan to begin our scheduled married life together," Francis informed his short, chubby inquisitive, landlady. "Well, I didn't wish to leave my steady employment at the five and dime store, so out of sheer spite, Elaine traveled against my wishes to New York with intentions of landing a role in a Broadway play. My girlfriend was a very good lead actor in her high school play. Was she being stubborn and stupid, or what?"

"It would be easier for her to land a burnin' asteroid on top of the Statue of Liberty's torch," Mrs. Purnell interrupted and loudly coughed. "Your hard-headed woman sounds like she's a science fiction space cadet!"

"You know how small-town Iowa girls are," Francis Perkins continued his tale of woe, ignoring the landlady's outlandish remarks. "Elaine had the leading role in her senior high school production, and naturally, believed that she had more talent than she actually possessed. Now, she's a tiny fish in an enormous pond, and is bound to get chewed-up and devoured unless I luckily find her, miraculously make her sane again, and then gallantly conduct her back to the Midwest where the hell she rightfully belongs. Have you come across anyone in your travels by the name Elaine Vashner?"

"What does your old flame look like?" Mrs. Purnell curiously asked. "I'll bet she's really pretty, with a nice tight ass, and a firm set of well-developed, very mature knockers!"

"Elaine's a fairly attractive damsel of medium height and slender build; around the average 34-28-34 I'd say. Her hair," Perkins added, pausing to rely on memory while mentally reflecting on nostalgia for a moment. "As I was saying, her hair is reddish-gold, and oh yes. Innocent Elaine has a black mole on her forehead just above her left eyebrow."

"Sounds like any of five thousand desperate hookers paradin' around Sixth Avenue as we speak," the sarcastic landlady pessimistically commented. "I swear to you Mr. Perkins, these rambunctious stage performers change their names more often than they change their sweaty underwear. I hope your frustrated woman friend hasn't turned to prostitution to pay her rent and food expenses after sadly experiencin' rejection after friggin' rejection in her play auditions. If your obstinate lady companion's wise and lucky, she's already entered a convent to study religion and salvation."

"Seriously M'am, I've inquired about her at every nickelodeon movie hall; at every chorus line rehearsal, and at every food kitchen in this part of the city, and yet I've obtained no vital information on the whereabouts of my beloved sweetheart," Francis sighed, feebly staring Mrs. Purnell directly in the eyes. "It's as if she's been mysteriously swallowed-up by some alien-but-powerful quicksand, and has entirely disappeared from the face of the Earth. If the blasted planet was so hungry, I wish it would gobble me up too, so that I could finally be reunited with my divine love."

"Don't be such a goddamned sentimental slob!" Mrs. Purnell loudly chided. "Learn and master the art of self-preservation. In a worst-case scenario, you're liable to commit suicide, and then your fickle girl will eventually meet and marry somebody else. That's just how bitterly fucked-up life in this insane city is, and most certainly always will be! A cold heart is about all that really thrives and survives here," the landlady emphasized. "In my accursed lifetime, I've seen too many spirits of naïve dimwits dampened, and too many pure and chaste spirits brutally crushed to convince me that fairy tale endings don't exist, at least not in this city. As I've already told ya', learn to be a selfish scumbag, and I guarantee that you won't drown in the very deep and treacherous New York City slime. Those fucked-up Grimm Brothers never knew how grim life really is!"

"Maybe someday, I'll finally shed my foolish nature and follow your sage advice," the young apartment renter replied. "Mrs. Purnell, you have no idea how much I'm right-this-minute yearning for my wonderful girl's love and affection."

"How about if we go down to the corner ice cream parlor after supper, and I'll treat you to a delicious banana split?" the flirtatious fat, ugly landlady suggested. "Yes, I'll generously treat you to a banana split, and when we come back to this deplorable dump, I'll pour some scrumptious hot fudge on your nuts, and you could then squirt some delectable whipped cream onto my cherry? What do ya' think Handsome? Overnight you could be the local rage; the exotic and erotic boss with the hot sauce!"

"No thanks," Francis politely answered. "Right now, I've only got the hots for Elaine Vashner from Des Moines, Iowa. But I could apply down at the ice cream parlor for a job as a soda jerk. After all Mrs. Purnell; I'm a dumb-ass sort of jerk already, aren't I!"

After the blunt landlady left Francis Perkins's melancholy company, and feebly descended the rickety stairs while holding on to the wobbly banister, the new third-floor tenant's eyes sadly surveyed his immediate environment. The ancient couch's brocade upholstery was ripped and ragged; the flimsy, small table looked termite-infested; the two accompanying wooden chairs appeared ready to collapse; the flea-laden bed's brass headboard was dull and cruddy; and finally, the begrimed icebox looked like it had been invented prior to the Revolutionary War.

'This dreary top-floor furnished room is so horribly confusing that it should've been mentioned in the Biblical city of Babel, a chapter and verse in the Book of Genesis, if my disintegrating brain still serves me correctly,' the sorrowed, callow man concluded. 'The threadbare rug underneath my shoes is far from rugged. The loomed weave is about as damned thick as a sheet of stationery writing paper. Surely, grotesque-looking squalor like this would be dynamited in Des Moines, or even obliterated in those enormous baneful hellhole ghettos known as Cleveland and Detroit. This apartment gives me the absolute creeps,' the peeved and dejected visitor from the Midwest determined. 'Hell-itself has nothing over this infernal room; that's for damned sure! I'd better open the window for some fresh air, before I fuckin' either choke or rot to death! This despicable room oughta' be first condemned by the Almighty, and then be condemned by the damned New York City building inspectors!'

Francis slowly walked-around the furnished room, and keenly observed every nook and cranny. The name "Marie" had been etched (probably by a miniature diamond) in the pier glass mirror separating the two small side windows. A great chunk of granite was conspicuously missing from the fireplace mantel, and several metal springs protruded from a corner lounge chair. The planked-floor was slightly warped, and the purple curtains ominously draping the rear window had seen better days.

'The most gorgeous call girl in the world would have trouble turning tricks inside *this* lowlife catastrophe,' Francis decided, shaking his head in utter disenchantment. 'Mary Magdalene, Delilah, and even that evil Jezebel never laid eyes on anything quite as atrocious as this so-called furnished room.'

Then, the young man's keen olfactory senses suspected that his nostrils had detected a familiar fragrance; a certain cheap French perfume that had been popular among the more frivolous ladies back in Des Moines. The rich odor made Francis simultaneously aware that it was the exact same aroma worn by his cherished Elaine Vashner, and traces of it emanated from various items of furniture inside the repulsive room. Perkins momentarily smiled, and imagined that Elaine was caressing his cheeks, and romantically running her lithe fingers through his curly locks.

'She's been in this room; my angel Elaine has been here!' Francis impulsively theorized. 'This particular perfume was only a big sensation in the Midwest, but not here in the East! What a fantastic revelation! Glory day! I believe I'm finally on the right trail! Heaven help me, Lord!'

The young man frantically rummaged through the inferior bureau and corresponding dresser drawers like an incensed maniac on the rampage. His crazed and hectic efforts resulted in finding four hairpins, a commonplace green scarf, and a used pink handkerchief, all objects that could indeed belong to any and all itinerant females. His further wild-ransacking diabolically yielded only the following cursory items: a three-year-old theatre advertisement program; a wrinkled pawnbroker's card; a decayed half-eaten marshmallow; two white blouse buttons; an informative, illustrated overdue library book on masturbation, and lastly, four sperm-less mothballs.

And then, the obsessed young fellow fanatically skimmed the room's corners where the thin walls met, and his anxious eyes uncovered not a trace of the relevant evidence the searcher so avariciously desired to discover.

'This lunatic behavior of mine is absolute insanity. I'm turning into a goddamned psycho case. I gotta' ask Mrs. Purnell where Bellevue Hospital is located, before I do something drastic, and either harm myself or someone else,' Francis irrationally supposed. Perkins's extended intensive investigation yielded only a half of a rotted bottle cork, and two tiny cigarette butts that had been wedged between the Lilliputian-sized cracks. 'Fuck! I must've been hallucinating all along! This nightmarish furnished room must be haunted! I mustn't let my imagination run amok! I'm so torqued-up right now that I think I gotta' take a wicked dump! Oh God! Here comes the diarrhea entering my colon! Oh shit! I'm loudly farting in rapid succession! I have no intestinal control! My vibrating asshole can't contain the fuckin' urge any longer!'

* * * * * * * * * * * * * *

The following morning, Francis exited the apartment house's rear porch and encountered the obnoxious chatterbox, Mrs. Edith Purnell, in the backyard where the landlady was diligently hanging her recently-washed bed sheets on a clothesline. Perkins very deftly and intrepidly initiated the conversation.

"Will you kindly tell me the names of the last several women to occupy the furnished room where I'm presently residing? I just got to know who the hell the girls were!"

"Yes Sir. There was Mary Wagner from Spokane, Washington; Tanya Glickman from Boston, and before her were the unforgettable duos of Sparrows and Mooney and Duncan and Schultz. Now Mr. Perkins, I do have twenty-twenty vision, but I can't say the same for my lousy hearing, or for my friggin' faulty memory."

"Well, Mrs. Purnell, for instance, what kind of a lady was Mary Wagner?" Francis persisted, his mind still in a quandary. "I mean, lots of aspiring women who come to New York use artificial names to remain anonymous."

"Mary Wagner was a virtual prima donna; a weird kind of crazy opera star diva that really and truly thought she was Jenny Lind reincarnated," Mrs. Purnell carefully described and enunciated. "And that irritatin' Tanya Glickman nutcase," the landlady continued her unorthodox narrative. "She was a neurotic, high wire tightrope walker employed with the traveling circus. The hot-tempered harlot deluded herself into thinking that she was a high-priced courtesan, but in truth, I gotta' give the old dame some credit; the demented high and mighty bitch still has the courtesy to send me a circus *cable wire* from time to time, ha, ha, ha!"

"Anyone else been in the third-floor furnished room recently?" Francis despairingly and desperately wanted to know. "My guilty conscience and my mental stability can't cope unless I soon find-out. You just gotta' help me!"

"No Sir, but a certain Emma Crowder practiced African voodoo up there in that modestly furnished third floor room five years ago. And then there was Lady Myrtle Doyle, a secretive charlatan tarot card reader. She ran-off to Chicago with the main bellboy over at the new ritzy Plaza Hotel across from Central Park. Basically, Mr. Perkins," Mrs. Purnell loquaciously editorialized, "everyone that ever lived in that moldy third floor fungus-laden, mildew-infested, apartment of yours has been totally fucked-up in one dumb way or another. And if ya' wanta' know my unbiased opinion," the talkative landlady added, "you're probably no damned exception, either!"

"My mind's a little disheveled," Francis acknowledged. "I think my cerebrum's suffering from neuron overload. I need to find some solitude, and sort-out all of the sordid details. I honestly feel like vomiting my cowardly guts out!"

Perkins returned to his dark and moribund living quarters, believing that he had been suffering from a rare combination of claustrophobia and agoraphobia. His accumulated hope was rapidly ebbing, and psychologically, the emotionally-defeated young gentleman's already faltering confidence was gradually waning.

'I'm getting the fuck out of here first thing tomorrow morning, and taking the morning express train back to Des Moines,' Perkins solemnly pledged to himself. 'I fear that Elaine has lost faith, and has deserted me, permanently. It's only a selfish theory, but this is what I now think. My girl has completely abandoned my precious love to sinfully cavort-around with some totally irresponsible big city gigolo!'

* * * * * * * * * * * * *

The next night, Mrs. Edith Purnell and her landlady neighbor, Mrs. Shannon O'Grady, shared some suds and libations in the former (as opposed to latter) woman's drab-looking kitchen. The subject of their dialogue was the transient nature of their tenants.

"It's time to get ripped," Mrs. Purnell proclaimed. "Yes, let's each chug-down our pints of beer, and then I'll get-out my bottle of rye. We might as well get drunk Mrs. O'Grady, because that seems to be one of the few coping mechanisms that we presently got at our disposal to deal with life's travails and worries."

"Right you are, Edith," Mrs. O'Grady amenably concurred. "Let's get so plastered that we'll fall to the floor, and eat the goddamned linoleum. Tell me, I understand you've again rented your third-floor furnished room. Your tenant is a handsome young man, I see."

"Oh yes, but he's just notified me he'll be leaving town quite soon to return to a hick place called Iowa," Mrs. Purnell confided as she imbibed a healthy snort of tasty whiskey, straight from the brown bottle. "The infatuated fool came to New York searchin' for his runaway girlfriend."

"What a pity! What a pity!" Mrs. Shannon O'Grady remarked. "I trust you never told him about the pretty colleen that breathed-in the toxic gas from the jets and committed suicide, did ya? What a waste of humanity, I tell ya'. If I remember right, the pretty girl's name was Elaine, and she had a large mole on…"

"Yes, a very huge black mole above her left eyebrow," Mrs. Purnell confirmed. "The girl had notions of bein' a dramatic stage actress. Another New York career snuffed-out because of constant rejection and failure."

"And Edith, you never divulged to the young man what had happened in your third-floor furnished room prior to his leasin' it?" Mrs. O'Grady pried. "I mean, you could've at least given him the address of the undertaker, who would've then directed him to her potter's gravesite!"

"Young Mr. Perkins would've never rented the bad-luck room if I had been honest and leveled with him," Mrs. Purnell assessed and opined. "Business is business, that's what the hell I've always believed. That strong concept had been instilled in me since childhood. Now Mrs. O'Grady," Edith Purnell articulated. "Take another lengthy swig of this here potent rye liquor, before it evaporates into thin air just like Mr. Francis Perkins will soon be vanishin' from our midst and headin' back to Iowa!"

"After Twenty Years"

The serious-minded policeman on his nightly beat moved along New York's Sixth Avenue, and his routine gait was seemingly maintaining a steady cadence. But pedestrian spectators were few and far between on that rainy November, 1913 Saturday night. The time was nearing ten o'clock, and most of the street's businesses had closed. Chilly gusts of wind had indeed dampened people's spirits, thus effectively depopulating the city's avenues and streets.

The guardian-of-the-peace occasionally stopped and checked to see if certain doors had been securely locked, those portals belonging to restaurant owners and retail merchants that the cop had known ever since the sergeant had been a fledgling Manhattan foot patrolman. The ordinarily busy thoroughfare on that lackluster damp and dreary evening seemed quiet and tranquil. All appeared copasetic in that central section of the big metropolis, because of the lack of regular human activity. Even those hard-nosed, stealthy individuals that were criminal-minded had apparently voluntarily taken the night off.

'Even the cigar stores and the pool halls have shut their doors,' the policeman acknowledged, as the steady rain continued to pour-down in sheets. Midway up the next block, the alert keeper-of-the-peace slowed his pace, when his keen eyes spotted a stouthearted fellow standing still as a statue under an awning, and the stranger was leaning against a wide doorway. The well-dressed fellow was in the act of placing an unlit cigar in his mouth, as the conscientious man-in-blue casually confronted him.

"Don't worry Officer! Everything's okay," the middle-aged gentleman addressed the fairly-concerned law enforcer. "I'm just waiting around to honor a special appointment a friend and I had made twenty years ago. I'll bet that all of this bluster must sound a little damned funny to you. Well," the gentleman proceeded with his intriguing narrative. "If ya' got the time, I'll explain it all in detail to you, just so ya' realize everything's straight and not goin' to hell in a handbasket. Two decades ago, there used to be a good decent restaurant right at this exact location where this hardware store is now. The place had really terrific Italian pasta. Yeah, I've always loved swallowin' down spaghetti and meatballs, and Big Joe Bradley's had the best damned Italian food in town."

"It was torn-down about five years ago, and then replaced by the hardware store," the accommodating policeman politely informed the stranger. “You’re right when you say Big Joe Bradley’s was a popular eatery, especially on a Saturday night! Most everyone around this neighborhood frequented it!”

The man standing under the awning then struck a match to light his expensive cigar. The instant flash had momentarily illuminated the existence of an exquisite pinky ring, featuring a two-carat diamond, and the temporary exposure revealed that the man’s square face had a short white scar right next to his left eyebrow.

“Tell me more about your scheduled rendezvous,” the inquisitive policeman implored. “It all sounds very interestin’ on a cold bitter November evening. The two-decade separation aspect you had mentioned is pretty nifty to think about, I gotta’ confess!”

“Twenty years ago on this exact date,” the short, stubby, handsome gentleman continued his unique story. “I had dined here at Big Joe Bradley’s enjoyin’ a delicious ravioli and meatball dinner with my old pal, Jimmy Watson. Watson and me were like two peas in a pod, yes, we were. My soft-spoken chum was the finest friend I could’ve possibly ever wanted. And we would do anything for one another if one of us was in a bind. At the time, back in 1893, I was twenty-two, and Jimmy was nineteen with hardly any serious whiskers growin’ on his face. Everyone we knew said that we were like blood brothers, always hangin’ around together, and pickin’ up the horny hookers that used to patrol this avenue, and then we’d be takin’ them over to the George Washington Hotel for some patriotic sex. But as I said, Officer,” the man summarized, “things were plenty different twenty years ago than they are today!”

“Well then, how come you and your friend got separated for two long decades?” the policeman asked, realizing that a nebulous void in logic evidently existed in the man’s exposition.

“You see, the next morning after the Big Joe Bradley meal, I was slated to board a train and go-out West to seek and make my fortune, which incidentally I had succeeded at doin’. And coming into town at the new Grand Central Station at 42nd and Park Avenue was a fantastic experience!” the returning visitor enthusiastically remarked. “Man, has the old city changed a lot during my twenty-year absence! And I gotta’ admit, Grand Central’s ornate architecture is a real work of art! Wouldn’t you agree?”

The rain began pelting with more intensity against the men’s faces, as the pair huddled closer to continue their casual conversation. “Before we get totally drenched and start growing fish gills, tell me more about your long-lost pal?” the policeman asked. “What sort of guy was he?”

"Jimmy was the absolute best," the man being casually interrogated remembered and claimed. "But ya' couldn't have dragged young Jim out of New York with a steam locomotive. Watson loved this place as if it was his own mother. To him, this city, especially Manhattan, was the only damned suitable place on the entire Earth. Well anyway, Officer," the garrulous stranger proceeded with his recollections before taking two deep puffs on his Havana cigar and then flicking the ashes onto the wet pavement. "We both had agreed on that particular November night way back in 1893, yes, we agreed that exactly twenty years later, and yes, no matter what had happened to us in our lives; that is, depending on us both still bein' alive, that we would meet and merrily review our mutual pasts. Distance would not be a factor, especially for Jimmy. We both figured that twenty-years would be enough damned time for each of us to pursue our individual destinies, whatever they would evolve into being!"

"Quite fascinating!" evaluated the captivated patrolman. "Haven't you heard from your old buddy since 1893? That really seems like an exceptionally long time to me!"

"Well, Officer. We had corresponded by mail for the first couple of years, but then over time, we lost track of each other," the well-dressed man explained. "You see, the West was a pretty damned big place, and I kept hustling around from Denver, to Seattle, and then on to San Francisco, and finally winding-up settling-down in Chicago. But I know Jimmy's a man of his word, and if he's still breathin', I have faith that he'll keep his promise for us to temporarily get back together. I've traveled over a thousand miles of railroad tracks to come back to New York, and be here tonight. So, I'm sure old Jimmy will find a way to walk his five blocks from wherever he lives now. But I assure you, all of my effort will be well-worth the time, if my old beer-guzzling dating partner and pool playin' buddy remembers to show-up."

The waiting man impatiently pulled out his hand-watch that was magnificently studded with sparkling diamonds, which reflected artificial light originating from an overhead electric sign. "It's now five minutes to ten," the city visitor announced, glancing down at his treasured timepiece. "It was exactly ten o'clock when Jimmy and I parted company. Watson was such a great guy, and if he presently needs any financial assistance, I'll be more than glad to help him out of his money crisis!"

"Done pretty well out West, huh?" the patrolman verbally guessed. "Please excuse me for prying!"

"You betcha'!" the apparently wealthy fellow bragged. "I had to deal with some of the keenest competition to be able to amass and then intelligently invest my large fortune. Now, I'm into gold and silver mines, real estate, chain stores, stocks and bonds, importin' and exportin', well just about into every damned thing that's associated with good old American capitalism! I only hope that Jimmy has done half as well as I have. But my pal was kind of a plodder," the New York City visitor recollected and shared. "However, he had a generous heart, and was always loyal, true-blue to the bone. I know that if he can still walk, and if his damned stubborn brain is still workin', he'll definitely be here."

The policeman twirled his nightstick like it was a drum major's baton, and slowly stepped-back several feet from under the protective awning. "I'll be on my way, Sir. Nice talking with you. Hope your pal Jimmy comes around soon! It's a perfect night to catch pneumonia, if that's your objective! Will you cut him ten minutes slack should he be a bit tardy in honoring his commitment?"

"I'll give him at least a half an hour leeway," the traveler from Chicago promised. "Yes, at least a half an hour!" the train traveler reiterated. "If Jimmy's not lyin' unconscious or completely out of commission in some friggin' hospital bed, or not buried six-feet-under and pushin' up goddamned daisies in some unkempt cemetery, I'm pretty sure that he'll soon be here at this special location! So long, Officer!"

"Good night, Sir!" the amiable patrolman replied before rattling several locked doors. "Every man should be lucky enough to have a dedicated pal like you!"

* * * * * * * * * * * * *

The falling drizzle and the continuous wind gusts remained a constant annoyance. The handful of brave urban souls walking the street all had their coat collars turned high, and their umbrellas held low. And despite the hostile, inclement elements, the man who had journeyed a thousand miles to re-unite with an old chum puffed-away on his Cuban cigar, and waited while exhibiting the patience of the Biblical Job.

After a grueling twenty-minutes had elapsed, a tall fellow wearing a heavy trench coat (with the collar turned-up to his ears) hustled across the desolate street, and then scampered through several rain puddles, splashing his way to the vicinity to where the visitor from Illinois was hibernating.

“Is that you standing there under the awning?” the new arrival yelled. “Is that you Bob?”

“Well, I’ll be damned and pregnant!” the stocky man from the Windy City joyfully greeted. “Is that you Jimmy Watson? Glory be, to the Father! I remember when we were wild, pugnacious sons-of-bitches looking for either a feud or a frolic; whatever the hell the event or excitement first would come our way!”

“Well, bless my grateful heart!” the newcomer boisterously expressed. “Sorry, I’m twenty-minutes late, but what’s twenty-minutes compared to twenty-years! I can’t believe it’s really you in the flesh Bobby Burns, sure as life! I was certain I’d discover you here, if you were still roamin’ the planet! Well, well, well; twenty-years have evaporated into history since our last meeting and dinner at the restaurant. I’ll swear to you, Bobby. I wish the old bistro’ was still churning-out big-portion lasagna and rigatoni dishes. Even Big Joe’s gone; the owner died of a heart attack three years back. Now tell me Bobby, how’s the West been treatin’ ya’! You look none-the-worse for all your wild adventures you had experienced on the other side of the Mississippi.”

“Bully, Jimmy. The West has wonderfully provided me with my own exclusive Gold Rush,” Robert Edward Burns gushed as the wealthy investor tossed his cigar onto the sidewalk and energetically crushed it to shreds by rotating the heel of his shoe. “But I gotta’ tell ya’ that you’ve changed lots since we last talked in 1893! I’m willin’ to wager that you’re at least three goddamned inches taller than when we last shook hands.”

“Oh, I was a late bloomer and grew a bit higher after I turned nineteen,” the other man laughed. “And speaking of bloomers, just think of all those *bloomers* we had tugged-down from the hips of those kinky hookers over at the George Washington Hotel! We must’ve screwed every damned whore from Times Square right through freakin’ Wall Street, all the way down to the Bowery.”

“Those were the good old days just before the Gay Nineties set-in, and being a homo’ faggot became both the rage and the vogue,” Bob Burns noted and concurred. “We were young, naïve, and reckless, yet we had great fun without ever havin’ more than a fuckin’ dollar in our pockets, after those hairy-cunt harlots got done with us! Doing well and earnin’ a nice living here in New York, Jimmy?”

“Moderately well, Bob,” the acquaintance answered, shrugging his shoulders. “I’m married with three kids to support, and work for one of the city’s bureaucratic departments. Come on Bob, we’ll stroll around the corner. I know a quiet bar that's still open where we can exchange new anecdotes and then reminisce old ones."

The duo started their hasty trek around the corner with Bob gripping his companion's trench coat at the elbow. Robert Burns began describing in detail all of his lucrative investments; his personal property deeds; and his corporate bonds and stock certificate holdings, while his reticent colleague listened intently as the New Yorker attempted to keep stride.

"Then, I bought two haberdashery stores just off Michigan Avenue, and parlayed the profits into steel mills, and also into these new noisy horseless-carriage machines that the inventive newspaper reporters across the country call automobiles. Say Jimmy," the egotistical wealthy investment mogul said. "I'm a little saturated and a bit fucked-up from talkin' my larynx out, so I need a breather. Let's stop for a minute at that lit-up drug store up-ahead so that I can catch my breath!"

Underneath the pharmacy's green-and-white-striped awning, the glare from the overhead sign immediately brightened the men's faces. Bob Burns believed that he had noticed something suspicious.

"Say, you're not Jimmy Watson," Burns loudly yelled, quickly releasing his grip on the other man's trench coat. "Twenty-years may be one-fifth of a century, but it's not long enough of a time to fuckin' change a man's nose from a Roman snout to a goddamned pug. What the fuck's goin' on here?"

"My nostrils are the least thing you oughta' be worried about," the man in the heavy trench-coat communicated. "You're right about transformation, Bob! Time can often change a good fellow into a dangerous criminal. The jig is up! I must inform you, slippery 'Silky Bob', that you've been under constant surveillance for the past three days, and you've been under arrest for the past fifteen-minutes. The authorities out in Chicago contacted us about the prospect of you headin' East, and possibly conveniently droppin' into Grand Central for a brief stay here in New York. And to add to your vexations, the Illinois State Police also want to interrogate you about certain gangster and mob affiliations!"

"Holy shit!" Bob Burns exclaimed. "If you aren't Jimmy Watson, you must be a goddamned city detective! I've been had by a no-good, low-salaried, goddamned gumshoe, who thinks he's a sleuth! Just my fuckin' bad luck! I was lookin' for a guy named Watson, and wound-up being nabbed by a middle-class jerk-off who thinks he's Sherlock Holmes! I gotta' get to a telephone and contact my lawyers!"

"You'll have plenty of time to accomplish that dumb-ass chore," the plainclothes detective assured his man-in-custody. "Now before we proceed to the precinct station, it gives me great pleasure to hand you this autographed note from one of the force's more dedicated personnel, Patrolman Watson.

Robert Edward Burns was at that moment mentally disoriented and emotionally nonplussed. The visitor from Chicago angrily opened the folded memo', and softly mumbled and cursed under his breath, subconsciously multitasking as the captive read and comprehended the full significance of the brief paragraph.

Bobby Burns,

I was at the designated place in front of the hardware store right on time at 10 p.m. Punctuality has always been one of my finer traits. When you struck the match and lit your cigar, I realized that yours was the face of an on-the-lam, pernicious culprit whose sketched drawing and description were being advertised on the precinct's bulletin board. The captioned words depicted you as a desperate-type syndicate villain, wanted in Chicago. Somehow, I didn't have the heart to arrest you myself, so I hustled over to headquarters and got a plainclothes detective friend to put the cuffs on you. Sorry about that, old friend Bob Burns!

Loyalty to duty,
Jimmy Watson

"The Gift of the Magi"

A measly one dollar and eighty-seven cents had been scattered all over the small living room coffee table; a paltry pittance even in this inventive age-of-machinery, Year 1910. That was all the saved money that Jim and Della counted, and sixty cents of that minuscule sum was in copper pennies. And the accumulated chump-change had been obtained from Jim, who had been arguing monetary trivialities with the neighborhood grocer, with the corner vegetable huckster, and with the parsimonious German butcher who often threatened his more belligerent customers with razor-sharp cleavers raised and held high above his bald head.

Sadness prevailed in the couple's hearts. One dollar and eighty-seven-cents wasn't enough money to buy a soap pack for two, or even a carton of sanitary napkins, and the worst aspect of this entire sad story was that the next calendar day would be Christmas, and no presents had yet been bought or exchanged inside the James Dillingham Young household.

Della flopped-down upon the apartment's tiny shabby couch, which was more of a miniature ratty loveseat than a bona fide comfortable sofa. The sorrow-laden wife sobbed while the more pragmatic husband speculated, 'Just look at that fuckin' bug-infested sofa! My last fuckin' name should be Davenport instead of Young. Why the hell doesn't Della go out and get a goddamned sweat-shop job and earn a few extra bucks, instead of foolishly sitting there crying and sobbing all day long about our destitute situation? And we don't even have any wise-mouthed kids' stomachs to feed! What a wagon load of horse manure this whole, rotten, domestic scene is!'

The Youngs' piss-poor flat was crudely furnished and cost eight dollars a week to rent. Jim, a lazy door-to-door mascara and perfume salesman, often wished that he was talented enough to sell encyclopedias, or girly magazines, or durable pots and pans, but the jerk had been emphatically rejected during thirteen separate short job interviews after Young had become overly argumentative and confrontational with his prospective employers. And besides *that* bad social habit of being both crude and rude, un-dynamic Jim had never learned how to read or write proficiently, flunking first-grade at Brooklyn P.S. #13 several years in a row.

The downstairs vestibule mailbox had a dysfunctional electric button that would surprisingly shock any finger that accidentally touched it, and the lettering beneath the flimsy container bore the accursed name "James Dillingham Young," but the "D" in Dillingham had been missing ever since Jim's weekly salary and commission had been diminished from thirty dollars a week to a mere twenty American bucks.

But on the positive side of the family ledger, whenever James Dillingham Young returned home at 6 p.m. with a defeated attitude and having his stubborn head crestfallen, Della instinctively hugged him dearly, yanked-off all her husband's sweaty and smelly clothes, kissed his ass and every other exposed part or organ, and then gave her chosen mate a really exotic and erotic blowjob, followed by some fantastic pussy penetration.

Then, after serving her love-mate a traditional supper of broth, bread and city tap water, Della would sit almost in a trance-like state and annoyingly weep on the small shabby couch, and with her avaricious fingers, physically recount the un-spectacular dollar eighty-seven cents over and over again. 'I've been saving-up this amount since the Fourth of July, but Jim had to curtail my weekly allowance because of the drastic decrease in his wages and in trying to survive in his present pauper status. Oh well; I can't afford to get him a decent Christmas present,' Della whimpered. 'Maybe by Easter, things will change. I suppose I'll ambush and attack him in the shower and give my adorable hubby another round of fellatio. Damn it! I knew I should've married my old high school beau Bill Lingus and changed my lousy first name to Connie!'

Della sadly gazed at her reflection in the living room's shoddy-looking and faded pier-glass mirror. The very self-conscious wife removed her barrettes, and next methodically pulled-down her long brown hair and simultaneously thought, 'I'm still pretty curvaceous and attractive, especially when I smile. I think I know what to do to get some additional cash to buy Jim a nice Christmas gift, and my solution doesn't even involve selling my gorgeous body to lowlife, dirt-bag men! Yes; I know exactly what I'm gonna' do!'

Now there were two personal possessions that the James Dillingham Youngs separately took great pride in having. One was Jim's highly coveted gold watch that he had (by sheer accident and serendipitous good fortune) found lying on a train station bench. The other prized item was Della's magnificent, long-brown, wavy hair that would have had the ancient jealous Queen of Sheba shear-off her nipples just to own. And had envious King Solomon lived in the dingy upstairs apartment across the hall, Della would have certainly teased and tempted his colossal libido by sending the greedy ruler photos' in the mail of her being stark naked and showing her long, wavy tresses draping-down and tantalizingly covering her more personal body areas.

'Holy crapola! My fabulous hair reaches way below my knees and must weigh at least ten pounds! No wonder I have a stiff neck! I guess I don't have to join the Hair Club for Women now after all!' Della mused as the wife assessed and admired her fantastic appearance in the tawdry pier-glass mirror.

The next morning, when Jim was wearing his retread shoe-leather out traipsing throughout dangerous Bronx ghettos, trying to sell perfume and mascara that both smelled somewhat like cow piss, Della donned her black wool jacket and meticulously arranged her old brown hat upon her head, and with a certain sparkle of determination in her big brown eyes, the goal-minded spouse walked six blocks west to a frequented Manhattan salon owned by entrepreneurial Madame Sofaronie, who also was the proprietor of a number of popular and well-patronized bordellos in the bustling city's five boroughs.

"My name is Della Young, better known as Mrs. James Dillingham Young. Oh, how I hate all of this aggravating male chauvinism bullshit, starting with women having to change their last names when getting hitched! Now tell me Madame, will you buy my hair?" Della asked as she dropped her extraordinary tresses down to her knees. "It hasn't been cut in over ten years!"

"We'll buy your pubic hair too if you'd like," Madame Sofaronie stated with a forced smile. "There's a big market in the pussy replacement business, you know. When teenage girls and regular housewives shave their crotches to pose nude, lots of times their domineering boyfriends and spouses become upset, so the dolls then glue my company's bushy crotch wigs that fit quite beautifully around their precious cunt cracks. I use the newly manufactured crotch wigs all the time in my network of prosperous brothels when certain discriminating male clients insist on having girls with nice pussies, even if the bushes being screwed are artificial! Even my most demanding lesbian and dyke patrons are showing more than a mild interest in my gorgeous pussy wigs! But I must tell you Mrs. Young, there isn't such a big black market for underarm hair!"

"No thank you about shaving and selling my pussy fur Madame," Della politely declined. "My husband James is an old-fashioned bush man, even though he was born in the United States and not in Southern Africa. And besides," Mrs. James Dillingham Young confidentially articulated, "my affectionate Jim usually likes to beat around the bush before he pumps me silly!"

"Well then, Lady, er, I mean Mrs. Young, I'll give you twenty dollars for your marvelous flowing tresses," Madame Sofaronie offered. "I figure I could make at least three-to-four fine wigs from your nice thick locks."

"Show me the money!" Della shrieked with great delight saturating her intense verbal reaction. "I'll return to your salon in ten years when my hair finally fully grows back. In a decade, I'll be able to feel decadent again!"

Two hours later, Della was euphorically parading up and down Manhattan's Fifth Avenue in quest of the ideal Christmas gift for her beloved Jim. Finally, the object that fit her special purchasing needs was observed through the sidewalk window of an exclusive men's shop. 'That's it!' Della imagined and realized. 'It'll make Jim have a premature ejaculation for damned sure! Maybe his sex rocket will even be able to blast-off twice!'

The totally thrilled wife paid twenty-one dollars cash for the handsome and expensive platinum fob chain that she believed would complement Jim's highly-treasured gold watch. 'I still have eighty-seven cents left in my pocket,' the ecstatic woman calculated. 'Hey, I still have enough change left over to purchase a high school jock sweater for Jim to wear on cold winter nights! Maybe I'll head over to Macy's right now!'

Prudence once again governed Della's delicate mind, after she had merrily reached and entered the dismal, all-too-familiar upstairs low-budget apartment. The wife found her curling irons stashed-away inside her bureau's right top drawer, and next, carefully began maneuvering the difficult short locks that remained growing from her scalp. 'Maybe I should trim my pubic area after all and paste some hair patches needed in the sparser regions of my head,' the wife whimsically considered. 'I now really look cheap and sleazy in the mirror, just like one of those Coney Island chorus girls that work their butts off on weekends at wealthy Madame Sofaronie's Brooklyn bordello, after the exploited chicks have done their exhaustive striptease dancing over at those disreputable Surf Avenue honky-tonk lounges. Oh well; at least Jim will have a tremendous orgasm when he sees his new platinum present!'

At six p.m. the coffee was perking on the hob, and the leftover pork chops were sizzling in the frying pan upon the corroded stove. Jim was a half-hour late, and Della began worrying. 'Maybe he's been mugged by some ruthless teenage hooligans, or maybe Jim's found another woman to pump the poop out of!' But then joy filled the woman's heart when her perceptive ears detected the sound of familiar footsteps ascending the antiquated, condemned building's fire-hazard stairs.

The husband slowly opened the apartment door, and his overall appearance seemed weak; his posture poor; his knees buckled, and his face pallid. 'My husband needs a new overcoat, gloves, pants and rubbers; yes, especially rubbers!' Della automatically thought. 'Yes, Jim indeed needs plenty of rubbers! What wife in her right mind wants a couple of bratty, snot-nosed, totally obnoxious kids further ruining her already-miserable life and crazily screaming their damned, infected tonsils out?'

A peculiar expression of alarm showed upon Jim's pale countenance as the man of the apartment gazed at and studied Della's new short hairdo. The guilt-afflicted wife approached the slightly-warped, wooden coffee table to expressly comfort and console her special man.

"Jim, darling," Della greeted, tenderly feeling and massaging his whiskered face with both hands. "Please don't stare at me that way. I've done some huge sacrificing for you; yes, I have! I couldn't have survived the holiday season without giving you a most appropriate gift that I'm sure will bring you much joy and happiness. And please don't fret, even though you never learned how to play a guitar," the wife jested, trying to get her mate out of his very obvious negative mood. "I just had to follow my conscience and do it. My hair grows pretty fast. Please now Jim', let's be happy and not be so glum! Wait until you see the nice thing that I've bought for you!"

"You've cut off your goddamned hair!" the husband squawked and protested, pounding and collapsing the frail, wooden coffee table with his clenched fist before it collapsed to the dusty floor. "Cut your hair off! That's just like me cutting off my dick!"

"But my hair will grow back and your magnificent penis wouldn't!" smartly argued the wife, thus gaining a definite advantage in their dispute. "Don't you like me for what the hell I am, either with or without my tresses? I had my sensational hair bravely cut, and I sold it for a good price just for you, Jim!"

"You'd better not have sold your pubic bush, too!" yelled the infuriated man of the apartment. "Della, you're saying to me that your majestic hair is gone? Where did you hide it? Where the fuck did you hide it? I hope not under the coffee table!"

"You needn't search for it," the wife soberly related. "It's sold for a handsome profit, I tell ya'! Sold for your benefit Jim! Maybe the hairs on my exposed scalp are numbered, but nobody could ever count or weigh my tremendous love for you! Are you now ready to eat your leftover *chops* and quite prepared to forget about busting mine?"

The disconsolate husband reached into his cavernous coat pocket and removed several objects that were guaranteed to be future family heirlooms of sentimental value. "Forget about the goddamned broken coffee table, and check-out these nifty items before you wrongly judge my character. This extremely bizarre coincidence has to be the ultimate irony imaginable! Not even that clairvoyant asshole Nostradamus could've predicted this incredible bullshit!"

Della stared incredulously at the two excellent and exquisite sterling silver combs being held in the center of Jim's right palm. "Holy dog shit!" the wife marveled and exclaimed. "I've worshipped these things in a certain ritzy Fifth Avenue jewelry store display window for over a year now! I never thought that *we* could ever afford to possess these beauties in a million years! Oh Jim; you shouldn't have done this for me! You're the finest husband a dumb-ass wife like me could ever desire!"

The appreciative spouse gladly threw her skinny arms around her man's thick neck and began smooching away incessantly. "Oh Jim! My hair grows pretty damned fast, including my fluffy pubic bush and the vexing bristles that are always-sprouting under my armpits! I think I'll be able to proudly wear these luxurious combs in six short months. Please forgive me Jim for acting so freakin' hysterical! I promise you! By the next Fourth of July, I'll be proudly wearing them in my new hair on the Coney Island Boardwalk!"

And then Della realized something very relevant and pertinent, and she quickly reached inside her bra and swiftly removed the fancy platinum fob chain she had especially purchased for Jim's cherished gold timepiece. The item's stunning precious linked-metal gleamed; the radiant reflection seemingly matching the wife's bright, ardent, upbeat spirit.

"Jim, take a look at this little article I've acquired for you this morning, my dear benevolent soul mate. I bought it on Fifth Avenue just for you to have and to own. Isn't this incredible specimen a real dandy?" the exuberant wife declared. "You'll have to admire your gold watch at least a hundred times a day now. Give me your timepiece so that I can immediately attach this most splendid platinum fob chain!"

Instead of obeying Della's suggestion, Jim tumbled onto the less-than-mediocre couch and momentarily cupped his hands over his face. Then, possessing a broken heart, the melancholy fellow had a rather extraordinary announcement to make.

"Della, let's put both our real and our imagined Christmas presents away for a while," the husband strangely prefaced his remarks. "They're entirely too superb for us to use, or even think about right now. Are you ready for a real shocker?" Jim rhetorically asked. "You have to understand that I had sold my gold watch so that I could purchase the sterling combs for your long brown hair; that is, for your now non-existent long brown hair! Damn it! Why couldn't I have attended and graduated from *Auburn* or *Brown* and made something big out of my boring, lackluster life!"

"Don't despair Jim," the supportive Mrs. Young answered in a bittersweet tone of voice. "It's not the expense of the gift that matters. In the final analysis, it's the true love in a fine marital relationship that genuinely represents the honest motivation for giving a special gift that really counts."

* * * * * * * * * * * * * *

The Magi were three important ancient Kings of the Orient, namely Melchior, Balthasar, and Gaspar, who had brought gifts of gold, frankincense and myrrh to the Christ Child lying in the stable manger in Bethlehem, expecting nothing in return for their heartfelt acts of kindness. Hence, the Magi are often referred to in literature and in standard Christmas carols as "The Three Wise Men". And in this magical chronicle of human wisdom, Della and James Dillingham Young discovered and confirmed the greatest gift of all: eternal and non-pretentious love for each other.

“The Last Leaf”

In the southern district of cosmopolitan New York City known as Greenwich Village, the narrow streets are arranged in an irregular configuration, and those small strips situated west of Washington Square are called “Places”. Many of the houses in that overcrowded section are apartment buildings; inferior tenements that are rented-out primarily to artists, actors, painters, sculptors, prostitutes, and musicians. The city canvas artists, along with the newspaper and magazine pornography sketchers, prefer the uppermost floors that feature eighteenth century gables, certain secluded Dutch attics that the avant-garde artists call “studios”, and of course, the modest dwellings command low-rents to accommodate the highly populated colony’s Picasso, Rembrandt, Norman Rockwell, and Thomas Nast aspiring wannabes’.

At the top garret of one of those antiquated old Dutch-style tenements, two young lesbians named Sue and Johnsy (that wanted fame and fortune as contemporary artists) resided in their cozy and modest “studio”. One frigid mid-December night, the pair had been impatiently standing inside Delmonico’s Restaurant, where the main dining room had been very jam-packed, and so the wishful artists (possessing similar interests and ambitions) had coincidentally met in the long reservations’ waiting line, and then ultimately agreed to share a table.

In January, just after the New Year had been celebrated in Times Square, an insidious villain identified in the newspapers as “Mr. Pneumonia” had infiltrated into the shadowed ghettos of New York City, smiting victim after victim, and the result of *his* wicked, heartless pandemic had rapidly filled virtually every remaining gravesite in the city’s cemeteries.

Sue was from New England, and had developed good resistance to rampant respiratory diseases, but Johnsy had lived most of her young life in Southern California, and was very susceptible to any bacteria or virus that the eastern winter atmosphere had to offer. The afflicted West Coast girl lay motionless in her single bed, and poor Johnsy steadfastly stared-out the studio apartment window, her body in a trance-like state; and her bloodshot, blue eyes being fixated directly on the rear red brick wall of the adjacent, crowded tenement house.

The second Monday morning of January, 1914, the overworked arts-community doctor climbed the humble tenement’s rickety steps, entered the back studio room, carefully examined Johnsy's pathetic physical condition, and then summoned Sue out into the hallway for a brief consultation.

"No, your blonde-haired friend does not have any life-threatening venereal disease," Dr. Wynan communicated to alleviate Sue's initial concern. "Instead, she's contracted the dreaded pneumonia that's been contagious throughout the city, and Johnsy has maybe a one-in-ten chance at surviving the current epidemic that's on an evil crusade. The mercury in my thermometer registered an all-too-high one hundred and three temperature, and I'm sorry to report that the local hospital's beds are all filled to capacity, and that they're not admitting any more patients. In fact, Miss Sue," the medical man elaborated, "there are no more large enough areas left in the facility to effectively quarantine the great number of extremely sick pneumonia victims. Even the goddamned undertakers are dropping like flies and dying from the major epidemic menace. If I may jest a bit Miss Sue, I'm even considering taking equestrian lessons and becoming one of the Horsemen of the Apocalypse! I mean, ya' gotta' have a flexible sense of humor to endure and survive this horrendous urban holocaust in progress! Wouldn't you agree?"

"Is that your definitive prognosis?" Sue lethargically asked Dr. Wynan. "Johnsy and I were just getting to know each other intimately, and were even thinking about inventing something called 'same sex marriage' right here in New York. We first met in line at Delmonico's. Now everything's being tossed into the hopper!"

"Your little lady friend has made-up her mind that she wants to die," the traveling physician sadly revealed. "Tell me Miss Sue; did Johanna, or should I say Johnsy as you affectionately call your girlfriend; did Johnsy have any particular interests or goals she wished to pursue before becoming so horribly incapacitated?"

"Yes Dr. My roommate wanted to paint the Bay of Nipples, er, I meant to say the Italian Bay of Naples," the aggrieved artist sobbed, blowing and then vigorously wiping her nose mucus upon her long dress sleeve.

"How the hell could she ever paint the Bay of Naples?" Dr. Wynan marveled and exclaimed. "That absurd project would require at least a million-million-million gallons of dark blue paint, and that's just the damned primer coat! Doesn't your gay roommate Johnsy understand that paint doesn't adhere to water?"

"No Dr.; I had meant that Johnsy wanted to paint the Bay of Naples on a canvas placed upon her easel," Sue clarified. "And after doing that, while still vacationing and working in that beautiful part of Italy, Johnsy had plans of painting Mt. Vesuvius, too; that is to say, painting the inactive volcano on a separate canvas!"

"What I had meant to articulate to you, Miss Sue, was this," Dr. Wynan said before removing a tin flask of hard liquor from his suit jacket's secret compartment, and then chugging-down several very ample swigs. "Excuse me! That imbibing you just witnessed was for medicinal purposes only! Now then Miss Sue; I meant to ask you if Miss Johnsy had any special man in her life to think about. That kind of hope might give her the necessary inspiration and the emotional strength she needs to valiantly combat the potentially-lethal disease that's taken over her body."

"No Dr. Wynan. Johnsy and I have a sort of civil union going where we share everything including our bodies," the slightly embarrassed roommate confided. "The plus side of our relationship is that neither of us has to worry about becoming pregnant or having an abortion. But that's all changed now that Johnsy seems to have purchased a one-way ticket to Heaven!"

"Well, Miss Sue. I'll provide you with some medicine and some pain pills, and we'll just have to let Mother Nature randomly practice her will," the local tablet dispenser and drug dealer bluntly summarized. "But as you're well aware, science can only do so much, and no more. Try getting your frail companion to speak and talk about fashion, or gay marriage, or anything else that floats her boat. Otherwise," Dr. Wynan predicted, "get ready for the Grim Reaper's lethal stalk. That roaming son-of-a-bitchin' prowler doesn't miss eliminating his targeted victim too damned often!"

After the bad news doctor departed the premises by tripping and then violently tumbling down the stairs, Sue darted into the small side room and cried her eyeballs out; her tears causing a quickly saturated Japanese napkin to turn to pulp. Then the young red-hair woman grabbed her drawing board and stepped into the studio where Johnsy was lying prone in a comatose state of existence.

'I'll start that pen and ink freelance drawing I plan on sketching for that literary magazine where the editor is a male homosexual that wants to see me succeed,' Sue fondly recollected. 'I should go into the asphalt and macadam business so that my road to success would be more easily paved!' the aspiring artist mused.

As Sue diligently sketched an Idaho cowboy wearing a monocle while riding a fierce bucking bronco, her concentration was suddenly interrupted as Johnsy began uttering a bizarre numerical sequence in her unconscious state. Immediately, the alarmed listener ceased her intellectual art experimentation, wondering what evil influence had been the cause of the suffering girl's weird, oratorical aberration. 'What kind of satanic bullshit is this? Whatever happened to the goddamned alphabet? She's obsessively counting her memorized numbers backwards!' the roommate recognized.

"Twelve, eleven, ten," Johnsy distinctly uttered those designations at three-second intervals. "Nine, eight, seven, six," she continued her strange countdown-in-reverse.

'Holy shit!' Sue nervously thought. 'Johnsy either thinks she's firing off a rocket, or counting the number of bottles of beer on the wall! What the frig' is this fucked-up anomaly all about?'

Then, the petrified woman from New England looked solicitously out the studio's window and quickly fathomed the reason for Johnsy's weird verbalizations. The neighboring brick house's rear outside wall was a mere twenty-feet away, and what had over the years climbed the residence's exterior was a gnarled ivy vine. Autumn's chilling winds had claimed most of the vine's withered leaves, and had shaken them to the ground but still, *five* extremely vulnerable growths still remained.

"What is it that you're counting?" Sue gently whispered into her roommate's left ear. "I can count on you to tell me!"

"Five," Johnsy spoke in a scary, monotone voice. "Four," was her next utterance three seconds later. "When the last leaf falls, then I must go, too," the girl answered and prophesied, sounding as if she were speaking from another dimension or world. "There're only four leaves left," the sick girl stated from her unconscious condition. "When the last leaf falls-off," the bedridden girl expressed, "that's when I'll fall and disappear, too!"

'Holy crap! I'd better not write all of this crazy shit down on *loose leaf* paper!' Sue's disheveled mind imagined. "Here Johnsy! Try to swallow-down some of this delicious broth! This tasty bouillon will make you feel like a billion. In fact, Johnsy, this tasty yellow bouillon is much better than gold bullion, as far as your deteriorating health is concerned!"

"Sue," the sick girl said from her horizontal, trance-like state. "When the last leaf falls, so do I. Four!" the infirmed roommate reiterated. "Four!" Johnsy frightfully repeated. "The fuckin' ivy vine seems to be stuck on four!"

"Keep your eyes closed and don't look out the damned window!" Sue imperatively commanded. "I need to sell a few drawings in a hurry, so that *we* can afford a friggin' window shade! Otherwise, if I don't, it'll certainly be curtains for you, my precious Johnsy!"

"I can't wait to die! I need to succumb! Come on, you stupid, goddamned leaves! Drop the hell off so that I can swiftly journey to paradise!" Johnsy scarily declared.

'I know what I'll do! I'll call old Mr. Behrman up here to pose as a miner sitting on a rock,' Sue decided. 'Behrman will be my model, and while he's up here, I'll tell the fossil-faced asshole all about poor Johnsy's dilemma. Maybe he'll be able to give me some sound advice, or be able to help my roommate recover from this shit respiratory disease called pneumonia! I've heard rumors that Behrman had once studied to be a voodoo witchdoctor before he ventured into painting murals, frescoes, and canvas portraits. Now the dumb-ass, drunken, old-coot, insane bastard has to settle for painting dilapidated rooms, shanties, and sleazy whorehouses!"

* * * * * * * * * * * * *

Old Wilhelm Behrman lived on the ground floor, and the dumb fuck honestly believed that he had been Michelangelo, Marie Curie, Cleopatra, a ferocious mastiff, and Moses in his previous lives. For forty frustrating years, Wilhelm Behrman had wielded a brush, and never once was invited to have an art exhibit, and never once had he ever sold a canvas painting while canvassing all of Greenwich Village. The ancient fool's major dream was to paint a masterpiece, but in order to pay for his next meal and his cheap apartment rent, Behrman often posed as a model, even though he wasn't a model citizen. And the old lush's severe drinking habit was indeed an abominable curse; drinking-down gin and tonic, often swallowing hair tonic stolen from another mentally confused and deranged apartment resident, who believed that *he* had been a Teutonic (two-tonic) knight during the fucked-up medieval period in European (Your-a-peon) history, a weird period when most the living, unwary, assholes frolicked amid-evil!

The inebriated Wilhelm Behrman gladly accepted the assignment of posing as a gold-panning miner sitting on top of a boulder, symbolizing to his degenerate mind that he was somewhere between a rock and a hard place and not getting any *bolder,* because of the very hard and uncomfortable huge stone.

Sue was encouraged to observe that Johnsy was sleeping soundly in her fleabag bed. She and Wilhelm then apprehensively paced to the studio window, and both were greatly relieved to witness that a single leaf still remained clinging to the ivy vine. Wilhelm then assisted the red-haired artist in hanging a bed-sheet over the window to serve as a makeshift curtain. After working-up a sweat from his most recent laborious ordeal, the exhausted old wheezer then further irritated his itchy hemorrhoids by faithfully sitting for four long hours, all the while pretending to be a determined Western gold prospector taking a five-minute break from his arduous toil. Unfortunately for Behrman's bothersome rectal discomfort, without *his* knowledge, Sue had left the apartment to go to the pharmacy, and then to the grocery store, to obtain medicine and nourishing food supplies to keep her soul-mate Johnsy alive.

* * * * * * * * * * * * * *

The following morning, after Sue awoke from a terrible nightmare, the loyal roommate brought Johnsy some cold orange juice to drink in order to lower the doleful girl's fever. "I'll give you a nice sponge bath to further cool you down, and I won't forget to thoroughly wash your personals. Don't worry, Johnsy! I'll take good care of you! What am I fuckin' saying? I can't even take care of myself!"

"Sue," the blonde young lady replied almost-miraculously, and then opening her swollen eyes. "Tear down that dirty bed sheet so that I can see if the last leaf has fallen."

Afraid of what might *not* be behind the opaque sheet, Sue reluctantly did as her dying friend had requested. And lo and behold; the fierce, gusty winds of the night before had not removed the last leaf, which still bravely clung to the ivy vine.

"I thought for sure that it would've dropped by now!" Johnsy said, almost with remorse. "I heard the strong gales blowing last evening, and without a doubt, tonight the leaf will plummet, and so will my soul; right into Hell for being a sinful, self-centered, practicing lesbian! If only I could've shown behavioral restraint. If only I could've been celibate, and chaste, and faithfully exercised good Christian abstinence."

"Johnsy, please get your mind off of dying and of going straight to Hell," Sue mildly reprimanded her dear friend. "If you won't worry about yourself, please think of me and my wretched circumstances! If you die like you want to, I'll have to masturbate at least four times a day until I finally find a suitable, cute, little blonde-haired replacement for you! It's not easy being a tough-chick dyke nowadays, let me tell ya'!"

But Johnsy was so weak that she again closed her heavy eyes without ever answering. The most lonesome thing in the world is a soul when it is making ready to take its journey into the unknown afterlife. The daylight hours slowly passed, and all night long, the extremely strong winds blew, and fierce torrents of rain pelted against the century-old Dutch eaves, but when sunrise gradually arrived, the amazing last leaf had not fallen.

Johnsy rested in her bed, and for several hours, her bloodshot eyes peered-out the garret window at the incomparable last leaf. After consuming her chicken broth and sipping-down a glass of cool refreshing water, the guilty-minded pneumonia victim confessed to her empathetic roommate, "I've been a naughty girl, Sue. That last leaf is still up there against the brick wall to show me how utterly wrong and selfish I had been; wanting to sinfully die and end it all! Bring me a little more broth, some milk and a glass of port wine," the indisposed young lady requested. "And also, please bring me two more pillows for me to prop-up my head. I'll sit-up in bed and watch you draw, and then later, I'll see you prepare lunch."

"If you get better, Johnsy, I promise to take you to Italy so that you can paint the Bay of Nipples, er, I mean Naples!"

Later in the day, Dr. Wynan paid the apartment's occupants an unscheduled visit, and the gentleman was astounded at noticing the vast improvement in health that petite "Johanna" was experiencing and exhibiting. "I'm not a gambling man, and I don't even play bingo at the local Catholic Church, but from what I can observe, I give her a fifty-fifty chance of beating it!" the M.D. told Sue. "With good nursing and tender loving care, she just might beat the despicable disease! Her spirit must be invincible after all the sickness crap that she's encountered! But now, I must go and visit another very sick patient downstairs."

"Who is it?" Sue curiously asked. "I know everybody that lives in this piss-poor tenement!"

"His name is Behrman; a kind of an oddball artist, so I hear," the beleaguered physician related. "He's somehow had the bad luck of contracting pneumonia, too! But I understand that he's an old weak fellow, and his attack has been both acute and severe. There's little hope for him, I'm afraid to say!" Dr. Wyman stated with mild regret. "I just hope that his Guardian Angel was alert and has already escorted him to the Pearly Gates."

The following morning, the on-the-go doctor again visited Johnsy and reported to Sue that her art partner was "wonderfully out of danger". Then, the family practitioner sagaciously advised, "But I warn you; no perverted lesbian sex for at least a goddamned week! I suggest that you now scamper over to the fish store and buy for yourself a dozen clams without beards to tide yourself over!"

Later that same day, Sue entered the secluded studio and had a brief-but-enlightening, meaningful-but-direct conversation with her recuperating companion. "I have some rather bad news to report Johnsy. Mr. Behrman had died at the hospital at dawn from the dreaded pneumonia. The cleaning lady had found him lying on the floor of his hideous, rodent-infested room. Wilhelm's shoes and clothes were soaking wet through-and-through, and icy cold, too."

"How did he ever get himself into such a horrible condition?" Johnsy wondered and asked. "He had often told me that he never wanted to visit either Siberia or Antarctica!"

"Well, there were some obvious tell-tale clues that hinted at what had actually happened," Sue joylessly informed her courageous girlfriend. "The cleaning lady had found a lantern, a ladder, and some scattered brushes, along with a palette with green and yellow colors mixed on it."

"Why is life such an ugly travesty Sue? You don't mean to say that…"

"Yes, Johnsy. I believe that your assumption is absolutely right! Just look out the window at that last stout ivy leaf! Didn't you wonder why it had never fluttered away?"

"Yes," Johnsy replied. "And it never swayed or moved when the wind blew!"

"That last leaf is Mr. Behrman's masterpiece that he always wanted to complete! He had painted it up there on our neighbor's rear brick and mortar wall; the same damned night that the last leaf fell!"

"The Higher Pragmatism"

This might be a marvelous story about Divine Intervention, or it might not be; the ultimate verdict would be depending on the interpreter's religious/moral/scientific orientation. Call it fate; call it destiny, or for the more cynical-minded, call it the result or the consequence of transcendent *chance*. Some critics will believe that an idea is only practical if it actually truly works. Regardless of the individual decider's unique perspective, positive thinking should always triumph over negativity, and then emerge victorious over skepticism and over doubt. And *that* particular sage conclusion is what is meant by the following appropriate nomenclature: The Higher Pragmatism.

I had found Richard (or "Big Dick" as the vagabond wanted to be known) lying prone on a park bench in Lower Manhattan's Washington Square Park. After Big Dick had routinely asked me for a meager quarter donation, and when I adamantly refused his panhandling solicitation, that perchance was the opportune moment when I half-heartedly initiated our rather remarkable conversation. For the sake of brevity, here's precisely how our minor chance encounter had actually occurred.

"Hi; my name's Mack, and I'm a struggling newspaper reporter searching for my next big scoop," I falsely began my salutation. "May I sit down and join your dignified company?"

"If ya' want a scoop, go sit your ass down inside an ice cream parlor and leave me the fuck alone," scruffy-looking Big Dick snottily answered. "If ya' ain't got a lousy quarter for me, then I ain't got the time of day for you."

I momentarily hesitated, but then reached into my pocket, removed fifty cents, and next reluctantly handed the loose change to the gregarious and pretentious mendicant. "Now Big Dick," I proceeded with my phony introduction. "My demanding editor has assigned me to document the experience of an unfortunate victim of fate such as yourself; a person that might be illegally loitering while occupying a park bench here near Greenwich Village this fine evening. Tell me Sir; what do you suppose might have heavily contributed to your downfall from our American culture's socio-economic graces?"

My rather corny-but-un-hilarious initial presentation was swiftly interrupted by a strong laugh, which soon morphed into a loud roaring guffaw. Then, the totally uncouth fellow identifying himself as Big Dick coughed-up a quantity of disgusting green phlegm, spit at and hit an unwary. slow-walking pigeon that was pecking-away at some discarded pretzel crumbs upon the ground, and then the itinerant philosopher addressed me in what my ears discerned as a facetious tone of voice.

"Okay, Asshole," Richard disrespectfully stated. "You ain't no goddamned newspaper reporter, that's for damned certain. A genuine story-seekin' gumshoe just pretends to be a city bum, and is usually disguised to look like one, too. You don't appear to be any hobo or tramp on the lam, or a freeloader that's just jumped off of the last freight train from St. Louis," Richard shrewdly determined. "Over time, us park derelicts get to be fine judges of human nature, and we're much more aware of reality than your goddamned average psychologist or college professor happens to be. We develop our keen insights by sittin' on park benches all day looking and seriously studyin' people's antics and semantics, so I don't give a flyin' fuck about the abstract quality of certain things like most academic assholes do! As a matter of fact," the tramp rambled-on, "I can size-up most any man much better than your average asshole tailor can! Well now, Sir; that's the true advantage of bein' a regular, fucked-up neighborhood bum like myself."

"Well then, Big Dick," I articulated with a degree of chagrin evident in my stilted intonation. "How do you size me up? Do you have a customized tailor-made answer for that specific inquiry of mine, too? Did you graduate from Prophecy University, or from What's a Matter U.?" I mockingly challenged.

"Look Mack, my initial assessment was that you were in the contracting business, but then I surmised that maybe you worked your ass off in a department store, or perhaps now you're a damned unemployed sign painter," Richard haphazardly speculated and guessed. "But I presently conjecture that you've stopped here in the park to finish smokin' your expensive imported cigar, and thought you'd amuse yourself for a few minutes by pickin' away at my pea brain. But still, ya' might just be a parasite lawyer, or a mobile wall plasterer lookin' for his next gullible customer. It's getting pretty fuckin' dark out," Big Dick observed and vociferated. "And my most recent analysis is that I think you and your wife just had a violent argument, because the untamed shrew won't let you smoke your malodorous cigars anywhere inside the house."

"I think you're full of shit all the way from your asshole right up to your hyperactive larynx!" I angrily replied. "You don't know shit about shit; so ya' can't just simply be an idle asshole who's laid-off from the city's sanitation department!"

"But judging again on hindsight," Big Dick continued his analysis, while completely ignoring my general diatribe. "On second thought, I'd say that you don't have any bossy wife after all; even though your intolerable disposition amply suggests to me that you're absolutely henpecked. Are ya' married or divorced?"

"No, no, no!" I exclaimed, wildly motioning my hands in animation. "I'm proud to say that I'm pretty evasive and have skillfully avoided Cupid's speeding darts. If I may say so, that..."

"I detect that you have a fucked-up story to tell me from either guilt or need," the vagrant accurately hypothesized and declared. "Here are your crummy fifty cents back, and a goddamned five-dollar bill to boot. Now's your one and only chance to have an unbiased, philanthropic expert objectively help you along the road of life! I won't even charge you a penny for my professional services."

Somehow, Richard's exceptional attitude and extraordinary demeanor caught my vulnerable fancy, and so I immediately gained some curiosity about the extent of his intelligence, and therefore, had to attempt measuring it through dialogue. "Confidentially, I've never disclosed to any of my friends my personal dilemma, so why not share my innermost thoughts and fears with you, Big Dick?"

At least that was my mental inclination at that specific moment in time. After all, my new, almost-anonymous acquaintance seemed perfectly harmless and innocuous. So, like the proverbial sentimental fool often featured in popular song lyrics, I've always been governed and influenced by inferior-minded people, ever since my early adolescence. Consequently, on that city park bench in late October of 1910, I naively opened my heart and confided the essence of my sorrows to that obnoxious, foul-smelling 'imperfect stranger'.

I told 'Richard the Mouse-hearted' that I had spent many months adoring a voluptuous, big-breasted, sophisticated doll named Mildred Ingram. I shared with Big Dick my grievous days of uncertainty; my vacillating hopes; along with my crushed romantic dreams, and finally, I divulged my countless hours of overwhelming emotional stress and duress that I had suffered. The devil-may-care night prowler even heard plenty of confessions about my perpetual frustration in not being able to overcome the lofty position that her distinguished family had maintained in genteel New York City high society. "Mildred has grace and dignity, and her parents have big bucks going back at least a century," I sadly lamented to my new guidance counselor.

"Why don't ya' just ask the rich bitch to marry ya?" Big Dick impulsively advised with a prodigious smirk showing above his chin. "Take the hot-to-trot hussy out to Coney Island for some honky-tonk entertainment, and during the height of your recreation and revelry, ask the high society bitch if she wants to screw and do sixty-nine before the wedding day!"

Showing deep cowardice when it came to expressing myself about one gorgeous Mildred Ingram, I explained to Poor Richard (lacking his almanac) that I had (like a total ignoramus) lost my entire savings gambling in the stock market, and also had amassed major deficits out at the local race track, and that I lacked the courage to hock my most prized possessions at the neighborhood pawn shop and purchase a cheap diamond ring that would accompany my belated marriage proposal. "When I'm in Mildred's illustrious company," I complained to my new shabbily-dressed consultation guru, "the only overt behaviors I can exhibit are stammering, stuttering, drooling and blushing. Mildred probably thinks that I'm the biggest jerk if not the biggest jerk-off in all of Manhattan!"

"The rich bitch sounds like a real professional when it comes to bein' a goddamned tease," the erudite Big Dick sagely evaluated. "You're overwhelmed by her dignity, her beauty, her family name, and her firm ass and big tits, aren't ya' Mack?"

"She's all of those things and much more," I remarked. "She's Venus reincarnated! She's Aphrodite's twin sister!"

My casual comment instantly inspired my lowest-income-level friend to again begin lecturing. "Tell me the truth; Mack; does this high society dame have any sisters?" my new-found psychologist asked. "Sometimes, ya' can cleverly use sibling rivalry to your own advantage in order to achieve the upper edge you're fuckin' lookin' for. Do ya' know any other girls that might make this Mildred jealous if she sees you grabbin' and feelin' their tits, or pinchin' and goosin' their tight, desirable asses?"

"I know dozens of beautiful girls, but none of them would ever permit me to do those vulgar things to them; either in pubic, er, I mean in public, or exclusively in front of Mildred," I revealed a little too honestly. "But I wouldn't be afraid to hold any of their hands in the dark over at the nickelodeon; that is, any of 'em but the most attractive Mildred Ingram."

"It seems that you're just basically afraid of this rich bitch, and no other woman seems to faze you," Big Dick perceptively theorized and concluded. "Now let me tell ya' *my* real-life case as a model example for you to study, and perhaps imitate. Just feel my muscle!" the almost-penniless bum said, flexing his right upper arm.

I consented and followed his strange command, and mechanically and obediently felt his upper right appendage. Then, I was flabbergasted at what Richard told me, because his profound wisdom amazingly pertained to my own personal, actual long-term problem with Mildred Ingram, but the comparative relationship existed in a rather ironic-but-convoluted way. Here's the exact, rather-incredible language that went down between him and me.

"Four years ago," Big Dick commenced his relevant narrative, "I could beat the shit out of any man in the city; and I often did just that," the unshaven and unkempt vagrant seriously boasted. "Now listen carefully, Mack, because your situation and mine are even more parallel than railroad tracks, and believe me; I know a fuckin' lot about railroad tracks, empty freight cars, cabooses and the like. I was in a pissed-off mood that particular night and feelin' pretty goddamned pugnacious, as opposed to you, usually bein' altogether recessive and pusillanimous. Anyway, Mack," the on-a-roll fellow resumed his bizarre braggadocio, "I was a formidable street brawler when I was only ten-years-old, and when I was twenty, I was the best amateur middle-weight fighter in the whole shit-eatin' metropolis, and nobody could go beyond four rounds with me. I had a devastatin' right cross and a Hammer-of-Thor left hook, not to mention my Herculean uppercut to the victim's jaw! I went undefeated boxing all over the West Side at charity benefits, at private parties, and at backyard barbecues, but never fightin' for money; just for the sake of sport."

"Did you ever consider fighting professionally, since you were so good as an amateur?" I sincerely asked. "Both you and my love Mildred Ingram do have something in common after all. You're both knockouts!" I idiotically commented.

Big Dick pretended that I didn't say anything, either smart or stupid. "Listen Mack; every time I got into the ring with a professional pugilist for money, my confidence dwindled; my knees buckled, and then I egregiously got the shit beaten out of me; really pummeled ya' might say! My face saw more fuckin' canvas than that crazy asshole painter Picasso ever did!" the derelict grossly exaggerated. "The minute I saw the large crowd in the arena that had paid big bucks to see me perform, I became terribly intimidated, and the minute that my opponent stepped through the ropes, I shit my pants, er, I mean crapped my trunks!"

"Well then, Rich; if I may call you that, you' poor slob," I bravely editorialized. "How the hell did you ever solve your perplexing confidence problem? You must've been in a friggin' panic mode with the advent of each successive professional bout crisis!"

"Well, after I quit jabbin' and parryin' as a failed professional boxer, I was so fuckin' pissed-off that I went around the city after dark and then wildly beat the shit out of anybody that looked at me the wrong way," Richard astoundingly communicated his general woe. "I even knocked the snot out of the nostrils of a couple of belligerent cab drivers; several hostile milkmen and mailmen; a handful of knife-wieldin' pimps, and a few loud-mouthed cops, too."

"Wow, you beat the crap out of so many people that no one in the entire city was full of shit anymore," I foolishly jested. "You should've focused your energies on all the bullshitting politicians, and done the rest of us an enormous public service!"

"Anyway," Richard proceeded with his illuminating commentary. "One fine evening, I was walkin' down near the Bowery lookin' for some self-satisfyin' fighting adventure. Seven drunken assholes came paradin' in my direction, all dressed in tuxedos, tails and carryin' canes; the group lookin' like a gaggle of fuckin' penguins. One of the brazen punks pushes me to one side of the pavement, and I didn't take kindly to his discourteous gesture. The jerk-off in question put-up a decent fight, just like the ones ya' see in those new-fangled silent motion pictures. In fact," Richard elaborated. "The other guy had some science and artistry, but then I creamed his ass with a savage right cross that could've been a five-hundred-pound crucifix as far as my doomed foe was concerned."

"Wow! What a tremendous story! Did ya' ever discover the unfortunate victim's name?" I inquired. "Did the dumb drunken shit require hospitalization? Was there any significant brain damage that you had so mercilessly inflicted?"

"Well, Mack, here's the goddamned irony that I had been tellin' ya' about," my ingenious new buddy proudly disclosed. "One of the unconscious jerk-off's friends, his manager, a clown named Easy Ed Elliott, then tells me right there on the Bowery Park scene, overlookin' the in-cherry-condition Statue of Liberty, that I had just brutally knocked out Reddy Burns, the reigning middleweight champion of the whole goddamned world. I learned that Burns had arrived in town just the day before, because the famous boxer was tryin' to get a promotional match with the invincible Jim Jeffries," Richard convincingly related. "But truthfully, if I had known I was fightin' Reddy Burns, I would've thrown in the towel and folded right away when the lousy arrogant bully had deliberately and roughly shoved me into the nearby shrubbery, because the fuck-head had thought I was a wimpy weakling *pushover* standin' in his goddamned way."

"I'm not a boxer. or any other breed of dog," I quipped, showing-off my fucked-up personality's comedy side. "What does prize-fighting have to do with *my* bewildering predicament involving Mildred Ingram? I'm not a fighter, and apparently, I'm not a very good lover either," I told Big Dick. "Perhaps I need some dynamic sex hormone pills, or maybe an effective aphrodisiac to get my sticky sperm juices flowing in the right freakin' direction, so that I could pop the mess right-out of my enlarged. erect love tube and directly into Mildred's warm and loving crotchola!"

"You're destined to fall even deeper in love with this enticin' Mildred bitch, just like I had been destined to get my ass kicked a multitude of times in the professional ring," Big Dick pessimistically predicted as the park-bench philosopher sat there next to me, his left hand vigorously scratching his testicles. "In boxing parlance, you're afraid to enter the ring and pursue the biggest conquest of your unenviable, piss-poor life! When it comes to this rich dame that you're so mesmerized with, you're a rank amateur, Mack. And I strongly recommend that you not stick your head through the three vertical ropes, because you're fuckin' afraid of entering the ring."

I was so impressed with Big Dick's oratory that I gave him a ten-dollar tip, which the contemporary "Bowery" Socrates eagerly and enthusiastically accepted as well-deserved compensation. At that 'epiphany moment', my mind was in a perpetual frenzy after hobnobbing with the modern-day genius for a full-hour.

But then, my suspicious and imaginative brain construed Big Dick as my personal enemy. 'I'll show this know-it-all two-bit tramp that I can fight the high society equivalent of Reddy Burns, and emerge as the victor. Within the last hour, I've miraculously turned into the foremost authority on the esoteric art of successfully proposing marriage. In fact,' I pledged to my growing ego, 'I'm gonna' demonstrate that I'm about to become totally invincible at love; just like champion Jim Jeffries is at boxing.'

I hurried to a nearby public telephone near Wall Street and Broadway, and excitedly rang-up the ultra-conservative, Uptown Ingram residence. I gulped as a female voice answered my dramatic rushed call. The moment of truth and courage had finally arrived.

“Is that you, Darling?” I asked, feeling quite omnipotent and virile in my presentation. “I need to talk with you, Honey, about a terribly urgent matter.”

“Yes, this is, I!” came back angelic, beautiful language in a very grammatically correct and utterly sweet female voice. “Who is this please? Your voice sounds awful, er, I mean awfully familiar!”

“Why it’s me, the inimitable and irresistible Mack Gordon!” I politely yelled, showing an excess of feigned anger at not having my masculine baritone immediately recognized by my favorite woman over the telephone. “And furthermore,” I very confidently added in my most mellow tone of enunciation. “I have a few rather pertinent items I need to speak to you about, so I might as well get promptly to the point and address them to you right now.”

“Dear me!” exclaimed the suddenly thrilled Ingram girl. “Oh; yes; it’s you Mr. Mack Gordon! You sound so energetic and so stimulated! What’s on your mind?”

“I just gotta’ get down to brass tacks,” I neurotically insisted. “You know, of course, that I’m madly in love with you; yes; ecstatically in love with you, right to the brink of insanity. I gotta’ confess that I’ve been incarcerated in this idiotic slave-like infatuation state for over a year now, so I guess it’s truly more love that puppy infatuation, or something like that!” I awkwardly expressed in circumlocutory language. “Now mind you; I demand a definitive answer right now, so be prepared to respond. I wanna’ truthfully know; will *you* marry me or not? Here’s a bland suggestion. Let’s be adults about this very crucial subject, and approach this matter with measured maturity!”

“Holy shit! Oh Mack; why certainly! I’ll be more than thrilled-to-death to be your ever-lovin’ wife! Oh Mack, please flag-down the next cab and come up to the mansion right this minute! I just can’t wait for your wonderful embrace! I want you to kiss and caress me all over!” Click.

* * * * * * * * * * * * *

Well, I hastily arrived at the Ingram’s Park Avenue palace as quickly as I could get there. I forcefully rang the harmony-toned doorbell and impatiently waited; twiddling my thumbs in the interim. A handsomely dressed butler, wearing a white, curly Revolutionary War era wig and matching impressive, red coat with an accompanying compatible white and blue uniform, greeted me, and then the benign servant formally announced my presence.

‘Oh well,’ thought I, with my big brown eyes turned upwards, closely examining the ornate, intricate cornice work, and also the delicate-looking crystal chandelier anchored into the foyer’s ceiling. Then, my wandering mind made a powerful realization. ‘I’m presently a big step up and above *that* obnoxious park bench scumbag Big Dick now!’ I thought. ‘His incidental knocking-out the notorious Reddy Burns has absolutely nothing over on me and my recently discovered love prowess! God; do I feel potent!’

Suddenly, my trembling knees began to knock as I heard footsteps descending the upper part of the Park Avenue castle’s magnificent spiral staircase. Foolishly, I looked around for a convenient window or trap door from which I could escape my sudden anxiety attack. But then fortunately, my rationality took command of my fluctuating emotions, when I plausibly considered exactly how much I actually loved the stunning and dazzling debutante, Miss Mildred Hortense Ingram. ‘The hard part is over!’ I rationally reckoned. ‘She’s already consented to my proposal over the phone.’

But just then, the side dining room door swung open, and in stepped little Betsy Ingram, Mildred’s charming younger sister, who at that confluence of space and time, looked like a radiant, glorified angel herself’.

“Hi Betsy,” I greeted, unaware of any impending surprise. “You look just as beautiful as Mildred always does, and I just gotta’ flatter you some more. Your impeccable blue eyes are a sight to behold, and also, your firm breasts, er, I mean your firm hands are indeed an alluring sight to be held.”

“Why Mack Gordon,” Betsy replied with a florid, blushing face. “All the while I thought it was my sister Mildred that you had the royal hots for. Oh my God! You don’t know how positively euphoric I am that you’ve asked me to marry you over the telephone! How original and daring! You do have audacity and style, Mack; I just have to concede you that!”

Amazingly, in conclusion to my small fascinating tale with a twist involving a certain degree of ‘Higher Pragmatism,’ I suspect that *that* pathetic failure known only as Richard or “Big Dick”, and me, Mack Gordon, will always be helpless amateurs no matter how long we each might live upon this majestic Earth. But in *my* singular matrimonial/marital bliss case, I’m mighty glad of my amateur status; and furthermore, I hope and plan to be married to my second marriage choice, vivacious Betsy Ingram, until “Death do us part”!

"The Cop and the Anthem"

As any above-average, acne-faced, eighth-grade student knows, O. Henry was William Sydney Porter's (1862-1910) penname. Porter's short stories are notorious for their "twist", or surprise endings, that usually involve the literary element of irony appearing in a parallel dual development situation.

Soapy sat uneasily upon a New York City park-bench, looking at the dying flowers that had been planted inside a circular Madison-Square-garden. A brisk, late autumn wind and overhead honking geese signaled the end of Indian summer, and the belated approach of nasty winter. The vagabond knew he needed a warm place to stay until the arrival of the next vernal equinox. A dead leaf fluttered-down from a tall oak tree and fell upon Soapy's lap, symbolically representing the dire coldness soon to envelop the city.

'It looks like the end of fall!' Soapy thought as he glanced-up at the now totally barren oak tree. 'Jack Frost is right around the corner, so I guess it's time for me to find a comfortable warm sanctuary to chill-out until spring before Mr. Winter pays the metropolis an unwelcome visit!'

The human indignity commonly known as the American "work ethic", along with the responsibility of maintaining a bank savings' account were both as alien to the whimsical tramp as much as tropical flowers and coconuts were to Eskimos. 'I gotta' commit some major misdemeanor, or some lesser felony, so that I can spend the winter as usual in a cozy *East River* jail cell on the Island!' Soapy thought. 'And now it's time to intrepidly collide head-on with the New York City justice system! I can only dream of exotic places like Mt. Vesuvius towering above the Bay of Naples, or a luxurious Mediterranean cruise ship to Greece that I've read about in vacation books over at the free library,' the idle tarrier mused. 'Those majestic places and things I'll proudly let my imagination visit, once I've guaranteed myself a bunk bed with a hard mattress on the Island! That's the splendid three-month vacation my heart truly desires!'

Some of Soapy's more fortunate old pals that had leeched off of rich old widows, or that had hit it big at the race tracks were now destined to Palm Springs and to the French Riviera that coming winter. But the disconsolate derelict had no alternative other than to connive an innovative way to facilitate his upcoming annual pilgrimage to 'the venerable Island'.

'Three discarded Sunday newspapers can't keep my chest, stomach and ass warm!' Soapy soberly realized. 'And I can't fall asleep at nights if my butt-hole is a degree under fifty on a standard rectal thermometer! A frozen ass is worse than a frigid woman; that's for damned sure!'

The happy-go-lucky drifter scorned the city's charity, especially crowded Bowery soup kitchens and raunchy fleabag hotel accommodations. The bum instinctively loathed dependence on institutionalized humanitarianism, thinking that some humiliation or obligation for the act of being socially reformed was attached to the taxpayers' benevolence. Soapy's plain and simple rationale was that the Law was more objective and logical about his future incarceration than any "Municipal Philanthropy" ever suggested or warranted.

'Those city shelters all make me shave, take a bath, and thoroughly wipe my ass after taking a shit!' Soapy considered in defense of his faltering ego. 'I'd rather have dirty brown-stained underwear on my own accord than a mandated clean lily-white ass any damned time,' the mendicant concluded as his eyes carefully scanned his immediate environment. 'Who needs a litany of questions and a dumb-dick inquisition for a lousy loaf of bread and a cup of coffee? It's my way or the highway; that's what the hell I believe!' the tramp rationalized. 'I friggin' hate when obnoxious do-gooders get their talons into my soul, and their snooty brown-colored noses stuck all-the-way up to my colon!'

Soapy rose from the hard, wooden, park-bench, stretched his arms out above his head, scratched his itchy balls, and then recollected exactly how he had managed to gain adequate residency during past harsh winters. 'I'll do something brash like dine at an exclusive restaurant,' the conniver whimsically imagined. 'And after I declare insolvency, the waiter will then dutifully notify a policeman; who will predictably notify an impartial city judge; who will quickly contact the sympathetic warden. Getting arrested and convicted is almost as easy as committin' the illegal act in the first place!'

Soapy departed the garden not far from Madison Square, and felt like a semi-*macho man* as the bum walked through throngs of apathetic Soho and Greenwich *Village people.* He kept strolling along concrete sidewalks and across asphalt streets until the vagrant came to the junction of Broadway and Fifth Avenue. The drifter turned-up Broadway, and soon halted in front of a glittering café, where local socialites, celebrities, and expensive horny prostitutes usually gathered to mingle, to conduct business, and to network their fame and fortune. The newly-arrived dinner guest had confidence that his superior scheme would yield handsome dividends in earning a very pleasurable hiatus at "the Island", conveniently situated away from mainstream civilization in the center of the *East River*.

The vagrant was unusually clean-shaven that particular morning, sporting only a two-day-beard. His black overcoat looked fairly presentable, and the necktie the tramp was wearing had been given to him on *Thanksgiving Day* by a *Salvation Army* lady lieutenant, trying to reform his chronic waywardness. 'All I gotta' do is reach a table in this fancy restaurant and success will ultimately be mine!' the old amateur swindler plotted. 'The tablecloth will conceal my shoddy trousers, which have indeed seen better days, months, years, and decades.'

'Ah, roasted duck and a glass of fine imported white wine will adequately fill my belly, and then I'll feel quite satisfied being ushered off the premises by a man in blue to later appear before my favorite sympathetic judge,' the big city hobo imagined. 'If only I didn't always have to go through all of this disturbing preliminary bullshit just to get to the damned courtroom!'

When Soapy set foot into the gourmet restaurant, the beggar's disheveled appearance was immediately recognized by the alert headwaiter, who was a veteran identifier of mendicant intrusions.

"Get your frayed trousers and scruffy-looking shoes out of this reputable establishment immediately!" the headwaiter commanded to the ill-starred (and now-thwarted) famished diner. And with that hostile evaluation being articulated, two husky assistant waiters savagely grabbed Soapy by the shoulders and by the seat of his wrinkled pants, and proceeded to hurl the destitute fellow out onto the hard, cold Broadway sidewalk.

"Fine hospitality you extend toward decent prospective patrons!" Soapy complained to his assailants as he got up and methodically dusted himself off from grime that had been caked onto his pants, prior to his ejection from the famous restaurant. "Give my damned regards to Broadway!"

"And don't come back here again until you're President of the American Telephone and Telegraph Company, or Commander-in-Chief of the United States Armed Forces!" the headwaiter yelled-down at the recently evicted trespasser lying on the sidewalk. "Your slovenly, unkempt appearance couldn't even evade detection if you were standing stark naked inside an overcrowded nudist colony!"

Soapy soon turned from Broadway, and trekked north to find another location in which to reconnoiter and loiter. Before reaching *Times Square,* the itinerant fellow was aimlessly pacing west on

Fortieth Street. 'Only three-thousand or so more miles until I enter the outskirts of San Francisco!' the homeless wanderer mused. 'That inhospitable restaurant headwaiter can't tell an epicure from a cancer cure!' the bum decided. 'Ya' might think that by now, the dumb-shit could accurately distinguish quality from quantity! What a friggin' retard that oversized asshole was!'

At the corner of Fortieth and Sixth Avenue, Soapy had a sudden inspiration. Electric lights and a storefront plate-glass window elaborately displayed an intriguing array of dinnerware, silverware, and cutlery sets. The fine China plates and soup tureens made the frustrated observer remember being recently, mercilessly, and embarrassingly tossed-out of the posh Broadway restaurant. The ambling derelict spotted a loose cobblestone on the street corner, picked it up, and then heaved the heavy object at one of the delicate gold-gilded place settings that had been neatly arranged on the other side of the plate-glass window.

A host of pedestrians had heard the window-glass shatter, and a horde of spectators soon gathered around the suspected perpetrator until a New York City patrolman arrived at the crime scene to conduct a proper investigation. "Okay, okay folks! I'm here to restore law and order!" the policeman imperatively indicated. "Ya' all can go about your business while I professionally perform my personal interrogation!"

After the curious crowd scattered in all directions, the policeman conducted a rather brief inquiry into the vandalism. The cop inspected Soapy, who was casually standing there with his hands in his pockets, and broadly smiling like the legendary Cheshire Cat. "Okay Mister; where's the criminal that's broken the window?"

"You're talkin' about me!" the big-city-bum shamelessly confessed. "I'm the villain that exclusively did the damage! And I gotta' admit that this ain't the first damned store window I've ever broken with a loose cobblestone, either!"

"Who the hell do ya' think your shittin', old man!" the cop snarled back. "Destructive scoundrels that smash windows don't hang around to get their asses' arrested! Do' ya' think I'm some kind of damned rookie officer that's still wet behind the ears?" the policeman rhetorically asked. "Do ya' think I'm some kind of goddamned virgin eunuch, or some kind of a friggin' faggot left over from the naughty-naughty Gay Nineties?"

"Don't ya' figure I had somethin' to do with this particular case of vandalism?" Soapy inquired to the cop in a very disappointed tone of voice. "I want ya' to know that my whole damned family is nothin' more than a bunch of violent criminals and dangerous convicts. My grandmother was a notorious safecracker, and my Aunt Harriet was a mass murderer, and my father was…"

The policeman turned and astutely observed a man running to catch a horse-drawn cab a block down the avenue. The dedicated keeper-of-the-peace drew his club and instantly sprinted in that direction yelling, "Stop running away; you' vile rogue!" as the determined officer took-off in hot pursuit of whom *his* mind had evaluated as the principal suspect in the quite mysterious storefront window-breaking offense.

Soapy felt disgust and depression accumulating inside his weak heart, as the drifter sullenly watched the policeman dash after a completely innocent man who just happened to be in 'a New York hurry'. The dejected wanderer next noticed an unpretentious-looking restaurant across Sixth Avenue that catered to the tastes of modest, casual clientele. 'That place has thick stone plates, thin soup, and watery coffee,' Soapy critically thought. 'But it's better than nothin'! I'll just have to eat a considerable amount of food, and then refuse to pay the bill; claimin' I got indigestion!'

The cunning, scheming, sly diner entered the busy eatery and remarkably made it to a comfortable seat unchallenged. The shabby-looking fellow parked his wide buttocks at a table-for-two, and successfully ordered and then consumed bacon, eggs, pancakes, toast, coffee, orange juice, more coffee, apple pie, a Danish, a chocolate doughnut, and finally, a huge slice of carrot cake. The busy waiter finally came around with the hefty bill, and presented it to his most satisfied, hefty, rapidly-farting customer.

"I ain't got no money to pay the tab," Soapy haughtily admitted, "so kindly call the police. I wanta' speak with a jerked-off law officer right now!"

"No goddamned cop is gonna' enter this establishment for street scum like you!" the aggravated, livid waiter hollered, drawing the instantaneous attention of fifty gossipy breakfast patrons. Two monstrous, muscular restaurant employees immediately emerged from the kitchen and came over to Soapy's table, latched onto the full-bellied leech, and then flung his ass out onto the Sixth Avenue sidewalk, which was equally as hard and cold as the Broadway pavement had been.

"I'd prefer *tossing* salad in the kitchen rather than having to slime-up my hands and have to toss scum like you outside!" the original waiter shouted-out the restaurant's front door at the slow-moving, bruised-up bum lying on the sidewalk.

"You're lucky we were very busy today," one of the huge muscular waiters yelled. "Anyone that's got the time to scrutinize ya' will quickly realize ya' ain't got two lousy nickels to rub together!"

"I've seen better scum on bathroom tile!" the third strong-looking waiter hollered-down at the sidewalk as the brute grabbed the handle to the restaurant's front door. "This is New York City and not Shanty Town!" the incensed waiter violently screamed.

Soapy slowly arose as pedestrians wove their way around his recently ejected shabby form. The notorious panhandler beat some dust from his black coat's threadbare sleeves, and then deftly noticed a policeman standing beside him.

"Ain't ya' goin' to arrest me?" the evicted diner asked the jovial-looking cop. "I just tried to scam that joint out of a decent meal."

"The restaurant has to register an official complaint for me to take that action!" the Irish-accented patrolman matter-of-factly informed. "They're too busy making money rather than havin' to spend time in court sendin' the likes of you to jail!" the experienced cop elaborated. "The business knows ya' ain't worth the time investment of a formal court appearance!"

"I gotta' do time at the Island for not payin' the bill!" the astonished tramp argued and insisted. "I deliberately committed a crime, and I wanna' be arrested!"

"I know your motives!" the shrewd cop verified. "And if I were you, I'd go out and get a freakin' job, earn some honest money, and then at least pay my simple restaurant bills!"

"I'd rather lose my fingers, my toes, and my mouth to frostbite!" Soapy nastily answered and protested. "I'd rather die of hunger than hold a despicable, sweaty, menial job anywhere in this shit-eatin' anti-beggar metropolis!"

"I think ya' was born on the wrong freakin' planet, not to mention the wrong side of the tracks!" the extremely-amused policeman bluntly replied. "The paradise ya' seek is supposed to be in the next damned world, and not in this stupid one! Ya' just happened to get off the *Eternal Express* train a stop too early! Ha, ha, ha!"

'It's easier for me to get laid with an expensive hooker than to get three months at the Island!' Soapy concluded as the failed fellow observed the jolly policeman stroll north on Sixth Avenue, twirling his nightstick as if it was a band major's baton.

The disgruntled indigent despondently walked five blocks south in a woebegone frame of mind. A rare opportunity to be suddenly arrested soon confronted his still-determined mental state. A young woman was standing, and apparently window shopping, looking at a store's handsome display of inkstands, clothes' stands, and umbrella stands. Six feet away a horny policeman was admiring the petite woman's hourglass figure, which was still quite evident outlined underneath her late autumn overcoat.

'If worse comes to worse, I'll just pretend I'm a masher and grab and squeeze her two chest spuds, and then wildly mash her potatoes!' the tramp imagined. 'That bitch's firm cantaloupes are nicer than any melons I can find or steal anywhere."

Soapy straightened-out his ready-made tie, exposed his rusty cufflinks by extending his arms out of his sleeves, and tilted his top hat downwards. The self-appointed masher swiftly approached his designated well-built female target.

"Ah, good to see you, Matilda!" the impostor began his cruel and calculated solicitation. "Don't ya' want to come and play some ball in my yard!"

"Why certainly," the woman surprisingly agreed. "I'm a damned horny high society hooker, but since that cop over there is waiting for me to solicit you," the lady of the night stated, "then there's not anything illegal about taking you up on you trying to hit on me! It might be a tad immoral, but certainly not illegal, if it's just sex without money involved!"

The promiscuous prostitute then grabbed the astounded Soapy's arm and proceeded south on Sixth Avenue. "After ya' buy me a couple of beers and a delicious steak dinner," the female continued, "we'll see how well ya' can perform in the damned sack! I hope ya' have more damned stamina than you're showin' me right now!"

"I don't need to get laid or have any blow-job!" Soapy shouted to his new-found female companion. "I don't even need any good blowjob! I just was fantasizin' about playing with your beautiful knockers! That's all I was doin'!" the dirty old rascal voluntarily and very honestly admitted.

"Well, ya' can massage, caress and lick both of them until ya' get tired, or until your' damned tongue falls off!" the bombshell blonde hooker promised. "But first, ya' gotta' buy me dinner and a few mugs of suds at Mickey's Bar over there!"

At the next corner, in front of Mickey's Bar, Soapy broke free from the hot woman's grasp, and hustled across the avenue, nearly getting run-over by a fast-moving milk wagon's team of brown horses. "Hey Bitch, I ain't had a decent hard-on in fifteen years!" the tramp turned and arrogantly yelled back at the totally shocked, well-proportioned harlot. 'And I ain't got a damned dime to even buy her an average cup of coffee!' the tramp thought and regretted as he continued scurrying away in the opposite direction from the aggressive blonde dame.

Four blocks later, the on-the-move vagrant abruptly stopped to catch his breath in the fifty-degree late morning temperature. Soapy was now situated in an upscale section of Manhattan, where the women wore warm fur coats, and the men were expensively clad in the finest haberdashery, being covered in rich wool great coats. 'I need to get arrested quick!' the visitor to that exquisite section of that glorious city thought. 'Maybe if I act like a complete imbecile and cause a major ruckus, then that dumb-lookin' gullible cop over there will put the cuffs on me for disturbin' the peace in a fine, upscale neighborhood!'

"Screw New York!" Soapy defiantly yelled. "This is the most ridiculous, fucked-up, shit-eating metropolis in the entire damned country! Fuck this rotten city!" the unkempt protester boisterously shouted as the charlatan whirled-around, raved, and howled like a confident maniac for the distinct purpose of being rudely apprehended by the vigilant law officer.

"Aren't you going to take that shrieking idiot down to the station?" a well-dressed pedestrian asked the equally-observant policeman. "His foul and vulgar language is offending my wife! Isn't that right Beatrice? That poorly dressed asshole is really fucked-up and deserves to be goddamned arrested!"

"Sir and Madam," the patrolmen said, doffing his hat out of courtesy to the fine citizens he was addressing. "I'm absolutely certain that the annoying fool is one of those obnoxious *Yale* students celebratin' the big victory in the football game against *Fordham University* last night!" the policeman incorrectly surmised and garrulously answered. "I'll wager he had drunk one-too-many brewskis, and is now not in control of his regular senses. Just ignore the zany idiot! He'll quiet-down once he realizes he doesn't have an audience, and can't bother or pester anyone!"

The sophisticated couple politely smiled and ambled into the nearest highbrow-oriented bistro. "Get along now!" the officer prodded Soapy with his nightstick. "You're a little old to be one of those insolent *Yale* students! I'll betcha' you're one of the university's deans that's downed one-too-many *boilermakers!* Been to *Purdue* lately? Ha, ha, ha!"

Soapy was rather disconsolate from again failing in accomplishing his noble objective. 'The Island today is as unattainable as my next damned erection!' the deeply saddened fellow imagined. 'The only functional things my dick can do is piss and stay limp, but not necessarily in that specific order; damn it!'

Soapy next glanced into a tobacco and cigar store entrance and observed a short, skinny man lighting-up a dollar "Cuban Special". 'The unassuming jerk has leaned his silk umbrella next to the entrance!' the tawdry-dressed observer perceptively noticed. 'I'll skillfully snatch that expensive baby and not run too fast or too far, before getting the long arm of the law's attention to interrupt my abbreviated escape!'

The conniving schemer keenly noticed a policeman stepping up the avenue, so Soapy reached inside the doorway and adroitly snagged the expensive black silk umbrella, and then fiercely banging the pilfered object against the tile floor, the demonstration designed so that its owner would turn-around and witness the theft-in-progress. At least, that was Soapy's clever strategy.

"My fuckin' umbrella!" the victim shouted at Soapy as the tramp stood on the sidewalk in front of the alarmed policeman, who was inspecting and assessing the characteristics of a crime in the making.

"Oh, it's not *your* umbrella; you lyin' bastard!" Soapy exclaimed in an indignant tone of voice. "Well, here's a policeman standing right here!" the brazen mendicant hollered at the appalled victim. "Protest to him what ya' claim to be true!"

The umbrella owner began stammering and stuttering. "I, I, er, I mean, er, I wanta' say that, er.."

"What the hell is goin' on here?" the patrolman questioned. "Who's the freakin' jackal here, and who's the friggin' coyote?" the cop asked as the patrolman curiously studied the behavior and the facial expressions of the two extraordinary men, who each claimed to own the black silk umbrella.

"Er Officer," the fancy-dressed gentleman guiltily responded. "Well, er, you know that occasionally, errors and mistakes happen sometimes when certain objects look similar," the pedestrian self-consciously continued. "But apparently this, er, this beautiful umbrella belongs to the other gentleman making the claim. I, er, had accidentally picked it up by mistake at a crowded restaurant over on Park Avenue this morning!"

"What the fuck' are ya' sayin'?" Soapy adamantly balked. "I just stole the goddamned. son-of-a-bitchin' thing from ya' out of the doorway! And now you're fuckin' claimin' to be a dirty crook, too?"

The formally dressed umbrella fella' retreated from the doorway as Soapy extended his wrists out, so that handcuffs could be suitably applied. At that moment, a woman's scream from down the block attracted the policeman's attention, so the cop devoted his dedication and energy to resolving what appeared to be a more dire emergency than an already settled mild dispute over the mere ownership of a black silk umbrella.

When Soapy walked away with the imported British umbrella, the poor bloke soon came to an area of recent building excavation and property renovation. The walker flung the closed silk umbrella into a heap of crumbled bricks and mortar, pretending that the rubble pile had been that last wifty New York City law enforcer he had most recently encountered. "If I didn't want to be apprehended," the tramp considered and lamented, "then I would've already been arrested at least a half-dozen times!"

The disillusioned stroller wandered east, and kept walking until he reached a certain Manhattan Avenue that, in the distance, paralleled the Brooklyn side of the East River. 'I'll just keep trekking until I finally make it safely back to Madison Square, just like the goddamned pigeons that inhabit that park always do,' the disappointed old mendicant thought. 'I've got more damned bad luck than Judas Iscariot and the Biblical Job put together!'

At an unusually quiet intersection, Soapy came to a standstill, and sized-up an old, historic church. The tramp ascended the granite-stone steps, entered the edifice, stepped to a rear pew, sat-down, and his bloodshot eyes admired the magnificent stained-glass windows. A low rumble of "Rock of Ages" filled the dim chamber, and the somber melody momentarily entertained the building's sole occupant, who was kneeling in a pew and praying to be arrested. The meditation of the audience of one was then rudely interrupted. A man's huge hand latched onto the tramp's weatherworn topcoat, and Soapy's concentration on the solemn church anthem had quickly become effectively fragmented.

"Why hello, officer!" the city's most luckless homeless man exclaimed. "I'm not preaching to the choir when I tell ya' that I was just prayin' for salvation while seekin' temporary sanctuary from the bitter elements!"

"I guess you aren't visiting here to redeem some grocery store coupons. If ya' can't resurrect a dollar from your pocket," the patrolman emphatically declared, "then I'm afraid I'll have to arrest your ass for vagrancy!"

"I was just in church prayin' for an exclusive job as a delivery clerk for a regional fur importer," the shabbily-dressed visitor disclosed and fibbed. "But now I see that my special wish has little chance of ever materializin'."

“Come along with me to the station!” the burly policeman commanded in a soft-but-persuasive voice. “I’m sure the Magistrate will confer on you three months of worthwhile rehabilitation on the ever-popular Island!”

“What a cruel and reprehensible world!” Soapy answered as the law offender rolled his eyes upward toward the church’s resplendent cathedral ceiling. ‘Thank God! My recent, solemn prayer has been heavenly answered!’ the grateful drifter concluded and relished with a wide smile.

"The Ransom of Red Chief"

As most everyone who is literate knows by now, O. Henry was the 'penname' used by William Sydney Porter (1862-1910), because the famous author couldn't think of an appropriate pencil name. After Porter moved from Greensboro, North Carolina to Austin, Texas, the future writer worked as a bank clerk, and got into a big heap of trouble. William Sydney was accused of embezzling money while transferring account funds. Porter became a fugitive from justice, and then swiftly fled to South America to avoid trial and certain imprisonment.

After being notified that his wife was seriously ill, Porter returned to the United States, was jailed, and then sentenced to a federal penitentiary. While incarcerated (with plenty of time on his hands), O. Henry wrote many of his classic short stories. It is believed that the author derived his famous pseudonym from the name Orrin Henry, a prison guard at the Ohio Penitentiary where William Sydney Porter had been sentenced by a judge that believed in short paragraphs in addition to long sentences.

O. Henry never produced or vended any candy bars of the same name, and spent a good deal of time in turn-of-the-century New York. The writer really loved that grand city, especially the Greenwich Village area. The author would often sit on a park bench and converse with derelicts, or with prominent citizens, getting fresh material for new stories from other people's lives. Porter's tales are notorious for their surprise or "twist endings", where an unexpected coincidence (or parallel coincidences) usually occurs. The author produced over two-hundred-and-fifty imaginative stories during his short forty-eight-year-life. Some of O. Henry's more notable tales are "The Last Leaf," "The Gift of the Magi," "Twenty Years Later," "The Cop and the Anthem", and "The Ransom of Red Chief".

The felony looked like a decent scam, but just let Old Sam the Narrator tell ya' everything that my forgetful mind remembers about it. Old Bill Driscoll and I were down South in Alabama, the armpit of *Dixie,* when this asshole kidnappin' brainstorm hit us like the midnight freight train out of Mobile. As Bill appropriately described our outlandish little scheme, "It was a temporary *apparition* that had more than a friggin' ghost of a chance at succeeding." Of course, my distinguished accomplice meant to say *aberration,* because at the time, both Bill and I were experiencing dual escapes from sanity, while also badly suffering from a lack of adventure.

Summit was a town down there in Alabama that was as flat as a Coney Island pancake. Its small hick population was comprised mostly of harmless, dull inhabitants, whose prime source of recreation was not doing anything except engaging-in perpetual gossip. Bill and I decided that the country bumpkins of Summit, Alabama needed some essential amusement as a diversion from their mediocre, brain-dead, level of existence.

Bill and I had a joint wallet asset of about *six hundred bucks,* an awful lot of male deer, but not nearly as much cash as we needed to get to a more prosperous city, and start pulling-off some big swindles that we were surreptitiously planning. We required just two-thousand-dollars more in capital to initiate our fraudulent town building lot scheme up in western Illinois, where (believe it or not) the citizens were actually dumber than we were. Bill and I talked it over in our informal sartorial splendor in front of the lackluster Summit Hotel, which looked on the outside like a cheap New York City Bowery bordello catering to drunken sailors and resident homosexual degenerates.

"Philoprogenitiveness," I academically said to Bill, "happens to be strong in these backwoods' quaint, semi-rural hamlets. Summit, Alabama isn't any damned different from the rest of the God-forsaken boondocks."

"Speak fuckin' plain English," Bill insisted and reprimanded. "I ain't got no shit-eatin' idea what the hell a goddamned hamlet is! Isn't that some kind of play by Shakespeare? Oh, I'm sorry Sam. I was thinking of omelet instead of hamlet!" Bill characteristically joked. "I got confused because both fuckin' plays have somethin' to do with breakfast foods!"

"I meant to say," I interrupted my expert-bullshitting colleague, "people around these parts love their children so much, that the strange local yokels are willin' to pay a handsome ransom fee for the safe return of their precious little piglets."

"What about police pursuit after we manage to kidnap some lucky little tyke?" Bill inquired.

"Well, the best they can muster-up around these parts are a few droopy, constipated constables, and several underfed bloodhounds with rotten teeth," I attested, employing a degree of hyperbole. "And the local gazette might feature a back page article about our great achievement, after we've cunningly skipped town with the ransom loot. The moon, along with all its moonshine, has more competent policemen on its surface than the lazy village of Summit does."

"Well, in that case," Bill amiably agreed, "let's give your prospective crime a serious go. Our illicit act will be a lot easier to accomplish if we could only catch some stupid-assed *kid napping* somewhere under a tree near a deserted fishin' hole!"

So, the fucked-up idea looked and sounded good to Bill Driscoll and me, right from the get-go. We did some diligent research on the matter, and selected for our targeted victim the only son of the town's prominent banker that answered to the weird Biblical-sounding name, Ebenezer Dorset. The financial wizard was a respected mortgage fore-closer that attended church every Sunday, and then the following Monday morning, repossessed the house of the parishioner that had been sitting next to him in the same damned church pew. Dorset's type was a patriotic citizen that had money to burn, or to throw away on an imaginative kidnapping of his only son, which, of course, would be skillfully executed by clever professional renegades on the lam like Bill Driscoll and me.

The ornery kid we had selected for bagging was ten-years-old, and had elevated freckles dotting his entire body, or at least the parts of his anatomy we could see from a distance. The kid's hair was flaming red, the color of certain alluring girly magazines you see exhibited for sale at a New York City newsstand. Bill suggested that Ebenezer Dorset would gladly fork-over a fair ransom of two thousand bananas to a cent, but wait until I tell ya' the entire damned hairy story.

A little mountain was situated about two miles outside Summit, so why the town (with the name it sported) wasn't built on top of that enormous molehill, defies human logic. Anyway, a dense forest of cedar trees covered most of the whole shittin' mountain. A cave without any prehistoric Neanderthal men living in its cavity was conveniently located on the ass side of the mountainous incline. Bill and I clandestinely stored our supplies in that dark, dank cave, as if we were preparing to commit the ultimate crime of the century, and then live like reclusive homosexual hermits.

Bill and I vigilantly went-out on surveillance patrols to scout the prospects of pulling-off our grand kidnapping heist. We drove our rented horse and buggy past Ebenezer Dorset's small brick mansion, and spotted the young rascal we had targeted throwing rocks at a meowing kitten, and its hissing mother, conveniently trapped between Ebenezer's and the neighbor's fences.

"Hey little boy!" Bill yelled in the startled kid's direction. "Would ya' like to have a bag of candy, and then go for a nice buggy ride in the country?"

“Don’t you clowns have any whiskey or chewin’ tobacco to offer?” the tiny tot criticized. “You two jerks ain’t child molesters, are ya’?”

“Why no!” Bill answered with surprise and regret. “We’re just two nice men lookin’ for juvenile companionship.”

“Then, fuck-off, assholes!” the little squirt yelled as the brat threw several rocks at our buggy, one of which clipped Bill above his right eyebrow.

“That act of defiance will cost old Ebenezer an extra five hundred buckeroos,” Bill promised me as my accomplice wiped-away some scarlet from his forehead with his right hand. “That little punk got an accurate throwin’ arm, and could be a startin’ pitcher with the *Yankees.*”

My loyal companion leaped-out of the buggy, and old William required my deft and daft assistance to effectively subdue the ornery young Turk. We finally got the screaming and cursing urchin on the ground, where the little critter clawed, scratched, and bit us like he was a cross between a welterweight cinnamon bear and a vicious bobcat. Bill and I tossed the still-struggling and bitching kid into the back of the buggy. I expertly applied a half-nelson around the boy’s left shoulder and neck, and then Bill adroitly took command of the wagon and hightailed it out of Summit to our cozy mountain retreat.

I hitched the horse to a cedar tree located in the hill’s posterior, and we tugged, dragged and wrestled the little scamp up to the dingy cave. After dark, I dutifully returned the horse and buggy back to the small livery rental business on the other side of Summit, where Bill and I had hired them, and then I swiftly paced the three arduous miles back to the isolated cave.

I spotted Bill pasting court plaster over a series of cuts, scratches, and bruises that decorated most of his facial features. My eyes looked to the right, and noticed the little smart-assed imp guarding a pot of coffee burning on a fire, all situated behind a small boulder at the cave’s entrance. I observed with fascination that the freckle-faced brat was wearing two buzzard tail feathers sticking-out like respectable erections from his flame-red hair.

The kid instantly detected my presence, and then menacingly pointed a stick at my throat and said in a feigned accented voice, “Ha cursed paleface! Do ya’ have the balls to enter the camp of the brave Red Chief, the no bullshit Indian terror of the plains?”

“Er, yes,” I replied with a weak grin. “Why do ya’ ask me that illogical question, Red Chief?”

"Because if ya' give me any crap," the kid tyrannically warned, "I'll cut off your vitals and hide them in the wilderness while you're too busy countin' stupid sheep in your sleep to do anything about it!"

I glanced over at Bill in a bewildered manner, looking for some rhyme or reason to what my eyes had been observing and my ears had been hearing. My usually dependable associate seemed rather perturbed and upset about his own singular predicament.

"Sam, the kid's all right now, ever since the lad finally calmed-down from his French hemorrhage," my partner nervously began. Driscoll then rolled-up his trousers to show me some rather nasty battle scars, which my distinguished colleague had already-received from his new-found junior nemesis.

"We were attemptin' to rehearse a few scenes from Buffalo Bill's Travelin' Show, Sam, but then the obnoxious kid wanted to change the venue from Buffalo Bill to a prolonged Indian hostage situation," Bill explained as my comrade applied some salve to a laceration above his right wrist. "I was appointed Old Hank the Trapper by that miserable little cutthroat coyote with the blazing-red hair," my super-sensitive friend angrily pointed-out. "And the little nefarious jasper then changes his illegitimate Indian name from Red Chief to Geronimo. I've been assigned to be his personal captive, and when I resisted him punching and clawing-away at my sensitive skin, the little jerk-off kicked me at least two dozen times in the shins, and then smashed me really hard in my already-sufferin' swollen testicles. Now Sam, the little terror has threatened to scalp me at daybreak," Bill lamented and reported. "Can't this little *scalper* do his thing outside some local *Minor League* baseball park?"

"Relax Bill," I calmly recommended in a disgusted tone of voice. "If ya' don't learn to relax, you're gonna' cardiac-out on me, and leave me all alone in this pathetic situation with this fifty-pound human alligator!"

Yes sir, that little rogue was having the time of his life at our expense. Immediately, the temperamental little Napoleon announced that he was changing his name from Geronimo back to Red Chief, because the twerp had heard somewhere that Geronimo was an "Indian-giver", and that Red Chief had no *reservations* about killing annoying trespassing palefaces like Bill and me.

Red Chief immediately labeled me Snake Eye the Spy. and claimed that I had been officially captured along with Old Hank the Trapper. Old Bill was still being sentenced to be scalped before daybreak, and *my* singular punishment for being apprehended was that I had been scheduled to be broiled at the steak at the morning sun's rising. I humorously told Red Chief I'd rather be broiled "at the *steak*" than "at the hamburger", and the dysfunctional lad didn't take too kindly to my Vaudeville sense of amusement. The little wise guy poured a cup of hot steaming coffee down my pants, and quite effectively scalded my sensitive rooster, along with my vulnerable sperm ducts.

After I recovered from the demented tyke's violent assault, *our* little abductee ate supper with Bill and me, and stuffed his mouth full with bread, bacon, gravy, and sausage, and spoke incessantly with his jaws full. The punk kid's thought patterns were erratic, and his words slurred by all the damned food in his mouth, but this is exactly what his speech sounded like:

"I like this here arrangement just fine. I ain't never camped-out before. I have a pet possum, and a pet skunk, and I was ten my last birthday. I ain't never had no sex with girls, or even felt their tits. I hate to go to school. Rats ate all twenty-four of Jimmy Taylor's hen's speckled eggs, and then Jimmy and I killed all of the raunchy rodents with baseball bats and clubs. That was really fun! Are there any real savage Indians in these here woods? I want some more gravy and bacon. Sam, can ya' still piss after I burned your thingy and your balls good with the hot coffee? Do the trees movin' make the damned wind blow? My dog has five puppies. Hank, how come your nose is so red? Are ya' an alcoholic? Are the planets and stars hot? My dumb-ass old man has lots of money, and thinks everyone else in the world is an asshole."

The tiny tyrant paused for a moment to gulp-down and devour the excess food in his mouth and throat. Then, Red Chief continued his incredible monologue. "I really kicked Ed Winters' ass good twice last Saturday for throwin' cat turds inside my bedroom window! I don't like girls, but only want to see and smell their pussies, and maybe feel their tits! Ya' can't catch toads right unless ya' use a string. How come some farts don't make noise? Why are oranges round and apples and bananas not? Have we got beds to sleep on in this shitty-lookin' cave? Amos Murphy has got six toes on both feet! I especially like to fart in the bathtub! A parrot can repeat some of the shit it hears, but a fish or a raccoon can't. Snake-Eye, why ya' holdin' your balls like that with both hands?"

Every few minutes, the pesky mop-head would remember he was supposed to be Red Chief, and pick-up a stick he pretended was a rifle, and point it threateningly at Bill and me. Then, the end of the stick the kid had been brandishing as a gun penetrated Bill's right nostril, and a stream of blood came trickling-out. And before Driscoll could latch on to the irritating pest, Red Chief ran to the front of the cave to feign being a sentinel waiting for more interloping palefaces to arrive and raid “the fort”. I looked over at Bill, and my chum had his bloody handkerchief held-up to his nose. My poor buddy was erratically shivering as if a sudden fever was invading his entire body.

“Red Chief,” I yelled at the young whippersnapper. “Would ya’ like to go home and be reunited with your parents?”

“Aw, what for Snake-Eye?” the pesky scamp rhetorically objected. “I don’t have any fun at home. My old man is just as corny as you two nutcases are when pop clowns-around. In fact, his jokes are even worse than the bullshit I hear from you two bozos, if ya’ can believe that horse manure! And if I’m home,” the little hot-shot persuasively continued, “I’ll have to go to school. I’d rather camp-out with you two ugly, fat, funny-lookin’ palefaces. Ya’ won’t take me back to my goofy old man now, would ya’ Snake-Eye?”

“Not right away,” I amenably replied. “Your father’s safer if ya’ stay put right here in the cave with us. I’m surprised your old man hasn’t appeared in the obituaries yet, as a suicide case havin’ an undisciplined little cannibal like you around to pester the hell out of his sanity.”

“That’s all right,” the ornery kid answered rather nonchalantly. “My uncle’s the town undertaker, and will know what to do with my old man’s body. I really like stayin’ here in this fort,” the weird boy admitted with a smile. “I never had such great fun playin’ torture with any of my asshole friends.”

At eleven p.m., I extinguished the fire, and we went to sleep on tattered blankets and goose-feathered pillows that Bill and I had confiscated from the last fleabag hotel we had stayed at somewhere in Missouri. We made sure Red Chief was safely stationed on a quilt, situated between Bill and me. The diminutive scoundrel kept us both awake, until three in the morning, with the miniature rascal yelling-out “Ready braves!” and “Let’s scalp the damned intrudin’ palefaces!” At last, I fell into a restless sleep, dreaming that a ruthless freckle-faced diabolical pirate had hostilely kidnapped me. The sadistic junior swashbuckler in my extensive nightmare had inhumanely chained me to a sassafras tree, and was making me eat and swallow fire from a blazing torch.

When daybreak finally came, I was awakened by a series of ear-shattering screams originating from Bill’s vibrant vocal cords. The shrieks weren’t masculine shouts or howls. Instead, the shouts were analogous to the sissy-type screams you hear when women see ghosts, mice, or slimy wall slugs. Naturally, I promptly leaped-up to determine the cause of Bill's sudden fright.

Red Chief was doggedly sitting upon Bill's exposed hairy chest. One of the runt's hands was inside Bill's curly black hair, and the other fist held the sharp knife we had been assiduously using to slice the bacon. The young ruffian was endeavoring to realistically remove Bill's scalp to satisfy the harsh frontier Indian justice sentence that *he* had unilaterally pronounced and was officially imposing and enforcing on my discomfited and totally-insecure traveling acquaintance.

I deftly gained control of the knife by smacking the kid on both sides of the head with a large metal spoon I had used to stir stew inside the black kettle. Luckily, the industrious little punk instinctively dropped the sharp knife, when the diminutive pretend Indian raised his hands to massage the outer covering of his thick skull. I instinctively picked-up the knife, and tossed it toward the cave's mouth. Then, I had to grapple on the ground with the little dynamo until I finally and decisively subdued him with a hammerlock, four exhaustive minutes later.

Bill's pipsqueak but un-daunting adversary had amazingly broken my partner's adventurous spirit. Driscoll just stayed on his side while lying on his blanket, whimpering like a petrified puppy dog about to be assaulted by a big ferocious tomcat. I didn't bother Bill, figuring that his mindset was not conducive to intelligent conversation, because of *his* extended emotional trauma. I then scrutinized Red Chief closing his eyes and succumbing to sleep a half-hour later, but I could not satisfactorily visit the Sandman, since I had remembered the adolescent Indian's personal pledge that I was to be burned and barbecued at the stake at sunrise.

Bill sat-up and noticed that I was still wide-awake, and seriously worrying about current circumstances. "How come you're up so early Sam?" William Driscoll curiously asked. "Ya' sufferin' from a bad case of insomnia?"

"Oh me," I said creatively faking emotional security. "I have a sharp pain in the shoulder, and I thought sittin' up would alleviate the intense throbbin'."

"Pain in the shoulder, my left nut!" Bill yelled so loudly that Ebenezer Dorset down in Summit might have heard him. "I think you're up all night, not because of any damned pain in the neck. Ya' can't catch forty regular winks because of that little pain-in-the-ass savage lyin' over there!"

"What do ya' mean?" I weakly and lamely challenged my paranoid and now-neurotic colleague.

"I mean that Red Chief sleepin' over there promised to burn your ass at the stake at sunrise, and you were afraid that the junior rogue would enact his mean-spirited prediction. Make sure we search his pockets for matches. Sam, do ya' really think any parent in their right mind would pay-out good American money to get that miniature demolition machine back home? I personally doubt that prospect very much."

"Sure, I do," I boldly lied. "That kid is so damned rambunctious, just because his parents placate him and dote on him all the freakin' time. That's why the little scoundrel is so damned fuckin' rowdy and insubordinate. He's an egotistical, spoiled, undisciplined brat. Now Bill," I continued my evaluation. "You and Red Chief get some wholesome breakfast prepared while I climb-up to the mountaintop to see if there's any activity goin' on searchin' for the missin' bundle-of-joy we got stashed here with us!"

On top of the mini-mountain, I expected to see all kinds of search and rescue teams combing the hinterlands for the missing little snot-nosed, third-grade pugilist. Instead, I saw during my reconnoitering a very peaceful landscape, devoid of human activity or minimal parental concern. One country farmer was tilling the soil with a dun mule. No couriers or constables were scurrying about, and no one was desperately dragging the nearby creek for a discarded body. It was as if no one in or around Summit gave a flying shit about the missing little ball-breaker. I decided to descend to the secluded cave, and have some nourishment and commiserate and prevaricate with Bill.

I found Old Driscoll standing-up against the cave's left-side-wall, breathing heavily like a person that was about to die from severe tuberculosis. The obnoxious boy was threatening to clobber some part of Bill's already-tortured body with a rock the size of a head of cabbage.

"Sam, that young lunatic put a red-hot potato along with one of *his* soft human turds down my back when I was dozin' off," Bill gasped. "And then the insufferable aggressor mashed them-down with his foot, and performed a brief war-dance all over my whole damned spine. I got-up off the ground and boxed his ears really hard, and I think I gave him the beatin' that his old man must've always been afraid to deliver. Sam, can I use your gun for protection?"

I gently removed the huge rock from the kid's sweaty hands, and attempted to patch-up the existing disagreement between kidnapper and kidnappee. In truth, I was not a very effective arbitrator.

"I'll fix you," young Johnny Dorset warned my exasperated and defeated colleague. "No white man ever violently struck the Red Chief before. My honor and name must be avenged in a wicked fight to the death!"

"See what I mean," Bill maintained with real dread showing in his eyes. "This toxic kid is very vindictive, and if I may add, extremely vengeful. He won't rest until I've been successfully castrated and assassinated."

"Don't worry Bill," I assured my disheveled friend. "I don't think anyone in Summit has yet realized that this blasted, peppery hooligan is missin'. His folks must think he spent the night at a friend's house, or at a relative's place. That's the way things are in these lazy rural mountain communities," I philosophically added. "Tonight, I plan to get the ransom note to Ebenezer Dorset, so that we can eagerly grab the two-thousand-clams and hastily skip town to pursue greener pastures."

"I wish ya' wouldn't make us sound like a couple of dumb mooing cows with all this 'green pastures' jargon," Bill answered and protested. "That Red Chief little varmint might be fixin' to slaughter us right now, so that the juvenile terrorist could sell our meat and testicles to the neighborhood grocery store."

"Hey!" Red Chief yelled in our faces, after awakening from his phony slumber. "Sally Norton once promised she'd show me her pussy, but then the little bitch pulled-down her pants, turned around, and showed me her asshole instead. The damned smelly red hole looked the same as mine does in a hand mirror!" our fake Indian captive vociferously complained. "Was I totally pissed-off!" the small villain continued his monologue. "Hey; either of you two guys ever had sex with a young girl?"

"Well," I replied. "Old Hank the Trapper and I try to keep our personal lives out of our professional relationships," I diplomatically returned to the despicable young wise-ass. "But we do prefer grown women to girls."

Just then a healthy war whoop was emitted from Red Chief's powerful lungs. The lethal kid had assembled a rudimentary slingshot during my absence from the cave, while Bill had been getting some much-needed shuteye. The repulsive twerp was whirling the ancient-looking weapon around his head, possibly pretending he was David about to slay the giant Goliath. 'Who knows what kind of crap is lodged in that kid's fucked-up mind?' I wondered as I ducked an errant stone heading in my direction.

I heard a heavy thud, and next a bone-chilling moan was emanating from abused Bill's larynx. A rock the size of a tennis ball had caught Driscoll just behind the left ear, making a good-sized gash. William felt the pain behind his earlobe, and then gaped in disbelief at a handful of wet crimson in his palm. The man became nearly comatose, staggered backwards, fell across the morning fire's flames, and nearly incinerated himself before my associate awkwardly tumbled to the rock-solid ground.

I altruistically dragged Bill outside the cave, poured cold water over his scalp and injured ear, and then cleaned the exposed cut as best as I could until the bleeding finally stopped. Then, I role-played being a psychologist and consoled my friend, who really desperately needed the advanced services of a skilled psychiatrist.

"Simmer-down Bill, before you're ready for either the funny farm or the county morgue," I sagely suggested. "Relax. Your heart is beating two-hundred-times a minute and is about to explode out of your chest! Take it easy, or you'll go into a wild seizure!"

"Ya' gotta' appreciate, Sam," Bill told me. "Do ya' know who my favorite Biblical character is?" my best pal erratically asked in almost a delirious state of mind.

I was going to answer 'David', but then realized that the recent stone incident might have been based on the slaying of Goliath of Gath by the Israelite boy hero, and Johnny Dorset might have been coincidentally impersonating the legendary David. "No, Bill. Please tell me if it'll make ya' come to your senses and not go deep into schizophrenia, or some other nasty and distasteful form of insane asylum psychosis."

"King Herod is my favorite Biblical character with what the monster did to the kiddies in Bethlehem, while his army was searchin' for the Christ child," Bill stressed under stress. "And I only wish that his royal highness was here right now to take care of that little banshee that's got my mind seriously reconsiderin' this entire lousy kidnappin' caper."

I stepped inside the cave, caught the young antagonist by the arm, and shook his frame until his red freckles rattled against each other. "If ya' don't behave Johnny," I shouted like a maniac, "I'll take ya' straight to your daddy, and then ya' could listen all day and all night to *his* asshole sick puns! Now are ya' gonna' honor my simple fair rules, or not?"

"I was only funnin' with Old Hank," the boy explained a little sullenly with a trace of guilt added-in. "I didn't mean to upset or injure Old Hank the Trapper. But I had to get even after he hit me hard behind my ears!"

"Then, you're hereby promisin' me that you're gonna' settle-down and quit clownin' around?" I demanded.

"I'll behave Snake-Eye! I promise!" the boy answered, crossing his heart with the pinky finger on his right hand. "I pledge I'll not cause any more ruckus if ya' let me play the Black Scout. I'm sick and tired of bein' the Red Chief, and sick and tired of bein' dumb-ass Geronimo, too."

"I don't know the Black Scout game," I honestly confessed. "So, that's up to you and Mr. Bill to invent the rules. Now come and sincerely apologize to the man ya' almost sent speeding to the nearest insane asylum!"

I made the insolent Black Scout and the shell-shocked Bill Driscoll shake hands, but was worried that the new truce wouldn't last too long. I told my co-conspirator I was heading over to Poplar Cove, a village three miles from the cave, the hamlet existing just north of Summit. First, I intended to glean some relevant scuttlebutt that might be circulating around the area concerning a "high profile kidnapping". Then, I also planned to mail a decent and reasonable ransom letter to Mr. Ebenezer Dorset.

"Sam, ya' won't leave me long with this small package of dynamite, will ya'?" Bill pleaded. "I oughta' curse that Nobel guy a thousand times over for inventin' the stuff."

"Just keep the boy amused and occupied with you playin' the popular Black Scout game with him," I strongly emphasized, without me having any knowledge of *that* particular form of recreation. "I'll be back sometime this afternoon, but first we gotta' organize the right language for the all-important ransom note."

Red Chief (or Geronimo or the Black Scout, take your pick) had wrapped a blanket around his shoulders, and was strutting back and forth "guarding the fort" from an imaginary posse of paleface fugitives. Bill had an urgent request to make before I prodigiously applied the fountain pen to the blank sheet of paper.

"Sam, it ain't human for any God-fearin' parent to surrender two-thousand-dollars for that chunk of freckled wildcat," Bill candidly pleaded. "I hate to sound redundant, Sam, but please lower the demand to fifteen-hundred. Ya' can charge the difference to my burgeonin' ongoin' expense account."

I tried to dicker with Bill, but then I reluctantly conceded and wholeheartedly endorsed his fairly legitimate request. We then collaborated on the following missive:

> Ebenezer Dorset, Esquire
>
> We got your nice shy boy hidden in a remote place far away from Summit. Not even the most highly-skilled detectives given good directions would be able to find him. You can have little Johnny back if you comply with the following plain and simple conditions.
>
> We demand fifteen-hundred-dollars for your boy's safe return. Leave the money tomorrow night in a box we will have set aside at a designated spot. Send a messenger tomorrow night at 8:30 p.m. to Poplar Cove Road. Have him stop just beyond Owl Creek. Three oak trees are clumped together there. Your cooperative messenger will find a cardboard box behind the first and second oak trees. Have him put the money in the box. We guarantee your precious, well-mannered son will then be safely returned to your splendid residence within four short hours.
>
> If you dare attempt any treachery or deviation from this well-designed plan, you'll never see your boy again.
>
> Two Desperate Desperados

I addressed the envelope to the very discreet ransom letter to Dorset, and placed it inside my coat pocket. When I was about to exit the cold and damp cave, the crazy kid came-up to me and said, "Aw, Snake-Eye. Ya' said I could play bein' the Black Scout while you was away on important business."

"Sure, play it with Mr. Bill," I defensively and suavely answered. "He said he'd give ya' his full adult cooperation. What are the rules to this special game?"

"Well, ya' see. I'm the Black Scout," the former Red Chief and Geronimo explained. "And I have to ride my horse to the damned stockade to warn the stupid deaf, dumb, and blind settlers that the Indians are comin'. I'm tired of being a dumb-ass Indian, so now I'm the Black Scout workin' on the side of the damned deaf, dumb, and blind palefaces."

"Mr. Bill will help ya' tame those wild hostile savages, won't ya' Bill?" I chuckled and asked my dismayed traveling-business partner.

"You're the hoss," Black Scout identified to Bill. "So, get-down on your hands and knees and start whinnyin' and neighin' like one. How the hell can I ride all the way to the stockade without a damned horse?" the bratty kid questioned.

"Ya' better keep him interested until I return," I mentioned to Driscoll with a cute wink. "I think we're truly dealin' with a dedicated juvenile delinquent with a complicated mercurial and mercenary conscience."

"When ya' return, ya' might discover both a homicide and a suicide here!" Bill yelled on his hands and knees before the terrified fellow was commanded again to whinny and then to neigh. "I just hope I'm alive to go to prison."

"Be a good *neigh*bor to the Black Scout!" I joked and advised Bill as I turned and rapidly exited the cave before the Black Scout could initiate any further disruptive interaction.

I briskly ambled-over to Poplar Cove, and parked my corpulent butt onto a wooden stool inside the combination post-office-general-store. I discussed some generic politics and religion with a couple of old chaw-bacons that came-in to trade money for food and merchandise. Both amiable hicks claimed that they had been lieutenants for the *Confederacy* during the *Civil War.* so obviously their overall credibility was suspect from the outset.

Then, one of the two bullshitting whiskerandos seated at a cracker-barrel, playing cards, and sitting next to a rusty black potbelly stove, disclosed that the population of Summit all had their bowels-in-an-uproar on account of elder Ebenezer Dorset's only heir being either lost or pilfered. I nonchalantly bought a pouch of smoking tobacco, checked-out the exorbitant retail price of a can of *black-eyed* peas, and had to chuckle thinking that Bill Driscoll was probably already "black-eyed" from the Black Scout's persistent abuse right that very minute. I furtively posted my ransom letter as unobtrusively as possible, and I overheard the postmaster remind a clerk that the mail carrier was scheduled to transport the daily post and a few parcels over to Summit in an hour.

When I arrived back at the dismal, dank cave, Bill was wobbling all around as if my confederate had been riding upside-down on a Ferris Wheel for forty-eight hours straight. My loyal associate removed his hat and appeared overjoyed to see me. Driscoll then also removed his bloodstained handkerchief from his soiled pants' pocket. I noticed that the irascible kid was stationed three-feet behind my then neurotic amigo.

"Sam, I gotta' confess that all the damned semen in my testicles has evaporated," Bill angrily began his testimony. "I'm a grown man with masculine proclivities and propensities," Sir William went-on, trying to impress me with his brilliant nomenclature. "But there comes a time when a man's proud ego disintegrates into plain vanity and basic survival. The boy has disappeared, run-away from the damned cave. I don't think any Biblical martyr had to endure the crazy crap that that young tiger has administered to me. I tried bein' faithful to our sacred criminal code," Bill summarized and sobbed, "but I guess ya' can label me a total failure!"

"That was some dramatic speech," I reckoned and commended. "Bill, what's the goddamned trouble?" I asked while keeping one eye on my suffering and apologetic accomplice, and the other on the predictably unpredictable child gorilla standing in the background.

"I was ridden the full ninety-miles to the stockade by the hyperactive Black Scout, not excluding an inch of dusty trail," Bill un-sentimentally disclosed. "Then, after four hours of heavy difficult ridin', Black Scout's horse was given oats to swallow without any damned milk to wash them down. I believe I would've preferred eatin' a pound of sand, instead. Sam, I tell ya'; I nearly choked to death on them stale dry oats!"

"Is that all?" I asked while fully aware that Bill was *unaware* of the terrible terror lurking behind him.

"Then Sam, I was forced to explain to the miniature cyclone why holes were empty; what makes the grass green, and why girls his age show him their assholes but won't show him their hairless pussies," Bill regretfully reported. "Then, the irascible scalawag asked me if I got hair on my balls, and if it looked like a goddamned toupee. I tell ya' Sam; a human can only stand so much freakin' physical and mental punishment, before the recipient distinctly rebels and outright murders someone."

"What happened next?" I inquired as I continued to survey the Black Scout, whose face was grimacing behind poor old Bill.

"Well, Sam. I dragged the little discipline problem outa' the cave, and then the little package of destruction kicks both my legs black-and-blue, and I ain't got no skin left between my ankle and my knee on my lower right appendage. I also need my left thumb and my right hand cauterized with a brandin' iron because of a vicious series of teeth bites applied by that junior juvenile delinquent."

"Bill," I slowly replied, so that my assistant could be somewhat rational for a minute. "Is there any history of heart disease or strokes in your family tree?"

"No," Bill softly answered in a seemingly vanquished tone of voice. "Nothin' chronic except maybe diabetes, malaria, alcoholism, consumption, migraine headaches, diarrhea, and numerous accidents. Why do ya' ask?"

"Just turn around and take a peek behind ya'," I suggested. "I don't think any Summit hospital ambulance wagons come-out this damned far from town!"

Bill turned around and all the blood from his head rushed somewhere else in his body, as my partner-in-crime clumsily fainted to the ground. I slapped his face silly and revived my colleague back to consciousness by pouring a cold bucket of water over his head and face. I then told Driscoll that the kidnapping scheme was all set to come to fruition, and that only a mere day remained for us to finally cash-in on the fat ransom.

"Let's reduce the ransom to a thousand-dollars just to be sure," Bill argued to me like someone under heavy sedation. "I think I'd rather be tortured by the Marquis de Sade than spend another hour with this freckled-faced midget barbarian."

"Okay, but until we get the money," I reminded my nervous companion, "ya' also promised the Black Scout you'd play the Russian in a Japanese war with him when our uncooperative hostage got tired of ridin' his well-trained hoss to the settler's stockade."

The next evening, Bill stayed in the cave playing a game of "pin the tail on the donkey's asshole" with the irrepressible young Johnny Dorset being the pinner, and beleaguered Bill Driscoll being the recipient pinned participant. In the meantime, I set-out to stealthily witness the ransom money being carefully placed by Ebenezer Dorset's courier inside the appointed cardboard box I had conveniently left behind the first and second oak trees in a clump of three next to Owl Creek. I climbed-up and hid inside the foliage of the third oak tree waiting for the messenger to deliver *our* hard-earned cold cash.

After the contemporary Hermes arrived on a bicycle, placed something inside the designated box, and then departed, I hastily slid down the tree's bark, nearly spraining my ankles with the last ten-foot leap, since I had been precariously hanging from a weak branch. I was extremely frustrated to find a written 'note' inside the box, rather than fifteen crisp, hundred-dollar government *notes*.

I anxiously read the correspondence, which contained the following disappointing words:

Two Desperate Desperados:

Gentlemen; I received your wonderful letter by post. In regard to the specific ransom that you're asking in return for my defiant and recalcitrant son, I consider you to be a little unreasonably high in your excessive demands. I hereby offer you a genuine counter-proposal.

You bring Johnny home and pay me two-hundred-and fifty-dollars, and I agree to take the little terror out of your custody. Please do it while my neighbors are asleep, because they might dynamite my house knowing that the kid's safely back home terrorizing the immediate environment.

Very truly yours,
Ebenezer Dorset

I took the creative letter back to the cave and showed Bill its entire unsavory narrative. "Great Pirates of Penzance!" my theater-going colleague lividly exclaimed. "The despicable kid's despicable old man's a much bigger and much more-clever, detestable thief than either you or I will ever be!"

"Don't be ludicrous!" I intelligently admonished. "The stubborn father's just stallin' to see how we're gonna' react to his wily subterfuge! Let's ignore his preposterous counterproposal."

"Hank," the rascally kid hollered over to Bill. "I'm tired of killin' ya' all sorts of ways in this stupid Japanese war. You're no longer gonna' be a dumb Russian hostage. Now I'm gonna' be Jack the Ripper, specializin' in removin' assholes, and you're gonna' be my first victim!"

"Sam," Bill solemnly cried and whimpered. "I ain't never had this much shit-stains in my underwear before! I'll gladly contribute the two-hundred-fifty-dollars to that rich son-of-a-bitch. No wonder why old Ebenezer Dorset can put on the *Ritz,* and enjoy the high-fallutin' lifestyle the shrewd bastard maintains!" Bill enviously regretted. "I've already reserved a stay in Bedlam when we finally get out of Alabama, return to modern civilization, and take the first scheduled steamer across the *Atlantic* to London."

We convinced young Johnny to accompany us home by telling him that his penitent "Old Man" had bought his cuddly pampered son a mounted silver rifle, a pair of Indian moccasins, a knight's metal uniform, with accompanying combat armor, and an authentic *Civil War* cannon.

Bill and I had little time to procrastinate. It was midnight when we knocked on Ebenezer's expensive, imported-wood front door. Bill counted out the designated cash into the shrewd banker's hands, and then at that very moment, young Johnny let-out a shriek that sounded something like a circus calliope gone amok with its shrill music. The violent, impudent runt kicked Bill four additional times in the man's already skinless right leg and shouted, "I didn't want to come back to this crappy shit hole so damned soon, and now I have to put-up with my old man's ridiculous happy horse crap!"

Before Bill and I ran down the street and headed for the railroad tracks leading out of Summit, I diplomatically said to the understanding Mr. Dorset, Esquire, "Here's your perverted kid back. Heaven help ya' after the potential nationally infamous criminal goes through puberty, and grows red hair on his enlarged brass balls!"

Bill and I sprinted as fast as our chubby legs could carry us, and although my good buddy was suffering from multiple leg injuries, I still had trouble keeping-up with *his* incredible speed for the first mile and a half away from Ebenezer Dorset's tranquil, fancy-looking Summit, Alabama palace.

“A Retrieved Reformation”

On February 13th, a blue-uniformed guard entered the prison shoe-shop where notorious inmate Jimmy Valentine was diligently preoccupied stitching leather.

“This shoe is a lot like a policeman,” Jimmy complained to a fellow prisoner. “It’s a big heel with no friggin’ *soul!”*

“Okay Valentine,” the guard began his announcement. “I gotta’ escort ya’ over to the front office. The warden wants to see your wise-ass right now!”

“Is the Warden a certified proctologist?” Jimmy humorously yelled to the martinet guard. “I want him to check my prostate while he’s probing away in *that* sensitive area.”

Five minutes later, the Warden transferred to Jimmy Valentine *his* official pardon, which had been signed by the accommodating state governor *that* very morning.

“Ya’ only served ten months on a four-year sentence,” the Warden griped. “That’s only just enough time for a woman to get pregnant and have a crying baby.”

“Warden, ten-month-sentences take a long time to write, and the grammar also must have a lot of commas and colons,” Jimmy joked. “Actually Warden; I had expected to be outta’ here in only three months, or just about as much time as a woman takes to have a goddamned abortion.”

“I guess your powerful high-society friends on the outside are dying-off and losing their influence with the state’s corrupt politicians,” the Warden sarcastically concluded and opined. “Look at it this way, Valentine. You’ve gotten ten-good-haircuts that cost ya’ absolutely nothing; not to fully mention a good bunk bed, along with three-square-meals to round-out your day. You’re luckier than most damned lottery and sweepstakes’ winners are after taxes!”

“Everybody on earth would be luckier if the dumb-shits were never born in the first place,” Valentine weirdly objected. “And stop talkin’ to me like I was born yesterday.”

“Now Valentine; I have a word of sound advice,” the all-too-conscientious Warden preached. “You’ll be officially outa’ the pen in the morning. Correct your errant ways, and lead an honest life. You’re not an evil person at heart, and you’ve got a good personality goin’ for yourself,” the prison director commended and praised. “Stop cracking safes, and start pumping safe cracks of the feminine variety, if ya’ know what the hell I mean!”

"Me?" Jimmy Valentine questioned while feigning surprise. "Why Warden; I've never cracked a blessed safe in all my life!"

"Oh no!" the Warden laughed. "Let's establish a little time line now, Valentine. How was it that you happened to get convicted on that widely publicized Springfield heist? Was it because your alibi might have compromised an important Congressman, or an unethical Senator?" the warden candidly accused. "Or maybe it was because a mean old jury finally decided to render an honest verdict based on the damned evidence? It's always some lame-brain excuse with you innocent victims that have somehow been deprived, depraved, and exploited by our unparalleled American free enterprise society!"

"Not me!" Jimmy answered with a broad smirk exhibited upon his face. "Why Warden; I've never been inside Springfield in all my life? I'm not too proficient at geography. What damned state is Springfield in, anyway?" Valentine virtuously replied.

"Okay Cronin, I've listened to enough of *this* wise-ass prisoner's arrogant malarkey," the Warden indicated. "Take Mr. Valentine to the prison tailor-shop, and have him fitted with some decent street-worthy haberdashery. Then, unlock Jimmy Boy at seven sharp tomorrow morning, *Valentine's Day*. What a fuckin' holiday misnomer in addition to being a bizarre fuckin' coincidence!"

"What should I do after that?" Cronin asked. "Sacrifice him to Zeus or Neptune?"

"Then take Mr. Valentine to the bullpen to warm-up. Keep him in the bullpen until it's time for us to release him after the tenth inning," the Warden jested and specified. "The barred room will help Jimmy V. meditate about reforming to an honest future. You'd better carefully weigh my advice, Valentine!"

At seven-thirty, on February 14th Jimmy Valentine impatiently stood in the Warden's outer office, studying and admiring the prison official's secretary's solid rock-hard breasts. 'Maybe I should imitate my throbbing dick and go straight!' Jimmy thought as the sex-starved jailbird squirmed-around in his chair, attempting to diminish his huge erection. 'Going straight with the right woman sounds like a pretty sound suggestion. But straight women nowadays are as hard to find as men with Z-shaped erections!'

Jimmy was villainously wearing a black pinstriped suit; a felt hat, and a pair of rigid squeaky shoes that he himself had personally stitched for his recently announced prison departure. 'These are standard items of apparel that the state provides for all its compulsory detainees,' Valentine deducted. 'God; I gotta' get me an inflatable rubberized woman to sleep with; one who has got solid firm tits like the Warden's knockout personal secretary has!'

The prison clerk presented Jimmy with a complimentary railroad ticket and a crisp five-dollar bill, which the naïve law establishment provided its former residents to hopefully rehabilitate into good prosperous, contributing American citizens.

"Here Valentine, take this cigar with my best wishes," the Warden requested. "I hope ya' don't choke on it before it explodes in your goddamned criminal face."

Jimmy thanked the prison operator for *his* exceptional wisdom and for his mediocre gifts, and soon "Inmate Valentine, 9763" was recorded on the books as being "Officially Pardoned by the Governor". At eight a.m., James Valentine stepped out of the front gates and into the dull February sunshine. The area winter songbirds chirping away in the barren deciduous trees seemed to be singing: "Go back to a life of crime, Jailbird! You have no fuckin' alternative! Go back to engage in crime!"

'I'll head for a restaurant and have a delectable meal,' Jimmy thought. 'I'll have some barbecued chicken, and a cheap bottle of white wine. Then, I'll puff on a new fancy Cuban cigar!' Valentine decided, as the released former convict chucked the lousy nickel cigar that the Warden had given him into a convenient street corner waste receptacle.

Having enjoyed his tasty meal, Jimmy leisurely exited the ordinary restaurant and headed toward the local train depot. After casually tossing a coin into a blind beggar's hat, the notorious safecracker purchased his railway ticket, and casually boarded a westbound train. Three hours later, the liberated man stepped off the *Pullman* and into a little hamlet located near the Illinois/Iowa state line. The paroled gentleman entered a popular local watering-hole and shook hands with the proprietor, a certain old acquaintance named Mike Donaldson.

"I'm sorry Jimmy my boy that we couldn't arrange this little conference seven months sooner," Mike whispered and confided. "But the big boys had that legal complaint from Springfield to iron-out, and the wimpy politician Governor had to be negotiated with. Now tell me, Doctor V. How the hell are ya' feelin' after your unfortunate tenure in the pen?"

"Just as fine as could be under the circumstances," Jimmy admitted. "Some shit-faced inmates tried to sodomize me on two separate occasions in the middle of the night, but I punctured one of the prick's balls with an ice pick, and I flipped the second fucked-up asshole into the other homo's bunk, and listened all friggin' night to them getting it on. Say Mike; doesn't anybody just jerk-off any more? The whole fuckin' world is getting into this perverted and gay sex bullshit!"

Mike Donaldson smiled and handed Jimmy the key to *his* old upstairs room, which had remained unoccupied since *his* ten-month incarceration. Valentine climbed the rickety steps, and then soon found that everything in the modest quarters was exactly as it had been situated the previous April Fools' Day. The detective Ben Price's collar button (that had been torn in an intense scuffle) even still remained on the floor. 'That police raid was rather rough and disrespectful,' the gentleman criminal remembered. 'Why the hell don't they go after blue-collar criminals like pimps, prostitutes, and transvestite bank robbers! This white-collar professional, namely me, felt friggin' humiliated when the rambunctious cops had the unbridled audacity to put the goddamned cuffs on my wrists! And that totally fucked-up extended two-month criminal court trial was nerve-racking, too!'

Jimmy slowly pulled-out the folding bed from the wall, and behind a well-concealed sliding panel was stashed his dust-layered suitcase containing his indispensable safecracking tools. Valentine gingerly opened the piece of luggage and admired the finest set of vault neutralizers in the entire Central United States. 'I feel like popping two loads just lookin' at these magnificent babies!' Jimmy laughed as the owner respectfully touched the fabulous assortment of drills, augers, clamps, special screwdrivers, "Jimmy's jimmies," braces, and drill bits. 'I've even meticulously designed and manufactured several of these tools all by myself'.'

A half-hour later, Jimmy Valentine was standing downstairs inside the small café, reminiscing shared history with his old loyal colleague, Mike Donaldson. The suave white-collar criminal was now dressed in more dapper apparel, which was reflective of his high society lifestyle. Jimmy's recently-cleaned black suitcase remained on the café's floor at *his* side.

"Got any jobs goin'?" Mike personally asked. "I really like harboring a person of your high caliber upstairs, and I treasure our memorable gigs done in area banks. Jimmy, ya' really taught me plenty about the profession."

"Are you referring to me?" Jimmy answered in a feigned bewildered tone of voice. "Mike, I'm now a top salesman for the California Amalgamated Short Crispy Biscuit, Cracker and Scumbag Frazzled Wheat Company, Incorporated!" Valentine imaginatively replied. "We specialize in distributing hookers and madams, all having shaved beavers of course, all over the country. Next year, my fledgling company plans to go international."

The safecracker's witty comment delighted Mike Donaldson, who had gone through three separate divorces, and had envied Jimmy Valentine's class and style with the ladies; those dolls having either shaved crotches, or those horny whores having wonderfully hairy bushes of all pubic colors.

The following week in late February, the Midwest newspapers accurately reported a well-performed bank-safe burglary in a Richmond, Indiana institution, with "no apparent significant clues left behind'. Two weeks later, a highly touted burglar-proof safe in Logansport had been opened; its contents heisted, and a large sum of stock securities, currency, gold and silver had been purloined. Detective Ben Price and his acclaimed team of rogue-catchers took immediate notice, and the federal authorities catalogued the pattern that was rapidly developing.

"It sounds like Valentine's on the march again," Ben Price informed his incompetent investigative partners. 'I'm targeting Valentine for a cardiac arrest! Ha, ha, ha!"

"How the hell can Jimmy V. be on the *march* when it's still only friggin' February?" Price's fellow detective answered and chuckled.

"Stop talkin' like a stupid shit-head and get serious about the art and science of detective investigating," Inspector Price chastised his wisecracking novice colleague. "You would make more fuckin' sense to me if you had been born in the China hinterland, and never learned a damned word of English!"

"Okay, the recent job's gotta' be Dandy Jimmy Valentine's signature," Detective Price's numbskull associate deduced and offered. "The tumblers were punched-out clean, and there was only one hole that had been neatly and skillfully drilled. That reminds me, Ben. My wife also has one hole including her ass, and I drill it all the goddamned time! In fact, sometimes three times a day! Every once in a while, my deep drilling hits oil!"

"When I capture the evasive bastard this time," Ben Price predicted as the renowned federal inspector gritted his teeth, "he'll serve his full sentence. The next time, I'll get my hanging judge brother-in-law to show Valentine no clemency for his incessant insolence to my regional authority!"

Ben Price was an expert on the proclivities of the criminals whom the detective adroitly followed, and the investigator kept a keen eye on every reported Midwest bank robbery. "Valentine's established pattern is long distances established between larcenies; rapid getaways; no accomplices, and a definite flair for high society vogues and habits. Yes Harry, Jimmy's a quick dodger of law apprehension," Ben told his pathetic apathetic assistant. "And the slippery felon is as elusive as a frightened cheetah fartin' its ass off in the open field. If I were a vile criminal, I would indeed model myself after stealthy Jimmy Valentine."

One morning in June, the accomplished safecracker and his heavy suitcase climbed out of a horse-drawn carriage that incidentally was used to send mail from one rural Arkansas village to another. Jimmy had landed in Elmore, a town of three thousand hicks, located five miles off the nearest railroad in the Arkansas blackjack territory. Valentine looked like a handsome *Yale* senior in search of his first authentic piece of ass. The visitor ambled down the board sidewalk in the direction of the *Planter's Hotel,* where all guests mysteriously always wound-up with gigantic in-grown warts on their feet.

A comely young lady wearing a semi-formal floral-designed dress and carrying a matching colorful parasol above her sophisticated bonnet, entered the Elmore Bank. Jimmy took one glance at the attractive vixen and immediately fell in love. 'Women like that make instant male erections and premature ejaculations possible,' Valentine mused. 'Even when those kind of gorgeous, cock-teasing, vivacious women have all their goddamned clothes on, the dolls still heighten a male viewer's sex urge into overdrive. Who the hell needs pornography with lovely, sophisticated bitches like her struttin' all around?'

Jimmy accosted a young boy, who was loitering in front of the livery station across the gravel street from the Elmore Bank. Valentine asked the acne-faced kid a catalog of questions about the special sights of the town. Jimmy kept transferring dimes to the receptive lad with every positive answer provided, as if *he* was an accomplished animal trainer rewarding a seal or a tiger with food after the creature had successfully performed each successive circus trick. Then the beautiful well-endowed lady exited the bank and acted unaware of Jimmy's or anyone else's presence. The gorgeous female then nonchalantly sauntered down Elmore's Main Street.

"Isn't that knockout bitch, er, I mean that proud young lady Miss Jennifer Sampson, the horniest and kinkiest woman in the whole southeastern United States?" Valentine very deliberately asked the callow lad.

"Naw," the ornery adolescent honestly returned. "Her name's Annabel Abrams, and her rich pa' owns the darn bank. Hey Mister;

that particular information will cost ya' a quarter instead of a mere dime. Say, Mister. Why in tar-nation did ya' come to a freaky, country-bumpkin town like Elmore for? Did ya' fall off the stage coach or something?"

"No son," Jimmy laughed. "I'm lookin' for a decent little community in which to settle-down in. I'm tired of travelin' all over creation searchin' for my seven-year-niche, ha, ha, ha!"

"Say Mister, is that a gold watch chain ya' got there?" the all-too-curious kid asked. "I'm savin' up money to buy a pedigree bulldog to scare the crap outa' senior citizens in wheelchairs that live in my neighborhood. Say Mister, ya' got any more dimes or quarters?"

Jimmy left the youthful informant's fantastic company, and ambled over to the *Planter's Hotel* that originally accommodated only vegetable and cotton farmers who habitually did only a *sow-sow* job. The Elmore visitor imaginatively signed the register as *Mr. Ralph D. Spencer*, pretending to be a prominent national salesman of primitive, prototype vending machines.

"What brings you to Elmore Mr. Spencer?" the amiable (but nosy) hotel clerk inquired. "Are ya' a Yankee trying to flee the Civil War fifty years too late?

"I wanta' get out of the machine dispenser business and find something more profitable and lucrative," Jimmy Valentine, alias Ralph D. Spencer, fibbed. "I've noticed you hicks around here ain't got no exclusive shoe store in this primitive-lookin' village, so I'm plannin' to open a fine shoe business right here on Main Street."

"The General Store down the block sells shoes," the slightly-offended clerk corrected in defense of Elmore. "But quite truthfully, its limited selection is rather shitty, er, I mean 'meager'. Most Elmore folks go into Little Rock to buy their foot-gear."

"Yes, but those obsolete-lookin' shoes in the General Store's window look like they're used leftovers from the time of the Massachusetts Pilgrims and the early western pioneers," Ralph (Jimmy) humorously maintained. "And if I ever need a diamond wedding ring, I'll surely go into Little Rock to purchase one."

"Well, Mr. Spencer, I'm really quite impressed with your city slicker clothes and shoes," the envious desk clerk confessed. "Show me how you achieve that exquisite tie-knot, and I'll introduce you to every damned whore in town that frequents the *Planter's,* and the *hot* bitches expertly giving their customers fantastic venereal warts rather than common ordinary planter's warts."

“This remote burg looks like a very pleasant community, and the people seem to be obnoxiously sociable,” Jimmy congenially responded. “Say, could I pay my bill in rare porno’ magazines?”

“Sure can,” the young hick clerk concurred with a smile. “I’ll buy ‘em from you, and then you can pay me back so that I could put the money in the cash register. But I warn ya’; I wanna’ see lots of wet pink hairy beaver slits, or it’s no damned deal!”

“Now then, I’ll stay here for three nights and check-out all aspects of beautiful metropolitan downtown Elmore,” Jimmy politely returned. “And you needn’t call a bellboy to carry my suitcase. It’s rather heavy and loaded with the latest porn’ mags’ from around the globe. Those Danish and French model bitches are really super-hot? I’d give ya’ one of my mags’ right now as a deposit, but then you’d be squirtin’ sperm juice all over the damned lobby, and that obviously would be detrimental to conductin’ civil business.”

Ralph D. Spencer felt like the proverbial *Phoenix*. He had risen out of his own criminal ashes, and now the free man had designs on leading a moral, straight life, especially with his new hard-on for Miss Annabel Abrams. ‘I’m gonna’ remain here in Elmore, run a legitimate shoe business, marry and screw Annabel Abrams, and then get promoted to vice-president of the bank.’

True to his promise, a month later, Ralph D. Spencer opened a modern shoe store with the latest available styles, and the handsome entrepreneur attracted a respectable trade, knocking the shoe department of the Elmore General Store into economic extinction. Socially, the new arrival instantly made many friends, and in a matter of three months, became Master Sergeant-at-Arms of the eminent “Elmore Perverted Sex and Dildo Society”.

Ralph finally managed to meet Annabel Abrams, selling her a pair of black leather army combat boots, and then smelling and licking her rancid putrid bare feet. Spencer soon became fascinated with Miss Abrams’s many appealing ‘charms’, and the reformed safecracker asked Annabel where she had purchased her glittering bracelet, along with all its dangling cheap, tawdry trinkets.

By the following April Fools’ Day, Ralph D. Spencer had been elected President of the Elmore Perverted Sex and Dildo Society, rising to that high privileged office in the shortest time of any newly sponsored member. His popular shoe store was prospering, and his kinky sex reputation was rapidly proliferating. Even Annabel’s stringent father, a demented pedophile child molester, found favor with the new Elmore businessman. Mr. Abrams already liked Ralph better than his other daughter’s irrelevant husband, Waldo, who was leading a unique double-life as an area Catholic priest in another backward Arkansas community. Martha and Waldo had two children, Agatha and *May*, who were both born in September of different years.

Jimmy Valentine was now happily reformed as the socially reincarnated Ralph D. Spencer. The satisfied gentleman sat-down at his apartment desk and authored a letter of regret and happiness. Then, the shoe entrepreneur mailed the informative missive to a former criminal confederate in St. Louis:

Dear Louie the Lip in St. Louie:

I want to meet you at Riley's place in Little Rock next Wednesday night at nine p.m. I intend to consummate some final details with you professionally representing me as my personal fence. My kit of precious tools is now available for instant black-market resale. You couldn't duplicate the special set for many thousands of bucks. Perhaps you can negotiate a sale to one of those new upstart male/female Little Rock amateur felony teams, either Bonnie and Clyde or Bill and Hillary.

Now, I shall regretfully review the personal sentimental crap. Louie, please don't give me any lousy lip about my expressed intention that I'm confidentially sharing with you. I've retired from the unpredictable safecracking banking business, and have purchased a fine shoe store down here in rural Arkansas. I'm making an honest living, and I'm going to wed the most gorgeous bombshell this side of the Hudson, or is it the Mississippi? Anyway, the straight life is the only life for me, Louie; and my throbbing dick also intends to go straight, along with my budding professional shoe store occupation.

After I get married, I plan to sell my upstart business, and take my new wife to California where Ben Price will probably never track me down, since his law enforcement office has a very scarce budget for traveling expenses.

I tell you Louie, my new girlfriend is an absolute angel, who believes in me as if I'm a true religion. I wouldn't perform another crooked thing in my life, especially with my erect straight pecker. Be sure to be at Riley's place in Little Rock to negotiate the final specifics of the anticipated transaction. From now on, I'll just be using the tool between my legs.

Your old buddy,
Jimmy V.

On the following Monday, after Jimmy's posting of the letter, Ben Price unobtrusively arrived in Elmore, searching for the whereabouts of an infamous, itinerant safecracker. The nationally celebrated detective casually strolled around the town, telling every inquisitive native who asked that he was a tourist in quest of founding a "Pet Shop" business in a vacant storefront situated off of Main Street. The clever detective carefully scrutinized Ralph D. Spencer's shoe store from a rented room's window above the Elmore Drug and Marijuana Shoppe, centrally located directly across Main Street from Ralph's flourishing commercial enterprise.

'Well Jimmy, I understand you have designs of marrying the banker's unsuspecting daughter,' the eminent detective imagined. 'Now that's what I really call an inside job! What a fuckin' impractical dreamer and schemer you are, Mr. Ralph D. Spencer!'

The next morning, Jimmy was enjoying a country breakfast at the Abrams' spacious kitchen. The conversation was both genial and genteel. But Annabel's always-suspicious banking father was quite inquisitive with his interrogatives.

"Why are you going to Little Rock?" Mr. Abrams asked his ambitious, future, favorite son-in-law.

"I'm going to *Little Rock* to buy a *big rock* for your daughter's hand," the gleeful soon-to-be fiancé ludicrously replied. "And I gotta' purchase my fancy wedding togs, too. This will be the first time I'll be leaving Elmore in over a month, Mr. Abrams, so I sorta' have island temperature living isolated here in Elmore, or cabin fever, or some other crazy mental condition like that!"

Two hours after consuming the very spectacular breakfast meal, Mr. Abrams, Mrs. Abrams, Annabel, Martha, along with her two daughters, visited Jimmy at his apartment to say "farewell" and to wish him "Godspeed" on his prospective shopping expedition to Little Rock, Arkansas.

"What's in the suitcase?" Annabel Abrams innocently asked Ralph. Then she tried lifting it. "It feels like it's got gold bricks inside. Are you a slippery, side-winding goldbricker!"

"Oh, it's just a few blacksmith anvils and plenty of nickel-plated shoehorns," the shoe store owner defensively laughed. "I'm gonna' sell them in Little Rock to cover the expense of your soon-to-be-coveted big rock, and also use the excess money to pay for my extravagant wedding costume."

“Okay,” Mr. Abrams lustily laughed. “Carry your heavy luggage downstairs. I’ve hired Adolph Jensen to take you in his buckboard to the railroad station. But Ralph, first I want to show you a surprise. Let’s all go over to the bank and inspect my most recent prized acquisition! It’s a real dandy!”

Everyone else hopped into two carriages, while Ralph D. Spencer (alias Jimmy Valentine) almost got a double hernia lifting the heavy suitcase onto Adolph Jensen’s classic taxi-buggy.

Five-minutes later, the merry entourage excitedly entered Mr. Abrams’ landmark Elmore Bank. The town’s financial kingpin (and the principal pillar of the community) had recently installed a new vault that had been especially obtained for holding safety deposit boxes and major cash storage. The new steel enclosure featured a modern-designed, patented door, configured with three solid bolts that latched simultaneously, and the massive safe also had an accurate clock timer, which constituted a novel, avant-garde technological addition. Naturally, the new vault represented an alluring temptation to one Jimmy Valentine.

“This vault is the most advanced one in this section of Arkansas,” Mr. Abrams proudly articulated. “And not even Bonnie and Clyde or Bill and Hillary could break into it.”

Martha’s children, May and Agatha, took an instant interest in the new contraption, but Ralph D. Spencer prudently showed a courteous-but-remote fascination with the new-fangled enclosure. While the family was marveling at the bank’s latest advancement, Ben Price strolled inside and observed the occupants chatting and complimenting Mr. Abrams on his impeccable judgment to safeguard his cherished customers’ accounts.

“I don’t want to make a deposit or withdrawal,” the master detective informed the listless teller, who was preoccupied reading the latest gay and lesbian county LBTQAKRFP pamphlet. “I’m just waiting to speak with someone I know who’s intendin’ to open a sizable savings account here.”

Suddenly, a loud, shrill, scream permeated the air, and the shriek immediately threatened to ruin the momentous occasion. The alarmed elders all turned their heads to learn the cause of the great commotion. Five-year-old May had been playing an impromptu game of “Hide and Seek” with nine-year-old Agatha, who had accidentally locked her younger sister in her grandfather’s shiny, new steel bank vault. The emergency presented itself as a tremendous mental dilemma to Ralph D. Spencer.

The elderly bank executive hastened to the vault and vainly tugged at its immovable handle. “I can’t budge the damned door!” Mr. Abrams bellowed and hollered. “The clock hasn’t been synchronized, and the combination hasn’t been set yet! Woe is me’! Woe is me’!”

Martha was screaming hysterically, as if a porcupine and a saguaro cactus had been shoved-up her sensitive love canal.

“Hush Martha!” Mr. Abrams admonished his older daughter as the rattled bank executive raised his right hand to fend the emotionally distraught mother off. “Your maternal instinct can only complicate matters right now! Shut the hell up, so that I can think rationally for a goddamned minute! Panic will not solve this friggin’ crisis!”

“My precious May!” “My precious May!” Martha hysterically and repeatedly yelled. “She’ll die of fright! Break open the damned door! Can’t anyone here do something!” the distraught mother wailed.

“The closest expert that can open this door is a hundred-miles away in Little Rock!” Mr. Abrams answered in a defeated tone of voice. “Spencer, what the hell can we do? May is an epileptic, and will surely go into convulsions, and soon have a wicked seizure! She’ll most certainly use-up all of the goddamned oxygen in that confounded airtight safe,” the melancholy bank director informed. “And in a matter of minutes, when May wildly rolls around the vault’s floor, swallowing her tongue, she’ll eventually be dead!”

Martha was frantic and began having her own epileptic fit, deliriously rolling around on the bank’s floor, and being awkwardly attended to by Annabel and by Mrs. Abrams.

“Ralph, can’t you do anything?” Annabel cried and pleaded from her kneeling position. “Why are you looking so dazed and puzzled?”

“Dynamite is not a dynamite idea!” Mr. Abrams boomed. “It might blast poor May and my expensive, uninsured vault all the way to Kingdom Come!”

Ralph D. Spencer momentarily studied Annabel’s large, bloodshot, blue eyes that profoundly reflected both anguish and fear. The former safecracker felt compelled to intervene in the dire situation to rescue May, knowing full well that his past clandestine activities, and his widespread disreputable safecracking identity, would be discovered.

‘Oh well; my inglorious past is gonna’ jeopardize my secure future,’ Jimmy Valentine realistically thought. ‘And I must do what is right and save May’s life, even though I despise with a passion the raunchy, little spoiled bitch!' Then Ralph D. Spencer gazed again into his woman's despairing eyes. A smile from his lips brought hope to her soul.

"Annabel," Ralph said. "Please give me that rose that's pinned on your dress. It will give me emotional strength."

Annabel stared at Ralph incredulously as if he was mystically speaking to her from another dimension. The future Mrs. Ralph D. Spencer did exactly as the safecracker had strangely requested, and gently handed him the flower, which Spencer immediately stuffed into his exposed vest pocket. With the transfer of the symbolic red rose, shoe-man Ralph D. Spencer instantly transformed back into the notorious high society rogue, Jimmy Valentine.

"Get away from the door, all of you!" Jimmy commanded the still-shocked, helpless family members. Valentine then dashed outside, obtained his heavy suitcase from Adolph Jensen's buggy, carried the necessary tools into the Elmore Bank, and then assiduously went to work practicing his ignoble craft. Jimmy laid-out his wonderful equipment upon the bank's white marble floor, and strangely (to the consternation of the Abrams' family members), whistled a cheerful tune. Everyone watched spellbound as the former convict confidently demonstrated his very remarkable (formerly secret) skills.

A minute later, Jimmy's favorite drill was smoothly biting a small cavity into the vault's solid steel door. Breaking his fastest entry record, Valentine adroitly moved back the three bolts and then easily opened the sturdy portal.

May was gasping and panting, wildly rolling around on the vault's metal base. Annabel dragged her niece out of the compartment, and used Jimmy's augers as convenient tongue depressors for both the almost-paralyzed girl, and next, *her* hysterical, epileptic mother, still rolling around on the white marble floor while frantically clutching *her* aching throat.

Jimmy Valentine put on his suit jacket, stepped outside the vault area, and paced toward the front doors as if in a mesmerized trance. The safecracker hesitated as he felt a hand on his shoulder, and a bass voice saying, "Hello Ralph!"

"Oh, hello Ben!" Jimmy greeted his old nemesis. "I figured you might catch-up with me sooner or later! Well, let's go and get my arraignment started over at the courthouse. Take me into custody, so that I can be spared the embarrassment of having to explain my arrest to my beautiful fiancée and her rather prudish, very wealthy, WASP family!"

"What the hell' are you talkin' about Mr. Spencer?" Ben Price surprisingly answered. "I don't believe I've ever met anyone by the name of Ralph D. Spencer before today. But I gotta' admit; that rescue was a damned wonderful humanitarian thing I had just witnessed, perhaps the greatest act of self-sacrifice and courage my eyes have ever seen."

"Do you mean I'm not goin' back to the slammer?" Jimmy Valentine asked in amazement, as the reformed criminal realized his possible retrieved reformation. "I mean, I've feared all throughout the Elmore bank caper that *that* was my ultimate fate!"

Ben Price simply winked at the new straight contributor to Elmore, Arkansas high society. The famed police investigator knew quite well when the exercise of moral justice should be warranted and justified, and now the acclaimed detective's keen eyes and mind had ultimately recognized it. A brief announcement ensued.

"Well, Ralph," Ben Price declared. "Strange and peculiar things often happen on April Fools' Day," the famous inspector coyly commented. The master detective courteously doffed his felt derby in respect to Ralph D. Spencer, and then slowly ambled out of the Elmore Bank onto gravel-topped Main Street. The flabbergasted, notorious safecracker now had permission to start a new life with a clean slate; thanks to the wise and sage discretion of the very judicious Detective Ben Price.

About the Author

Jay Dubya is author' John Wiessner's pen name. John is a retired New Jersey public school teacher, having diligently taught the subject for thirty-four years. John lives in Hammonton, New Jersey with wife Joanne, and the couple has three grown sons.

Counting *O. Henry: Obscenely and Outrageously Obliterated*, John has written and published sixty-two total books. *Pieces of Eight, Pieces of Eight, Part II, Pieces of Eight, Part III* and *Pieces of Eight, Part IV* all contain short stories and novellas that feature science fiction and paranormal plots and themes. *Nine New Novellas, Nine New Novellas, Part II, Nine New Novellas, Part III, Nine New Novellas, Part IV, One Baker's Dozen, Two Baker's Dozen, Snake Eyes and Boxcars and Snake Eyes and Boxcars, Part II* are short story collections all written in the spirit of the *Pieces of Eight* series.

Other Jay Dubya adult-oriented fiction are the works *Black Leather and Blue Denim, A '50s Novel*, and its exciting sequel, *The Great Teen Fruit War, A 1960' Novel. Frat Brats, A '60s Novel* completes the action/adventure trilogy. Jay Dubya also has produced two irreverent Biblical satires, *The Wholly Book of Genesis* and *The Wholly Book of Exodus.* A third satire *Ron Coyote, Man of La Mangia* is a parody on Miguel Cervantes' classic novel, *Don Quixote* published in 1605. *Thirteen Sick Tasteless Classics, TSTC, Part II, TSTC, Part III* and *TSTC, Part IV* are satirical works that each corrupt thirteen classic stories from American and British literature and from Greek mythology. *Fractured Frazzled Folk Fables and Fairy Farces* and *FFFF & FF, Part II* satirize and corrupt famous children's literature stories. *Mauled Maimed Mangled Mutilated Mythology* is another popular adult-oriented satirical/parody work that pokes fun at twenty-one famous classical myths. Finally, *Shakespeare: Slammed, Smeared, Savaged and Slaughtered* and *Shakespeare: S, S, S and S. Part II* poke fun at the famous works of the great playwright.

The author has also penned a young adult fantasy trilogy: *Pot of Gold, Enchanta* and *Space Bugs, Earth Invasion. The Eighteen Story Gingerbread House* is a collection of eighteen new children's stories. And last but not least, two non-fiction works are *So Ya' Wanna' Be A Teacher* and *Random Articles and Manuscripts*.

Jay Dubya really likes '50s music and he also listens to songs by the Beatles, *ELO*, the Carpenters, the Beach Boys, Fleetwood Mac, the Eagles', the Rolling Stones, John Mellencamp and by John Fogerty.

Author Biography

Born in Hammonton, NJ in 1942, John Wiessner had attended St. Joseph School up to and including Grade 5. After his family moved from Hammonton to Levittown, Pa in 1954, John attended St. Mark School in Bristol, Pa. for Grade 6, St. Michael the Archangel School in Levittown for Grades 7 and 8 and then Immaculate Conception School, Levittown, Pa. for Grade 9. Bishop Egan High School, Levittown Pa was John's educational base for Grades 10 and 11, and later in 1960, the aspiring author graduated from Edgewood Regional High, Tansboro, NJ. John then next attended Glassboro State College, where he was an announcer for the school's baseball games and also read the nightly news and sports over WGLS, GSC's radio station.

John Wiessner had been primarily an English teacher in the Hammonton Public School System for 34 years, specializing in the instruction of middle school language arts. Mr. Wiessner was quite active in the Hammonton Education Association, serving in the capacities of Vice-President, building representative and finally, teachers' head negotiator for 7 years. During his lengthy teaching career, John had been nominated into "Who's Who Among American Teachers" three times. He also was quite active giving professional workshops at schools around South Jersey on the subjects of creative writing and the use of movie videos to motivate students to organize their classroom theme compositions.

John Wiessner was very active in community service, being a past President of the Hammonton Lions Club, where he also functioned for many years as the club's Tail-Twister, Vice-President and Liontamer. John had been named Hammonton Lion of the Year in 1979 and in 2009 received the prestigious Melvin Jones Fellow Award, the highest honor a Lion can receive.

John also was a successful businessman, starting with being a Philadelphia Bulletin newspaper delivery boy for two years in the late 1950s in Levittown, Pennsylvania. After his family moved back to New Jersey in 1959, John worked at his grandparents and his parents' farm markets, Square Deal Farm (now Ron's Gardens in Hammonton) and Pete's Farm Market in Elm, respectively. He later managed his wife's parents' farm market, White Horse Farms in Elm for three summers.

Also, in a business capacity, for 16 summers starting in 1967 John Wiessner had co-owned Dealers Choice Amusement Arcade on the

Ocean City, Maryland boardwalk and also co-owned the New Horizon Tee-Shirt Store for eight summers (1973-'81) on the Rehoboth Beach, Delaware boardwalk. In addition, "Jay Dubya" was a co-owner of Wheel and Deal Amusement Arcade, Missouri Avenue and Boardwalk, Atlantic City. And then, for 18 summers beginning in 1986, John had been the Field Manager in charge of farm crew-leaders for Atlantic Blueberry Company (the world's largest cultivated blueberry farm), both the Weymouth and Mays Landing, New Jersey Divisions.

After retiring from teaching in 1999, writing under the pen name Jay Dubya (his initials), John Wiessner became the author of 62 books in the genre Action/Adventure Novels, Sci-Fi/Paranormal Story Collections, Adult Satire, Young Adult Fantasy Novels and Non-Fiction Books. His books exist in hardcover, in paperback and in popular Kindle and Nook e-book formats.

In January of 2022, John Wiessner (Jay Dubya) was nominated into Marquis Who's Who in America, and in April of that same year, was one of nine distinguished Who's Who in America members honored with Lifetime Achievement Awards, all nine sharing an article of recognition appearing in the Wall Street Journal.

Google: Jay Dubya books

www.ingramcontent.com/pod-product-compliance
Lightning Source LLC
Chambersburg PA
CBHW070459120726
47910CB00003B/1069

* 9 7 8 1 5 8 9 0 9 6 7 7 6 *